CHASING THE LIGHT

CHASING THE LIGHT

A BENEFIT ANTHOLOGY OF SPECULATIVE FICTION

Edited by
EMILY LAVIN LEVERETT

ROARING WRITERS PRESS

CONTENTS

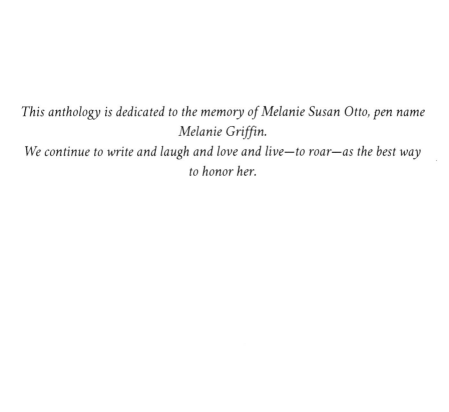

This anthology is dedicated to the memory of Melanie Susan Otto, pen name Melanie Griffin.
We continue to write and laugh and love and live—to roar—as the best way to honor her.

ACKNOWLEDGMENTS

The Roaring Writers gratefully acknowledge our mentors Faith Hunter, David B. Coe, and John G. Hartness. You inspire us with your own stories.

We appreciate the dedicated contribution of our anthology editor and fellow Roaring Writer Emily Lavin Leverett for helping each of our stories shine brighter.

We thank Melissa McArthur of Clicking Keys for her unparalleled attention to detail in proofreading.

Thanks also to Natania Barron for the design of the beautiful cover.

We are grateful to John G. Hartness for his generous assistance with the technical aspects of publishing this anthology.

Thanks to the generosity of our mentors and contributors, all profits from sales of this anthology will be donated to Melanie's lifelong partner, Judith Bienvenu.

INTRODUCTION

Writers are strange folk. They look at the world and the people in it the same way most people look at the cover of a book. There's something there, a picture, maybe, and a title...but there's so much more inside. Writers seek out stories, a burning desire to fill in the blanks, to form coherent narrative from scattered experiences. Writers reveal truth through beautiful fiction.

Photographers, too, are strange folk. They look at the world and the people in it the same way most people look at the cover of a book. There's something there, a picture, maybe, and a frame...but it is one moment in time, ephemeral. Photographers capture moments, a burning desire to freeze time, to imbue a single image with a lifetime of experience. Photographers reveal truth through a single perfect shot.

The title of this anthology, *Chasing the Light*, is a phrase most photographers know. Losing the light—to nightfall, to shadow, to time—means losing the shot forever. Writers have a similar pursuit of their own, to harness the words before they slip away.

Melanie was a writer and a photographer, and she persisted in her craft, chasing the ideas, the light, wherever it took her. Her writing and photography dovetailed, both ways to understand the world. In her story included below, "The Purple Planet," Melanie muses on the planet of lost things, leaving the comic story with the beautiful possibility that those things which are lost might ultimately be returned.

We too persist, catching such moments as we can, seeking the return of lost things, remembering our friend. This collection is a tribute to Melanie—each story and author touched by her in some way—and we offer it to the world, a reminder of the benefits, the rewards, and the beauty of chasing the light.

~Emily Lavin Leverett, 2018

THE MAN FROM THE PURPLE PLANET

MELANIE GRIFFIN, AS RECOUNTED BY JANET BUHLMANN

Melanie and I were roommates the second half of freshman year. One morning I was running late for class. I was frantically searching our room for my keys and couldn't find them. I searched everywhere to no avail, cursing under my breath, when Melanie told me, don't worry, the man from the purple planet had them and I'd eventually get them back. I looked at her and said, "Huh? Guy on a purple planet?" She then proceeded to tell me this story.

You see there is this purple planet, and on it lives a man who loves shiny things and is somewhat of a kleptomaniac. He will see something and just can't resist taking it. Every time he picks something up, he'll drop it on his planet, which is covered with all the things that he's collected. Now, because he can't stop picking up things that catch his eye, there's a delicate balance of all the stuff on the planet. When he picks up something that throws off the balance, something will fall back to where it was. So, when you go back and look somewhere and find your missing item, it's fallen back from the purple planet.

I didn't find my keys and finally had to go to class. Melanie reassured me not to worry. Eventually the purple planet would give me back my keys. When I got back from class, I started looking for my keys again, checking my desk where I'd looked before. Lo and behold, what did I find but my keys. Of course, I had looked there before and nada, but voila, there they were. The purple planet had given them back to me.

To this day, every time something goes missing, I think of the Man on the Purple Planet. And Melanie.

WHAT'S YOUR YEAR, DARLIN'?

MELANIE GRIFFIN

One

Ellie traced the engravings of the silvered revolver, slipping her exploring fingers around the gun's guard. Her brown eyes sighted down the barrel. She wasn't a bad shot. And spelled silver plating like this increased accuracy. What a mess Lovin' Boy's russet curls would become if she let her trigger finger just...

At the pang in her heart, Ellie shook her head. Damned silver. There was no way it wasn't tied to her banishment sure as it was necessary for her true calling. Less than a handful of people out here even knew anything about *that*. Besides, she'd miss Lovin' Boy's intensity. Money on her dresser, too. But whatever was haunting the Jemez Mountains wouldn't miss any of these, especially not his gunslinger talents—unfortunately needed frequently.

Dipping to inhale the burnt powder, Ellie brushed a stray blond hair aside. This scent was none of her making; her continued freedom required strategic anonymity. With a resigned sigh, she spun the cylinder and dropped the six-shooter's chambers open.

"Ellie, darlin', that's my best gun." Lovin' Boy—nobody considered calling him elsewise—didn't even turn around. Bent over the papers scattered on her vanity-turned-desk, his arm was tensed like he was facing down a mountain beast. But he was only working a stick with lead in its middle.

True lead was in short supply. Most metal, for that matter. Ellie wouldn't reveal her connections, but now and then an unusually heavy package arrived at Mama Rollins' Tumbling-Weed Palace via canyon messenger. It came through the wide doors escorted by a smartass grin if the rider was male—all the way to her upstairs bedroom if he could get away with it. A sniff of perfume, a knowing glance from her painted eyes, that would usually keep those boys in sweet dreams for a week.

If the rider was female, the only sniff Ellie got was a nose in the air and package slung with a thump onto the downstairs bar. Rare it was any woman messenger even collected the mighty-obliged-to-ya Jumper's Slingshot of whiskey. Ellie's ample bosom lifted her chile-pepper-red camisole and silk shawl as she shrugged. *Their loss.*

"Best gun? You're the one that left it on my vanity." She shouldn't scold; deputy or not, Lovin' Boy kept his mouth shut tight about the contents of her packages. Though in plating this revolver, the material hadn't come from her... She gave his gun chamber a speculative tap, bullets spilling onto her palm with a cold, pretty clinking. "Lordy, L.B., you have silver in here!"

The chair creaked as Lovin' Boy stiffened. Turning this time, he grumbled, "Don't be saying so's your neighbors'll hear!"

His adorable thatch of reddish hair made Lovin' Boy's hazel eyes more prominent. Distracted by how soft his jawline beard must feel, a flush rose up Ellie's cheeks on both counts. "Pardon. Haven't handled such before. Least," she frowned at the ammunition, "I don't believe so..."

Bullets augmented by silver poisoned an ojáncanu so fast it would get nary a pace—a damned good thing. The Western Territories' perilous mountain beast's reach was fifteen feet. Shot, they fell noisy as a thunderclap, their outsized height comprising another ten to fifteen. Ellie shivered under her shawl. Not that she'd seen the monstrous beasts but hauled in dead. Worst nightmare of a scaly,

4

ram's horned devil mixed up with an ant-eater snout big as your leg, they were.

"I-I'll polish these right up." Setting the clutch in a rumple of her bed's duvet, the bullets chimed. Yes, and they were bespelled all right. Who'd done this work? A furtive freelancer like herself? She glanced in Lovin' Boy's direction.

Crowding her perfumes and lotions aside, his leather gun belt and second pistol tilted toward him. Ellie tsked. Look at that proximity! Good thing she'd withdrawn the revolver. Keeping activated spells like it separate from incomplete lead compositions was critical. Every spellsmith knew that. Power drained off quickly. She waved it under his nose. "Shame, setting this nigh atop to your lesson!"

"Well... Most people don't go messing with a law-bringer's weapons."

"Humph."

Lame retort or not, he was right. Most people didn't pretend to engage her horizontally in order to learn how to compose spells, either. Ellie shrouded a private smirk. Hard not to overhear rustic boys—fortified with a stirrup-cup from Jake, their bartender—strutting and crowing how they better pleased her than other cowhands frequenting the Tumbling-Weed. Jake was smart enough to nod, saying he'd look forward to seeing the fella again.

And back they did come. Mama Rollins smiled her own invitation at them every time. Ellie didn't mind. Better than living back East, a town's unincorporated spellsmith. Out here, sweetly earned coins, or sometimes gold nuggets, kept supply packages coming. And lead pencils, her most precious. Watching Lovin' Boy scribe the page, Ellie frowned.

This man kept his secrets tighter to his vest than a winning hand of cards. He still hadn't revealed who had directed him to her. *Dangerous*, she fussed, wiping the sullied bullets to a shine. "Lead's costly. If you want to redo—"

"Eliza Margaret Spencer!"

Ellie froze stiff as a January corpse. "Mama Rollins!" she hissed. Racing to jam the pistol back into the empty holster, she draped her shawl messily across the compositions, praying it looked natural. Pulled off in passion. "Drop those drawers, deputy!"

With two expert wrenches, Lovin' Boy lost his boots, Ellie dragging his rucked-up denim pants to his knees. She swiped her lipsticked mouth hard beside his lips, straddling him quick enough to make the wooden chair creak and him gasp. "Ellie!"

"Yes?" she purred.

"Darlin'," he groaned. "I can't—"

Mama Rollins afforded the scarred door one rap as she barged in.

"Mama!" Ellie exclaimed, not feigning alarm.

The bordello owner smiled at her star girl mixing positions up, keeping clients interested. Mama's voice, however, wasn't giving one inch. "Child, I know you heard me calling."

His flush genuine, and unable to stand, Lovin' Boy stammered, "M-Ma'am."

Mama Rollins clucked, "Don't you worry, sweetheart. I won't tell who had the jump on a law-bringer." She inclined her head toward the hall, her gray-concealing hairstyle shifting. "I wouldn't be interruptin' if it t'weren't important. Sheriff is here, as hot and sweaty as you, but not for as fine a reason."

By now rumor and gossip would have brought Lovin' Boy's whereabouts to his fiancée's ears even if the woman hadn't lived but a mountain and mesa over. In this narrow canyon, regular visits to Tumbling-Weed couldn't be easily disguised. The blond spellsmith wondered if L.B. would reveal his true reason once married. He was mad in love with Sadie.

Ellie slipped off his lap and adjusted her skirt. Hunched over, the deputy snatched his pants upward, trying to arrange what wasn't inclined to fit well behind those wooden buttons. Ellie suppressed a snicker. Paying for spelling lessons on the sly didn't mean a well-endowed, flirty woman couldn't affect a man. Lovin' Boy, wedging his loosely socked feet back into the warm boots, grunted, "What's Kyiahl in a lather 'bout at this hour?"

A bow tip jutting from behind the shoulder of the shadow looming at Ellie's door offered a clue. Sheriff Kyiahl nudged the wood and leather-hinged door open, his stern mouth fighting amusement. "Practicing for your wedding night, deputy? I should carry the word to Sadie."

Visiting a brothel wasn't unusual. Women were few. No male chosen wanted to bring his woman less than pleasure abed. But females frequently still reviled others who didn't pursue opportunities to bear needed daughters. His question likely only echoed what Sadie's family thought. Hoped. Still, L.B.'s lips flattened.

"No? Then no grumbling."

The sheriff had a point. Unnecessary conflict was engendered by too many single males—those dangerous ojáncanus didn't wipe away, anyhow. Subsequently, newspaper advertisements back East—'Better Income than Mining or Farming'; 'Protect the United Territories'—spurred candidates to seek law-bringer employment. Certainly 'Live a Life of Adventure!' generated interest despite risk. With things as they'd become, Ellie reflected grimly, eighteen-eighty-seven provided a good year for opportunities. Her relocation was a variation. Why was her business—if she could just remember all of it.

The snowflakes lazily filtering down into the mountain shadow made her frown. Earlier dusk came to canyons than open range, but winter days were short nonetheless. Surely trouble arriving nigh on any dusk wasn't anything but bad.

Casting a furtive glance toward her obscuring shawl, Ellie chirped, "So what brings you, Sheriff?"

The Gyusiwa Pueblo man wordlessly surveyed the three. Mama Rollins fluttered a folding fan before her lips. Kyiahl grunted, then shut Ellie's door, dropping the fussy latch soundlessly into place. His long queue of gray-streaked braided hair bobbed at his nod northeast. "Valles Caldera bison. Atin found converging tracks. Many. So many, the muddy trail was arrow-deep."

Lovin' Boy stalled in his intricate lashing of gun belt. "A *single* trail?"

Kyiahl's grimace didn't hide the unwanted answer: Not a large, meandering swath of hoofprints drummed across miles of open flat, but this unnatural convergence behavior. Now and again a handful of

Ellie's cowboys had confided crossing such worrisome findings. As if the intractable and sacred beasts had docilely trotted off, single file, vanishing to somewhere no eye or power could see.

Only a few dazed bison had ever reappeared, their curly silver coats stripped. Instead, abnormal, scaly, mud-colored hides drooped loose at their flanks. Efforts from tribal healers and Easterner spell-smiths failed to return their spirit or canny wits. And these survivors never again reproduced.

Opinion argued ojáncanus were getting them. Others, bad Medicine. Neither made sense. But incidences were increasing. And it affected not only of the shrinking number of bison; these wild children linking earth and air held in balance the love that Sky-Father wrapped around Earth-Mother. Ellie bit her lip. All Peoples were part of this. Offspring weren't being conceived, and those successful, often delivered weak. Everywhere crops and stock were failing.

The Land was dying.

Feeling unworthy, Ellie gently toed the hide heating her room with its energy. With great herds diminishing, gifts bison provided were even more sacred.

L.B. searched Kyiahl's dark gaze. "Trail's hot?"

"It yet holds the silver glow of Passage."

Hoofprints left a tinge of power wherever they touched. But a Passage trace—and trail—lasted a scant few hours. Valles Caldera, the ancient volcano bowl plain, was thirty miles away or more by conventional travel.

She looked up. "Will you make it in time?"

"Could be." Kyiahl's considered grin was reassuring. "Saddled wapiti wait outside."

"Elk Jumpers?" Ellie gasped. The huge, grand animals moved through geo-ether, location to location, not in between. These wapiti—Easterners called them elk—occasionally accommodated riders for travel. They judged it a small trade for sweet white corn all year round. Messenger services abundantly provisioned herds in exchange for such 'jumping.'

"Let me get my chaps and duster." Lovin' Boy tugged them from the peg on Ellie's door, only to find her beside him, swiftly lacing him into the rawhide. He dropped a kiss on her forehead. "Till we take up where we left off."

Mischievousness quirked Ellie's lips. "Better be careful. I'll teach you a lesson."

Her student raised a brow. "Can't wait."

The older two snickered, successfully misdirected.

L.B. settled his wide-brimmed hat. "Sheriff?"

Kyiahl turned to both women. "To avoid reaping panic, it is best not to sow fear."

"None's welcome in my house," Mama Rollins answered with a majestic nod. News wouldn't travel. "Go safely, return well." She followed their coattail rush out with a more leisurely roll of hips and a wave of...something—apology?—for Ellie. To the younger woman, she moved very much like a plump and self-satisfied cat.

Ellie thudded her door to the jamb, a puff of relief escaping. No one suspected her as but what she appeared. Silently looping her bespelled leather cord around the latch, she fiddled with the cord's turquoise bead. This, her last permitted casting—a 'lock'—was three times as strong as banks back East requisitioned for safes. *Strong.* Ellie's hand drifted to her throat. *Almost as strong as the—*

She shoved away from the door, likewise this line of thought.

Retrieving her shawl set the dislodged papers beneath to a whispered shuffling. Lovin' Boy had the Touch. A shame Mama's interruption had come just then. His precise inscription left his unfinished composition virtually thrumming under her fingers. This needed only its final rune. A sealing drop of blood to bring it into being. Destruction to release it.

Ellie sucked her lips tight. If only she dared utilize her own spells...

The spellsmith piled evidence of their collusion atop her unarmed compositions and shoved them inside her longhunter's fringe bag. Swaddled so in thin lead revealed no trace of energy, even those readied for release. Ellie wrapped the bag within a tattered corset. No one would trouble that. She shut her storage trunk with a thump and flopped backward onto her bed.

Spelled silver jingled in her ear.

Ellie scooped up the shiny cylinders, staring in horror. Sherriff Kyiahl likely had his obsidian arrowheads dipped and spelled, but Lovin' Boy loading silver in his lesser revolver?

"Lordy, lordy!" Ellie stamped, mind hop-scotching. Revolver... Bison... Valles Caldera... Elk Jumpers...

She whirled from her room, red shawl slithering to well-trodden backstairs as she ran.

"Jake!" the blonde hissed to Tumbling-Weed's bartender.

His otherwise average face with fancy signature mustache turned, quizzical. Two cowboys were bellied up to the far end of the bar. Duster coats and woolly bison chaps hung, dripping, on the antler rack a pace from her by the entrance. Drinks were fresh. They'd be staying awhile.

Ellie frantically gestured Jake closer. His clomping behind the polished ponderosa slab picked up speed to the piano player's start of a raucous favorite.

Shooting a backward glance toward his customers, he murmured, "Trouble afflicting ya, Miss Ellie?"

"Midweek messenger come yet?"

"Nope." He squinted through the crack of the swinging doors at the failing light. "Oughta be soon. Expecting one of yer bundles?"

She fidgeted. "Listen, honey, if the carrier's a man, you tell him come right on up the front stairs. I'm waiting to see his handsome face at my door."

"And a woman?" Jake's eyebrows rose in some sympathy.

Ellie's resolve strengthened. "Press that whiskey shot upon her. Any abstainer might reconsider in this weather. If she still declines, tell her I'd be pleased to discreetly pass along the name of a fine man it might benefit her to meet."

"Sure enough." Jake bent to whisper in her ear, "But Lovin' Boy is Sadie's, ain't he?"

Ellie pecked his cheek. "Don't you worry your sweet whiskers off. Just make sure any messenger doesn't leave till I have a word." His nod was as agreeable as the man, she thought, darting back upstairs.

Thick purple silk stockings first, then a close-fitted chemise. Ellie stuffed her chilled derringer into her warm cleavage—my, how unpleasant! Next, a cowboy's abandoned green shirt, not flattering but warm. She sighed ruefully at the candy-striped knee-length bloomers. No easy remedy for that clash. She'd add a concealing skirt soon. And tuck her red shawl to wrap her neck. Couldn't forget that fashionable Filly style top hat. Now the bullets...

Ellie paused, heart hurting for Sadie if this didn't work.

Her blond braid swung wide as she hooked the spell collection from the trunk.

Two

The bullets, swathed in a handkerchief, were barely cached in her longhunter's bag when the sound reached her: Soles tapping up the flight. Man in a hurry.

Ellie jammed pencils and lancet in beside the packet of spelled compositions, no time to choose which extras to leave. She positioned herself behind the door, silver mirror gripped like a hatchet. Conjuring her most alluring voice at the knock, she purred, "Yes? Do come in."

A gauntleted hand wiping a reddened nose preceded the Jumper. Fringe swayed on sleeves and bison chaps at the inward stride, the traditional, thick leather cap's loosened earflaps dragging over a collar upturned against snow. Delicate six-sided flakes were still melting on the jacket's shoulders. "You have word for me?"

Ellie's jaw dropped.

The black-haired, blue-eyed Jumper pulled off her gloves, staring at Ellie's gape. "So? Lessons in collecting Grandmother Spider's flies? Those I do not need."

"What a shameful lack of manners! Please forgive me." Ellie plunked the hand mirror down and leaned to peek outside her room. She eased the door shut. "I thought Jake would send for me for a, uh—"

"Squaw?" the Indian messenger said with distaste.

"What? No! Female."

"Then neither shall I call you a vulgar name," said the ruddy-skinned woman. She balanced one high-laced fur boot on her opposite knee, sliding away a long, flat obsidian knife Ellie hadn't spotted. Sheathed it solidly, like something was settled.

The Jumper examined Ellie from beribboned, feathered, and netted top hat above pale skin, down from bundled in mismatched clothing, to dainty boots. "I have no package for you, Easterner woman. Perhaps I should." She tipped a glance between Ellie and the rich, warm carpet. "Yet with Brother Bison's gift, I do not understand how you are cold."

"I..." Ellie thrust up her chin. "I aim to go out."

"Where? Night comes." The messenger's eyes sparkled. "Ah. Perhaps to hide those clothes within its darkness?"

"Fashionable, I am not," Ellie allowed, cheeks warming.

The rider's flashed smile revealed fine lines around her striking eyes. She wasn't young. Jumper messengers always were.

Ellie gave a saucy grin at their shared societal defiance. "Yes, out. Out to help save the Land and Peoples." The messenger's raven eyebrows rose, skeptical. "Ah...so I hope."

"Not saving by bearing yearned-for daughters to bounce upon your knee?"

Ellie's face blanked. "No," she whispered.

She unwound the shall scarf, gaze planted on the silver bison hide.

At her touch, links tattooed around her bared collarbone glowed. Lightly scarred skin where, unknowingly, bites of passion most frequently locked. Where Ellie always prayed one would somehow sever the spelled circle. And none ever did.

"You are Chained!" At the inward hiss of breath, Ellie looked up. Any remaining iciness to the Jumper's demeanor had melted. The woman hesitated. "What is your year count? Will you share this?"

Ellie drooped. "Five. Two remaining."

"On what were you tried?"

The rider's melodic tones softened the inevitable sting, but Ellie couldn't still her fingers from twisting the limp shawl ends. "My memories were...taken. Stolen. I search my mind always, but..." She clenched her jaw. "I am not a bad person!"

"One with so large an aim, who seeks to save others, she, I'll believe." The fringe of coat sleeve swayed as the rider reached out. "I am Antoinita—Nita. My people sometimes call me 'Atin' because I start at the end of things. So they *say*." Humor twinkled in her pale blue eyes. "I find it is good to surprise them."

A tight laugh sprang from Ellie. She offered her hand. Instead, Nita's clasp came at her forearm. As a friend's would. Ellie paused in surprise, smiled, then returned it with strength. "Your people?"

Nita shrugged away her polite confusion. "Jemez. Walatowa Pueblo. Even after the invading Spaniards lost, some preferred our place on the Land. They left traces," she gestured toward her blue eyes, "and names. What are you called by your people, Sister?"

"I..." Eliza gently tucked her shawl closed around her throat. "I prefer 'Ellie.'"

"Ellie, then," Nita agreed. "Outside, by night, your help is expected?"

"I..." The canyon's dimming now felt claustrophobic, coming on much too fast. "I thought to lure a messenger into my room, then steal —" She flushed. "*Borrow* his wapiti. I would bring it back after making my delivery."

Nita scratched at her chin. "Do you know how to direct them?"

Ellie's blush darkened. "Not...really. A rider speaks to them. Instructs where to go..."

"And to what markpoint?"

Her fancy room turned overfull of uncomfortable silence. How much to tell? Minus augmented bullets, Kyiahl and Lovin' Boy were relying on resources they didn't have. And Nita's newly-chanced trust needed honoring. Unlike her own dishonorable past. Supposedly dishonorable. Ah! If only she could remember!

Ellie shook off the hesitation, daring Nita's disgust. "To Valles Caldera. To return Lovin' Boy's silver bullets. In foolish curiosity, I removed them. I've never handled spelled silver ones." The nagging feel of untruth made her frown. But it *was* what she'd done. "He and the sheriff rushed out before I remembered."

"Kyiahl and Lovin' Boy?" Nita's brows lowered in a squint. "Seeking bison?"

This time Ellie kept from gaping. "How did you know?"

"Did they say who informed them?"

"Atin." One of Nita's eyebrows rose. "Oh! Your name—"

"Reversed." Nita snorted. "Just because we're of different pueblos—"

Ellie clenched her leather satchel strap painfully. "But then you know the whereabouts of the Passage!"

"And how to Jump with wapiti. My people arranged that treaty." Nita matched her gaze, held it, then nodded. "Your reason is worthy. I will bring you, Ellie."

Choosing to accept her word, not worry the cause of her Chaining? Ellie took a clean, blue-sky breath. Somehow she would merit this trust. But at the Jumper's prolonged frown toward her mismatched outfit, Ellie cheeks heated again.

"Have you nothing more protective for your legs? Wind kachinas dance in Valles Caldera. Any skirt must stay."

"Protective?" Ellie gnawed at her lip. Who—? She snapped upright. "What measure do you judge the pair of cowhands drinking at Jake's bar to be?"

Nita's uncomprehending stare transformed to knee-slapping

giggles. "Ooh! One too tall, one just right! Go. I shall make an argument with your soon-empty room."

Heedless of the damp jacket, Ellie caught her in a hug. "I'm beholding to you."

The Jumper waved it away, untying a pouch from her belt. "Take this. Offer my wapiti, Avanyu, the corn meal. He will endure your company until my arrival."

"Wait." Ellie fished a gold nugget from her satchel. "Buy those cowboys another round."

Nita eyes sparkled. "As you say."

Ellie managed the back stairs in a quiet patter, then slunk close to the coat rack. Yet upstairs, Nita's rising volume preceded her. Patrons' conversation faltered as their attention turned. In a forward dive, Ellie snatched the shorter curly-coated chaps from their prong. She eased back out of sight. Well practiced in negotiating apparel bindings, the blonde laced on their warming length, simultaneously evaluating the racked dusters.

"Such insults I shall not forget!" Nita's soft boots somehow managed a loud stomp down the main stairs. Music stopped.

Ellie braced herself.

"'Tender! My whiskey," the Jumper demanded in a tone no male would cross—not if he wanted to remain intact, anyway. A familiar growl sounded: the full shot glass slung down the bar.

The cowboys muttered. Something hard whacked onto wood, halting the glass. Subsequent clatter gave Ellie no need to peek: the gold nugget was rolled across to Jake.

"These friends would also not accept poor treatment upstairs. Take care of them."

To the cowboys' distracted cheer, Ellie waltzed a duster off the rack, onto her shoulders, and slipped between the swinging doors. Though not as valuable as silver that gleaming gold chunk was sufficient: rounds Jake poured tonight would ensure they'd trip over their own spurs.

While L.B. and Kyiahl freeze. And maybe die. Because of me.

Blinking away chilly tears, Ellie wrestled her arms into the long coat. If this Avanyu wapiti skewered her, it was naught but just desserts.

Three

Jumper pairs were held sacrosanct. That wapiti were both sentient and clever encouraged this. They had to be for navigating geo-ether.

"Using some kind of compass?" Ellie guessed as Nita helped her settle into the saddle. Avanyu turned his head with its incredible antlers and rolled a big dark eye at her like he had when she arrived. He gave a snort and two steaming huffs. Nita clapped him on the neck, saying something Ellie didn't understand, and gracefully vaulted the five feet up behind her.

"Wapiti are a collective culture." Nita hummed a complex rise and fall of notes. Avanyu huffed in return. "You do not know who carried the men, nor exact markpoint?"

Uncertain whom to address, Ellie stuttered, "I-I'm sorry, no."

"Then we shall reuse Avanyu's. His name is now recorded as Jumper for that mark. Collectives share," Nita continued as the massive animal took a few steps gauging their combined weight and balance. "Wapiti memorize thousands of markpoints. Within a territory, points are so crowded they overlap like stars in Sky-Father's bright belt. A Jumper companion must memorize them the best she is able."

Avanyu snorted.

"There *are* too many," Nita objected.

He made a soft um-hum.

"Disrespectful wapiti! I shall find another," Nita announced with a practiced sniff.

Ellie smirked. Long-suffering affection warmed her heart as well as the chaps did her legs. The town of Jemez Springs, rose and pale rock, was nearing full hibernation among the leafless cottonwoods. Mountains protected them from much of the worst weather, which swept that section of country. Canyon hot springs did their part. But it was still January—and snowing.

From the corner of her eye, Ellie glimpsed Nita draw that wicked obsidian boot knife. She stiffened. The gewgaws on her top hat, were they trailing into Nita's face, or—?

"Wrap your hands in the harness leathers," the rider murmured at her ear. "Landing is not always easy. There is no knowing how any markpoint will be."

A familiar energy rose. Different but familiar, Ellie thought, her tense awkwardness easing. It was like Avanyu was weaving a sp—

"Oh!" Beads of blue energy blossomed at the tips of each antler branch. They grew until strands as fine as web silk radiated between them. "A tree of light!"

"Just so." Nita's free hand wrapped around Ellie's waist. "Now grip tightly."

Dropping his glowing crown, Avanyu charged forward. Its upward swing in his sudden leap threw the riders back, hauling forward into a silent, blinding explosion.

Ether shredded.

Combined.

And the four-legged landing dashed them forward, snow scattering up into their faces. Ellie exhaled; they were through.

Avanyu's violent headshake tore remaining ether to shreds, and it streamed away from his antlers. A childlike squeal of joy burst from Ellie at the unleashed energy. Its glowing ribbons wreathed her—then flared to a choking burn. Gasping, Ellie clawed open her scarf.

"What is it?" Nita said.

"Chain," Ellie wheezed. "Can't—"

The loosed energy collapsed into itself. Remains of joy lay like blackened ash upon the floor of her soul. Fighting a sob, Ellie twisted her fists tighter on the harness straps. She was forbidden to spell. To bring something into being. To create life—or take it. What evil *had* she done, justifying such punishment?

Nita swung down. In the dimness, she patted Ellie's knee. "Do not allow in what is not welcome, sister. Come." She pointed. Just beyond the fallow grasses poking through crusty snow hung a pale line like scintillating fog. "Avanyu's Passage."

Ellie sniffled, eyes widening. "Mercy!"

Wind-scoured ground crunched beneath their steps to the yard-deep rut. She instinctively cupped the sparkling light. It pooled, tingling, into her hand. At verge of her mind flitted indistinct shadows. Ellie caught her breath. Memories! A pair edged into the hollowness of her heart. And dissolved. She closed her eyes. Another two years. Did she even want the answers?

Into the wind burst a soul-shaking howl. Ellie whirled. From a snow squall lumbered a scaly, mud-colored mountain beast. Enormous ram-like horns curled above the ojáncanu's slathering, jawless face. Claws as splayed as tree roots drove toward them.

Avanyu bugled and leapt. A grating crack of antlers and claws clattered as Nita launched into a sprint. A hooty trumpeting of pain came from grappling ojáncanu and wapiti. Avanyu'd scored. The mountain beast batted him aside, rending his flank. Twisting the wapiti's antlers, it pinned him, lowering its widening mouth-tube, acid dripping, for Avanyu's eye.

Ellie's shriek was lost to a war-scream.

With a leap, Nita crested the ojáncanu's bent back, burying her black knife in the top of its spine. Wheezing, it staggered sideways, flailing. Nita clung on, giving a vicious twist. Still prone, Avanyu carved his rack across its legs. The beast stumbled. Clutching one horn, Nita heaved, completing the deadly slice. Its grotesque head tumbled as she sprang from the twitching corpse, the fall's impact thundering beneath their feet. Both raced for the wapiti. Avanyu struggled to stand, his ribs protruding amidst gouts of blood, and fell back. "Brother, stop!"

Freezing tears tracked down Ellie's cheeks. Avanyu was dying because of her meddlesome curiosity. She smeared at her eyes to find six staring back. "Nita! Behind you!"

Three ojáncanus fanned out, low howling promising an ugly end.

Concealing her bloody blade against her forearm, Nita's eyes tracked the beasts. "Have you a weapon?"

"My derringer. One shot only."

"Stay with Avanyu." Nita began a slow stalk to divide the ojáncanus' attention.

Ellie bit her cheek. Three years she'd acquiesced to her sentencing. Even when she'd lit upon a loophole to casting spells for a greater good, she'd hesitated. To regain what? An uncertain past? Each balk was to retain anonymity. *I'm a selfish coward.*

"Nita, wait!"

"Sister?"

"I-I'm a spellsmith. Chained, I cannot cast. Help me."

Nita's guarded glance flicked between Ellie and the ojáncanus. "How?"

Ellie dug frantically in her satchel. "This spell. It creates a wall of wind." Handing the folded square, she said, "It'll block their advance. Use—" Ellie hesitated, loathing herself. She was delivering coming pain. Pain she dared not own.

"Use...?"

The beasts circled inward, gurgling sick laughter.

"Avanyu's blood to arm it, then tear it. Fling the pieces toward them."

"I trust you, Sister."

Ellie grimaced and turned away. She flinched when Avanyu moaned at the bang and blast of air; empowering the spell's invocation stung him mightily. Counting rapidly through spells, sick with herself, Ellie murmured to Avanyu, "Lie still. Your injuries shall quickly mend." Using his blood again to prime the next spell would bring agony as it healed. Ellie bowed her head, positioned the unsealed composition, and released the sheet, whispering, "Forgive me."

The furious wind plastered it against his wound.

It soaked in blood.

Dissolved.

Invoked.

Avanyu stiffened.

Ellie forced her ears to endure his bellow. Watched his pain-glazed eyes clear.

Rocking onto his hooves, the wapiti slashed air with his rack. Death upon sharp antlers. And not toward her.

Voice quivering, Ellie called to Nita, "We're again three."

With a hiss-snap, an arrow embedded itself in the nearest ojáncanu's clawed hand. The monster's trumpeting iced through Ellie's body. She jumped as a gunshot nicked scaly flesh from its shoulder. Gusting snow wavered, and her heart leapt. Kyiahl and Lovin' Boy! The ojáncanus saw them as well, all three lumbering after the mounted law-bringers. Simultaneously both men took aim, their wapitis drawing off.

"How do we break through?" Nita called above the defending wall's rush.

Ellie snatched out a pencil and hurled it into the blast. The spell-wind vanished. "Lead absorbs power!"

"Good." Nita's growl to Avanyu came deeper than she was tall: "You kill it, I'll cut off its horns." His only response was slowing to catch her vault.

Scrabbling into her cleavage, Ellie hollered, "Take my gun!"

"Too inaccurate," filtered back. "Better up close!" From the thick falling white came Nita's muffled war cry.

Too inaccurate. Ellie clenched wrapped silver bullets. *But not spells.*

Gunshots sounded. And again. L.B. was missing.

"Lovin' Boy!" Ellie's chaps flapped heavily as she ran, falling snow stealing sight, cold searing her lungs. She would not have him taken from Sadie. Not see him die. Never again like with her and— Ellie stopped. Who? Movement stirred to her left. "L.B.!"

If fiery eyes could smile, the ojáncanu's did.

"Ellie!"

Shadow-memories rushed her mind. The lost. Hers.

Never again.

Tree root claws slashed. She dodged.

"God love ya, Ellie, get down!" came Lovin' Boy's distant holler.

Distant. *Too inaccurate.* Ellie wrenched out her derringer. *Better...* Shaking, she stepped inside the monster's reach. *...up...* Acid spittle dribbled from its lowering tube-mouth. Ellie inhaled. Raised the gun. *...close.*

"Eat lead, you son-of-a-bastard."

Her spelled bullet meeting blood stole Valles Caldera from under her feet.

"El-*lieee!*"

Four

"E llie?" Lovin' Boy's voice was hesitant, like a child waking parents, uncertain if he'd catch trouble for it.

Chill drops spattered her cheek. One eye cracked open. Melting snowflakes clung to russet hair above her. "John...ny?"

"Uh, my mama named me Luke." Lovin' Boy squashed her into the smell of his wet rawhide. "Oh darlin', I feared you were gone!"

"I didn't know if I..." Her voice trembled. "If that would count."

"Count?" Kyiahl's tone was odd.

L.B. gently raised her to her feet, but Ellie's shamed gaze stayed down. "Chained spellsmiths may not personally invoke. I am one. If we do, we..." She took a deep breath. "Die."

"So." L.B. touched her neck softly. "Wondered why you never cast."

Ellie's smile ached regret. How she would've loved what Sadie was getting. Just a taste. She shook her head and met Kyiahl's gaze.

"I'd inscribed that lead bullet. Whether the spell's blood-arming without my direct touch would count as casting—yet I'd propelled it —well, that I hadn't known. It took fire, and..." Ellie's eyes widened at burnt patches in her clothes, hand flying to still tender cheeks. "There was acid!"

"Lovin' Boy reversed your acid-death," Nita interrupted. "I revealed you, telling them of your spell papers." Avanyu, great antlers bobbing with blue light, nudged her with his soft nose. She chuckled. "So it is; *Brother Wapiti* told them—through *this* interpreter." Nita grinned, eyes gleaming. "And Lovin' Boy finished his 'lesson' with one of your leads."

The deputy's face was flushed but proud. "Mine was the only healing comp'sition. You used t'other on Avanyu, she said." His bashful smile couldn't suppress his excitement. "It worked, Ellie! I mean, I knew it, but..."

"Mightn't've troubled yourself. What's the point of wasting it on a thief?" Ellie dragged out her handkerchief and untied her 'lock' rawhide cord. "Bad as a worm ruining an apple, my curiosity endangered you all." Ellie proffered the bullets to L.B., to Kyiahl, her binding cord and wrists. "Sheriff, my foolishness added to your burden. Whatever your judgment, I shall abide it."

When Kyiahl made no move for the cord, Ellie looked up. He searched her brown eyes. "No Peoples are free from mistakes."

"But—"

He held up a hand. "Actions speak: To correct your mistake you risked your life. Atin—"

"Uh..." Ellie fidgeted. "She prefers 'Nita'."

An edge of his mouth quirked. "Easterners talk too much. I require one thing only."

Ellie swallowed. To leave the Jemez. Unincorporated spellsmiths were unpredictable, not invested in a town's interests, and—

"Never have I witnessed ojáncanu together. It is unnatural. What lies buried beneath all of this, I do not know. Nita and my deputy, they grant you trust. You protected us. Aid us again."

Ellie gaped.

Nita elbowed Lovin' Boy. "Watch. Ellie teaches how to catch flies like Grandmother Spider."

The Easterner girl's eyes sharpened. Ellie snapped her jaw shut and attempted a failed curtsy. "I shall gladly, though I am undeserving." She looked about. True night had settled in. The snowfall had abated, but fading wind hadn't cleared the sky. "Which way?"

<hr />

Five

"Worse than hide-n-seek in a gol-durned sugar bowl," Lovin' Boy swore with a puff. Steam spiraled out of his wapiti's nostrils into the blue antler glow. In the snowy range's peculiar half-light, sweat vapor was rising from everyone.

"Together we make waha—a cloud." Kyiahl's dry humor contradicted his body language, Ellie noted. It gave away far more about what men prided themselves as keeping secret. His said frustrated.

"We blend in mighty fine with th'hot springs and fumaroles," Lovin' Boy grumbled. "If that's what we're aimin' to be."

Nita tsked. "We do not smell so bad as a fumarole."

The wide swath to which Avanyu's Passage had led was empty but for the sulfurous stench from low humps of earth. These fumaroles with their piss-yellow stains, visible even without the advantage of wapiti antler glow, warned of choking fumes, just as hot springs steam alerted of other treacherous ground. The four were safer for it, having spent the last hour crisscrossing the snowy reaches in pairs.

"Ojáncanu tracks?" Kyiahl asked Nita. The silvery bison trail had faded, Passage rut healed with it, leaving only the surprise discovery of disordered hoofprints way out here. Their best guess for this herd's dispersion? Another unheard-of massed attack. Frowning, Nita kicked her fresh-shorn pairs of ojáncanu horns lashed to the saddlebags and shook her head. There'd been no bison carcasses either.

Feeling herself but a burden, Ellie asked, "Is there aught I might do?"

"Got a 'find it' comp'sition?" L.B. drawled. "Elseways only prayer'll help."

"Prayer!" Kyiahl swung out of the saddle to plant his feet and fished inside his coat. "Deputy, blessings upon your skill at speaking the obvious. More obvious and a snake, I would be bitten." He poured a small something onto his palm. Beginning a quiet chant, Kyiahl raised his hand of corn pollen skyward.

"For guidance?" Ellie murmured to Nita.

"Just so." Nita's own breathing words of the cadence tugged deep in Ellie's spirit, and she offered silent thanks. Kyiahl blew the fine pollen gently in each of the four sacred directions. One puff hung several heartbeats, the rest falling away. "Ah," Nita whispered. "Our parents guide their children."

The three wapiti turned straight east into the dead volcano's largest flatlands.

W ith each hunting pass, Cerro la Jara loomed higher from the darkness. Squatting alone on the Valles Caldera plain, two hundred and some feet tall, the pine-covered rock dome was as a pebble tossed in a horse watering trough—a lonely souvenir of the volcano that once formed such an enormous basin another mountain fit inside.

Ellie's skull began to pound as they swept closer. Lovin' Boy rubbed his own forehead. "This's indirect as herdin' cats," he grumbled. His mount bounced several strides, swinging glowing antlers as if to Jump; nobody was enjoying this.

Mouth grim, Kyiahl reoriented northward.

Fast as a whip-crack, L.B. spun his wapiti south. "This way!" The sheriff's posture pulled tight. Confused, Lovin' Boy massaged his temples. "Ain't you feelin' somethin'?"

Avanyu, giving the age-weathered sheriff a great, dark eye, plodded several steps after Lovin' Boy, vote unmistakable. Nita shrugged. "Your deputy has the Touch. Listen."

"Fine, you lead," Kyiahl grunted.

Ellie laughed, clapping a glove across her lips too late. "Begging pardon! You sounded as resigned as my—" Her eyes widened, hands snatching after the memory flicker as her Chain choked it again.

Ellie struggled not to scream. Her reestablished life centered around Tumbling-Weed, its expectations, pleasures, troubles, not endangering her life for her stolen past. Ellie blinked. Her pistol shot: She'd taken a life with a spell. And nothing had—

"Look!" Lovin' Boy's wapiti charged forward.

The others nearly lost sight of them rounding a crumbling rock outcrop. It was as if wind kachinas whirled sparkling snowflakes into their eyes; what Ellie first took for moonlight breaking through clouds wasn't.

In a rocky chute, Lovin' Boy braced beside his mount, agog. A veil of light, hazy-bright like a frosty sky, hung rippling across a wall of stone bigger than a covered wagon. Within its spill hoofprints, all leading into this rocky defile, ended at its brilliance.

Seizing bow and quiver, Kyiahl leapt down. "Something lies dying."

Thrashing in the mud were a bison's hind legs and tail. Its faintly braying front, partially visible, lay halfway through the veil. Lovin' Boy drew his gleaming revolver.

"Wait!" Ellie flipped a leg forward to avoid Nita in dismount, only to discover her, knife drawn, speaking rapidly to the wapitis in that odd language. The veil's undulating pattern beat into her skull like a drumbeat. "Do you feel that?"

"Like a mother," Lovin' Boy groaned. "Pardon, Ellie."

Kyiahl shook his head. "I do not, but this calf does." Its writhing matched—was making?—the disturbance. The sheriff handed Ellie his bow. Gauging the footing, he positioned strong hands on the calf's hocks. At its next kick, he hauled backward. Several hundred pounds of young bison slid free, its bellowing ending on a querulous note.

As they watched, the tarnished gray hide resumed healthy silver. The yearling, muddy but hale, hauled itself upright. It picked its way to Kyiahl. Everyone tensed. The man scratched kinks of hair between its short horns. It gently head-butted him, giving a series of grunts. At Avanyu's address, they changed.

"His herd is inside there," Nita translated. "A great hole in the hill. Adults went, but confused. He begged explanation. None answered him."

Kyiahl rubbed his jaw. "Dee-pah-law—long-time-ago—was such a Hole, grandparents say. On the other side were a different People, different Land. Some disappeared there. Almost none returned. But some did. There is a way."

A different People...

Forms, like reflected in window glass by candlelight, danced in Ellie's mind. A large...door? Room? Strange shapes... The sting at her collar vacillated, her hands itching to grip what wasn't a bow.

"The Hole. It's fading!" Nita called.

Avanyu's distressed bugle was echoed by the other wapitis. Ethereal blue shine was tearing from their antlers like tattered flags, streaming toward the Hole.

"They say it is stealing their power!"

Lovin' Boy lifted the bow from Ellie, tossing it to Kyiahl, who nocked an arrow.

"Wait! I've a sustaining spell!" Ellie withdrew it, and hesitated. "Blood's needed to arm it."

Nita passed over her obsidian knife, offering an open palm.

"Invocation will briefly hurt."

Her wave dismissed it. "Had worse."

"Let me catch." L.B. lifted the composition.

Mouth grim, Ellie delicately pressed in the blade tip until a drop ran free. At the spell's surge to readiness, Lovin' Boy almost dropped the pulsing paper.

"Cast it into the ripples."

In one stride he tore and flung it. A smell like iron arose. The veil blazed, bright flame withdrawing to solidify at its edges. Lovin' Boy turned, eyes equally alight. "Teach me this!"

"Once we're successful," Kyiahl intervened. "How long will this hold, Daughter?"

"Normal circumstances, one hour," Ellie said. "Here..."

"Even half must be enough. Deputy?" Lovin' Boy checked his revolvers, chambers properly loaded. He nodded.

Ellie gritted her teeth. "I'm coming."

"Ellie, darlin'..."

"Not wise, blocking the way of a determined woman," Nita remarked, re-gloving her pricked hand. "Married, you will understand. Sister, take that knife."

"I couldn't!"

"What is it you think?" Nita laughed. "I have two!" She clasped forearms. "Blessings go with you. We'll keep watch." The wapitis had formed a defensive arc beyond the narrow defile.

Ellie gave Nita a hug. "Thank you."

With a shared nod, the trio stepped warily through the veil.

<hr>

Six

They stumbled into a herd of uneasy bison.

The cavernous chamber of pale volcanic rock had strange inverted, cradle-like boxes hung overhead shedding dim illumination. Kyiahl startled as his shiny arrowhead flared, quenching to a pewter dullness matching the tarnished bison coats. "Spelled?" Ellie guessed.

Lovin' Boy swore. His silvered revolver clattered down, the metal forge-bright. Kyiahl ducked, hauling Ellie deeper into the apprehensive animals before any gunpowder exploded. But the firearm winked to an equally dull gray. L.B. cautiously picked it up.

"No longer," Kyiahl replied, wryly.

Ellie stuck her hand in her bag. Cool paper rustled. "Your corn pollen?"

The sheriff patted his unscorched coat. He shook his head.

She nodded. "Then only 'live' spells are extinguis—"

The skin at her collar flamed molten hot. Ellie gagged, view swimming. She could feel Kyiahl's arms lowering her. Hear Lovin' Boy's tautly whispered, "Is she...?"

<hr>

"Ellie!"

Reddish brown curls bobbed into sight. Johnny and little Emma were so much alike, Ellie smiled. Hand in hand, her husband and daughter parted the line of respectful bank patrons. "Sorry we're late. *Someone* needed to finish her ice cream."

"They don't let it in here," Emma informed her mother, offended.

"Bank presidents don't want sticky money," Ellie agreed, resetting her filly-styled top hat. "Dearheart, he's interested in engaging us after the other commissions."

Her husband beamed. Their renown as security spellsmiths was soaring. "More agreeable than silvering bullets, government contracts or no!"

"What are you—?" echoed from within the brass vault. "How did you gain entry? Leave that! Guards!"

John leapt the banker's desk, beating both uniforms through the foot-thick door, their seven-year-old trailing him like an eager puppy.

"Emma, no!" Ellie yelled.

Gunfire rang out, bullets pinging.

Patrons screamed and ran. Ellie's heart climbed her throat. She fought Victorian skirt and bustle to the vault, cursing.

Seared flesh and acrid smoke stung her sinuses. Blood smeared the wall. Guards lay like broken marionettes, holes in their chests. Trapped within a pulsing sphere, Johnny fought a green, bulbous-headed humanoid reaching for Emma. Another clutched the silver bullion. The third alien leveled a wand at the banker.

"Don't shoot!" Reversing his silvered revolver, grip out, the banker raised his hands. "Don't—"

A thin ray of light blasted through his heart, spinning him to the floor, gun clattering to Ellie's feet. She swooped. Its silvered steel chilled her palm as she sighted—

"M a'am, put the gun down. Slowly."

Ellie blinked. "What?"

Death times three lay before her: banker, two guards. She looked around wildly. "Johnny! Emma! Where—?"

"Ma'am!"

Her heart fell. No one alive—except the uniformed bank guard braced to fire.

E llie clawed at the fire choking her. It too vanished. Like the alien creatures had with—she brushed away tears—her husband and child. Who were now her reasons for reckoning. Ellie stilled. Had they suffered ill-luck in time and place? Had the creatures stolen that silver as well?

"What new hell is this?" Lovin' Boy mumbled.

Ellie rolled onto her curly-wooled chaps, waving the surprised men aside. She peered between milling bison. A green figure with a bulbous head and oversized dark eyes stepped through a door at the top of a ramp. She jerked back, hissing. "Are we visible?"

"Our sisters and brothers shield us," Kyiahl answered, meeting her eyes. "You are..."

"UnChained." Ellie measured the green-skinned being pushing a large button. "And I remember my enemy."

"Anasazi," the Gyusiwa Pueblo man spat. The literal translation as "ancient alien-enemy" prickled Ellie's spine. Yes. What was the chance?

Low, pulsing hoots sounded. The shimmering Hole began contracting. L.B. swung around. "How do we get back through?"

Ellie inhaled. Held it. "Will that gun fire?"

He glared at its tarnished length. "Sure'll find out!"

She extracted the lancet and compositions. "First one's 'open.' Second is 'memory.'"

L.B. stared. "For the Hole and...?"

"Your guiding of the herd, that they return with wits, and...maybe you'll remember me."

"You're not com—" Kyiahl's hand fell on L.B.'s sleeve, silencing him.

Her eyes narrowed. "Anasazi steal lives. Not anymore."

Kyiahl nodded. "You granted us aid. We'll honor your wishes. Do what you need."

Need...

Ellie seized L.B. in a dizzying kiss. She laid a palm along his bearded jaw as his blush reached her heart. "Go to Sadie. Raise good daughters. Sons. Teach them..." Ellie swallowed. "Love."

Kyiahl pressed his leather pollen bag into her palm. Ellie blinked. "The Great Spirit does not care in what language you pray. Keep faith always."

She hugged him. "Tell Nita I'm sorry about the knife."

"My, uh...this gun? It-it's yours," stuttered Lovin' Boy, shoving it at Ellie. "I got this other'n, see? And I-I'll study on how to spell it." He smudged brimming eyes. "Promise."

Ellie drew a shaky breath, turning away. Sadie deserved L.B.; the Peoples deserved Kyiahl. Time to close the Hole. Permanently.

Gaze measuring the green alien, Ellie resettled her top hat. "Cast both. I'll then fire."

Primed paper tore. Bison rallied, bright-eyed and bellowing. In alarm the Anasazi drew its peculiar light-wand.

Ellie's gunshot cracked, cleaving the herd as she dropped him, one tarnished bullet between the eyes.

Seven

Cool gray passages greeted her entrance. To one side of the floor snakelike ropes were bundled, humming. Spells flowing? But to what purpose? Ellie clenched her hand, rediscovering Kyiahl's pouch. *Keep faith.* She stared, then nodded, comprehending. Spells effectively drew from a smith's essence. Spirit was a gift, like that provided the bison. Time to be worthy.

Reverently Ellie puffed corn pollen outward, whispering, "Please, aid me to protect the Land and Peoples." Pollen condensed into a sunshiny sphere. In wonderment, Ellie shadowed its bob through maze-like hallways, encountering no one. Reaching a dimmed room, it faded.

Inside, blinking lights covered the walls. A giant glass tube whirled with naked energy beyond subterranean windows, green-skinned Anasazi poking waist-high panels. At a garbled inhuman command, light rays stabbed into a half-dozen penned bison. Their guttural bellows cycled to howls like ojáncanu. Burned bare, they collapsed.

Implacable rage suffused Ellie. Lives sacrificed. Johnny and Emma's. Hers. To what end? Anasazi stole them without regard. Feet shifting with fury, her boot-tip bumped something: hallway spell-snakes. Spell-snakes leading directly to the boards. Feeding them. Ellie's startled eyes turned steely.

Nita's obsidian knife bloodied a finger to arm the chosen composition. Crouching low, Ellie hurriedly looped it around the Anasazi snake cords. She levered the blade inside the sheet's encircling cuff. There was a Great Spirit. Was there not a just afterlife?

"Johnny," Ellie choked, tears sliding down her cheeks. "Emma, I-I'm coming."

"Glrphrshyt?"

Vacuous, black eyes loomed balefully from the doorway. Ellie raised her chin. Sliced the composition.

Everywhere, power reversed. A juddering boom convulsed the passage. Hums through the tunneled rock climbed to screeches. Cradle-lights shattered. And the threatening Anasazi, its torture room detonating brighter than the sun, shredded into uncountable globs.

The explosion hurled Ellie's crouched form into the opposite wall, its door ripping backward, her tumbling body fetching up hard across stair treads. Surrounding stone trembled. Above, the stairway quivered. Held.

Silence and sifting dust descended.

An excruciating breath seared Ellie's lungs. Again. She wedged open an eye. Blurred in her tears, the golden globe reformed. "Wh-y?" she croaked. "Why...am I...alive?"

The globe circled her, then rose.

Weakly, Ellie lifted an arm. "Am I not done?" She'd honored her promises. Reversed the Anasazi spells. Sealed the Hole. Tears smudged her hand. Destroying it all left no way home.

The globe waited, swirling.

Ellie wheezed a laugh. "So, no rest for the wicked."

Bruised and limping, she collected her battered top hat, sighed, and staggered slowly upward behind the sphere.

Eight

Perspiration was breaking out everywhere. Ellie fanned herself with her hat, gave up, and opened coat and shirt only to realize how scantily and ill-clad she was beneath them.

No remaining Anasazi had appeared the whole way out of their rock warren. At the disguised exit in a snowless pine wood, her blessed globe had dissipated in morning sun, leaving her strangely revived. Aimless, Ellie followed a curiously dense, striped black road. Several times she had dodged from right marvels: speeding horseless carriages, glossy and rainbow colored. Humans inside, seemingly unperturbed, hadn't spared her a glance.

A peculiar green sign, wastefully *metal*—she tapped it with the gun —read *Los Alamos 3mi.s.* Ellie sighed in relief. Los Álamos, not far from Jemez Springs, was mostly Puebloans and cattle-running Easterners. Maybe one could explain the spring-like budding cottonwood trees— if they weren't somehow locked under Anasazi control...

Ellie shivered, wishing for Avanyu and Nita. But would she Jump back?

From the UnChaining revelation, pain and loss ravaged her heart again. Happily married, mother with daughter, all three of them spell-smiths... Once.

Ellie sniffled, forcing her boots forward. She'd become UnChained early. Keep to the Western Territories, she told herself, and no one would know. Lovin' Boy could get incorporated in Jemez Springs. She'd find a town and do the same. Maybe this one. There'd be work. Surely horseless carriages required mighty composition skills....

A plank-porch saloon showed around a curve. Painted red on its whitewashed adobe was 'Los Ojos', black pupils peering from the second 'O's. Tethered saddle horses outside flicked their tails beside several shiny carriages. Ellie approached, biting her lip, revolver tucked behind a chap. De-spelled, it still killed Anasazi.

Fancy-duded up cowboys, leaving, tipped their hats and held the swinging door. *All the better to get a longer look*, Ellie thought wryly. What a picture she must make.

Unable to curtsy, she raised her hat. "Gentlemen."

Inside, she stalled, adjusting to the dimness. No piano was playing, but it was early. Whiskey scent tickled her nose, but it was the tang of onions, green chilies, and steak sizzling as set Ellie's mouth to watering. The bartender, an older woman, gave Ellie a once-over, nodding at the tarnished revolver. "Check your gun at the door, sweetie, alongside the others."

"Beg pardon." Ellie racked it beside several beautifully finished rifles. Her finger traced engraving on a silvered double-barrel. "This metal costs a fortune, let alone the talented spellsmithing."

"Ain't cheap," agreed the 'tender. She squinted. "What's your year, darlin'?"

Ellie froze. How might she guess she'd been Chained? The tattoo would be gone. Straight-faced, she purposely misunderstood. "Eighteen-eighty-seven, same as yours."

The bartender's sun-leathered face creased with a smile. "Not mine. Altair there's twenty-three-aught-six. Laverne, nineteen-seventy-two." At Ellie's disbelief, the woman nodded. "Los Ojos keeps watch. Lemme introduce our spellsmith. He—they—escaped captivity in their year of eighteen-eighty-four. Like everyone, slightly different history. And Easterners, y'understand, but good people." She led to a corner table. "Hey, Johnny? New Traveler, your era."

Familiar brown eyes under a fringe of russet hair grew enormous. *"Ellie?"*

Ellie froze. "John-ny?"

"Emma!" he hollered, hoarse. "Emma, come quick!"

"Whaaat, Daddy?" preceded a coltish ten-year-old girl, scribed papers in her hand. Her mouth formed a silent 'O'. "Mom...ma?"

Ellie swallowed. Shaking, she drew them tightly into her arms. "Dearhearts, I'm...I'm *home.*"

STASIS

MARGARET S. MCGRAW

The reptilian gold eye never blinked, his head hovering motionless above mine as I hunched over the kitchen counter. His slow breaths warmed my back against the Chicago winter cold that seeped through the high-ceilinged loft, no matter how heated the buildings were. Of course, the human living quarters on the Complex weren't kept nearly as warm as the Nest.

I looked up with a smile and rubbed his snout. "You've been very patient tonight. I'm about done here," I said in the deep voice he found most soothing. I pulled my hair away from my face and twisted it into a messy bun before returning my attention to my work. He rested his chin on my head as I slid bead after bead onto the long needle, tugging them down the thread into place on the glittering statue I would sell in the Complex gift shop. I tied off the last line of glass beads and stood up, stretching, to admire my night's handiwork.

"Not bad," I thought of the four statues before me. I hardly painted anymore. My quilled and beaded creations sold much better. All my living expenses were taken care of on the Complex, so my art sales went into savings for my future—not that I gave much thought to a future away from here.

I hardly saw the movement as he bent down and snapped up all four figures in a hungry gulp. "Tyr!" I yelled. "I worked all night on those, you big jerk!"

I clapped my hands and stomped my feet—loud disapproving sounds that made him duck his head and look somewhat guilty. The statues weren't large enough to do his iron-clad stomach any real harm, but dammit, I spent all night working on them!

The cat chose that moment to leap up on the counter and saunter across, swishing her fluffy white tail. She did seem to love lording her mammalian status over him. Suddenly, Tyr's claws were around her waist, lifting her up. He chuffed, and she ignored him with her usual aplomb. Was she that brave? Or just stupid? I never was sure. But she calmly waited as I reprimanded him yet again.

"Tyr. Put. Her. Down."

He hung his head and lowered his torso to release her gently on the floor. She brushed up against him as she wandered away. No hard feelings, apparently. He swung his head over to me, and I absentmindedly reached up to scratch along his jaw.

"I guess it's time to get you home, big boy. The Professor doesn't like you to be out of the Nest so late."

We headed out to the parking lot behind the enormous warehouse apartments, and I climbed in my gold hybrid VW Beetle. As I rolled down the window and started the silent engine, Tyr crouched behind the car and swished his tail. I was tired after a long night focused on the beads—and still frustrated over the wasted effort—but I grinned as I eyed him in the rearview mirror. He *loved* street chases, and obviously we could only indulge in that particular treat in the wee hours when there would be virtually no cars or pedestrians in our path. I led him out through the Complex gate and along our favorite loop, a combination of long stretches on the lakefront and some of the reliably deserted office areas downtown—avoiding any residential areas of course.

No matter how sanguine the city had become about the Professor's dinosaurs *inside* the Complex, someone always freaked if they saw a Tyrannosaurus Rex chasing a Beetle past the deserted office buildings or warehouses. Best keep *that* sight to the occasional beat cop, garbage truck driver, and stoplight camera. They'd seen it all.

Someone would see, of course. Someone would get a video. Tomorrow would be the inevitable wave of social media frenzy. The Professor would grumble, but he didn't read me the riot act like the first few times. It wasn't actually <u>illegal</u>, after all, and we always saw more tourists after videos cropped up showing one of our late-night chases.

Tyr loved to run, but I had to keep his body limits in mind—his heart and lungs were meant for short bursts, not long races. We returned to the Complex, and I led Tyr around to the back of the Nest Center, where it was easier to get him in the dock bay doors. My fingers danced over the control pad to swing the doors open and quiet the chirping alarm before it rose to a claxon.

I didn't bother turning on any additional lights—I could walk all over the Nest blindfolded. I took the dare for an easy twenty bucks from every new grad student. Tyr's steps thudded dully on the specially-made rubberized floors as we made our way in the dim emergency light amber glow back to his nest.

He slowed outside the Parasaurolophus nests. I scratched his leg soothingly and whispered, "No, Tyr. No chasing now. We'll see if they want to run in the fields in the morning, okay, big boy?"

He leaned down and gently butted his head against my back, pushing me forward. I laughed softly.

"Okay, come on. Let's get you settled in Stasis."

Stasis was the Professor's triumph. After the first dinosaur DNA was successfully cloned into viable eggs, there was a huge outcry over the "Jurassic Park" dangers, and all research was in danger of being permanently shuttered. The Professor discovered an energy field that allowed each saur to be bred, raised, and confined within their own "signature resonance."

Stasis combines all these SRs and weaves them into an invisible dome that covers the entire island Complex: buildings and open spaces. I'm a neo-paleo Artist, not an engineer Tech, so I don't really understand *how* it works. But I often think of Arthur C. Clarke's wonderful line, "Any science sufficiently advanced is indistinguishable from magic."

The energy feels like the slightest breeze on your skin, or a buzz under your feet, like music you can't hear. None of the Complex residents notice it after a while, but tourists always do. Each saur's SR keeps them alive and safe on the Complex—they couldn't survive more than a few hours outside. Just long enough for the occasional educational program or festival photo op. And, of course, Tyr never gets to go on those.

With the Techs' constant fine-tuning of the Stasis SR for each saur, they can be lulled to sleep in the Nest or taken out anywhere on the vast Complex grounds—which gives them freedom to run in the fields—under close supervision of their Sponsors.

Turns out, every saur *needs* to imprint on something when it hatches. The Professor had a long line of Sponsors-in-Training, and he personally screened, chose, and trained a Sponsor for each newly hatched saur. We often debated among ourselves why he chose which person for which saur. I have no idea why he chose me for Tyr. I mean, what made him think an Artist would be suited to a T-Rex? But the Professor was notoriously successful—and closemouthed—about how he determined his choices.

I came into the DSIT program while I was finishing my art history thesis at Mount Holyoke, and I've lived on the Complex ever since Tyr was hatched. The Professor encourages all two hundred or so staff to live on campus, and he provides everything we could need or want. After my parents died in the Amtrak crash of '23—returning home from my graduation—I rejected offers from family and friends to go live with them. I quit looking for academic positions. The Professor assured me I would always have a home here.

I turned all my attention to my art and raising Tyr. I used to sneak him into my apartment to sleep with me, all wriggling tail and needle-sharp claws. When he became too big for that, I would climb in his nest and curl up with him, listening to his slow heartbeat and feeling his deep breaths push my head up and down in a steady rhythm. I love that big lunk.

Aside from his occasional mischievous habit of eating my night's work, of course. I suddenly giggled, as an image of his next glittery poop sprang to my mind's eye. I wondered what the Keepers would make of that. They had to go through each and every steaming pile as part of the careful tracking program on each saur's condition.

We reached Tyr's nest, and he snuggled down. I leaned against his head and scratched over his eye and along his snout as he tiredly huffed his pleasure and closed his golden eyes. As he settled into Stasis, I gave him one last hug and headed for the door.

Suddenly, I heard a noise. But that was impossible. Nothing should be moving in Stasis—nothing! I froze. Then I heard it again. A soft shoe step, not claws, on the padded floor.

"Who's there?" I demanded. No one should be in the Nest this late! The security system would have been off when we arrived if another Sponsor or Keeper were here. Suddenly I was afraid—had someone snuck in to hurt the saurs? Some people still didn't believe that imprinting on humans made the saurs completely unable to hurt us.

A couple of young teenagers crept out of the dark, clinging to the wall. Tourists? How had they managed to sneak past the closing security sweep in the Nest?

I hissed angrily. "What the hell are you doing here?!"

"Please! Help us! Get us out of here! We don't know how long we've been in here..."

They were wild-eyed and disheveled. I could feel fear flowing from them, and I rolled my eyes. They were just kids. They really were scared half to death—even though no saur *would* hurt a human—and I realized they were in no shape to do any harm. I couldn't figure out how they'd gotten in or why they were here, but I decided questions could wait until I got them out of there. They were clearly on the verge of a full-on freak, and I didn't want that spreading to the sleeping saurs.

"Okay, you're okay." I soothed them like I would a baby saur. "Follow me, and we'll get you out of here."

They started forward, then paused and looked at each other. "We have to get the others," the girl said. The boy hesitated, looking behind them, then suddenly he dropped back into the gloom of the Nest.

"Hey!" I called as quietly as I could, mindful of the sleeping saurs. "Come back here! What others?"

Silently, people began to emerge from the dark. Mostly college kids, a few older people, and even a few young kids. What the hell was going on? I watched in stunned silence as a dozen became twenty. They all shared the same disoriented looks of the original pair. I didn't understand what was happening. My mind raced, searching for answers or explanations.

With more coming into the pale amber light, my questions turned to concern for the saurs. I needed to get this crowd out of here before I got them talking. I waved my arms to get their attention, made quieting motions, then waved for them to follow me. They held on to each other and glanced around fearfully as they shuffled along behind me. I shook my head in disbelief. I knew I was going to have to call the Professor as soon as we got to the dock bay. I didn't know what was going on, but I had a growing feeling that this was all kinds of bad.

As we rounded the final nest, we disturbed a huge Pterodactyl, who sleepily raised his long snout and yawned. His scissored rows of four-inch teeth gave even me pause, I will admit. I held still and whistled the soothing low tune that always settled Tyr. The Pterodactyl lowered his head and ruffled his wings as he closed his eyes again.

When I turned back to my following crowd, I was dumbfounded to find them all crouched in terror on the floor. I bent down to the first teens I had found. "Come on. It's okay," I stage-whispered. "He's back in Stasis. Let's get moving—quietly please!"

They cautiously raised their heads and stood when they saw me standing there, waiting as patiently as my burning curiosity would allow. I urged everyone up on their feet and moving once again. I led them through the wide hallways, steps muffled on the floors, until we passed outside through the dock bay doors.

Almost a hundred people crowded around me in the open dock bay, staring at the rosy sky in stunned silence. "Okay, someone start talking," I demanded. "What the hell are you all doing here?!?"

They all started talking at once, of course, and I couldn't make out a single word. I held up my hands and gave a loud whistle. Saur herding works on people too, apparently, as they all shut up and froze.

I saw two sweatshirts I recognized and pointed at the girls clutching each other. "You—are you from Mount Holyoke?"

The blond smiled shakily. "Yes, just graduated in May. Class of '89!"

I stared at her. Everyone else did too. Noise erupted again, and this time I heard snippets—dates.

"'89? What are you talking about? I graduated Class of '35—two years ago!"

"What do you mean? It's 2048!" cried a woman who wore a t-shirt proclaiming "2048 National Volleyball Champions."

"It's 2012!"

My eyes still locked on the girls, I pointed to myself.

"2023," I said, through the din around us.

The brunette's eyes widened, and she replied, "2089."

Sixty years? How was it possible? But what was the last date I could actually remember? I wasn't on social media, and I didn't watch the news. I didn't care about the rest of the world outside the Complex. I'd left it behind when Tyr was hatched. I'd never thought about it leaving me behind as well. But even if I had chosen that, none of this made any sense. How had all these people been trapped in the Nest for so long?

Did the Professor know?

I sank to the floor, deaf to the shouted confusion, suddenly conscious of the warm buzz of the Stasis field all around us. My hand trembled as I pulled out my phone and thumbed the Professor's photo to call him.

I hesitated. As soon as I made this call, everything would change, and I had no way to stop it.

I wanted to run back through the building and climb in Tyr's nest. Listen to his slow steady heartbeat and hide from all of this. As dawn brightened the sky, I rubbed my eyes, more tired than I had ever been. My head whirled as the truth of it sank in.

The dinosaurs weren't the only ones locked in Stasis.

THE INTERN

KEN SCHRADER

I looked at my phone, and it flashed the time at me. Eight forty-five.

I'm going to be late.

I looked at the people in line in front of me, at the harried barista, struggling to keep up, taking orders and making drinks by herself.

Crap.

I got out of line and left the shop. The morning sun was bright, and I put on my sunglasses as I beeped my car unlocked.

"Maura?"

I stopped. Dread and a warm thrill joined hands and skipped through me as I turned.

"Erik, hi!"

Erik Schardt stood on the sidewalk looking amazing. He wore running shoes, shorts, and a damp Oakland Raiders t-shirt. An earbud dangled over his shoulder.

"What are you doing downtown?" he asked, his breath coming out heavy from running. He brushed coal-black hair away from his face. "You're not usually down here on a Saturday."

"Job interview," I said, fighting the urge to smooth my dress or play with my sunglasses. Erik and I were passing friends...well, we knew

43

each other by name. I'd have liked to get to know him better, but we didn't move in the same circles.

But he did stop to talk...

And here I was, out on the street with him, looking pretty good myself, and I was running late.

"Good luck on the interview," he said, putting the bud back in his ear. "You look great." His voice came out louder, to overcome whatever he was listening to, and a few people turned from him to me as he jogged up the street.

Smiling, I watched him for a few seconds, then I jumped, mentally. *Interview. Damn.*

I got in my car.

***

My best friend, Zoe Talbot, waited for me on the steps outside Doat Incorporated where, hopefully, I would land an internship and knock out an additional college credit or two before I graduated high school. It was a paid internship to boot, which made it a pretty popular destination this morning. There were more people here than I thought there would be, clustered in small groups on the sidewalk.

"Where have you been?" Zoe hopped off the step and gave me a hug. She wore a black pantsuit with a rust-colored shirt under the jacket, setting off her brown skin. I hugged her back, nearly losing my grip on the folder with my resume and a pen clipped to it. She stepped back, her eyebrow arching. "And no drinks?"

"There was a line. Sorry."

Her face spread into a warm, wicked smile. "What else?"

I flushed. How did she always know it when something happened? "Nothing."

"Come on, spill it," Zoe said. "You're practically glowing."

"Fine," I said, and my own smile bloomed. "I met Erik outside the coffee shop. We talked."

"Talked?" Her eyes sparkled.

44

"He'd been running." I frowned at her, but it didn't last. "So, yes, we talked." I paused. "He said I looked great."

"I knew it!" She turned as the doors opened. A tall, willowy man in a black suit stood in the doorway. He had white hair that shuffled in the breeze and pale skin. He would have seemed cold, but his smile thawed him out.

"Applicants for this summer's intern positions," he announced. "Follow me, please."

Nervous anticipation brushed aside my excitement, pushing me toward the door. Zoe was a step behind me.

"You can fill me in on all the details, later," she said, catching up to me. "Good luck."

I flashed her a smile.

"You too."

T he morning went by in a blur. I remember looking around the building as we followed the tall man inside. There was a lot of wood in the lobby and front hall, dark and warm looking. Tall windows let in the morning sun, adding to the overall warmth of the place. The dormant reception area counter looked like it was marble. I felt a little out of place, like I had stepped back in time. Zoe loved it instantly. She was crazy for old buildings and their history.

He led us to a long conference room where I sat, waiting, while the group of people with me gradually vanished. Eventually, it was just me and Zoe sitting alone. I glanced at my phone. Eleven-thirty flashed back at me. As soon as I knew what time it was, my stomach rumbled. Zoe glanced at me, but before she could say anything, the door opened, and the tall man who had met us at the door stepped in.

"This way, ladies, if you please."

Hoping that my stomach would stay quiet for the next few minutes, I stood.

Zoe and I followed the man down a hall, through a small office space done up with the same warm tones as the lobby, and to an open wooden door. He stood aside extending his arm.

"Please have a seat."

The office was enormous. The ceiling had to be twenty feet high, a wooden fan spun lazily overhead between two globe lights. The walls were lined with bookshelves.

More tall windows, with thick wooden frames, let in light. Through the blinds, I saw traffic passing on the street outside. A small table with a couple of chairs stood nearby, but my eyes fixed on the desk on the other side of the room.

Made of a dark wood and polished so that it gleamed in the light, the desk was expansive. At least as wide as I was tall. Okay, so at five-five, I'm not a giant, or anything, but that's pretty big for a desk.

The top was totally empty except for a closed laptop. Behind the desk, on a filing cabinet between two windows, was a small printer.

"What do you think?" The tall man walked across the room. Behind the desk, he pulled back a black leather chair and settled into it.

"It's pretty open," Zoe said.

"I love the bookshelves," I said, nearly right on top of her. I took a second to glance at the titles. I didn't recognize many, but I knew some. *Treasure Island*, *For Whom the Bell Tolls*, *The Wendigo*. I blinked. *War and Peace*? They didn't seem like the kinds of books that you'd find in a business office. Jane Austen? Agatha Christie? I could get used to working here.

He gestured to a pair of comfortable looking chairs on the opposite side of the desk. We sat, and it felt like I sank a mile into the cushions. The chair was wide enough for me to curl up in, and I wanted to take it home.

"Miss Talbot, Miss Hearne." He leaned his arms on his desk and looked at us. "My name is Mortimer Thaddeus Doat."

I sat up a bit straighter at that. The owner of the company, interviewing interns—on a Saturday?

"I'm not one to mince words," he continued. "So let me get straight to the point: you're hired."

I nearly dropped my folder.

Zoe was quicker on the uptake than I. "But there was only one position available."

"You're both hired," Mr. Doat said. He looked from Zoe to me. Had his eyes changed color? I thought they were light blue when he met us at the door, but now they were on the greenish side.

"I happen to have an inside track with the boss." He smiled. "And my gut tells me that the two of you would complement each other."

I flashed a look at Zoe. Her eyes were wide, and I was sure her smile was going to hop off her face and turn cartwheels any second now.

Mr. Doat removed two folders from a desk drawer and slid them over to us. "We'll have you start on Monday afternoon. Please fill these out and bring them with you."

"Thank you, sir!" I said.

He stood and swept out from behind the desk. Behind him, the printer hummed to life. We rose and Mr. Doat walked us back to the front door.

"See you on Monday, ladies." He shook our hands. His fingers were long and thin, and his grip was firm. His skin felt dry. "Enjoy the rest of your weekend."

Zoe and I skipped down the steps to the sidewalk.

"Squeeee!" Zoe said, and she gave me a hug.

"I'm so glad it didn't come down to either one or the other of us."

"I'd have totally kicked your butt back in there," Zoe said. She stepped back, and we headed toward the corner.

"You didn't even have a copy of your resume." I waggled my folder at her. "It was your butt that would have gotten kicked."

"Hah! The only thing my butt is getting is some lunch. You interested?"

My stomach rumbled, and that was the only answer we needed.

Monday, after school, Zoe and I met at Mr. Doat's building. We stepped into the lobby, and a woman with an infectious smile was waiting for us. She wore brown slacks and a deep blue and white blouse. Her shoes clicked on the floor as she approached.

"Hi." She shook our hands. "I'm Abby Greyson. I'll be showing you around today."

Abby collected our folders and led us back into the back offices. The place was filled with the quiet buzz of voices, the click of keyboards, and the hum of printers.

Our desks were located in a cluster in one corner. Mine had a half-dead spider plant in a white, plastic pot sitting on one edge. Embarrassed, Abby started to clear it away, but I stopped her. It added a bit of color—or would, if I could revive it.

I went to get some water while Abby got Zoe logged onto the computer. I found a water cooler in the break room and filled a coffee mug. On the way back to my desk, a man reading from a folder strode around a corner and nearly ran me down.

I gasped, pulling back. Water sloshed over the rim and splashed onto the carpet.

"Idiot." He stopped reading and gave himself a quick once-over. His gray suit was immaculate, down to his brown leather shoes. A deep, black stone flashed from the slender expanse of white tie that hung from around his neck. When he was sure I hadn't gotten any water on him—or near him—he aimed dark eyes at me. "You're not supposed to take anything out of the break room."

"I'm sorry," I said. Great, I was going to get fired on my first day. "I was just—"

"Who are you?" He looked down at me, his eyebrows coming together. "You're not supposed to be back in the employee area. Who let you in here?"

"I'm—"

"Do you know how much trouble you're in?" His face darkened, and he took a step toward me.

Around us, heads popped over the tops of cube walls. We were now, officially, a "scene." This day was getting better and better.

"Miss Hearne is one of our newest interns." A quiet voice broke through my thoughts of water sloshing down that gray suit, giving the urban prairie dogs something to talk about later. Mr. Doat stood to my right. I hadn't seen him approach.

He turned to me. "And Mr. Reeves is in acquisitions." He nodded from one of us to the other. "Maura Hearne, meet Aron Reeves."

"Pleasure to meet you," I said. I extended my left hand.

Reeves had to juggle the folder to his other hand to shake mine. I smiled.

"Likewise," Reeves said. He squeezed my hand, but I've got three older brothers. Reeves was no contest, even if his hands were on the cold and clammy side. He released my hand and turned to Mr. Doat. "Excuse me." Tucking the folder under his arm, he vanished back the way he came.

Mr. Doat turned to me, eyebrow quirked. Had his eyes changed color? They looked darker, almost brown. "Making friends already?"

"That man is..." I decided to play it safe, "intense."

Doat chuckled. "Yes, that's a good word for it." He glanced down at the cup in my hands. "Enjoy the rest of your day, Miss Hearne."

"Thank you." I watched him head in the direction of his office. I glanced at the mostly full mug, remembering Reeves and his stance on taking things out of the break room, then hurried to get back to Abby and Zoe.

My average day consisted of answering phones, answering emails, making sure there was coffee in the break room, and talking with Zoe. It could have been any office job in the world, but one thing made it unusual.

A large printer stood in the intern area and, seemingly at random, pages would print out of it. Sometimes it was a single page, other times, great piles of pages would print. The paper was thick and perforated so you could split it up into twelve cards, like business cards. On each card was a name and address.

The cards were our highest priority. When a page printed, we took it and split it into twelve cards. There was a different color for each of the people working in acquisitions: blue, fuchsia, green, and gray.

Once the cards were sorted, we took them to the acquisitions offices. This was my least favorite part of the job, because, whenever I went, I always ran into Reeves.

No matter when I went, even if I didn't have any cards for him—which was rare—I always seemed to be passing by when he was coming out from someplace. I'd pass by a doorway, and there he'd be, looming, looking down at me. We never spoke.

Delivering cards to him was the worst. His were the gray ones (naturally) and his office was sterile and lifeless. The furniture was a dismal storm-cloud color, and the office had to be at least ten degrees colder than the rest of the building.

I didn't like the place, and I never lingered. One time, after dropping off some cards, I turned to hurry out, and he was standing in the doorway. I'd never admit this to Zoe, but I made a tiny squeaking sound at the sight of him. I don't think he even noticed. He stared past me at the small pile of cards, like he was a starving man and I'd just delivered a steak dinner. It was like I wasn't even in the room.

I stepped aside so that I wouldn't get run over if he made for the cards, and that was when he noticed me. The look in his eyes made me uncomfortable in a noise-behind-you-in-a-dark-parking-lot kind of way. He stalked into the room, his eyes following me as I arced around him to the door and got the heck out of there.

When the people in acquisitions finished doing whatever it was they did with their cards, they returned them to the intern area, and we entered the information on the cards into a spreadsheet. Every day there was a new, blank sheet titled with the date. I couldn't see why we didn't just import the names from wherever they were printed from.

Zoe returned from delivering a batch of cards to Reeves and flopped into her chair. "That guy isn't right. The way he looks at you, it's like we were delivering cash or something." She shrugged. "He's in acquisitions, so maybe we are, in a way. I don't know."

"None of the others do that," I said.

"True," Zoe said. "But none of the others are as creepy as he is."

I couldn't argue with that. Everyone in acquisitions had their own thing. Gil Porter (blue) was a huge rugby fan. One day, I made the mistake of admitting that I didn't know much about the sport, and I wasn't able to leave the room for the next fifteen minutes.

Evony Malkin (fuchsia) was the biggest Sci-Fi and Fantasy geek I'd ever seen. She had an actual light saber on a plaque on her wall and a life-size cardboard picture of Gandalf from *The Lord of the Rings* movies in one corner of her office, next to a huge map of Middle Earth. I didn't mention it, but I'd have gone with Faramir, myself.

Ruth Belcourt (green) had an office full of plants. The spider plant on my desk came from her collection, and she was glad to hear that it had recovered. Going into her office was like stepping into a terrarium.

They all had their own preferences when it came to the cards, but none of them reacted the way Reeves did when they showed up.

"Hey, check this out," Zoe said.

"What?" I looked up from sorting piles of cards. It had been a busy Friday afternoon with several big print outs.

Zoe held up a card. At first, I didn't notice anything beyond the gray color, but when I looked closer, I saw the name.

Erik Schardt.

Zoe waggled it in the air in front of me. "It's got his address," she sang.

I frowned at her. After he told me I looked great a couple of weeks ago, we hadn't said more than two words to each other.

"Stalker much?" I asked. I plucked the card from her fingers. "And I already know where he lives, thanks." We'd ridden the same bus to school until we could drive.

The smile faded from Zoe's face. "He'll come around, Maura."

"I don't know." I turned to put the card on my gray pile. "Sometimes I don't think it's—" I stopped, looking at the address on the card.

"What is it?" Zoe asked.

"This isn't Erik's address."

"Typo?"

I shook my head. "No, it's not even close."

"Somebody must have gotten their records messed up."

"Must have." I hesitated. I wasn't sure what to do with the card. Abby had never explained what to do when the address on a card was wrong. I didn't even know who was printing them out, so I couldn't go tell anyone about the mistake. Ultimately, the idea of Reeves getting a card with Erik's name on it decided me. I put the card in my pocket, intending to mention the error to Abby on Monday.

I never did.

When I got to school on Monday, everyone was quiet and subdued. During the second period, I got called into a councilor's office and that was when I found out that Erik was dead.

I sat in shock as the councilor relayed what she knew. Erik and four others were killed in a car crash over the weekend. I barely remembered the rest of the conversation, or of walking through the school. The next memory I had was of Zoe hugging me while I cried on her shoulder.

I left school and went home to find a light flashing on the answering machine. Mr. Doat's voice drifted from the speaker saying how sorry he was for my loss and that I could take as much time as I needed before returning to work.

He was so nice. My vision blurred as I listened to the message a second time. Sniffling, I went to my room and turned on my laptop.

I checked the news for what information they had about the crash. I didn't want to know, but I couldn't keep myself from looking. The accident happened late Saturday night. I read the location where the accident happened, and my blood ran cold.

I pulled the card from my pocket and looked at the address. It was the same. That had to be a coincidence. I shut down my laptop, got into my car, and drove to the address on the card.

The police had done what they could, but they couldn't erase the skid marks. They couldn't clean up the damage the car did to the tree. I sat in my car, pulled onto the side of the two-lane road, and stared across the blacktop at shattered bark and splintered wood. Sunlight glinted off a piece of glass at the base of the tree. A car whooshed past me without slowing, and my car rocked gently in the backdraft.

I read the address on the card. This exact address was where Erik had died. I told myself that it was just some kind of mailing list mix up, though a part of me wondered if there were four other cards back at the office with the same address.

You're being silly, I thought. *There's no way—*

"What are you doing with that?" A sharp voice cut into my thoughts. Aron Reeves was outside my window. He lurched into the car and grabbed at the card.

"Get away from me!" I beat at his arm, trying to pull the card out of his grip. What was he doing here? The paper tore, and he stumbled back, a ragged corner of the card pinched in his fingers.

"That was mine!" he shouted. I put the car in gear and floored it before Reeves could come back at me. The engine roared and gravel spat from my tires.

As I pulled away, I looked in the rear-view mirror. Reeves stood on the side of the road, growing smaller. Where was his car? He stretched an arm out toward me. I thought he had pulled a gun but, an instant later, a brilliant ball of green light appeared in his hand. It shot toward me and hit the back of the car with a crash that lifted the rear wheels off the road. I screamed as my car bounced and skidded to the side, crossing the middle line and stopped, pointing in the wrong direction. I looked out my window. Reeves stood in the middle of the road. He was smiling. Then he vanished. I don't mean that he got in a car and drove away; he just wasn't there anymore. I blinked at the spot where he'd been.

A horn blared. There was a screech of tires, a horrible, jolting crash, and the world went black.

I opened my eyes, and I wished I hadn't. White light speared into my head and punched holes in my brain. I groaned.

"You're awake!" Zoe's voice drilled through my ears. "How are you feeling?"

"Stop shouting." My mouth felt dry and crackly. The rest of the world started to filter in. I was in a bed, my head raised a little above my feet. The ceiling was a blaring white. I turned my head. My neck ached. The walls were light blue, and a table stood next to the bed. Zoe stood by the table, her eyes red and glistening. She dabbed at one with a tissue.

"What happened?" I rasped. I glanced at the table. A tiny white cup with a blue straw poking out of the top sat next to a vase of flowers. I reached for the cup and stopped. My forearm was bandaged almost from my wrist to my elbow.

As if my noticing it had been a signal, every ache and pain—and I had a lot of them—flared to life. My head was the worst. I reached up and found another bandage there—and a bump that felt like it was the size of my fist.

"You scared the hell out of me is what happened." Zoe handed me the cup, and I took a sip. Blessedly cold water washed the dryness away. "You really don't remember what happened?"

I shook my head and regretted it. Pain throbbed in my temples. "No."

"You were in an accident. The police say that you must have lost control of your car when your tires blew. There was a truck—a big one—that was going the opposite way." Zoe blinked a couple of times. "He couldn't stop in time and..." She trailed off and took my hand.

I closed my eyes. In my memory, I saw Reeves standing in the

54

road, throwing that green blob at me. I felt it hit my car. I saw him smiling before he vanished into nothing. It was almost as if he knew what was coming. He knew. How could he have known? How could he have done those other things?

"Maura?" Zoe's voice was soft. I opened my eyes. My friend's face was strained. "I'm sorry. I wasn't sure if you'd fallen asleep."

"It's okay."

Zoe paused. "Maura, what were you doing out there? Isn't that where Erik—"

I cut her off. "I had to see. Had to be sure."

She straightened. "Sure of what?"

"It wasn't a typo."

"And you've lost me." She cocked her head. "What wasn't a typo?"

"I hope I'm not interrupting anything."

The words died on my lips. Aron Reeves stood in the doorway, his gray suit looking immaculate, black tie pin gleaming in the light of the room. I shrank back into the bed.

"Maura, what is it?" Zoe turned, and a scowl shuttered her features. "I don't think you should be here."

Reeves slipped into the room. He waved his hand casually as Zoe took a step forward. She froze in mid-step.

"Zoe?" I asked. She didn't move. I turned to Reeves. "What did you do?"

"What makes you think I did anything?" He stood at the foot of my bed, looking down at me.

"I'm not stupid," I said. The pain in my head bled into anger. "I may not be able to explain what I saw you do, but I saw you doing it."

"Indeed?" A smile spread across his lips. It didn't reach his eyes.

"I catch on pretty quickly."

"The scope of your ignorance is staggering."

"Yeah?" I sat forward. My whole body felt like one big bruise, but I wanted to punch holes in all that smugness. "Well, I know that you had something to do with—" I paused, not wanting to give him Erik's name, "—with that accident."

"Is that what you think?"

"And I know that it has something to do with those cards."

"You don't know any—"

I plowed over him. "And I know that you're never going to get another card from me, or any of my friends. I'll shred them first."

The smile froze in place. "That would be foolish."

"Would it?" I sat back, feeling pretty smug myself. "I might not know why the cards are important to you, but I know they are, smart-guy. You just showed me that. And, because you want them, I'm going to make it my job to keep them from you."

He leaned forward, his knuckles going white on the end of the bed frame. His eyes flashed a sickly green. The groan of metal echoed through the room as the frame bent under his hands.

I felt much less smug.

"You don't have the first idea of the powers you're playing with." He straightened, releasing the bed frame. It was crumpled where he'd touched it. "I will only say this once." He looked down at me. "Walk away. Leave the company. Never return."

He glanced at my vase of flowers, and his eyes flashed green again. The vase exploded. I yelped as cold water and pieces of glass, peppered me. Reeves stepped around the end of the bed. Green light swirled in his eyes as he stood over me. I shrank into the bed. "Do I make myself clear?"

"Mister Reeves."

The voice flowed through the room like an arctic wind. I shivered, but maybe it was from the water on my face and arms. I tore my eyes away from Reeves.

Mr. Doat stood in the doorway. In his black suit, he seemed to take up the entire space. Lips pressed tight, his eyebrows furrowed over storm-gray eyes. "I think you've been here long enough."

I wanted to shout out to Mr. Doat to be careful, but not with Reeves standing so close to me. I glanced up at him.

The green light in Reeves' eyes faded. He turned.

"Morty."

My eyebrows rose. Snark dripped from the word like the water dripping from my bedside table.

Mr. Doat stepped into the room. He took in Zoe—still frozen in place, and the shattered vase. He faced Reeves. "Whatever you've come here to do, it's finished."

The room echoed with a silent pop, and Zoe started moving again.

"I don't think so," she said. "You need—" She cut herself off, head cocked in confusion. She turned, spotting Reeves standing next to me.

A drop of water plinked into the silence.

Zoe turned. "What just happened?"

"Miss Talbot," Mr. Doat said, "there's been an accident. Would you please go find some towels?"

His eyes didn't flash, he didn't move, but when Mr. Doat spoke, even I felt a need to get up for towels.

"Sure." Zoe glanced at me. "I'll be right back." She went out into the hallway.

"Mr. Reeves," Mr. Doat said, "you were just leaving, correct?"

Reeves was silent, fists clenched behind his back. They relaxed, and Reeves glanced down at me. "I don't think there's any need to continue our conversation." He stepped away from the bed, heading for the door.

"See that there isn't," Mr. Doat said.

Reeves whirled in the doorway. "You won't always hold the position you now have." Reeves stabbed a finger at him. "Your time will come."

"It comes for all of us, Mister Reeves," Mr. Doat said. "Even you."

Reeves swallowed whatever he had been about to say and left.

"What an ass," I said.

Mr. Doat turned his head to me, an eyebrow raised. The corner of his mouth quirked up for an instant.

"How are you feeling?" he asked.

"I have a massive headache." I grimaced. "And I can't figure out what the hell is going on here."

"What do you mean?"

I glared at him. "Don't you start. My tires didn't blow because I ran over something." I looked out the door into the hallway. I didn't want any nurses to hear me and toss me into the mental ward. "Reeves threw...something at my car. Something that blew out my tires and spun me into the path of an oncoming truck."

A chill flowed over me as I gave voice to the thought that had been swirling around my banged-up head since I woke up. "He tried to kill me."

"Miss Hearne," he said.

"I'm not crazy," I said. I pointed at the foot of the bed where Reeves had crumpled the metal. "He did that, and he smashed my vase with just a glance." I gasped. "And Zoe. What he did to her. She's out there with him!"

I sat forward, struggling to untangle my legs from the sheets. I had to get out there. I had to—

"Look at me, Maura."

Mr. Doat was at my bedside. I hadn't seen him move, and his voice surprised me. I looked into his eyes, and a wave of calm washed over me, the pain in my head eased.

"Zoe will be fine," he said.

"But—"

"Rest."

I didn't want to rest. I wanted to ask him about Reeves, about what he did, about the cards, but my eyelids had other ideas. They were so heavy, and I thought it wouldn't hurt to let them down for a little while.

I tottered around the house for the next couple of days. My headaches faded, but I wasn't allowed to go back to school or to work. If I'd have let them, my parents would have wrapped me in cotton and packed me away in my room. I can't say that I blame them. My dad came home on Wednesday with pictures of my car for the insurance company, and he showed them to me.

My poor car had been squished by the truck. I looked at the pictures with a kind of detachment. I didn't remember any of what caused the kind of damage I was looking at. I only remembered Reeves, standing in the road, smiling at me before he vanished.

I clicked through the pictures, stopping when I got to the rear of the car. It was mashed and warped. I zoomed in. My license plate was folded back under the car like it had been crumpled by a giant fist. It looked scorched. The rear bumper was crushed in, and the sticker that was there was blackened, like it had been burned. Both rear tires were melted. Nobody said anything about a fire, and the pictures didn't show any other sign of it. Everyone thought the damage was all due to the truck that hit me, but I knew what really happened. Reeves.

During the week, Zoe stopped by to fill me in on everything that was going on at school. People found it weird that I was hanging around where Erik's accident had happened. By extension, they thought I was weird and were talking about it.

I shrugged it off. In light of what had been happening, school politics seemed petty. It bothered Zoe, though, and she went out of her way to try and keep me distracted. One day, she brought a printout of some building plans. The address at the bottom said that it was Mr. Doat's office building.

"It's a historical building. Used to be a post office, or a bank, but check this out." She pointed to a spot. "This should be Doat's office, and that," she slid her finger a few inches, "is a spiral staircase that runs from the attic to the basement." She looked around, then said in a stage whisper, "Goes all the way down to the Batcave."

I couldn't help it. I laughed. It felt good. Then, like an idiot, I asked about work.

Zoe told me that Reeves had been getting even creepier. He hadn't been returning any of his gray cards. Zoe said that she'd even seen him snatching stacks of cards from Gil, Ruth, and even Evony. As she spoke, I pictured a confrontation between Evony and Reeves. Evony with her lightsaber glow-humming and Reeves with his green goo facing off over a pile of cards.

The image made me smile until Zoe mentioned that Gil had tried to reclaim some of his cards from Reeves and Reeves had knocked him down.

It all came down to those cards. I told Zoe about the one with Erik's name on it and how the address was the place where—well, you know. Zoe didn't remember it, and when I tried to show her the card, I found that it had turned to mush after my mom ran my jeans through the washer without checking the pockets.

I resolved to go back to work the next day, but I couldn't get anyone to agree to sign my doctor's note until Friday. I had to push my parents who wanted me to wait out the weekend, but all I could think of were the sheets and sheets of cards that printed out every day. Of Reeves getting his hands on as many as he could and doing whatever the hell it was he was doing with them.

I hated knowing that Reeves was somehow involved in Erik's death, hated knowing that he was out there causing harm, hated knowing that no one would believe me if I told them, maybe not even Mr. Doat.

That meant it was up to me to stop him.

———

On Friday, I stayed in school for a couple of periods, ignoring the whispers and side-looks. Just before lunch, I went down to the nurse's station, claimed I had a headache—which wasn't exactly a lie—and signed myself out for the day. I waved off the nurse's offer to call my parents to come get me. I had driven to school, I said, and I could make it home all right.

I drove to work. When I got there, I badged my way into the back, taking the long way to my desk to avoid passing too close to Reeves' office.

On my desk was a "Welcome back" card leaning against the monitor. I opened it and saw that it had been signed by everyone in the office—except Reeves. I smiled at Ruth's flowery message and Evony's "Dammit, Maura. I'm in acquisitions, not a doctor..." Gil mentioned something about scrums and large vehicles—whatever a scrum was. I set the card on my desk, logged onto the computer, and opened the spreadsheet of all the names we entered.

On a second monitor, I opened up the obituary page at the *Times'* website. I chose the first name in the list and did a search in the spreadsheet. A second later, I found the name and the address.

I chose the second name in the list and did a search. I found the name. It had the same address. Frowning, I opened up a new tab in the browser and Googled the address. It was a hospital. Both of these people had died in the same place.

Something caught my eye, and I looked from the string of numbers to the obituary page and back again. The numbers matched the date on the obituary. I looked at the rest of the numbers, and the room seemed to spin. Time.

Behind me, the printer hummed to life, and I jumped. A single gray sheet printed out and dropped silently into the paper tray. I picked up the paper. Names, locations, and, now that I knew what I was looking at, dates—down to the second. Every name on this page was someone who was going to die. I had to do something. I could call the police...but what would I tell them? I looked at the page. Twelve people. I couldn't be in twelve places at once. What could I—

My eyes landed on the final name on the page, and my blood ran cold.

It was mine.

I burst into Doat's office, the sheet of cards in my hand—minus the card with my name on it—and came to an abrupt halt. He was gone.

"Dammit."

Frustration and fear washed over me until I had to sit down. Even empty, the office felt heavy with Mr. Doat's presence. I sat at the little conference table and took deep breaths. My hands trembled, and I flipped the paper over so I couldn't see the names. I took the card out of my pocket and looked at it.

Maura Elizabeth Hearne. It took me a second to recognize the address. Almost against my will, my eyes dropped to the line of numbers.

Today.

22:45:13.

I was going to die in this building in just under ten hours.

No, I'm not.

There is no way I'm going to be anywhere near this building tonight. I'm not even going to be in this city. I'm going to take my car, find Zoe, and we're going to hang out somewhere. It's Friday. We could crash at her house, and I'd never be here. This card could be wrong. It would be wrong. I wasn't going to—

"What are you doing here?"

I jumped. Whirling, I grabbed the card off the table and stuffed it into my back pocket.

Reeves stood in the doorway.

My eyes flashed around the room, looking for another way out. There was a door in the wall to my right, but I didn't know if it was locked, and I wasn't turning my back on Reeves.

"What is that?" His eyes flashed green, and the paper flew off the table, blown by an unfelt wind. He plucked it out of the air and looked at it.

"What are you doing with this?" he asked. "These are to come directly to acquisitions." He shook the paper at me. "Where is the last one? Is that what you've got in your pocket?"

He took a step toward me.

"If you touch me, you'll regret it," I said. I hadn't realized I was backing up until I ran into something—one of the chairs by Mr. Doat's desk.

Reeves laughed. He actually laughed, like I'd said something unexpectedly funny.

"Really?" He crumpled the paper in his fist, took another step. "What is it, exactly, that you think you can do?" His lips split into a horrible grin.

"Stay back."

"Whose name was it?" he asked. "Someone you care for? Zoe, perhaps?"

"You keep away from her."

"Or...what?" His voice was graveyard cold.

"I'll—"

"You'll stop me?" Reeves stalked forward. "Because you catch on pretty quickly?" I slipped around the chair, putting it between us, and backed into the desk.

He raised his hand, and the chair lifted off the floor. It rose, spinning slowly, until it was level with my head. I stared at it.

How is he doing that?

"You can do nothing," he said. "You are an insect among gods, and you don't even know it."

I slid along the desk, watching Reeves and the chair, angling for the door. "Small doesn't mean insignificant."

"No," he said, turning. Following me. "It means you're easier to crush." The chair dropped with a hollow boom that I felt through the floor. I jumped, backing into a bookcase.

He laughed. "Keep your card," he said. "After tonight, it won't matter."

My mouth went dry. "Why?" I was nearly at the door.

"Because I'll be the one in charge. Not that idiot, Doat." A smile spread across his face. "And when I am, I am going to take great pleasure in ripping your life to shreds before finally taking you."

"That's not going to happen," I said.

"I assure you it will." He stepped back and sat on the edge of Mr. Doat's desk. "Now get out of my office."

I stood in the doorway, not wanting to turn my back on him. "It's Mr. Doat's office."

"Not for much longer."

I edged into the hallway and ran.

I thought I was running for my car, but I found myself back at my desk. If Reeves didn't know about my card, then what made tonight so important? I brought up the office calendar and frowned. Mr. Doat had blocked off time on his calendar for tonight. I couldn't see the details, but the appointment ran from ten to eleven. He was going to be here.

That's what Reeves was talking about. Why bother with a corporate takeover when you could blast your competition with nasty green goo and disappear?

I had to warn Mr. Doat about Reeves. I glanced at the calendar again. The rest of his day was full of meetings. Some of those meetings overlapped, some of them even conflicted with each other, and they were all somewhere else.

I thought about emailing him but dismissed the idea. I don't think I'd even believe an email from me that read, "Watch Your Back! Reeves is going to try and kill you!" More likely, he'd have me packed away somewhere for observation.

I was going to have to try and catch him between meetings and convince him, somehow, of Reeves' threat. I put the information for the remaining meetings in my phone, shut down my computer, and headed for my car.

I only had to sit for thirty minutes before it became apparent that I'd staked out the wrong meeting. That, pretty much, sums up how the last day of my life went.

I chased him around the city for the rest of the afternoon, either missing meetings or going to the wrong ones altogether.

Why the heck would he book two meetings, for the same time, in two different locations?

Eventually, I caught up to him just as he pulled into another private lot. Dammit, I was going to have to find a place to feed a meter and wait.

This meeting was the longest scheduled for the day, and as I shoved change into the meter, I studied Mr. Doat's car. It was a pure white Rolls Royce. I eased my seat back and wondered how he managed to keep his car so clean.

The sun was warm, and a nice breeze blew through my open window as I waited. I remember thinking that I should have brought a book or something as I listened to the traffic *shoosh* past me in fits and starts. I glanced at my phone—thirty minutes to go. I tipped my head back, looking at the roof of my car, wondering if I had time to grab something to eat.

My phone rang, snapping me awake. I sat forward, blinking. Zoe was calling. Probably wondering where I was, since I wasn't at work. I sent the call to voicemail.

I looked at the parking lot, and a wash of relief flooded me. Mr. Doat's car was still there. I pulled my seat forward, mentally kicking myself for dozing off. I glanced at the phone. Mr. Doat was going to be done any minute.

The door to the building opened and Mr. Doat stepped out. He was wearing a black suit. His pale skin seemed to glow in the bright sunlight. He walked down a short flight of steps, headed for his car.

I scrambled out of my car and slipped through a gap in the thigh-high wall surrounding the lot. A tree had been planted there, giving me enough room to get through.

"Mr. Doat," I said.

He turned as I approached. "Miss Hearne. Shouldn't you be at work?"

Anything I had planned to say evaporated. I stopped in front of him, his hand on the door handle of his too white car, and I couldn't put two words together.

A look of concern crossed his face. "Are you all right?" He paused. "Maybe you should take the day off. Come back on Monday."

That jolted me. Monday would too late. For both of us. The wind picked up. I glanced in its direction and saw clouds moving in. There would be a storm later.

He opened his door. "Get some rest, Miss Hearne."

"Reeves wants to kill you," I said.

Okay, that could have gone smoother.

He stopped, one foot still in the air. "What?" He turned, left the door open, and stood in the gap like he could fall into the safety of his car if the crazy intern in front of him went even more batty.

I took a deep breath. "I know about the cards," I said. "I know what they're for." My hand twitched toward my back pocket where I kept the card that said I was going to die in this man's office at ten forty-five tonight. A chill washed over me. Was I making a mistake? The card never said how I was going to die—or who would be there when I did.

"Names, places, and dates," I said. "Of people who are going to die. Printed on color coded cards that you have your interns separate and deliver to your—" I made air quotes with my fingers. "Acquisitions team."

Acquisitions. The truth hit me like the truck that smashed my car. They all did it. Gil, Ruth, and Evony. They all got cards.

"What the hell is going on?" I asked.

"Miss Hearne—"

"Don't give me that crap." Dammit, I *liked* Evony. "What, exactly, does your acquisitions team acquire?"

"Maura—"

"They're killing people."

"No."

Even as he said it, I knew I had it wrong. Reeves never saw the card with Erik's name on it. They weren't killing people. What were they doing?

Zoe's ring tone started playing. I ignored it.

"That's your phone," Mr. Doat said.

"It does that sometimes," I said. "You're not going to distract me off this. What is going on?"

"You wouldn't understand."

"Explain it to me."

Zoe's ring tone exploded from my phone. Dammit. I was getting worried now. Zoe never attack-dialed me like this. I looked at Mr. Doat. "Don't go anywhere."

I clicked the phone on. "Zoe? Now isn't a good—"

It wasn't Zoe on the other end, it was her mom.

She was crying.

For the second time that week, I was in the emergency room. Being in the waiting room was worse than being inside.

I had left Mr. Doat in the parking lot without saying a word and raced for the hospital. Zoe's mom met me. There'd been some kind of accident. A car had jumped a curb and plowed through the front wall of a coffee house that Zoe liked. She was cut up pretty bad, and her leg was broken. It was going to need surgery.

It was a couple of hours before I could visit her. I stood in the doorway taking her in. She looked awful, and beautiful.

"Hey," Zoe said. I stepped inside, and my vision blurred as I crossed the room.

"We've got to stop meeting like this," I said. I took her hand and squeezed gently.

She let out a tired laugh. "You started it."

The corner of my mouth turned up. "You win. I don't want to know what would top this."

"Good." She reached for a cup of ice water. I grabbed it and handed it to her. She took a sip and rested her head on the pillow.

"God, hit by a car in a coffee shop," she said. "How dumb is that?"

"You do like to put your own spin on things."

She snorted. "I would not have chosen Beans-n-Things."

"I don't know about that," I said. "You loved that place." I paused, realized I had put it in the past tense. "Love that place."

We were both quiet for a moment.

"It was so weird, Maura. I was sitting there with my coffee and my phone, and I catch this green flash out of the corner of my eye. I turn and there's a car coming right at me." She shivered. "I can still see the driver's face. Eyes wide, mouth dropped open, like he had no idea what the hell was happening."

The room seemed to tilt under me, and I put a hand on the bed rail. "A green flash?"

She shrugged. "Something. Probably just light off the windshield." Zoe looked at me. "It probably saved my life. If I hadn't seen it and turned...that car..."

"But you did, and you're here." I took her hand. "And you're going to be fine."

And I'm going to make sure you stay that way.

I stayed until visiting hours were over. Night fell, bringing rain with it. Thunder rumbled, and lightning flashed outside Zoe's window, and I couldn't keep from coming back to the thought that Reeves tried to kill my best friend.

Because of me.

"Maura?"

I blinked, startled out of my thoughts for the second time in the last half hour. "I'm sorry."

A look of concern crossed my friend's face. "You're not usually this scatter-brained. What's wrong?"

A maniac tried to kill you, because of me. I have to stop him, and the only place I know where to look for him is where I'm scheduled to die tonight.

"It's nothing," I said. I glanced at the clock. Nine forty-five.

"Bull." Zoe quirked a smile. "And it's gotten worse the later it gets." She paused, looked at me. I tried not to squirm. "You have to be somewhere." Her eyes gleamed. "Somewhere you should be telling me about? You know I can always tell when it's something big."

It was like a freaking superpower, but it sent her in the wrong direction this time.

"It's nothing like that." I huffed out a laugh. "One, I'd have told you if I had a date and, two, if you think I'd leave you in the hospital to hang out with some guy, they should x-ray your head to see if there's anything wrong. I don't have anywhere I have to be."

And I didn't. If they were going to kick me out, they'd have done it already. I could stay here. The card in my pocket could still be wrong. I didn't have to go out and die tonight. I didn't have to get involved in whatever struggle was going on between Reeves and Mr. Doat.

But, if Reeves won, what would happen?

He said he'd tear my life apart before killing me. He already tried to kill Zoe. I didn't know what I could do against someone like Reeves, but I knew I had to do something.

Thunder cracked outside.

"Maura?"

I shook my head. *Dammit.*

"I'm sorry, Zoe. It's just—"

"It's okay," Zoe said. "I'm getting tired, and you're not looking so good. Maybe you should get some sleep."

I swallowed. "All right. Get some rest." I leaned down and hugged Zoe for what was probably the last time. My eyes stung.

"Ow, easy," Zoe said.

I winced. "Sorry." I straightened, blinking away guilt.

"You sure you're okay?"

I exhaled, wiping at my eye. "You just scared me today is all."

She took my hand and squeezed. "I'm fine." She paused. "Well, I'm getting better. Go on. I'll see you tomorrow."

I nodded, not trusting my voice, hating myself for the lie, and stepped to the door. I turned, took one last look at my friend, and left before I lost my nerve.

I drove through the storm, headed for my office building, unsure of what I was going to do when I got there. All I had on me were my keys, my phone, a pen in my back pocket, thirty-two cents, and the card that said I was going to die in twenty minutes.

I could call the police, but what would I tell them? They might take a bomb threat seriously, but who called in a bomb threat against an empty building? How do I know they wouldn't just treat it like a prank?

No, I had to be sure Reeves was stopped. The police would only delay him, and that wouldn't be good enough.

I parked my car and raced through the rain toward the entrance. It didn't occur to me to wonder if my badge would work after hours until I was half-soaked with my hand on the handle.

The door tugged open. It was unlocked. Shivering from more than the rain, I slipped inside.

The entrance was dark. Beyond, service lights spilled pools of light at regular intervals while lightning splashed light everywhere at random.

I cut through the office, drawing small comfort from Gandalf as I passed Evony's door. Grimly, I wondered if a real lightsaber would make a difference against Reeves.

The door to Mr. Doat's office was closed. Green light slipped from the crack underneath. My hand hovered over the handle. Reeves' voice came through the door. I didn't understand the language he spoke, but the skin on the back of my neck prickled. That wasn't good.

As I touched the door handle, there was a crash. It felt like the entire building shook. I heard another sound. Mr. Doat, growling in pain and effort.

I admit it. I almost ran. This was way out of my comfort zone. I thought of Zoe, that what happened to her was, partially, my fault.

I took a deep breath and turned the handle as quietly as I could. It didn't budge. Frowning, I tried again, harder. Still nothing.

"Dammit," I said. I stepped back and scowled at the door. Reeves must have locked it. I looked around for—I don't know what. It wasn't like I was going to break through the door with a chair or—

Wait.

My mind flashed back to the plans for the building that Zoe dug up...had that only been Monday? It seemed like a lifetime.

Zoe had pointed out some stairs that came out by Doat's office—

stairs to the Batcave. Lightning flashed, turning the hallway white for an instant. I turned and ran for the fire door, hoping that Zoe'd been joking about the bats.

The door closed behind me with a quiet click. Service lights puddled the dark. Even down a flight, the roar of thunder reached my ears. At least I thought it was thunder making the building rattle.

I stepped down the hallway, unsure of where I was in relation to the floor above. Finally, I found myself in front of an unmarked door. It could have been a storage closet for all the attention that it drew to itself, but this had to be it.

I turned the knob and the door opened with a creak. Light rushed into the space beyond to illuminate a staircase made out of black metal that spiraled up into darkness.

"Great," I said. "Freaking Batcave."

There was a boom, like something heavy hitting the floor above me. The sound echoed up and down the stairwell. I put my hand on the rail and started to climb. Three steps up, the door clicked shut and blackness swallowed me.

"Oh come on," I said.

Why the hell hadn't anyone put a light in here?

Three more steps and I completely lost the sense of which direction I was facing. I kept climbing, spiraling up through blackness. Suddenly, the rail stopped. I reached out with my foot and found that I was on a flat space, probably a landing. Keeping my hand on the rail, I turned and reached out with my other hand. Fumbling, I found a door knob and turned it. The door swung out and, in my haste to get out of the stairwell, I walked through a bunch of cobwebs.

"God!" I brushed the strands away, trying not to think of spiders, and looked around. Lightning showed me a short, empty space. I turned at the sound of struggle coming from behind a wooden door nearby. The other door to Doat's office. I went to the door, took a deep breath, and turned the knob. It clicked open. I pushed the door open just a crack and looked through.

The office was a wreck. Books had been thrown everywhere, and paper swirled around the office, caught in a howling wind. I opened the door wider. One of those beautiful bookshelves had been ruined, the shelves were broken, and books spilled from them onto the floor.

Reeves and Mr. Doat stood at opposite ends of the office. I stared, trying to make sense of what was going on. Reeves, in his gray suit, was surrounded by a glowing green goo that swirled around him. He had a hand stretched out in a weird claw shape, and more goo flowed from it, making a kind of tentacle that pounded on a purplish dome.

Mr. Doat crouched, his hand held out, projecting the shield that kept the tentacle from reaching him. He looked terrible. His black suit was ripped and torn, and blood trickled from his ear and the corner of his mouth.

Neither of them noticed me. I pushed the door open wide enough to slip through. The broken frame of a chair scraped the floor, and I winced.

I edged along the bookshelves toward Mr. Doat's desk. I hadn't gotten more than a couple of steps before the door slammed shut. I turned. Reeves leered at me.

"Well, if it isn't the intern," he said.

"Maura, get out of here!" Mr. Doat turned his gaze back to Reeves, straightened, and thrust his hand forward. An orange column of light leaped from his palm. It hit Reeves in the chest and pushed him backward into the wall where he hit with an almost gentle thump. Reeves laughed.

"You old fool." He crossed his wrists in front of him, and the orange light shattered. He stepped forward, his tie pin glowing green. "You can't harm the living." He swung his arm like he was going to punch Mr. Doat, even though he was across the room.

Mr. Doat made a wuffing sound as something picked him up and threw him into the wall. He hit with a crash that I felt through my feet. He bounced off the wall and fell to his knees.

Mr. Doat looked at me, his eyes wide. "Go!"

72

"She isn't going anywhere," Reeves said. "And you—"He raised his fist. Mr. Doat gasped. His body rose from the floor and hung in the air. "Your time here is nearly—"

The book I'd grabbed and thrown at Reeves hit him in the face. It was the hardcover of *War and Peace*, and it hit with a pretty good thump. Reeves stumbled back, his hands going to his nose.

Mr. Doat dropped to the floor. "Run, Maura!"

"You miserable, little, nothing!" Reeves raised his hand toward me.

I dove at the conference table. A hissing, green blob struck the books behind me, and I smelled burning paper. I scrambled to my knees and tipped the table over in front of me just as another green blob struck. It splashed against the table top, and a few drops of it hit my arms and got into my hair.

The green goo burned. I rubbed at my arms and clawed the stuff out of my hair, but it didn't stop the pain. I huddled behind the table. What the hell was I doing here? I couldn't fight Reeves. What was I going to do, throw books at him until it hit ten forty-five? I threw my gaze to the clock. It was ten forty-four.

I was going to die here. That damned card was—

An idea exploded in my head. I fumbled the card and pen from my back pocket and scribbled.

The table flew across the room and shattered against the wall. I scrambled to my feet.

Reeves raised his hand; it glowed a sickly green-black, and tendrils of mist trailed from his fingers.

Mr. Doat struggled to his feet. I sprinted toward him, stretched out my arm, held out the card to him.

"Die!" Reeves shouted.

Pain shot through me, and I screamed, falling to the floor. A black tendril, sickly green light threading through it like lightning, pierced my leg and numbing cold flowed in. I couldn't feel my legs. I tried to rise, but my arms felt cased in ice.

"Maura!" Mr. Doat fell to his knees in front of me. He took the card from my numbing fingers.

"She's mine."

A blast of green goo hit Mr. Doat, picking him up and hurling him into the wall next to the printer. Some of the goo might have gotten on me, but I was so cold and numb, I didn't feel it.

Mr. Doat rose to his feet behind his desk. He eyes glowed white, and he stood straight. In his hand, he held the card I had delivered to him. I'd scratched out my name and written: Aron Reeves.

"That changes nothing," Reeves said. He curled his hand into a fist.

"Actually," Mr. Doat said.His voice was strong, and it echoed through the room. "It changes everything."

The cold reached my head, filling my entire body. I couldn't move. It was hard to breathe, and I couldn't feel the floor beneath me. I heard the printer start up, and I knew that my name was going to be on one of the little cards it printed. As darkness crept around the edges of my vision, the last thing I heard was Mr. Doat's voice.

"Mister Reeves, you're fired."

"Maura?"

The world felt thick and muzzy, but comfortable. I wanted to stay there.

Warm fingers touched my forehead, and a tingling washed through me. I opened my eyes. I was in a hospital room. Again. Zoe stood on one side of the bed. Her head was turned up, and her mouth was open. My mom stood on the other side of the bed. Both were frozen in place. My dad was at the foot of the bed, equally stuck.

Outside, thunder rumbled.

Mr. Doat appeared next to Zoe, bending over to look at me. As I watched, his eyes changed color from green to yellow.

I blinked up at him. "What happened?" Memory returned, and my eyes widened. "Reeves?" I struggled to sit up.

"Easy." He put a hand on my shoulder, his thin fingers warm and strong. "You've had a busy night."

"But—"

"Aron Reeves has been dealt with." His voice was cold, but it warmed again. "Thanks to you, he won't hurt anyone again."

My eyes fell to my leg beneath the blanket, to where that black thing had touched me. I shuddered, remembering cold filling me, making it hard to move, to breathe. I remembered the printer coming to life. The machine that printed the names of people that were going to die.

"Maura?"

I looked back up at him. His suit was whole, and there were no traces of the blood I had seen earlier. A chill that had been lingering at the edges of my awareness gripped me.

"Who are you?" I asked.

"I think you know." The corner of his mouth turned up. "Or, at least, I think you suspect."

"You're him, aren't you?"

He straightened. "Say it, Maura. Who am I?"

"Death," I whispered.

He inclined his head.

"But—"

"All of your questions will be answered, but now is not the time."

"One question," I said. "I think I've earned that much."

Death paused. "Ask," he said.

"Reeves was...what?"

"Reeves was someone I should have kept a closer watch on," Death said. "He was a Gatherer." My eyes widened, and Death held up a hand. "Gatherers can see the souls of the deceased. They help those souls to move on. They don't kill anyone. They can't. None of us can harm the living."

A memory of cold flowed through me, and I shivered. "But Reeves..." I trailed off, not wanting to remember.

Death started to speak, stopped, started again. "Souls are both a part of this world and the next. Reeves collected them, used their energy. That is why he was able to do what he did."

"What happened to the souls?"

A breath slid from him and his shoulders sagged. "The ones he used up, ceased to be. Those he partially used, were...damaged." He paused. "They will remain, drifting. In time, they will heal enough to move on, but until then, they will be vulnerable to those who would use their energy."

"That's horrible."

"Yes it is."

He leaned forward. "Maura, I need people I can trust. Good people who aren't afraid to do what is right." He hesitated. "People like you."

"I can't see souls."

"You could, if you're willing."

I thought about it. Could I work for Death? Gather the souls of the dead and help them to move on? What if I had to gather someone I knew?

"You are compassionate and strong, Maura," Death said. "And you would be helping untold numbers of people who need you."

My mind flashed back to Reeves, a black tentacle piercing my leg. The cold. All powered by souls. Did I want to risk someone I cared about falling into the hands of a monster like that?

"Can you change me back? If I want to stop seeing?"

"No," Death said. "Once your eyes are opened, they can never be shut again."

Would it be worth it? If I could keep a vulnerable soul from being consumed? These were people. They had hopes and dreams. They deserved better than being turned into batteries for things like Reeves.

"How can I protect them?" I fumbled for the words. "Without using them up?" I thought back to my poor car. "Reeves could do things."

"I will show you how to defend yourself and others."

I let out a long breath. The world seemed so much bigger than it had an hour ago, and heavier. *What about school? Can I juggle both it and this?* I hoped so, but Death said I couldn't go back to the way I was. *Would I eventually have to give up school?*

I pressed my lips together. *No, I'm not going to give up my dreams, but if I could do some good, shouldn't I? I'll figure the rest of it out as I go.*

"Okay," I said. "I'll do it." I set my jaw, wondering what the hospital would look like when I could see the souls of the dead. "Show me."

"Not now," he said. "Wait until you can return to work." He glanced at my parents. "The police found you unconscious in your car. Your doctor is going to blame it on the accident. I'm afraid that you will have to endure closer observation for a while." He patted my shoulder. "Give it a week or two."

My head sank back onto the pillow, and I closed my eyes. Two weeks? And then what, go back to work like normal?

I opened my eyes, questions on my lips, but Death was gone.

"You're awake!" Zoe cried.

CASSIE'S STORY

DAVID B. COE

By the time Cassie was shot, I'd been covering the story of the vigilante killer, Hell's Fury, for a couple of months. The assignment landed on my desk because I was the Metro beat writer, but the story had become front page news and they'd kept me on it. Biggest story of my life.

I interviewed the cop who fired the shots the night of the shooting for an article that ran the next morning. As he told it, he and his partner were patrolling their usual beat when they heard a girl screaming in the alley. The cop's partner reached the girl first; the guy who attacked her was already dead. But the guy's killer—a woman— was still in the alley. She ran from the partner and straight at the first cop. He shouted for her to stop, and when she didn't, the cop fired. He only got off one round before he was flung against the alley wall, but he was certain that he hit her. That's what he said at the time, and even when I interviewed him again, giving him every opportunity to change his story, he stuck to it.

Turns out the woman he shot, the woman who killed the attacker, was Cassie Sloan. Cassie, my colleague at the paper. Someone I dated briefly, after her husband died. Well, not really dated so much as slept with one night and then avoided for weeks afterward. Not my finest moment.

Now Cassie was in jail, a convicted killer. And I had come to interview her.

She didn't look the part. If you could find someone in this country who'd never heard of Cassie Sloan—who hadn't read or heard accounts of what she was said to have done—and you showed that person a picture of her, he might guess she was an actress, or a sports star, or a news anchor. He might even peg her as a newspaper reporter. Anything but a killer. That was part of the fascination. The crimes themselves, lurid and mysterious, could feed headlines for months. Add in her angelic face, the long dark hair and pale blue eyes, and you had a spectacle.

Staring at her now, through the small glass window in the door, her features framed in one of those diamonds of wire embedded in the glass, I noticed lines around her eyes and mouth that hadn't been there before. The last few months had taken their toll. People who didn't know her wouldn't have seen it, but I did.

She sat on a metal chair, her hands resting on the wooden table before her, which was bare save for a pack of cigarettes and a book of matches. She looked small, solemn. Back when we'd worked together at the paper, before everything happened, she always seemed to be smiling. Not friendly, necessarily. More like she was amused by something the rest of us hadn't heard or wouldn't have understood. Now she looked so serious. Not scared. Just...somber. She gave no indication of dreading this conversation as much as I did.

"You ready?" the guard asked me.

I took a breath, nodded.

He unlocked the door and stood back, allowing me to step past him into the room.

Cassie looked up, her eyes widening at the sight of me. "You've got to be kidding me. They sent you?"

"I've been covering it from the start. You know that."

The door closed behind me, and I started to panic, my heart trip-hammering, my breath catching in my throat. I thrust my trembling hands into my pockets so she wouldn't see.

Cassie shook her head, her lips pursed. "Fine then," she said. "Let's get this over with."

I remained where I was, watching her. She wore her hair in a loose ponytail, and her lips were dry, cracked. She'd always been pale, and she would have been the first to point out that she hadn't spent much time in the sun recently. But in the flickering glare of the fluorescent lights she looked positively ghostlike.

"Well?" she said, impatient, seeming to read my thoughts.

I forced myself into motion, crossing to the chair opposite hers, willing myself to inhale, exhale. As I sat, I pulled a digital recorder from my jacket pocket.

"You mind?" I asked. "I've always been terrible with notes."

She shrugged, but then a change came over her, as if she had decided something. "Sure," she said. "Go ahead."

I switched the recorder on and placed it on the table.

"Thursday, September fourteenth." I glanced at my watch. "Nine-forty a.m. I'm with Cassidy Sloan at the Fuller Correctional Facility. Cassie, why don't you—"

"I don't think it's working." She stared at the recorder. "Shouldn't there be a light or something?"

I leaned closer, checked the LED. She was right. Nothing was happening.

"Damn it." I picked it up, moved the switch to "off," then back to "record." Nothing. I took out the batteries and put them back, though they were already loaded correctly.

"Looks like you're stuck taking notes. Just as well. They say writing things down helps you remember them better."

Our eyes met for an instant. Something in her expression...a hint of amusement.

"All right." I put the recorder back in my pocket and pulled out a pad and pencil. I jotted down the date, time, and location before looking up at her again. "Why don't you start with your husband?"

A reflexive grin touched her lips and vanished as quickly as it had come. "I did."

I shuddered, and she grinned again.

"Why do you think everyone's so interested in this, Eric? Is it me? Is it the way I look?" She paused. "Is it the way I did it?"

"How did you do it?"

She eyed me. After a moment she reached for the cigarettes. "I'd ask if this was going to bother you, but I don't really care. It's pretty much the only vice I'm allowed." She lit up and took a long, deep pull, closing her eyes. After what seemed a long time, she exhaled through her nose, a billowing cloud of blue-gray smoke enveloping us both like a mist.

"My husband." She opened her eyes. "You met him, didn't you?"

I nodded. "At one of the office parties, I think."

"That sounds right. It would have been several years ago. He stopped coming after my promotion." She took another pull, rested her elbow on the table so that the hand holding her cigarette hovered just beside her head. "Kenny was..." She shrugged. "I think I was drawn to him because we were so different. I wasn't looking for cerebral; I got enough of that at work. I liked him because he was physical—muscular, broad, like an action movie hero."

I jotted down notes, avoiding eye contact, feeling weak and small.

"The first time he hit me, I was...shocked, you know? But I figured it must have been my fault."

"When was that?" I asked.

"April twenty-second, five years ago."

I frowned and looked up.

"It was our anniversary." She smiled faintly. "A girl remembers. We'd just finished dinner and were...well, the evening was moving along as you'd expect. And then I said something. I don't even remember what it was, but it made him angry and before I knew it, we were arguing. Finally, he got so mad that he hit me. His hand was open. It didn't even hurt that much. But it was...We crossed a line, you know? I knew it immediately, though I didn't admit it to myself.

"Kenny said he was sorry about twenty times. He got real tender.

We went to bed a little while later and he was so gentle—more than he'd ever been. I tried to put it out of my mind, but the whole time we were making love, I kept thinking to myself, 'He hit me. Kenny hit me.'"

"How long was it before he hit you again?"

Cassie took another drag. "Not long. A couple of months maybe. Another argument. We were at home again. We were always at home when it happened. This time he hit me hard, with his fist." She pointed to a spot high on her cheek. "Right here. Really rattled me. For a couple of minutes I could barely see, like I'd been staring into the sun too long. You might remember the bruise. I said I'd gotten it rollerblading, that Kenny and I had been trying some silly trick and we bumped heads."

I did remember. Hearing this now, I was ashamed that I'd believed her.

"When was that again?" I asked to mask my discomfort.

"I don't know exactly. Early summer. After that..." She shrugged again and smiled, though it looked more like a grimace. "The hits just kept on coming. A black eye that I blamed on an inadvertent elbow during a basketball game; a swollen jaw that I blamed on my dentist; another bruise on my cheek that I couldn't explain, so I just stayed home for a week until it faded enough that I could cover it over with makeup. I think I pleaded flu on that one.

"I once did a piece on battered women," she said, looking at me. She took one last pull from the cigarette, dropped it on the linoleum floor, and ground it out with her foot. "Were you at the paper yet?"

"I don't think so," I said.

"Maybe not. I remember thinking that their stories were sad, but also a little pitiful, you know? I mean, he's hitting you, so leave him. I might have even said as much to some of them. 'Why don't you just leave?' As if it were that easy. As if shame and love and need didn't amount to whole lot more than—" She made air quotes with her fingers. "—'being strong.' And a few years later, there I was, just like them, trapped in love with a guy who knocked me around every now and then.

"Women like me—professionals; independent, bright, educated women—we're not supposed to be victims of abuse. Turns out that's horse shit."

I wanted to ask why she didn't leave him, just as she had asked those women. Because I didn't understand. I couldn't get past what I knew about her. Cassie was beautiful and smart and confident. She should have been able to walk away and make a new life for herself. But I didn't ask her about it. Instead, I kept to the story. "When did you decide to kill him?"

She cast a hard look my way. "You know that's not how it happened."

"I know what you said. But I'm still trying to understand. All of us are."

Cassie reached for the cigarettes and lit up again. She'd once been such a health nut; it was hard to believe this was the same person. I kept that to myself, too.

"It got really bad," she finally said, each word emerging from her mouth as a puff of smoke. "He'd gotten his contractor's license not long after we were married, and for a while business was pretty good. Not great, but he was getting by. But then he had a problem with a client—some rich guy up in the Crescent area. The guy sued and suddenly the rest of Kenny's clientele began to shy away. Pretty soon, he had nothing. No clients, no prospects, no way of paying his crew. I was making enough for both of us, but that just made things worse, you know?

"He was angry all the time, and he started drinking." She closed her eyes and winced. "God. Listen to me. Somewhere along the way my life turned into a goddamn soap opera cliché."

I didn't say anything. I simply watched her, my pencil poised over the paper.

"One night he came home drunk and was yelling at me before he'd even closed the door. It wasn't just the beatings I was afraid of at this point. For a couple of months, I'd been thinking that it was just a matter of time before he killed me. And this was the night. I was sure of it. If I hadn't—" Cassie looked away and lifted the cigarette to her lips. "I would have died that night," she said softly.

"Instead he did."

She nodded. "I'm still not sure how I did it. One minute he was coming at me, his fist raised. The next he was on the floor by the table, a gash on his forehead. You wouldn't have believed the blood."

Actually, I'd seen pictures, and I'd been appalled. You always hear that head wounds bleed like mad, but good God. Blood everywhere. The police investigated it as an accidental death and concluded that Cassie had called nine-one-one as quickly as anyone could have expected. But Kenny never had a chance. And as to her killing him—a man that big? The lead detective said it was impossible. The coroner agreed. Case closed, at least for a time.

"How did you do it, Cassie?"

"I just told you, I don't know."

I stared back at her, silent, waiting.

"It felt..." She stopped, shook her head, took another smoke. "You'll think I'm nuts."

"That would make me stand out in a crowd."

She looked startled for an instant. Then she burst out laughing. "Yeah," she said. "Yeah, you have a point."

"You started to tell me what it felt like."

Cassie nodded. "Right. It felt like I...like I pushed him. But with my mind, you know? I knew what I wanted to do to him. I was scared and angry and sick to death of feeling that way. Of being afraid of the man I was supposed to love. Just once I wanted him to feel what it was like to be weak and helpless. I wanted to hurt *him* for a change."

She puffed fiercely on her cigarette. "So it was like I took hold of him somehow. I grabbed him and threw him at the table. Not with my hands, but with my mind." She shook her head. "I know how it sounds, but it's the truth. I was trying to make him hit his head. He...he did just what I wanted him to."

"You mean the way he fell?" I asked.

"I mean the way he died."

I didn't know what to say. I cleared my throat. Cassie smiled, enjoying my discomfort.

I forced myself to meet her gaze. "Then what happened?"

"Very good, Eric. For a second there I thought you were going to leave."

I looked down at my pad and realized that I'd stopped taking notes several minutes ago. Not that I was likely to forget any of this.

"What then?" I asked a second time.

Cassie shrugged. "I convinced myself it hadn't happened. I'd never done anything like that before, and I couldn't explain how I managed it this time. The cops all said it was an accident, so that's what I told myself. I went back to living my life. I wrote. I slept around."

I felt my face turn red.

"Our night together came, what? Two months after Kenny died? Didn't that strike you as odd?"

"I didn't really think about it," I said.

She gave a short, harsh laugh. "Right. And afterwards you avoided me like I had the plague. Or was it the clap?" Still grinning, she narrowed her eyes. "What was the matter, Eric? Wasn't I any good?"

Panic flooded my chest again. "That had nothing—"

"Don't," she said. "It was a joke. That's all."

I wasn't sure if she was referring to what she had said, or to sleeping with me. She was right, of course. I had avoided her, but only because it had been an incredible night for me and, I was quite certain, far less than that for her.

"How long after that until you killed the second guy?"

"All business, huh?" she asked. She puffed on her cigarette for a few moments. "It was probably six months after I killed Kenny. I'd had a late night at work, and I wasn't ready to go home yet. I went to the Oasis, instead. You know the place? Over on Sixth, near Woodbine."

"Yeah, I know it."

"I was drinking white wine at the bar. Nothing very good. But I was chatting up the bartender, this pretty college girl, and wondering if I was ready to take a woman home for a change. And then I heard them." She shook her head. "It was like being pulled back in time to a part of my life I thought I'd escaped forever. I heard them arguing, I heard the way he was talking to her, and I knew. I just *knew* that he was beating her. Not there, of course. But at home. He was Kenny. She was me. I knew it.

"I listened to them, and when they left, I followed. I was lucky, I guess. They lived nearby, and they covered the distance on foot. They went in and I watched them through a window. And sure enough, as soon as they were inside the house, he started screaming at her and slapping her around. I don't know what he thought she'd done, but he was pretty pissed. She was crying, bleeding from her nose. I could see it all. I could tell that she hated him, that she wanted to be rid of him, just like I'd wanted to be rid of Kenny."

She'd sucked her cigarette down to the filter and she mashed it out on the table. Immediately she reached for the pack again, but then seemed to reconsider. After a few seconds she looked at me.

"I did it pretty much the same way. He'd smacked her, and she'd flown across the room. She was this tiny thing—that asshole must have had a hundred pounds on her. He was stalking her now, and she was cowering against the wall next to the television. Before he reached her, I pushed, hard this time. I knew what I was doing and I did it good and hard.

"He hit his head on the set and landed next to her. And then for good measure I made the TV fall on him. For a while she didn't move. She just sat there crying, staring at his body, saying, 'Oh no, oh no,' over and over again. I thought maybe she was upset that he was dead, you know? But pretty soon she pulled herself together and called for help. Then she got herself a glass of water. I figured she was okay, so I left. I didn't want to be there when the cops showed up."

"That was when you started going to the bars?"

Cassie nodded. "At first I wasn't sure why I did it. I mean, I knew what I was listening for, and I guess I knew what I was going to do when I heard it. But it wasn't like I decided, you know, 'Okay, now I'm going to start killing guys who beat their wives and girlfriends.' A part of me just wanted to hear those conversations. In a way it made me feel better. I wasn't the only one, you know? There were all these women out there who were just like me, who were afraid of their Kennys. They just didn't know how to do this...this thing that I did. Do."

She stared at the cigarettes for several seconds before finally giving in and lighting up another.

"Pretty soon I was noticing other stuff, too," she said, breathing out a haze of smoke. "I could tell when guys were cheating. It didn't matter if they were with their wives or their mistresses, I always knew. After a while I could tell with the women, too. But I left those folks alone—the men *and* the women. That was..." She shook her head. "I didn't want any part of that; it's just normal relationship stuff, you know? But then there was a night when I saw this guy slip something into his date's drink. Them I followed. And when he tried to rape her, I killed him. I don't even think she noticed he was dead—that's how out of it she was."

"How long was it before the papers started writing about you?"

"The first story appeared the next morning. I had to take a cab to keep up with them, and the cabbie remembered me. His description was way off, but that's when the headlines started. Pretty soon they started putting other things together. People remembered seeing me at several of the bars where I found the guys I killed. Without meaning to, I'd been wearing my hair differently from night to night, so the police sketches weren't very good. But they were looking for me."

I nodded again. The headlines had been sensational right from the start. "The Avenging Angel," they called her at first. But when that proved too tame, they went the other way: "Hell's Fury." From that famous quote: "Heaven has no rage like love to hatred turned, Nor hell a fury like a woman scorned." That was Cassie.

"You didn't stop, even after the stories started," I said. "Why?"

"I wasn't scared. I didn't think anyone could stop me." She took a long pull on the cigarette, her eyes locked on mine. "Do you have any idea what it's like to have the power I have? I can make people do whatever I want. I can kill with a thought. I can..." She trailed off. "You don't believe me, do you? You don't believe any of this."

87

I couldn't say what I believed, but in that moment, I was terrified—of her, of the anger I saw in her eyes.

"I just...I'm just wondering why, if you can do all these things, you're still here in this jail."

"Is that all you're wondering, Eric? Aren't you wondering if I ever considered killing you? You bought me drinks, you drove me back to my place, and you screwed me—twice as I remember it, though that first time didn't amount to much. And then you ignored me. You didn't call, or speak to me, or acknowledge what had happened in any way. After I was arrested—after you read and heard everything they were saying about me—you must have wondered."

She was right about this, too. I did wonder. I was wondering at that very moment. If she really was all she claimed to be, all she appeared to be, then she held my life in her hands. Or in her mind.

"Yeah," I admitted. "I thought about it. I'm out of my depth here, Cassie. I've never dealt with anything like this before. The things they're saying about you—the things you're saying about yourself...I don't know what's real."

"Yeah, well, welcome to my world."

She stared at me for a moment. And then without warning, my chair flipped backward. My pad and pencil went flying. I crashed onto the floor, the back of my head smacking the linoleum, the air leaving my body in a rush. I lay there for several seconds, trying to breathe, waiting for my vision to clear.

"You okay?" Cassie asked, her voice calm and even.

Before I could answer, the door swung open and one of the guards stepped in. "Everything all right in here?"

I rolled off the upended chair and climbed to my feet. "Everything's fine," I said.

The guard eyed Cassie and then me. I think he was trying to decide if we were both crazy. After a few seconds, his expression curdled and he left, pulling the door closed behind him.

"You didn't have to do that," I said. I rubbed the rising bump on my head.

"Didn't I? You believe me now, don't you?"

88

I nodded, righted the chair, and retrieved my notes and the pencil. Sitting down, I touched the bump again, half-expecting my hand to come away bloody. It didn't.

"You should put ice on that," she said.

"Yeah, thanks."

"Don't be pissed. I needed you to understand that I'm not making this up. Now you know."

I nodded, sullen, embarrassed. My whole body hurt.

"One of the cops swears that he shot you, says he couldn't have missed. The others say he's nuts. But..."

I stopped, my mouth falling open. Cassie had taken hold of the collar of her shirt and pulled it down so that I could see the top of her left breast. A small white crater marred the skin there. It was about the size of a penny, perfectly round and slightly puckered in the center. I levered myself out of the chair and walked around the table for a closer look, all fear of her forgotten for the moment.

"He did hit you," I whispered.

Cassie nodded. "It hurt like a sonofabitch, but only for a second."

"Tell me how it happened."

"I was at some diner, listening as this older guy tried to pick up my waitress. I stayed 'til closing time. So did he. He hung around the diner, and I pretended to leave. When the waitress came out a while later, he offered to walk her home. One thing led to another, and eventually he forced her into an alley and tried to assault her. I killed him before he could hurt her, but I was still in the alley when the cops showed up. I guess there were two of them—cops, I mean—and they entered the alley from opposite ends. I ran from one of them and ended up face to face with the other. I tried to shove him aside..."

I looked up from my pad. She shook her head.

"Not literally. I used my...I did it the same way I knocked you over, the same way I killed Kenny and the others. Anyway, I wasn't quick enough, and he managed to get a shot off."

That was pretty much the story I'd gotten from the cop.

For months before that episode the press—mostly the tabloids—had been writing about the supposed supernatural powers of this "vigilantess" known as Hell's Fury. Not only could she kill with her eyes, but she could make herself invisible. She could fly and summon the dead to her aid. The police, of course, dismissed all of this as nonsense. As far as they were concerned, she was just another wack-job serial killer who happened to be taking out creeps instead of more respectable people. Then patrolman Peter Silofsky told his story about shooting her through the heart. After that, no one was certain of anything anymore. Not the cops, not the press.

Even as I stared at that tiny crater on Cassie's chest, I didn't know what to think. I didn't say anything. I stood over her, not believing it, yet having no choice but to believe it.

"There's a mark on my back, too," she said, "where the bullet left my body."

I straightened, then hesitated. "May I?"

She nodded.

I stepped around to the back of her chair, and as she leaned forward I lowered the back of her collar so I could see. Sure enough, there it was: larger than the entry wound, less perfect, but still vaguely round. Spidery lines radiated from the scar in every direction so that it resembled a child's drawing of the sun. Given where the bullet had gone in and the path it had taken through her body, I didn't see how it could have missed her heart. I let go of her shirt and backed away from her. After a moment, I returned to my chair, happy to have that table between us. I felt queasy, though whether from the smoke or the sight of that wound I couldn't say.

"You should be dead."

"I know," she said. "But they can't kill me. No one can. You want to know why I'm in jail? Why I let myself get caught? Why I haven't escaped? Because I'm tired of killing. And I'm tired of being hunted. It was either kill myself, keep going, or get caught."

"You could have left," I said. "Gone somewhere else and started over again."

"I don't think so." She smiled, though sadly. "I'm Hell's Fury, remember? Those sketches would have followed me anywhere I went."

"They didn't look that much like you. Cut your hair, maybe dye it; no one would have recognized you."

"It's not that easy. Given the chance to kill those bastards again, I'd do it in a heartbeat. Even Kenny. Especially Kenny. I don't feel guilty at all. But that's no way to live. And I would have kept on doing it. I'm sure of that. Once I started hearing those conversations, the violence hidden in those words, I couldn't get away from it. It's everywhere, Eric. What I said about you before..." She shook her head. "I didn't mean that. I never for a moment thought about doing anything to you. You're clueless, like most guys. But you were sweet that night, and I don't think you're capable of hurting anyone."

I kept my mouth shut, sifting through my past, fearing that I'd find something—anything—that might prove her wrong.

"But the violent ones," she went on. "There's lots of them. More than you'd believe. And if I was out there, I'd still be killing them. I wouldn't be able to help myself. How long do you think a person can do what I've done before it starts to eat away at their soul?" She lifted the cigarette to her lips, only to find that it had burned to the end.

I made myself look her in the eye. "I don't know."

For a while neither of us spoke. She lit up again. Her eyes wandered the empty room and one of her legs bounced impatiently. A few more minutes and she would put an end to this interview.

"So what will you do?" I asked. "If they can't kill you..."

"I'll do it myself," she said. "But first I wanted to get my story told. I wasn't happy when I first saw they had sent you."

"Yeah," I said. "I noticed that."

Cassie smiled faintly. "Well, maybe I was wrong. There's hope for you, yet." She toyed with the matches. "Anyway, once the story's out..." She shrugged.

Probably I should have said something, tried to talk her out of killing herself. But had I been in her position, I would have been thinking along the same lines. She deserved more from me than empty words about not throwing her life away.

"You'll write it, won't you?" she asked.

"Of course I will. That's why I came."

"But you don't think they'll print it."

I exhaled, a frown on my face. "I don't know, Cassie. It's...it's quite a story."

"You believe it, though, right?"

For one last time, I forced myself to meet her gaze. "Yes, I do. Every word. I've got the bump to prove it." I smiled. She didn't. More seriously, I added, "And I've seen your scars."

"You think the scars would convince other people? You could take pictures." For just a moment she looked so hopeful. Then she shook her head. "Pictures wouldn't convince anyone, would they?"

"Probably not. Pictures can be doctored." I closed the pad and put it back in my pocket. "I'll write it," I said. "And I'll do what I can."

Another half-smile touched her face, and for a fleeting moment I saw the old Cassie, the smart-mouthed beauty with the wry sense of humor. "You haven't asked me the obvious question," she said.

I hesitated, then pulled the pad and pencil out once more. "Why you?" I asked. "Why do you think you wound up with these powers? Or whatever you want to call them? You're certainly not the only woman who's been abused."

"The short answer is that I don't know."

"And the longer answer?" I asked, knowing she wouldn't have brought it up if she didn't want to talk about it.

Cassie regarded me. After a few seconds, her gaze strayed toward the door. Her expression was wistful, sad. Watching her, I thought she might get up and walk out. And after all, who could have stopped her had she chosen to?

"I don't think I'm special at all," she finally said, her voice so low I had to lean in to hear her. "I think the power resides in all of us."

"But Cassie—"

She lifted a hand, stopping me. "It's in every one of us, Eric. But I found it. I was scared and I was pissed and I'd had enough. And somehow I found it."

"You can't be the only woman—the only person—who's felt those things," I said, expecting her to cut me off again. "And lots of them die at the hands of their abusers. How do you explain that, if they have this power, too?"

"I can't explain it. You're right: Lots of us don't manage to save ourselves. For some reason most of us can't find the power that I did. But I believe many of us do. More than you'd think."

I tried to keep the skepticism out of my expression. Didn't work.

"How many guys die each year in ways the cops can't explain or only think they understand?" she asked, sounding so reasonable, so sure of herself. "That was Kenny for a long time, until they reopened the investigation. How many times have women protected themselves the way I did, but without actually killing the guy who was hitting them? We don't know, do we? Because it never draws the attention of the police or the press. It happens, then it slides by, unnoticed.

"If I could describe how I did it, if I knew some secret to finding the power, I'd write the damn article myself and make sure all of those women know." A sad smile settled on her face. "Maybe what made me different wasn't the power itself, but my willingness to use it. I mean really *use* it. If I'd stopped with Kenny, we wouldn't be having this conversation. I'd still be working at the paper, getting laid now and then, leading a normal life. Maybe I wouldn't even believe it myself. But I couldn't leave it alone." She let out a small laugh. "Turns out I was different because I liked the way it felt. It felt good, you know? I wanted to do it again."

I could think of nothing to say. As explanations went, hers didn't amount to much. But I could tell she believed it and I wasn't sure I wanted to challenge her.

"Go," she said. "I'm talked out. And you need to write this thing if it's going to run tomorrow."

I stood, reluctant to leave her like this. "I can come back—"

"No. Like I said, I'm talked out."

"How soon...?" I trailed off, not certain how to ask the question.

She wouldn't look at me. "Take care of yourself, Eric. Be good."

I lingered there for several seconds, then nodded, crossed to the door, and knocked once for the guard. "If you change your mind," I said, my back to her. "If you decide you want to talk again, call me."

Cassie didn't answer. In the next moment, the door opened.

As I started to walk out, she said, "Sorry about your head. And also about your recorder."

The recorder? I hesitated, my hand straying to my pocket. All I could do was laugh and shake my head.

A guard waited for me in the corridor, a tall, rail thin white kid who couldn't have been more than twenty years old.

"Is that girl crazy or what?" he asked, grinning like a ghoul.

I grunted a response.

He led me through the twists and turns of the hallways and buzzed me through a series of locked, steel doors. I'd noticed the doors coming in and had meant to count them while leaving, but I didn't remember until after I'd signed out and was outside, beyond the fences and the razor wire. The air felt cool and clean. I must have reeked of cigarette smoke. It had rained while I was in the jail, but now the sun shone, and faint wisps of steam rose from the damp blacktop.

I started toward my car. As I walked, I pulled out my cell and dialed Beth's work number. We'd only been seeing each other for a couple of months, but already it felt substantial, like something that might last.

She picked up after the second ring. "Beth Danbridge."

"Hi," I said. "It's me."

"Hey, you." She sounded happy to hear my voice.

I smiled in spite of myself.

"I didn't expect to hear from you 'til later," she said.

"Yeah. I just wanted to say hi."

"You all right?"

"I'm fine."

"How'd the interview go?"

"All right. It was hard."

"I'd imagine."

I didn't say anything, and for a moment we were both silent.

"You sure you're all right?" she asked.

"I haven't hurt you, have I?"

"What?" She sounded confused. I could almost see the frown on her face, the crease in her forehead above those dark brown eyes.

"Never mind." I took a long breath, rubbed the bump on my head. "I'm sorry I bothered you. Why don't we eat out tonight? My treat."

"Yeah, all right. That sounds nice."

"I'll come by and get you around seven-thirty."

"Okay. See you then."

"Right. Bye."

Before I could end the call, she said, "Eric?"

"Yeah?"

"You haven't. We're doing okay."

I smiled. "Thanks." For a heartbeat or two I said nothing. I enjoyed the silence, the feeling that she was enjoying it too. "Bye."

"Bye."

I returned the phone to my jacket pocket. Reaching my car, I glanced back at the prison, taking in the institutional brick, the small barred windows and the floodlights, off for now, but gleaming in the sun. I couldn't help thinking that it looked like a terrible place to die: sterile and cruel and lonely.

Not that there was much I could do about it. Her death, her choice. She'd made it clear that she didn't want my help, at least not with that. There was only one thing Cassie expected of me.

I climbed into the car and began the long drive back to the office. In my head, I had already started to write her story.

GAME OVER

MINDY MYMUDES

"Honestly, Kevin, if you keep your eyes plastered to that computer monitor, they're going to get stuck there, and we'll need a spatula to peel them off," his mother said as she smoothed his hair back out of his eyes.

He suppressed a smirk as she glanced warily at the little eyes on top of the monitors.

He didn't acknowledge her. If he could just kill one more manticore, he would reach level 52,000. That would just ash Joey's butt. His score already doubled Joey's all-time personal best.

His mother sighed. "Dinner will be ready in a few minutes. Wash up. We're having fish tacos. That's your favorite."

He took his eyes off the monitor in time to see his mom shake her head and leave him to his world. A huge fireball rolled across the screen and engulfed his avatar in flames. Game Over. He stretched and groaned. His cell phone vibrated and blasted out the theme to the game he'd just lost. He would need to download a new ring tone. A quick glance alerted him it was his best friend, Tom.

He hit answer on his cell. "Hey! What's up?" the teen asked. He put his feet up on some old computer CPUs that he was hoping to scavenge for parts. Surrounding him was a tangle of copper tubes that kept his computers cool. Multiple screens made a semicircle around him so he could keep track of several games at once. Skype was always up so he never lacked for company. His mom thought his room looked more like a factory than a bedroom, and the disembodied voices creeped her out. It kept her out of his room, for the most part.

She was warned his peeps could see her.

"Listen, remember those games Kyle was bragging about? He got access to more of them. The real shit! Are you in? Gotta know now!" Tom spoke fast, tripping over his words in excitement. Kevin could picture his friend foaming at the mouth.

"You're saving me from fish tacos. Even if you wanted to tag cop cars, I'd be there. So where's 'there'?" Kevin heard his family sliding chairs, clacking dishes, and laughing. He'd have to make a break for it, fast, before he was called down for dinner.

"Behind the Walgreen's on Frame. You'll need seventy-five bucks. I can't believe how cheap the dude is selling them for. He swore they were straight out of the Starflight labs. Guess he doesn't have any overhead. These games're hot!" He laughed at his own joke.

Kevin checked the time on his phone. "I can be there in ten."

"Any faster? No, never mind, you're home and biking it. When're you gonna get your license? One of us has to be able to drive! Whatever. Just get your ass over there."

Tom disconnected, leaving Kevin looking at the phone. He'd have to empty his stash, but from what he'd heard about these games, he would've sold everything he owned, including his Manga. Well, maybe not those.

He opened his closet and reached into the back. He snagged an old gym shoe his mom said smelled like rotting fish and his brother swore was covered in dog shit. Which it was. It was better than the bank—no one would reach in and steal his bucks. Except him.

Taking the steps two at a time as he pulled on his jacket, he almost missed hearing his mom shouting from the kitchen. Kevin stopped at the hallway to see if she'd say anything important. Eh, she was just calling him.

Not important.

"Hey, Ma, I gotta go do something. I'll be back in a few." Kevin reached into his back jeans pocket to make sure the money was still there and escaped out the back door. His banged-up mountain bike was leaning against the garage where he'd left it. He'd tried to save up for a new one, but there was always something else more important.

Like a new game no one else ever played yet.

He rode to the meeting place high on an adrenaline rush.

Kevin skidded his bike to a stop in front of Tom. Tom's bike might be better, but at least he got the better scores. Where was the guy with the game? He didn't see anyone else, although the shadows were getting long.

"Maybe we're early?"

"No, man. Maybe he got held up. You got the cash?" Tom asked. His eyes were huge and shiny with excitement. If Kevin hadn't known him his whole life, he might have thought Tom was on drugs.

Kevin nodded and patted the bulge of his pocket.

A small gold grandma-car pulled up next to them. The driver's window rolled down. A geek with shaggy hair and taped-together glasses poked his head out.

"You kids ready for the ride of your lives?" the guy asked. The ride thing was weird, but he looked like a gamer. "Let's see the green."

The boys pulled out their hoards. The guy presented two memory cards with a flourish, and the boys exchanged their money for them. After a quick count of the cash, the man peeled out of the lot, leaving the boys in the dust.

"I can't wait! Bet I beat this bitch before you." Tom took off, Kevin not far behind. They didn't even say goodbye as they went in different directions toward their homes.

Kevin tossed his bike in the drive and started to make tracks to his room before his mother caught him. No such luck.

"Where have you been, young man!" his mother scolded. She shouted over running water and clattering dishes. "You are grounded for a month and taking over your brother's chores! And if you think you're getting any dinner, think again."

"Yeah, Ma, whatever." Kevin made the break to his room and shut the door. The lack of a lock bothered him. A chair tucked under the doorknob worked in the movies. He hoped it would keep his brother out.

He booted up his computer and slipped on his VR goggles.

He drummed on his desk with a couple of pens as he waited for the slowest machine on Earth to accept his treasure. His parents just had to pony up for a new one. This model was already six months old and out of date, even with the additions he'd made. He could make out the muffled voices of his mom and dad. They were probably arguing about him. Whatever. As long as they left him alone. Grounding suited him just fine. Maybe he'd get his ass suspended from school.

Abstract blobs in various colors rolled across the screen. "Confidential" flashed in red capital letters. Next, a series of numbers and letters scrolled over the shapes. A list of names followed.

Sweet! Not even a title yet, he thought. Knowing the wicked excellent games the lab produced in the past, this one…he couldn't wait.

A green and purple swirling vortex appeared in the center of the screen. Kevin touched it. The picture shattered and reformed into a bustling town. A box asking for his screen name and avatar popped up. He entered WIZ KLR, and downloaded his favorite picture of a hooded figure, cloaked in black, wearing black leather boots, and carrying a burning staff.

The picture spun and fleshed out. A three-dimensional version of his character stood in the center of a dirt road. The WIZ KLR's cowboy-booted foot was in a pile of steaming horseshit. Whoa. Instead of his normal avatar's costume, Kevin was wearing Western gear. His cloak was a fancy black duster, and he was wearing cowboy boots and a black cowboy hat. Kevin could swear he smelled the manure. Sweat, rotting garbage, and mud completed the scent picture. Women in boring dresses and men in jeans, hips with low-slung guns, ignored him as they did whatever people in what looked like a Western did.

The VR goggles' speakers pumped out obscenities, screams, laughter, grunts, and whinnies. A wood plank sidewalk ran along a few gray clapboard buildings. Posts had horses hitched to them. The general store, complete with a wooden Indian in front, was up against a courthouse and jail with barred windows. Next door was a two-story saloon. Two men sat playing checkers in front.

A red-and-white-striped pole announced there was a barber in the next storefront. A hand-lettered sign declared, "Teeth Pulled, 5¢ Each." Across the road, smaller wooden houses bracketed a large brick home. Kevin's scuffed, horseshit-covered boots crunched on the debris in the street. *Sweet!*

He had no clue how it worked. Other than his goggles and controller, he wasn't rigged to the computer. However, with only a thought, what appeared to be his body moved like in reality through the goggles. This was so much cooler than *World of Warcraft*. He didn't even see the edges of the monitor. It was so real, like he was in the midst of downtown Old West. He could even feel the heat pound on his cowboy hat. Grit blew into his mouth and crunched. A blue bandana appeared around his neck, and Kevin pulled it up over his mouth and nose.

From the corner of his eye, he saw a suspicious-looking dude. The guy, who needed a shave, had a blanket around his shoulders and wore a strange-looking, flat-topped, wide-brimmed cowboy hat.

Kevin's hands crept to his hips.

The man glanced at him. "Make my day, punk. Don't get between a man and his spaghetti." The stranger shuffled off, spurs jangling, as he whistled a familiar tune.

A dark blur streaked down the wall of the saloon. No one seemed to notice the person dressed entirely in black. *A Ninja! Cool!* Peering out over a mask were brown eyes that looked straight into Kevin's. At the Ninja's side was a long scabbard tucked into a sash. A long silver sword suddenly appeared in the Ninja's hand. Without thinking, Kevin pulled guns out of the holsters strapped to his waist. The Ninja's sword whistled through the air. Two bullets hissed at the same time. One bounced off the sword, wrenching the arm wielding it. The other went right through the Ninja's heart.

The crowd turned toward the action and clapped. A man with a shiny star affixed to his leather vest walked up to Kevin and offered his hand.

"That was one hell of a shot. We could use a man like you here. That Ninja has devastated the town, and many of our families have left. Being a deputy ain't great job, but you'd get good grub and sheets. Might be a few bed bugs. Whaddya say?"

Kevin thought about it. This could be a trap. Maybe the sheriff was on the take. Maybe not. Well, it seemed he was a crack shot, so if there was a problem, he figured he could take him out, too. This should have racked up a shitload of points. He didn't see where the score was tallied, though.

"Sure, Sheriff. I was considering a place to settle. This place looks as good as any. Tell me why a Ninja was in your town."

The sheriff pointed to the saloon. "Let's talk over a whiskey."

The crowd cleared a path for Kevin and the lawman. Before Kevin got through the swinging doors, colors swirled around him. He felt nauseous and hurled whatever he'd last eaten. It added color to the vortex he was caught in.

The kaleidoscope stopped, and he was standing on the deck of a ship. Swelling waves washed over the sides, making his black leather, square-toed boots wet. His feet were cramped, and they hurt. His arm felt funny, and he nearly screamed when he saw it ended in a hook.

He swallowed his fear and reminded himself it wasn't real. "This is so cool! I'm a pirate. I have to think like a pirate!"

Kevin muttered under his breath, "Arrrr," deciding to growl like a real pirate.

He was disappointed there wasn't a parrot on his shoulder. The frilly shirt seemed girly for a real pirate, but the long black jacket was cool. He touched his hair. It was greasy and stuck together. *Gross!* He snapped his hand away. There was a hat, which he gingerly removed to inspect. Small insects scuttled away into its three corners. He scratched his head and realized they were lice. *Oh. My. God!* He didn't realize how disgusting pirates were. That meant the stench of unwashed body was him. Maybe even the fish guts. So not cool.

If this game was at all typical, the first level was a gimmee. As sweet as the special effects were, level one was boring. He looked forward to more action.

The boat rolled and creaked. There were ropes everywhere, and it was amazing no one tripped over them. There were also bones and garbage strewn over most of the deck.

It was almost as bad as his room.

He looked up and saw a crow's nest on top of a tall pole. A black and white flag with skull and crossbones flapped in the stiff breeze. Dirty beige sails billowed in the wind, pushing the ship like a toy across a huge puddle.

As he looked up at the sails, a disc with blue, green, and red flashing lights weaved through the clouds. At first he thought it was a Frisbee until a brilliant gold ray-beam shot out and boiled the water next to the ship.

"Oh shit! It's an alien UFO!" Kevin looked around at the chaos on the deck. Men pushed their way to get a better look at the flying saucer, mouths gaping like giant carp. He had to do something, or it was "Game Over!"

There were two large cannons off the stern. Bow? He couldn't remember which was which. It wasn't important. How did one use a cannon?

"Hey, you! Bald dude with t' eye patch and earrin'! We need t' get these six pounders ready t' fire!"

"Every man t' himself!" The bald guy jumped into a small dinghy and cut the rope that held it above the deck. It hit the water with a splash and was immediately incinerated. Kevin wondered how many points the pirate lost him.

"You scurvy dogs! Get those lazy dungbies t' t' six pounders!" Kevin wasn't exactly sure what he had yelled to the crew. It sounded piratey, though. This game's translator feature was awesome. The scruffy men only gave him a brief glance. They fought for spaces on the two lifeboats or jumped overboard. Rats abandoning a sinking ship. Zapping noises followed by steam and the scent of crockpot stew surrounded him.

Well, dammit. The game wasn't over. His ship hadn't sunk yet.

"Any man who stands with me will receive his weight in booty. For the rest of you scurvy dogs, if the aliens don't get you, I'll see you swing from a hempen halter from the yard arm!" Great threat. At least, he thought it was a threat. It would be hard to carry out if he didn't know what it meant. As Kevin gestured for the men to get their asses to the big guns, he discovered a cutlass swinging at his side. He reached for the sword, forgetting he had a hook until it tore his trousers, and grabbed it with his other hand.

Several men in tattered clothes took Kevin's threat seriously. Or they didn't want to contribute to the crew stew in the water. Rather than risk being tossed to Davy Jones' Locker, the men took their places at the cannons.

The spinning aircraft hummed closer, wires bristling from the surface of the UFO like whiskers. Now that the ship was closer, Kevin could see it wasn't flat like a Frisbee. It was made up of two charcoal gray dimpled balls squished together so there were two bumps. From between the bumps sprouted two longer antennae. The ship resembled the head of a really ugly caterpillar. Two hooks jutted out from beneath the ring of flashing lights, and a gangplank slowly eased down.

"FIRE! FIRE ON THE DAMN SHIP!" Kevin couldn't believe that his men were standing around, pointing at the foul thing above their heads. He just knew the "Game Over" sign was going to flash across the sky soon.

He conked the man closest to him with the butt of the cutlass and pointed to the cannon.

"Look lively, you scallywag. Where's your powder monkey? We'll all be feedin' t' fishes if you don't shoot that big gun o' yours. If we go down, I'll be takin' your little gun with my big blade." Kevin pointed his cutlass at a particularly sensitive portion of the man's anatomy. The pirate blanched, poked the kid next to him, and they returned to their cannon duty.

Kevin went to the other men, cursing a blue streak as ray-beams of gold cut along the edges of the sails. It became apparent cannons weren't meant to be shot straight up. The heavy balls didn't soar toward the UFO as much as spit out of the cannon before hairpin curving back to earth. The sail sheets fell flaming from the masts. The cannon balls rained down.

Where was the "Game Over" sign? Where was the music? Where the hell was his chair? Was there a glitch somewhere he could use to level up?

A whirring-buzzing sound attracted his attention. A golden haze surrounded his heavily damaged ship. The men were frozen in whatever position they were in. The flames that chewed the wood and cloth were as still as a light bulb.

The gangplank tapped to the deck. A hoard of tiny red-eyed fairies danced down, wicked fangs dripping with gray slime. Their gauzy wings fanned open. Closed. Open. The haze swirled faster in the wing-breeze around the defeated pirate ship.

"What be you?" Kevin's voice was strong. His hook trembled.

Tinny voices tumbled from the fairy flock. "This is a day of independence for all the fairies. And their descendants. Yes, let the joyous news be spread. The wicked old pirate is at last dead!"

Jeez, they sound like the Munchkins from The Wizard of Oz, Kevin thought. Besides, the pirate wasn't dead. That is, assuming he was the pirate they were singing about.

A gray-skinned fairy with dingy wings landed on Kevin's shoulder. Ugly little fairy-feet grasped his shoulder like the parrot usually associated with a pirate. If parrots smelled like rotting broccoli and dog farts. If parrots had silver needlelike teeth. If parrots had long, skinny fingers with suction pads on the ends. If parrots... Kevin shook his head to clear the images.

He struggled with the winged wretch. The fairy's feet dug in deeper, drawing blood. The fairy's nostrils flared at the metallic scent. Gray slime pooled on his shoulder as the fairy drooled.

This wasn't fun! It hurt! What the hell was going on? Was there a glitch in this game and that's why it wasn't released yet? How could he reset it from here?

He looked around for the button. No button. Just a heavy weight on his shoulder where a fairy was staring at him.

"What? What do you want from me? You got my boat. I don't have anything else," Kevin said with as much bravado as he could gather. Which was to say, not very much with a scary-fairy on his shoulder.

The fairy put his tiny scary-fairy face up against Kevin's.

"I believe humans would call this a shit. I mean, ship. No, right the first time. This is a shit. Your species build fragile structures to house your fragile bodies."

A miasma of wood-smoke, cooking meat, rotting broccoli, tinged with a whiff of fairy feces clouded Kevin's mind.

"We don't want much. Just a little blood. You won't miss it. A lot. In return, we'll get you home. With a special gift," the tinny sounding fairy said as he unhinged his jaw and struck like a snake at Kevin's neck. The flock of fairies decided the dinner gong had rung. They rushed in, tearing at Kevin's clothing to bite a bit of the booty.

Kevin was staring at his computer monitor when his mother came in. "Kevin? Tom's mom called, she said he has some new virus. How do you feel?"

She walked behind him to try to see what was so addictive about his computer that he couldn't break away even to go to the bathroom. At least, she didn't think he'd used it since she hadn't heard it flush.

Her youngest son had on a mask. On the computer screen a blue Lava Lamp display of blobs were bouncing up and down, merging, separating. A wax dance. "Game Over" scrawled across the screen in big black letters. Under it, "You've Lost Ha Ha" flashed in red.

"Kevin, are you all right, dear? Kevin?"

Kevin slowly turned to her. He slowly removed the mask covering his face. His eyes were strangely focused, clear and bright.

"Am I back? Am I home? I thought I was fairy food for sure!" He looked at his computer monitor, disbelief clouding his face.

"You've been in your room all this time, unless you snuck out." She moved to his window and stared out. Nothing seemed out of place.

"No, just…" His eyes widened to the size of Ping-Pong balls as his mom came toward him.

She sniffed the air, and drool dangled from the corner of her mouth. "We're so sorry you missed dinner. We had your friend, Tom. He came over to check on how you liked the game…" She grabbed him before he could twist away, sharp teeth exposed.

"Mom! No! I don't understand? What's happening?" Kevin tried to roll away, his mom was insanely quick.

She smiled. "We wanted you to share dessert with us." His mom shouted, "Family, come upstairs!" His mother bent over his head, as if to kiss him. "You know, I never could resist dessert. Perhaps I should have a little taste."

She struck like a shark, sharp teeth biting into his skull. She spat out the bone and hair that filled her mouth and licked the brain she found resting inside. A pearl resting in an oyster.

"Hmm, I really should've let you use the computer more often. I never knew what education could do for your mind. And they say, a mind is a terrible thing to waste." His mother gently placed his body on his bed, propping his head up on some pillows. "Hurry up before I overeat!"

A swirling cloud of color illuminated a small door next to the bed. The computer monitor flashed again. "Bonus round over. Gift of life lost. Too bad, so sad."

STEAM MAKES THE MIRRORS MOVE

LILLIAN ARCHER

At the scene of the crime, upon which our heroine is discovered to be a non-believer.

I fiddled with my camera, thick fingers moving over the metal parts, setting dials from memory. My gaze marked the flow of light in the room. Tonight was another seance, another chance to photograph the ghostly realm, another grieving loved one to deceive. The dishonesty did not sit well with my conscience, but as a woman with the need to work, I had to take whatever jobs came my way. For now, that employment was photographer to the famous Fox sisters.

"Remember, Merriweather, the left light will move more than the right." James Turret, our technical director, took a swig from the flask in his pocket. "Let me check the valve one more time." He fiddled with a wall sconce, the wayward left one, until satisfied. His job was to pump the bellows, building the fire that created the steam that traveled through the pipes to make the room alive. His gadgets would seal the deal, create belief where there was only miserable hope, perpetuate the myth that spiritualism was real, that the dead really did still care about the living and our petty issues. If his moving mirrors and flickering sconces left any doubt, my fake pictures convinced the most hardened skeptic to believe in the supernatural.

I arched my back, twisted since birth. Mother decried my deformity, announcing it a burden on the family, as if any one of them had to toil under the twisted muscles and sinew. I set my camera for the proper settings. "I bet they ask about the buried money in the backyard."

It was a common game between James and me, guessing what the grieving family wanted most from the dead. The typical fare of hidden money, questions about updated wills, or stolen goods jaded my worldview, coupled with my mother's callous brand of maternal love, compacted any compassion I once had into a strange and foreign sensation. No one ever wanted to talk with the deceased one last time, to balance a ledger of regret. They all just wanted something for themselves.

"I have warned Miss Fox that the mirror mechanism is faulty. The valve needs replacing, and I cannot risk opening that channel. I do hope she remembers." James, full of unrequited love for his employer, saw no wrong in what they did. It offered a family peace, and reassurance, if not the gold or money so many sought.

"She will remember. Make sure the book mechanism works and the table rises. That is always such a satisfying way to convince the family."

"You should have more faith."

I tapped my camera. "I will, when I see a ghost on my negatives."

James turned from the switches and valves of his creation to stare at me. "Why then work for the Fox sisters if you have no belief in the good they offer?"

"Their money pays my bills."

"You are too young to be so calloused."

"You are too old to be this naive."

"The ghosts come if you believe."

"They come because I fake pictures for the Fox sisters for good money."

James's placid face contorted with rage. His hands clenched into fists. "Don't you dare talk about Maggie and her sisters like that. They are real. The ghosts are real."

I backed away, hands raised like with a wild animal. "I am sorry for offending. I thought you might feel bad about deceiving the living."

"We aren't deceiving anyone. They are real, I tell you. I can hear them." He unclenched his fists, burying his face in his hands. "I have to believe. I take the money for the same reasons as you."

"Yes, the world is a cold place without a place to heat your bones. You of all people know that. Now, let me set my camera in the south corner—if the left sconce doesn't catch like it should, I can still have enough light to take a good picture of the family there."

I turned my back on the believer in miracles and busied myself with the special lenses I made for my camera. They each had a particular purpose—one to blur the background, another where I painted the outline of a spectral figure that for all the world appeared to be an organic part of the photo. A green tinted one with a small guide ring could distort various parts of the lens, making the proportions of the room appear differently, as if under a spectral spell. I researched each of our subjects to familiarize myself with the intent and type of grief to better give them what they want.

Tonight, we met with Mrs. Weston, a grieving widow of the worst circumstances. Her husband, the dear late beaver hat maker for the rich and famous, Mr. Winthrop Weston, had inconveniently passed, leaving all the worldly possessions and his will in the loving care of his mistress, the lovely and talented stage actress Miss Cordelia Laughton.

James reached for my tripod, his hands shaking from too many years of alcohol. I helped steady the heavy piece, and we grunted and moved it to my desired place.

"Thank you," I said, squinting and touching the camera, rechecking the lens mounts.

"You care more for that camera than you do people."

"The lens never fails me. It tells me the truth. Not like people."

James sighed. In his mind, my reticence to believe was a testament to my youth. "I need to check the boiler in the cellar. The widow will be here in a few hours. As Shakespeare said, 'There is more to this world than your own small perspective.'"

I giggled. "I don't think that is the proper quote."

"Close enough." James laughed.

Leah Fox, oldest of the famous Fox sisters and manager for her two little sisters, burst into the room. She reminded me of a disapproving aunt, her hair in a severe braid, always dressed in black out of deference to the clients, but I felt she was mourning a life lost to chicanery. "Miss Merriweather, do you have a lens for a small boy? I just received word from a source that the widow lost a young boy of seven last year, and that led to the estrangement with her husband. I want to be prepared in case she asks about him."

"No, I have not made a spectral lens for a young boy." I frowned and hobbled over to my trunk of equipment. "But I can alter the one of a young man who was short, you remember the widow from Williamsburg?"

Leah Fox clapped her hands, nodding her head in remembrance. "She paid up front in gold coins from her inheritance."

"Yes, the one who miscarried her child from her lost husband and wanted to see if they were reunited in Heaven. That one. I can change the perspective with my spectral lens, overlay that with the figure, and with some careful tilting of the camera make an acceptable youthful figure."

Leah waved her hands, dismissing my expertise. "Yes, yes, just make sure you can do it if asked."

Nightfall, when the truth is blurred in shadows.

The room creaked and ached under the weight of expectations of the small assemblage. The wallpaper, a beautiful gray silk in the daylight, transformed into a shiny backdrop for suffering, anger, and desperation at night. The wall sconces, carefully prepped by James, flickered on command at the touch of a switch from his control room behind the fake mirror to the left of my place. Bookshelves with tomes about grief and loss and the afterlife lined the wall opposite of the mirror. Maggie Fox, resplendent in her black silks and pale skin, presided from her place near my camera setup—she would move her shoulders or hands in certain ways during the seance to signal to James and me for certain effects. Her little sister, Kate Fox, a talented voice medium, sat silently across from Maggie.

Mrs. Weston, a lovely woman with a loose bun and a tinge of gray at her temples, sat with her daughter at the circular table, her hands twisting a knotted handkerchief in her lap. "My friends say this is all fraudulent."

Her daughter, all of fifteen if she were a day, reached to clasp her mother's hand. "If Dad could just tell us anything, who cares what others believe?"

Maggie Fox nodded smartly from her seat at the table. "Your daughter is wise beyond her years. We have helped ease the suffering of many a family with our talents."

"You can leave now, if you prefer. No need for distress. The afterlife is eternal. Your husband's spirit will always be waiting." Kate spoke, voice barely above a whisper.

"Merriweather, you may leave. We have no need for your photographic skills tonight."

Mrs. Weston threw her handkerchief on the table. "No. We do this now and move on." She looked at the two Fox sisters. "You say you are the best. Prove it."

Maggie smiled, graciously bowing her head. "As you wish."

On cue, James lowered the flames in the sconces around the room, plunging it into dusky overtones. Mrs. Weston exclaimed, "Oh!" and her daughter covered her head with her hands.

Maggie reached for the widow's hand. "The spirits are ready. Are you?"

"Yes," she said. "I think so."

"Then let us begin."

They all joined hands. I touched the lenses in my pocket, reminding myself of the order arranged in the special pockets on my apron. I bent to peer through the lens of my camera, ready for my cue.

"Whom do you wish to contact?" Maggie intoned, her voice rising, theatrical, swelling to fill the room with the force of her showmanship.

Mrs. Weston faltered, voice cracking. "I wa-want to contact my husband. Winthrop Weston."

Maggie cleared her voice. "Spirits, I beseech you. Come to the sound of my voice, apparate to my will, find Mr. Winthrop Weston, and have him appear."

James would be flicking switches to make a small fan above Miss Weston crank a few puffs of air across her neck. I hit the shutter button on my camera, taking a "before" picture for comparison to my "after." It takes great skill to have any pictures develop with such a darkened room. The Fox sisters had no idea what talent I possessed to make every one of their seances live.

Faint music sounded from a listening trumpet in the ceiling. James would be starting the sequence now. Trumpet, bell, then another rush of air. Table, book, and apparition in the crystal ball.

I readied my apparatus, holding two lenses precisely in front of the aperture of the camera, finger on the trigger.

"Spirits, I beseech you. Come to the sound of my voice, apparate to my will. Find Mr. Winthrop Weston and have him appear."

A bell sounded, and Mrs. Weston cried out, her daughter clenching her hand. Another puff of air, and I hit the shutter release.

Counting to twenty softly, I fumbled in my apron for the combination of lenses that will make a loved one appear.

"Spirits, I beseech you. Come to the sound of my voice, apparate to my will. Find Mr. Winthrop Weston, and make him appear!"

I swapped the lenses in my hand, ready for the picture. Maggie swayed in her chair, eyes rolled back in her head, chanting. Kate sat ramrod straight and began to talk in a masculine voice.

"Amalie? Amalie, is it you?"

"Yes! Winthrop, it is me."

Kate threw her head back, her voice reedy and deep and masculine. "It is cold and dark. I cannot see you."

Maggie swayed more, chanting, "Winthrop Weston. I command you to appear!"

"Amalie, it is cold, and I cannot see."

"Appear!"

Books started falling off the shelf behind Mrs. Weston. She shrieked, cowering in her seat and sobbing.

"Amalie, it is cold. I cannot see!"

"Winthrop! Where is your will? We cannot find it."

"Amalie, leave me in peace."

"Winthrop, I will haunt you every day until you tell me where your will is."

"It is cold and dark. I cannot see."

A small childish voice answered. "I can see you, Papa. Come and play with me."

A larger gust of wind fluttered my camera cloth. The scones flickered erratically. Maggie moaned, clutching at the hands on her wrists.

Kate sat ramrod straight. "Momma. I want to play with Papa now. Papa, hold my hand."

I hit the shutter button, cursing myself for not having time to prepare a lens with the two of them together.

Mrs. Weston sobbed. "Richard? I love you, son."

"Goodbye." Kate slumped over the table, Maggie stopped swaying, and the room lights brightened. Mrs. Weston and her daughter sat stunned, looking at the havoc wrecked in the room.

"My word, I did not believe you."

"We are not frauds. This has been proven multiple times, in front of crowds and confirmed by men of science."

"But Winthrop did not answer my question. Where is the will?"

Kate rose from her fugue. "It is in the hands of the mistress, Miss Cordelia Laughton. Your husband told me before he vanished."

Mrs. Weston threw herself on the table and sobbed. I collected my things and went to join James in the cellar to develop my prints.

R ed light made the shadows flee. I swirled my prints in the usual developing solutions tweaked for my own purposes. Tonight I wanted to try a green tint for the apparition shot.

James pinned my finished prints on a line and fiddled with a fan to dry them quickly. "Too bad about tonight."

"What do you mean? I thought it was a smashing success."

"I mean, this photo is ruined."

"It is not!" I hurried over to peer at the drying sheet. "What do you mean?"

James pointed to a place beside the mirror, in the background of my second shot. "Here."

I squinted. A dark figure of a man lounged against the mirror, arms crossed, a top hat tilted at a rakish angle and the cut of a long, tailored coat blending into the background. "My God." I blinked and looked again. "Go get Leah," I told James.

Ten minutes later, Leah huffed into my darkroom. "This had better be good."

I pointed to the arranged prints. "We cannot give Mrs. Weston five prints. One is not...appropriate."

"But her package is for five prints."

"Refund her part of the money."

"Any refunded funds will come out of your salary."

"Look at this. I did not make a mistake." I pointed to the picture in question.

Leah gasped. "We really, I mean, you captured...?"

"Yes. A real specter. And it appears to be taunting us."

Leah chewed on her fingernail. "No need to refund any money. Can you make a copy of this picture so we can have one for ourselves?"

"Of course."

"Do it. And still give Mrs. Weston the five prints. I will tell her the 'Tophat Ghost' is our spirit guide and brought her son and husband to greet us tonight."

She hurried back upstairs. I sighed, and went back to work, not certain if the Tophat Ghost was the spirit guide I wanted.

A new bit of business.

Tuesday dawned bright and cold, with a penetrating chilly rain that seeped into your bones. Leah called an emergency meeting for everyone this morning, and I trudged into the sunroom still cold from the difficult walk from my home.

Leah, dressed for business, sat at the head of the conference table in the sunroom. Maggie, still in a sleeping turban and robe, lounged on a chaise near a potted plant. Kate, eerily alert, sat straight-backed beside Leah. James, hands shaking, helped me with my cloak.

Once we were settled, Leah clapped her hands. "Let us begin. You each have two days to pack your things. We leave from the train station at 8 a.m. on Thursday. We have been summoned by no less than the First Lady, Mrs. Pierce."

Maggie bolted upright. "To commune with her son?"

Leah beamed. "Yes. The dead Bennie Pierce, eleven years old and taken too soon in a train crash last October."

Maggie asked, "We have to travel to the White House?"

"Yes."

James cleared his throat. "If I may be..be..be so bold, Miss Fox. Will I have access to the seance room to best prepare for your talents?"

"No." Leah beamed. "But we don't need gimshaws and gimmicks. We have the Tophat Ghost."

I groaned. "Then I need to be paid more money."

Leah turned to me, and sneered, "This may be the only chance you have for notoriety. None of us are paid for this trip. This is for posterity."

Maggie whispered, "I don't think this is a good idea, Lee."

"I manage this endeavor. You run the seance. I book the client. You talk to the dead." She stood, rearranging the folds of her skirt. "I am off to purchase our tickets at the station. I suggest you all apply your-selves to preparing for this auspicious occasion."

Upon which the auspicious occasion arises.

We stood gawking at the famous Red Room of the White House, the butler droning on about the furnishings. The Pierce household was still in mourning, black bunting draped over the mantel, tied to the backs of chairs, swaying in the drafts from the chandelier. I shuddered, thinking of the drab room and my photographic needs.

"Bennie is such a good lad. I am sure he will be easy to contact," Mrs. Pierce, First Lady of the United States, whispered. Her whole demeanor seemed deflated, gray, washed out, grief sucking the life out of her as surely as the train wreck smashed the life out of her son.

Leah reached for her hand, hesitating before making contact. "May I?"

Mrs. Pierce nodded, and Leah engulfed the grieving mother's hands in hers. "We have brought such peace to so many. It is an honor to help you in this time."

My stomach heaved at the false sympathy.

James took a swig of his flask and whispered in my ear, "You up to this, Miss Merry?"

"I am not the spiritualist. I am a documentarian only. Why does everyone keep thinking I am the secret to this success?"

James swigged from his flask again, nervous. "Because you are. I cannot do any of my usual assistance, so the success of this endeavor is all on you. Remember that. We all go home heroes, or off to prison for bilking the President and his wife. Our destiny is in your hands."

"No pressure," I muttered, wondering if I fled now how long it would take them to find me.

James clapped me on the back. "No pressure at all. They will appear if you believe."

The Tophat ghost and other spirits.

Night fell, and the Red Room transformed into a seance parlor. A circular table now sat in the center of the room, directly beneath the chandelier, wisps of bunting flirting with the surface the table. White linen draped over the wooden surface, and three standing candelabra appeared in the corners to help with lighting the space. Shadows flickered across the walls, and a faint wisp of moonlight played about the windows fronting the lawn.

Leah swept into the room, glancing about at the setup, commanding the butler to move this candelabra there, and to raise the bunting off the table, if you please. Maggie followed, circling the table slowly, hand trailing along the white cloth. Kate, alert and quiet, sat in a corner stroking the brocade of her chair.

I hunched over my camera, set in the western corner to get the best of the feeble light available. My lenses snug in my apron, I fingered each one, reminding myself of their order. James, standing to my left, awaited my command. His job was to collect my frames and scurry off to the darkroom established in the adjoining salon.

"I don't like this," I stated, worried at the pressure placed on me to make a hoax appear real.

"I would bear this burden for you if I could, Miss Merry, and you know that. I have full confidence in you."

"What if the film is corrupted? What if it does not develop?"

"Then I am sure Mrs. Pierce will be mollified knowing that is the work of the special sphere, and not one we can control."

A cold wind blew, sending the cloths aflutter in the invisible draft. "This place is so drafty, I worry the bunting will obscure my picture."

"You are a documentarian. I am sure you will overcome."

Leah, satisfied with the preparations, clapped her hands. "Let us all assemble!"

Mrs. Pierce, stooping under the weight of her grief, settled in the chair Leah indicated. Maggie, hair especially tight and worry around her mouth, sat on the eastern end of the table. Kate perched her chair opposite, straight as an arrow.

"Will the President be joining us?" Leah intoned solicitously.

"I... I.. No. He is busy with other affairs and is sorry to miss this opportunity." The First Lady sobbed, wrenching sounds of grief shaking her whole body. Maggie, alarmed, pulled a handkerchief out of her bodice. "Here, please take my kerchief."

Leah tutted, patting the First Lady on her back awkwardly. "Now, now, you are but moments away from talking to Bennie, but you must be strong to help us guide him to you. Can you sit up and dry your tears? We need your help."

Kate, never moving from her spot, said, "The spirits are waiting. I can feel them."

Another cold draft through the unseen door.

Mrs. Pierce mumbled, "Let me try," blew her nose loudly, and settled in her chair. "Please, let us try again."

"Then let us begin." They all joined hands, and I hit the shutter.

"Whom do you wish to contact?" Maggie intoned.

"My son, Master Bennie Pierce."

Maggie said her part with a rolling, stern voice. "Spirits, I beseech you. Come to the sound of my voice, apparate to my will. Find Master Bennie Pierce and make him appear!"

I hunched over my camera, hand reaching for the green lens to take the next picture.

"Spirits, I beseech you. Come to the sound of my voice, apparate to my will. Find Master Bennie Pierce and make him appear!"

My fingers closed around the lens, raised it out of my pocket.

"Spirits, I beseech you! Come to the sound of my voice, apparate to my will. Find Master Bennie Pierce and make him appear!"

Kate flung her head back, strange garbled sounds forced from her throat. Maggie looked at her sister, alarmed. I hit the shutter again as a new shadow played behind Maggie's chair.

A second cold blast rattled through the room. I dropped the lens, glass shattering on the hardwood floor.

"Damn!" I cried softly. My hands reached for the lens with the little boy.

The pocket was empty.

"Oh no!" I cried softly, hands franticly patting my apron.

Another cold wind flung the draperies behind me to whip around my apparatus.

James asked, "What is it?"

"I dropped the lens, the one I needed."

"Give me the pictures you have taken so far. I can start to develop them."

Kate's voice broke the eerie tension building in the room. It was the sound of a young child. "Mother! Please do not cry. It bothers me to see you upset."

"Bennie? Oh God, Bennie?" Mrs. Pierce clutched Maggie and Kate's hands, searching the room for her little boy. "Bennie? Oh God, how I love you son! I miss you!"

I snapped a photograph with a plain lens, hoping something would show on at least one of my prints.

Kate spoke again, eyes rolled back in her head, body swaying erratically in her seat. "It is warm and beautiful here. I can see you in every reflecting pool, hear you in the birdsong, and feel your arms around me in the warm breeze. Please do not despair. I only wish I was bigger and stronger so that I could tell you more often that I love you."

Mrs. Pierce wailed, the full measure of her grief in her words. "Oh, Bennie. I want you to know how very much you are loved and missed."

"Mommy, I love you too."

I scrambled to place another lens on the camera. My hands fumbled in my apron.

The pockets were all empty.

Cursing myself and how I could miss such a thing, I hit the shutter again, hoping against hope to have some image that would save this evening.

"Bennie. Stay with me. Can you do that for mommy?"

Kate twitched, her voice garbled. "Mommy, I want to give you a hug, but my arms are small, and I am terribly tired. It is hard to talk." Her voice faded, scratchy and weak.

"No!" Mrs. Pierce screamed. I hit the shutter again, my feet sliding around on the floor to feel if I had absently dropped my lenses.

"Take your time with Father. I will be waiting for you when you arrive with a hug and flowers from your favorite spot. I can watch you, you are not alone…"

Kate slumped in her chair, the silence more eerie than the shouting and crying. Maggie cleared her voice. "Thank you, spirits."

Kate surged upward, voice growling and menacing and masculine. "Leave us be. Leave us to our eternal peace."

I snapped the shutter again.

Maggie stated, "I have command over the spirit realm, and you, spirit, will not dictate to me!"

The candelabras winked out. Mrs. Pierce screamed, and three security men rushed into the room with lanterns to escort her out.

James appeared beside me. "Miss Merry, you must come look at your pictures."

I sank to the ground, exhausted, my lenses clinking gently in my apron.

"Dear heavens, they are here! James, how could I be such an amateur? The lenses were here all the time."

"No, they weren't. I took them from you while you were concentrating."

The lights were back on in the room. Maggie wiped her forehead with a cloth, while Kate sat in her chair, back straight as an arrow.

"Why would you do such a thing?"

"You need to see your pictures."

I followed James to the makeshift darkroom. He'd followed my instructions meticulously, and the photos hung in a tidy row, developing fluid dripping into the pan beneath them.

"Just look."

I stared at the scenes, tears rolling down my face. The figure of a small boy, arms wrapped around his mother filled two of the pictures.

The Tophat Ghost lounged against the back wall in one picture, then held the young boy's hand in another picture, as if leading him off to play.

I pointed to Kate's slumped form. "Look, here!"

James gasped, and took another swig from his flask. A man-shaped figure with tentacles for arms embraced Kate's slumped form, a thin wisp of white lights drawn from the top of her head into its gaping maw.

"Do you know what that is?"

Leah flew into the room. "Please tell me you got something."

"Oh, we captured what you wanted."

Leah scoured the images. When she saw the picture of the creature behind Kate, she giggled. "That's what Kate gets for being a show-off. She completely upstaged Maggie, and that simply won't do moving forward."

"You aren't going to tell Kate about this...this...creature?"

Leah grabbed the print off the line, tearing it into pieces. "No, and you aren't either, if you know what is good for you."

She stomped off.

James sighed. "She can be disagreeable when she is excited."

"Let's pack up." I asked him to go back to the Red Room to collect and pack up my camera. As soon as he left, I dunked the photographic plate from the last picture in the remains of the developing solution. Leah could not tell my conscience what was right and wrong.

A photographic documentarian specializing in grieving souls.

"Hold your head still, now tilt your chin to the left." The young man smiled and did as he was told. His hands were brown from ground-in dirt that didn't come off in the wash. His bare feet dangled above the floor.

It was three years since I left the employment of the Fox sisters. We all went our separate ways. I still saw James occasionally out and about in Philadelphia—he worked at one of the theaters as a lighting specialist.

"Who do you want to be in the picture with you?"

"My dad." He grinned, black cavities staining his smile. "He was a soldier, died in a place called Vicksburg, and we don't know where he was buried."

"Then let us hope your dad heard you and was paying attention." I adjusted my focus and hit the shutter.

I didn't use the special lenses, although some students at the Philadelphia College of Photography still asked about my time with the Fox sisters. I shared my techniques for making and grinding my lenses, and they were mostly pleased. None were able to re-create my spectral photographs, and that was fine.

As James said, if you believe, then the ghosts will appear.

"Smile and hold still."

The little boy smiled again. I hit the shutter, the caress of cold air across my neck all the assurance I needed that the Tophat Ghost had delivered another soul to my film again.

JAZZ CITY BLUES - A QUINCY HARKER HISTORY

JOHN G. HARTNESS

New Orleans, 1994

I pried my eyes open through a crusty film and found myself face-to-face with a concrete curb. *Facedown in the gutter again. My life is starting to resemble a country song. Starting to smell like one, too.* I heaved myself over and flopped onto my back, the bright sunlight stabbing into my head like icepicks through my eyes.

"Fuuuuuuck," I groaned, struggling to an upright position. I looked around, taking stock of my situation. I was lying in the gutter on a city street. Cobbled brick sidewalks meant an old city. Beat up streets. No traffic to speak of, which was good for me since my long legs were now sticking out into the road. I wiped the sleep from my eyes and looked up, regretting as more sunlight daggers poked me in the retinas. Wrought-iron balconies. Lots of plants. Jewel-tone buildings. Smelled like stale beer and piss, with just the slightest hint of vomit on the wind. A steady stream of water ran under my ass, and I felt something fetch up against my hips. I felt around behind me and pulled up a stream of rainbow-colored beads, the cheap ones that drunken guys throw down to even drunker girls in hopes of seeing a flash of boob in...

"New Orleans?" I croaked.

"New Orleans," a voice behind me said.

I'd like to say that I leapt to my feet, ready to meet whatever threat loomed over me, but that would be bullshit. I kinda half-turned, half-rolled around until I saw the trim black woman sitting on the stoop of the shop directly behind me. She had a spectacular afro shot through with white and wore a flowing robe of bright oranges, reds, and purples. Gold and silver bangles festooned her wrists, and a pile of necklaces that Mr. T would envy encircled her neck and cascaded down her chest. She sat on the concrete step, her feet pulled up under her and elbows on her knees, clutching a black coffee mug in the shape of a skull. She looked like a cross between a kindly grandmother and a voodoo priestess.

She was the second.

"Good morning, Madison."

"Good morning, Quincy. Why are you lying in the street in front of my shop at eight in the morning?"

"I'll do you one better. Why am I in New Orleans?"

"Have you been drinking again, Quincy?"

"Apparently, I have not been drinking enough, Madison, because I find myself talking to you in an unpleasant state, which is to say stone fucking sober. Do you have anything that can remedy that for me?"

"I do, but I am more likely to give you a hangover remedy and a place to recuperate than to give you another drink right now."

I struggled to my feet, finding it difficult since this chunk of Bourbon Street decided to buck and roil like the Pacific Ocean under me, but after a few stumbles and the assistance of a very kind lamp-post, I managed to stabilize. "While I appreciate the offer, I believe I will be better served by continuing my quest for perpetual inebria-tion. After all, the perpetual inebriation machine has been one of mankind's great quests since the dawn of the Industrial Revolution, has it not?"

I leaned in toward the genteel black woman. "And if we're being honest, hasn't that revolution won yet? I mean, really?"

Madison looked at me, pity in her eyes. "Luke told me it was bad. I didn't realize he meant it was this bad. I'm sorry for your loss, Quincy, but you need to pull yourself together. The girl died six months ago, and you barely knew her."

Anger rushed through like a wildfire, burning the last vestiges of drunkenness from me, and I glared at Madison. "You don't get to tell me who I knew. She was everything that was left of Anna in this world, and now she's gone. No children, no grandchildren, just some octogenarian cousins in Switzerland who can't remember her face. *I can't remember her face!* I can hear her voice, still right there in my head every night, but I can't remember her face..."

And that was it. I dropped to my knees in the street, ruining a pair of jeans that was, if I'm being honest about it, already pretty well fucked, and curling up into a little ball at the foot of a streetlight in the Louisiana morning sun. New Orleans, that regal old bitch that she is, just looked down on my tears in the same stoic silence she gave to everything that happened in the city of jazz. Madison was better, though. After I got the most gut-wrenching sobs out of me, and when I was at least somewhat less likely to blast anyone who touched me with eldritch power, she wrapped an arm around me and helped me to my feet.

I stood, still trembling with barely contained sobs, and she led me up the chipped steps into the narrow entrance of her voodoo shop. "Be careful," she said. "It's tight quarters in here. Go straight on to the back and strip. I'll put some fresh coffee on while you get yourself wrapped up in one of the clean robes back there."

I opened my mouth to argue, and she grabbed my jaw. Madison wasn't a young woman anymore. Not as old as me, but no spring chicken. But when she latched onto my face and spun me around, her grip was iron. "Do not argue with me, John Abraham Quincy Holmwood Harker. I have known you and your uncle far too long to take any shit from you at this hour of the morning. Now we are going to wash those clothes, and what can't be salvaged, we're going to send out to the swamp for alligator bait. You are going to get yourself a quick little whore's bath in the sink back yonder, and you're going to put on that silly robe I wear when I read cards or cast the bones for tourists. Don't worry, I don't ever wear it when I'm doing any kind of real working, so there won't be any residual energy in the hems. You don't have the defenses right now to protect from any of that. While you do that, I'm going to call my nephew Joseph and get him to send his boy Alexander over to Cafe du Monde for some beignets. Then we gonna sit down in my back office and make us a plan."

"A plan for what?" The words came out jagged, through the ruin of my throat. It sounded like I hadn't spoken to anyone in days, maybe weeks. For all I could remember, I hadn't. My last memory was of being in Arizona, getting a phone call I expected but still wasn't prepared for. Then I woke up in the gutter in front of Marie Laveau's House of Voodoo. I idly wondered what day it was, then what month. The last time I lost myself, it took four years and Luke's intervention to pull me out. This didn't feel that bad, but it wasn't good, either.

"A plan for how we going to put Quincy Harker back together, and how you going to help me get rid of all these damn zombies in New Orleans, boy. I figure if you here, and in this kind of shape, somebody up there must have seen that we need one another, and I ain't one to ignore divine intervention." She grabbed one of her necklaces without looking, a silver crucifix, and brought it to her lips.

"Now go get changed, and tie up the garage bag you put them clothes in. Come to think of it, throw the washrag in there, too. You stink, boy."

Fifteen minutes later, I hovered over a steaming cup of Cafe du Monde's finest coffee with white powdered sugar coating my fingers and face. "Thank you. Madison. I needed that. Now, do you have any Irish whiskey to put in this coffee? I'll settle for bourbon, if that's all you have." I held out the cup to her, but she just shook her head.

"Luke told me you were well off the reservation, Quincy, but this is ridiculous. You have work to do, boy. Get your ass together and do it."

"Boy? I'm older than you, old woman," I growled.

"Call me old woman again, and you won't get any older, *boy*. Now if you so damned old, why don't you quit acting like a baby and pull yourself together. I know full well that you lost your lady love, but I know it was also forty years ago, across an ocean, and a lot of bad people were doing terrible things then, and you did some pretty terrible things yourself when that happened. And I know that this woman you are mourning was the cousin of the woman you loved and that she died half a year and half a continent away from here. And I know that you spoke to that woman maybe half a dozen times since she moved to the United States and never mentioned that you knew Anna or that she meant anything to you."

She knew a lot. Seemed Uncle Luke had been telling tales out of school again. I figured he and I would chat about that the next time we saw each other. But Madison wasn't finished raking me over the coals, apparently. "But what I know now is that you are needed here, and you are needed whole and sober. At least a little bit."

"I suppose I could stand with a day or two of sobriety, just to remind my liver what it feels like," I said. "What's going on?"

"We got a zombie problem," Madison said, taking a bite of beignet without getting powdered sugar all over her face. After all these decades, I've met two people who can manage that feat. One of them is my uncle Luke, who also happens to be the most famous vampire in history. The other is Madison. I'm not sure which one of them is more unnatural—Dracula or the voodoo priestess who eats beignets without making a mess. "We've always had our fair share of the walking dead, but most of them are raised for a purpose, and the priests tend to put them back where they found them when they're done."

"Or else," I muttered.

"Well, I have been forced to give a little persuasion from time to time," Madison agreed. "But this…infestation seems to be coming from a new player. Someone not interested in playing by the rules."

"That's pretty rare, isn't it? How long has it been since a new player came to town?"

"Sister Evangeline was the last, and that's been no small number of years. And I think I was the newcomer before her, so that takes us back more years than I care to reveal."

"And Evie's been here for twenty years at least," I said. "Are they voodoo or necromantic zombies?"

Madison laughed, a rich, honey-coated sound that wrapped around me and warmed me rather than made me feel ridiculed. "Oh, child, I know you are old, but sometimes you sound like such a babe. Voodoo *is* necromancy. Your spells and Latin and circles are just a different way to focus the power. It's all the same thing. But to answer the real question, which is if I have any idea who is raising the dead, I have no idea."

The bell over the front door *dinged*, and I heard Alexander greet the newcomer. He stuck his head through the beaded curtain into the back room where we sat. "Gran, we got a customer. She say she here for her reading."

Madison smiled. "Yes, baby, that'll be Miss Cheryl." She turned to me. "Cheryl comes in here every Thursday morning and has me read the cards for her weekend. She's convinced that a husband is going to come through the front door of Big Daddy's one night and sweep her off her giant high heels and into a lap of luxury. Every Thursday I tell her she ought to save her money for community college instead of getting her cards read because if she gets off that pole, she's gonna have a lot better chance of finding the lap of luxury."

"As opposed to just a lap dance," I said.

"Exactly. But she don't listen. None of you children ever do. Now get your butt back over yonder and wait in my office while I do a reading for this girl. It won't take but about fifteen minutes. Then we'll see about sending Alexander out to get you some fresh clothes, and you can see about helping me with my zombie problem."

I did as I was told and settled into Madison's desk chair, putting my feet up on the desk just long enough to hear her yell, "Get your feet off my desk, Quincy!" I grumbled, but I did as she asked. I try not to really piss off the few friends I have left by being rude.

I heard the *clump-clump* of heavy heels and the slight rattle as someone pushed aside the beaded curtain. Madison's chair scraped across the worn hardwoods, and I assumed she stood up to greet her customer. "Hello, sweetie. How you doin' dis mornin'?" Madison was deep into her "customer voice," ramping up the Cajun accent and pouring molasses over every word as she spoke.

"I'm fine, Maddie, thank you. I...I ain't here for a reading. I just stopped by to tell you I probably ain't gonna be coming around anymore." The woman's nasally voice quivered with fear or excitement. I couldn't tell which through the wall, but I leaned forward, pushing my heightened hearing so I didn't miss anything.

"What's wrong, Cheryl, sweetie? What done happened?" Madison's voice had a hint of steel in it. I recognized that protective tone. She cared for this girl and was going to rain down hellfire on anyone who hurt her. Maybe literally. I didn't know the full extent of Madison's abilities, but she was no slouch as a medium and probably had more than a few tricks up those billowy silk sleeves of hers.

The newcomer laughed. "Oh no, Maddie, it ain't nothing like that. I done found myself a good one. He come into the club a few nights ago, and he's been back every night since, asking just for me. Look at all this!" I heard a zipper, then a *thump* as something soft and heavy dropped onto the cloth-covered reading table.

"That is a pile of money, baby girl, that I can see."

"He gave me all this just in three nights, Maddie. It's almost enough to get me that cherry-red Ninja motorcycle I been wanting, with a matching helmet and some sexy riding leathers. And Maddie, he wants me to come over to his place tonight! He says he's having a private party and wants me to entertain. Says I can make ten grand, and I don't even gotta fuck nobody."

"Sweetie, are you sure you trust this guy enough to go to his house? You want me to send Alexander with you? He ain't real tough, but he's big, and he's black. That's enough to keep most white boys in line." The women laughed, and I had to smile. Even in the relatively progressive nineties, she was right. Most white people in the South wouldn't try anything with Alexander in the room because they'd just see a six-foot man with dark skin. They wouldn't notice the soft hands or the posture that said he never expected to have to be in a fight.

"Oh, Maddie, it'll be fine. There's gonna be three more girls from a couple other clubs there. Nobody would try to hurt us with a bunch of people around." I could almost hear Madison sigh through the wall. Usually by the time they've been at it for a while, strippers have a very clear understanding about humanity. This girl, however, was the Pollyanna of pole dancers. She had no idea how much trouble she could wander into.

"Okay, darling. I reckon you knows best, after all," Madison said, and I felt a sinking feeling in the pit of my stomach. Madison was not the type to give up easily, and if she did, it was because she had another plan. I had the distinct feeling I was the other plan.

"Well, I just wanted to stop by and give you this. Since I'm probably going to be riding out of the Big Easy on my new red Ninja in a couple weeks, I won't need little Jude anymore. So maybe you keep it and give it to somebody else that needs guidance from the Other Side."

"Oh, baby girl, I will make sure this goes to the person who needs it the most. Now you come over here and give Aunt Maddie a hug." I heard the *clump-clump* of those shoes again and Madison's chair scrape.

"Thanks, Maddie," the girl said, then I heard the rattle of beads. A few seconds later, the bell over the door *dinged*, and I heard Madison call for me.

"Come on in here, Quincy. I know you heard every word."

I stood up, smoothing down the wrinkles in my robe and gave a fleeting thought to the timeline for getting me some pants. I didn't relish the thought of me going around New Orleans after dark in this rainbow robe. I sat down in the chair opposite Madison, who had both elbows on the table and a medallion dangling from her right hand. "Saint Jude?" I asked.

"Patron Saint of Lost Causes," Madison replied, passing the silver necklace over to me. "I need you to—"

"Track the girl using the medal, make sure this sugar daddy is on the up and up, and beat his ass if he isn't. That pretty much cover it?"

"Pretty much, but be careful, Harker. This one feels bad. It feels bad in my bones."

When the closest thing you have to family is the world's oldest and most famous monster, you're pretty well-connected to the criminal underworld in every major city in the world. With New Orleans holding one of the top spots for murder in the late nineties, Luke knew everybody who was anybody in the city. That meant that it was ridiculously easy for me to walk around the French Quarter less than twelve hours after waking up drunk in the gutter with a fully restocked wallet, a new set of fake identification, and a nice Colt 1911 pistol in a holster under my arm. The only thing missing in my equipment was the serial numbers on the pistol. Funny how those have a tendency to vanish around Uncle Luke's associates.

I stopped at a beer stand wedged between two buildings and grabbed an almost-cold Budweiser. It tasted like horse piss, but carrying something around made me look a little less conspicuous. I was decked out in thrift store jeans, a pair of ill-fitting Air Force surplus boots, a New Orleans Saints t-shirt under a light denim jacket, and a black baseball cap with some sort of athletic logo on it. Cheryl's Saint Jude medal was in my jacket pocket, close to my left hand, the tracking spell I cast on it making a steady tug in one direction. I parked myself at a table by the window at The Famous Door across the street from Big Daddy's Topless & Bottomless and kept an eye on the entrance.

Madison gave me a rough description of Cheryl, but it was hard to narrow the stream of skinny white girls with big boobs down to just the one that I was looking for. But as one particular girl stepped out into the neon glow of the night, the medal in my pocket gave a harder tug than normal. This must be her. I fixed her in my memory, making sure I could find *this* stripper in the Bourbon Street crowd. She was tall and that special kind of skinny that speaks of a little too much indulgence in Bolivian Marching Powder. Her hair was a platinum blond, and I was impressed at the attention to detail she used to make sure that her roots were dyed a nice deep brown. She'd traded in the clunky heels she wore into Madison's shop for a pair of white Keds, but I would have put money on there being shoes with Lucite platform heels in the duffel bag she had slung over one shoulder.

Cheryl wiped her nose and turned left toward Canal Street, and I got up to go follow. My path was blocked by a wall wearing a black t-shirt, who put a hand on my chest and growled, "Two drink minimum, asshole. You owe ten bucks for the rent on the stool."

I looked up at the goon, who had a thick Magnum P.I. mustache, despite Tom Selleck being off the air for a decade, and more muscles than sense. *I do not have time for this shit.* "Here's a ten. Have a nice life." I peeled a bill off the roll in my pocket and stuffed it into the neck of his skintight t-shirt.

His hand didn't move, but his eyebrows lifted at the sight of the roll of cash on me. "I said fifty."

"You said ten," I said, scowling. I needed to hurry, but this guy was quickly pushing me past the point of discretion.

"Now it's fifty."

"Now you can go fuck yourself." I took a step back, making sure to give him room to swing. I was happy to give him one free shot. I could take it, and if I couldn't, I heal fast. But I didn't want to get in a wrestling match with some jackass the size of a grizzly bear.

He obliged and punched me in the jaw, spinning me around and dropping me to one knee. I concentrated as much as I could with stars exploding across my vision, and muttered, *"Ferrum."* My fist flashed white, then reddish-brown as the flesh on my hand turned to solid iron. I spun around and landed a punch of my own, right on the point of Magnum's jaw. He dropped like a sack of potatoes, and the band on stage froze at the *crack* that rang out through the bar.

I dispelled the magic wrapping my hand and turned to the room. "Y'all saw it, right? He hit me first. Now I'm leaving. But you might need to call a doctor for Mr. Glassjaw here." I stepped over the unconscious extortionate bouncer onto the sidewalk, letting the tide of insanity that is Bourbon Street envelop me and carry me along. I dodged beads, breasts, and spilled beer as I wove through the crown toward Canal Street, following the insistent tug of the necklace in my pocket. I moved through the crowd almost unnoticed, using my unnatural speed and grace to navigate the sea of humanity. I reached the mouth of Bourbon Street just in time to see Cheryl get into the back seat of a waiting Town Car and pull out into traffic heading away from the crowds and north into the night.

"Shit," I muttered, then flagged down a taxi. I slid into the back seat, wrinkling my nose at the smell of stale sweat and barely-cleaned vomit. "Follow that Town Car," I said.

The driver, a black dude with short dreads, looked back at me and grinned. "You joking, right, man? Where you really want to go?"

I shoved a hundred-dollar bill in his face and said, "I want you to follow that goddamn Town Car and not let it out of your sight. If you can stay on it, there's another hundred for you whenever it stops. My girlfriend is in that car, and I think she's cheating on me. I want to beat the shit out of the guy who's screwing her, and then I'm gonna win my girl back. Now drive!" Somehow, he bought that line of shit. Or he just didn't give a fuck and took the hundred. I didn't care which; I just cared that he put the cab in drive and peeled out after the black Lincoln.

We drove north for several miles, then turned right on Jefferson David Parkway back into the heart of the city. A couple more twists and turns later, and the Town Car pulled up to the back gates of St. Louis No. 3 Cemetery. The driver cut the lights and pulled over, turning back to me. "You sure she's meeting a guy here? 'Cause that's some kinky shit, man. I don't know if I want a chick so freaky she wants to fuck in a cemetery."

I handed him another hundred dollars and opened the door, saying, "I don't want a woman who *doesn't* want to fuck in a cemetery." Then I slid out of the cab and pushed the door closed slowly so as to muffle the sound. Ahead of me, Cheryl stepped out of the Lincoln, flanked by two no-neck goons in double-breasted suits. They each took an elbow and guided her to a section of fence that swung open at a touch from one of the men. I followed, but the fence locked behind them, and I had to jump to the top of the fence, then spring over to the top of the nearest crypt. Jumping from tomb to tomb made it easy enough to follow Cheryl and the goons through the graveyard without being seen, and it also gave me a good vantage point to see what was coming up ahead of me.

I did *not* like what I saw ahead of me.

A man stood in front of a huge family crypt, in a circle with candles at the five points of the pentacle. And, of course, this guy was facing away from the top of the circle and working widdershins, sprinkling a dark liquid around the circle counter-clockwise as he turned and chanted. I strained to hear him, but just a few words of Latin drifted to my ears. Nothing specific sounded familiar, just some gibberish about doors, portals, and breaches. *Yeah, that sounds pretty much awful. I can't think of any time some asshole in a long black bathrobe in a cemetery has ever said something about breaching portals, and it's turned out* good *for anybody.*

I hopped to the roof of a nearby crypt, then leapt into the lowest-hanging branches of an old live oak and scurried high into the tree. Inching out over the walkways gave me a better vantage point on the proceedings and provided better cover against discovery on the off chance that somebody decided to look up. Bathrobe looked over to where Goon 1 and Goon 2 stood with Cheryl between them and drew back his hood.

"Hello, darling. I trust you are well this evening?"

The worried look Cheryl wore vanished at the sight of his face, and her broad smile lit up the walkway. *Dammit. She actually likes this douche.* "Babycakes! I was getting scared out here. I don't like creepy stuff like cemeteries, and these goobers you sent to give me a ride wouldn't tell me where we was going or nothing." She took a step toward Bathrobe, but Goon 1 grabbed her arm and held her in place. I could see the pain flash across her face as he yanked her back, but she wiped it away with the practice of a woman who's spent a long time pretending not to be hurt. "Hey, asshole! Let me go. I want to go lay some lovin' on my man. Or does that make you jealous?"

Bathrobe spoke again, and his oily voice matched the greasy dark hair that he wore slicked back from his receding crown. "Cheryl, my love. I am so happy that you could join us for this, the finest night of my ascension. I only regret that you will not be able to share its completion with me. But fear not, my sweet. You shall play a crucial role in our festivities."

"What are you talking about, babe? I thought we was leaving town tonight. And where's the party? There was supposed to be other girls and a bunch of rich dudes. And ten grand..." Cheryl pulled against Goon 1's grip, but he didn't even have to work at keeping her still. Cheryl was maybe a buck-fifty soaking wet, and both of these goons were double that if they were an ounce. I kept my attention on Bathrobe but tried to scoot along the branch so that I'd land on one of the goons if I dropped out of the tree.

"Oh, you are, my love. You are most definitely leaving tonight." Bathrobe reached behind him and drew a silver *kris*, a wavy knife that magical wannabes like to use in their faux rituals. Real practitioners use a nice little *athame*, or just whatever's handy. It's the blood that's important. The knife very seldom matters, unless it has some residue from the last person to bleed on it. Me, I usually just use my pocketknife. I try not to use blood magic, but when I do, it's my own blood. Bathrobe very obviously had other plans.

Cheryl started to struggle in earnest when she saw the blade. "Nah, Victor. I done told you, I ain't into all that kinky stuff. A little bondage is fine, especially the silk scarves, I kinda like that. But no blood stuff and no wax. That stuff got in my hair last time, and I had to melt it to get it out. I almost burned my scalp off! So, I'm sorry, baby, but if this is the way you wanna roll, I'm going to have to go back to Big Daddy's. This whole scene is starting to creep me out, anyway." She yanked against the goon's grip, and after the third hard pull, she reared back and kicked him right in the shin. That's when I noticed she had changed shoes into the big clunky heels I heard at Madison's shop earlier. Goon 1 let go of her arm and jumped back, cursing, and

Cheryl bolted off into the cemetery, wobbling on her platform shoes but making pretty good time. Goon 2 took off after her, with Goon 1 limping along behind.

Bathrobe watched them go, shaking his head. I couldn't help myself. I laughed. Bathrobe's head snapped up, and he clapped his hands together with a shouted, "*Illuminus!*"

The branch I was sitting on burst into a brilliant white, throwing everything in our part of the cemetery into stark daylight. I winced at the onslaught of painful brilliance, then hopped down. I bent my legs to take the impact of the twelve-foot drop, but otherwise didn't do anything to show that it had been any big deal. The very minor levitation spell I cast as I jumped insured that it wasn't a big deal at all. "Hi there," I said, looking at Bathrobe. "Quincy Harker. You are?"

The skinny man looked completely flummoxed at the sight of a man dropping nearly two stories to land in front of him in what I'm sure he thought was a deserted cemetery, except, of course, for him and his folks. His brown eyes were wide in his pale face, making his thin beard look even patchier along his waxy skin. "Who the hell are you?" he asked.

"I think I just mentioned that. Quincy Harker—magician, problem-solver, all-purpose badass. And once again, you are...?"

"I'm Maeve the Mighty!" He puffed out his skinny chest and put his fists on his hips.

"I thought your name was Victor. And isn't Maeve a woman's name?" I asked, as much to see his chest deflate as anything else. He didn't disappoint.

He shrank in on himself, and his face reddened. "Do you think I would tell that harlot my true name? I am indeed the legendary Maeve the Mighty!" This time the pose didn't seem quite as heroic. More pitiful, really.

"Never heard of you," I said. "But whatever. What are you doing with the nice young lady? She thought you were whisking her away to be married. I'm guessing that isn't the case, what with all the trappings for dark magic and all."

Trappings was being generous, frankly. Now that I was close

enough to see the details, his candles weren't black—they were white pillar candles that somebody, I assume Maeve the Ridiculous, had spray-painted. Melting spray paint stinks to high heaven, by the way. His circle was also broken in two places by a crack in the concrete sidewalk, and the Enochian runes were almost all upside down. And they didn't say anything. It looked a lot more like he'd copied symbols off of Led Zeppelin and Slayer albums trying to cast a spell.

"I am going to summon a zombie horde the likes of which this city has never seen! They will all tremble before the coming zombie apocalypse, and only my magic will be able to save New Orleans from the tide of undeath that is coming!"

I managed to stop myself before I asked him how long he rehearsed that little speech. Instead, I said, "So you're responsible for the increase in zombies lately? Good to know. What does Cheryl have to do with all that? She's missing one critical part of zombie-ism. She's not dead."

"Oh, but she will be," Maeve said with what I'm sure he practiced as his evil mastermind grin. Really, it just looked like a shitty preteen ogling his dad's *Sports Illustrated Swimsuit Issue*. "She shall be the final sacrifice to raise my army of the undead! All my efforts up to now have been but minor workings, using the life force of animals to raise a few of the creatures. But with Cheryl's energy, the life force of a virgin sacrificed under the new moon, will...what?" His monologue trailed off, and he glared at me.

It took me a minute, but I wiped my eyes and managed to stop laughing. "What was that about her being a virgin? How the fuck do you figure that? Son, she is a thirty-year-old stripper in New Orleans. You're going to have a better chance finding a virgin at a Tulane frat party than you will on Bourbon Street. That girl is no more a virgin than I am a teetotaler, or you are a wizard. So let's just end this charade now. You quit fucking around with magic you don't understand, leave the goddamn neighborhood cats alone, and go back to whatever kind of bullshit you do for money. That way I don't have to rip off any pieces of you that you might want to use later."

"Do you have any idea who you're speaking to, you piece of worthless English trash?"

Now, I'll admit, my accent does come out more when I've been drinking, and by the best of my reckoning, this was the first sober night I'd spent in six months, so I could handle the "English" bit. But my family was pretty solidly middle class, maybe even a little better, and for the past seventy years or so, I'd been hanging out with Luke, who is a legitimate Count, so I was not going to stand for being called trash by some asshole in his father's bathrobe. I walked toward him, my pace even, slow, and very predatory. "I don't know who you are. I don't care who you are. I don't give a fuck if you're Prince Charles or the grandson of John F. Kennedy. Right now, you're just another fuckwit magician with a spellbook he can't read, a circle he can't scribe, and the barest hint of power he can't direct. So if you don't want to learn what it means to fuck with Quincy Goddamn Harker, you'd better change your name to Vanished." I walked right up to the outer edge of his ten-foot casting barrier and stopped.

He stood in his circle, his half-drawn chalk circle with its fucked up symbology, and glared at me with his arms folded across his chest. "You cannot breach my magical wards, fool. I am protected inside this circle from all threats, be they physical or metaphysical."

"I don't need to get metaphysical with you, jackass. I'll stick to the physical and just beat your ass." Then I reached out, grabbed him by the front of his robe, and dragged him out of the circle. His feet dragged, making even bigger breaks in the ward, and the tiny bit of energy he had dancing across the half-assed barricade flickered out.

"How? You can't do that! The books—"

He stopped talking when my fist connected with his nose. I turned his pointy little snoot into a flattened mass of blood and cartilage with three quick punches, then I flung him six feet to sprawl across the concrete. He rolled to a stop right at the feet of Goon 2, who looked down at his unconscious boss, eyes wide.

"What did you do to Melvin?" the goon asked.

"Melvin?"

"Yeah, Melvin de la Rocque. His dad's Marvin de la Rocque, the businessman," Goon replied.

"Businessman," I repeated. That was a good word for it. Marvin "The Rock" de la Rocque controlled all the hookers and drugs in the Quarter. Not the weed because that was purely the domain of Papa Greenleaf, a witch doctor and marijuana dealer who had been known to imbue his crops with some "special encouragement" from time to time. Papa's weed was the best shit I'd ever laid my eyes on, and I've been almost everywhere on the planet.

"Yeah, he's a totally legitimate businessman," Goon 1 said, stepping back into the light from behind a crypt. He had Cheryl slung over one shoulder, unconscious.

"Well, his totally not legitimate half-baked wizard son has been murdering pets to make zombies. Tonight, he planned to kill that woman to raise a zombie army."

"I know," came a new voice. A man stepped out from behind Goon 1. He moved like money and power crammed into a double-breasted suit. He had the same nose as Maeve, or Melvin, and the same hair-style, but on him, it looked classy and styled, while on his kid, it just looked greasy. "Melvin has been getting more and more involved with the occult lately and neglecting his duty to the family. I am very disap-pointed in him."

"If he'd managed to raise a fuckton of zombies tonight, I think we'd all be a lot more than disappointed," I said.

"With that spell? With those workings? Come on, Mr. Harker. You and I both know he would have been lucky to raise three half-crazed ghouls with this magic. The city was never in any danger."

"Cheryl was." My voice was low, and from the glint in de la Rocque's eyes, I could see he knew I was *pissed*. I don't like powerful people using normal people and throwing them away. It bothers me.

"She was," Melvin's dad agreed. "That is why I sent Gog and Magog here to look after her. They were under strict orders to step in should Melvin fail to come to his senses before he harmed the girl. She was in no danger, and when she awakens, she will be at home, in her bed, with a note of apology from me and double the money she expected to receive tonight in cash on her dresser."

"Gog and Magog? Really?"

"An affectation, yes, but convenient. After all, can *you* tell them apart?"

"I'll give you that. So you knew what your kid was up to, and you sent Heckle and Jeckle here to make sure he didn't kill anybody, but now what? You're just going to take him home and pretend this never happened? He's played with power, and he knows it's real. He's either got to be trained, burned out, or killed. That's the deal. Otherwise, he's just going to go back into the same shit."

De la Rocque stepped up to me, his jaw set. "Are you going to kill my only son, Mr. Harker?" He wasn't a big man, but I could feel the power coming off him. Not just magic, even though there was some of that. No, most of what he exuded was authority. This was not a man accustomed to being fucked with.

"Not tonight, Mr. de la Rocque. Not tonight. But if I hear of any random zombies popping up around New Orleans, I'm going to come back down here. And if I come back down here, whoever is causing trouble is going to die. If that's Melvin, so be it. If it's you..."

"It it's me, what?" de la Rocque asked, his voice almost a whisper.

"Then so fucking be it," I whispered back. "Clean up your house, Mr. de la Rocque. Because if I have to clean it up, you aren't going to like what I do with the trash." I turned to Goon 1. "You so much as cop a feel on that girl while she's knocked out, and I will cast a spell that will make your balls shrivel up and fall off. You got me?"

The big man nodded and took a step back. I looked around at the bunch—the crime lord, the ineffectual wizard, the bodyguards, and the stripper. I wondered, not for the first time, if I was doing the right thing even saving them. Then I saw the face of a young Jewish woman, her pale skin in stark contrast to the dark brown hair that framed her face and made her hazel eyes stand out. I saw Anna's face in my memory, and for the first time in nearly fifty years, I didn't break down in tears at the thought of her. That's when I knew that no matter how broken, stupid, or pitiful these people were, they were my broken, stupid, pitiful people to save, just like Anna had once saved me. She died for saving me, and if that's what it cost me to save all these idiots, then I guess I'd be tilting windmills 'til Sancho rode his last.

I turned and walked back to the entrance of St. Louis Cemetery No. 3 having been reminded in that place of death exactly why I was alive.

PRESERVATIVES

LAURA S. TAYLOR

The glass-and-chrome behemoth on the office kitchen counter loomed with all the pretention of a wealthy hipster. Not surprising, given who'd acquired the monstrosity after the old microwave kicked it last week. Tiffany was on another of her holier-than-thou cleanses, and something like this seemed to fit with her litany of kombucha, quinoa, and kale. But I was starving, I'd timed my break to avoid Princess Probiotic, and my lunch was in serious need of therapeutic radiation, so I didn't have much choice.

I savored the muted aroma emanating from the foam box I'd pulled from the fridge, then dumped its contents on a plate. Emperor Ho's made the best chicken chow mein in town, and the Phokas College union contract mandated an hour for lunch. After yet another harrowing morning, I was ready to take my MSG-laden comfort and escape into the June sunshine. I opened the machine's wide door—

"Chinese food, really?"

She was at my side as if I'd summoned her, derision dripping from her voice like a leaky faucet. "Ellen, I thought we talked about this."

No, you talked at me. Red-faced, I glanced away. "They're just leftovers."

"That's still not an excuse, you know. You should really consider your health." Her auburn ringlets bounced as she strode to the fridge to retrieve her own lunch—a salad, naturally—before turning back to eye my food. "Well, at least that thing will see some use."

Right. The microwave. She'd made such a grand gesture of donating it on Friday—right before declaring yet another holy war on processed foods. How could I forget?

I glared at the back of her twin-set as she strode off. There she went again, trying to force everyone to conform to what she thought was best. *Dammit.* Svelte and fit she might have been, but Tiffany was the biggest cow I knew.

What was it about losing weight that made a person think they were superior? As if we were all failures if we didn't kowtow to her ideas, do what she'd done just so we could be as "successful" as her. The sad thing was, for the most part, everyone in our department had fallen in line—even our boss. Not that Milo was much for conflict. Ever. And so Tiffany and her quinoa reigned supreme.

While I stuck to the one defiance I could still get away with: my lunch.

So what if I spent more on eating out and facial degreasing than clothes?

A pang in my belly reminded me of what really mattered. I stuck my food inside the machine. The door closed with a *clunk* as it locked, and I studied the rows of buttons on its not-so-standard panel.

Oh, the usual options were there. Cook. Power level. Clock. But one button in the panel's lower left corner struck me as odd.

Incinerate.

I snorted. Clearly the machine's creators had a sense of humor. And then I thought, *Why not?* The faster I could enjoy my calorie-laden therapy in peace, the better. I punched in ninety seconds, hit the button, and popped into the nearby washroom.

I shouldn't have left.

I'd heard the microwave beep while I peed. The office walls in our department are pretty thin, and the kitchen produces a linoleum echo not found in the rest of the carpeted halls. But when I returned, the room lacked the distinct mouth-watering scent my greasy leftovers usually produced.

The box was gone. In its place was a dense green mass on a squarish glass plate.

I eyed the palm-sized glob, cold with disbelief. That was *not* my chow mein.

Somehow, in the two minutes I'd taken to empty my bladder, someone had switched my carton of scrumptious snackage with this—this—

Whatever the hell it was, I sure didn't want to call it "food."

Growling, I yanked on the microwave door. It didn't budge. I rolled my eyes, jabbed the release button, then pulled. A cloud of noxious fumes poured out.

It was all I could do not to gag.

I dumped the offending mound in the trash, set the glass square in the sink with more calm than I thought possible, then stuck my head through the window and sucked in deep gulps of air. Anything to get that smell out of my lungs. When I was recovered enough, I turned back to the fridge.

My lunch bag was empty. I'd only brought the chow mein and a drink.

Screw it. Woman cannot survive on lemon FizzUp alone. Time for another one from Tiffany's "don't" list.

Fresh grease.

"This is really starting to get on my nerves."

Nora stole a french fry. "Only starting? Ellen, I think she crossed the line when she announced her office health plan."

"Or when she tried to make the department pay for a subscription to her favorite yoga magazine?" I shook my head. "Yeah, I know she's out of line. But try telling that to her face. She'll argue you cross-eyed until her faulty logic proves she's right."

"I'm surprised no one's filed a grievance on her."

Nora worked in the Registrar's Office, so she always had a finger on the pulse of the entire college. She was great to have lunch with, and even better for sharing a bitch session. We both shopped in the double-XL section and could have traded clothing; but while I stuck to cotton and corduroy, my brown hair tomboy-short, my Filipina friend always rocked impossible heels with dresses and skirts, her sleek black locks in a stylish chin-length bob. Like Tiffany, Nora had a lot of strong opinions. The difference was, hers I could handle.

"And tangle with the queen of self-righteousness? Everyone's too scared to try." I took a bite of my Dot burger and washed it down with a swig of pop.

Nora scowled. "And there's nothing you can do?"

"Not without proof," I sighed, then dipped a fry in ketchup. "I just wish I could get her to leave me alone."

"So get some."

I laughed. "Like what?"

She glanced at me for permission, and at my nod, took another fry. "That's easy. Trick her into getting caught."

E llen's food! HANDS OFF.
I stuck the neon orange post-it on the cardboard box of fried chicken. That would get her attention without being blatant. Like I'd told Nora, I wasn't ready to level accusations (no matter how true they may have been), but maybe she'd finally get the message. This time, I wasn't going to back down.

Her sigh broke the kitchen's cool silence. "Are you honestly eating that? You should have more respect for your body."

I kept my eyes on the box. Stuck it in the microwave. Punched in ninety seconds, hit Incinerate, and for a few brief moments watched the food cook.

Deep breaths, deep breaths—

Too late. I pushed past her and went straight for the ladies' room.

Someone once told me that when we feel threatened, it's easy to resort to shallow breathing. If we don't keep calm, pressure builds up in the blood and affects the awkward things, like tear ducts and the bladder. Great advice. But remembering that around Tiffany, who'd had me hyperventilating since I entered the kitchen? Not as easy as it sounds.

How she always found me when I made a point of taking my break at odd times from the rest of the department, I had no idea. Like she waited for me to step out of my cubicle every day, just so she could pounce. I crushed the wad of toilet paper in one hand. Ripped it in two. *Why can't she just leave me alone?*

The microwave beeped. I wiped, flushed, washed my hands, and went back to the now-vacant kitchen.

I bit back a cuss.

She'd done it again. My chicken had vanished, and that same awful green atrocity sat in its place.

I ripped it from the microwave, dumped it at once, then held the empty square glass plate in my hands, knuckles white. I hadn't looked at it much yesterday, just tossed it in the sink and left it, unwashed.

It wasn't your average dinnerware. For all that it was just plain glass with rounded edges, there was an understated elegance about it that was hard to explain.

So it was probably the sort of thing only snobs would buy.

So it was probably pretty pricey.

So it was probably Tiffany's.

Numbness crept up my spine as a small smile formed at one corner of my mouth.

Glass was such a fragile medium.

And she always *said* I was careless.

My grip loosened—

As I tilted the plate, hands shaking, tiny etchings flashed across its surface, catching the light.

What the— I fumbled, trying to keep hold, but it slipped from my hands, and my stomach lurched as it crashed to the floor.

And rattled as it settled on the linoleum, unbroken.

Damn. Luck? Plexiglass? But it looked so real—and felt cool, like porcelain or crystal. I decided I didn't want to know, set the plate in the sink, and made for the cafeteria.

I chose my words carefully that third day.

Please stop stealing my lunch, I wrote. *If this continues, I will file a grievance with the union.*

Surely that would work. I knew I wasn't good at telling her off to her face like she deserved, but maybe if I invoked the threat of our righteous staff powerhouse, she'd finally back the hell off.

"Junk, again?"

I darted my eyes to her. Wow, she actually had her hands on her hips.

Her crimson nails gleamed against her navy pencil skirt. I stared in her direction, but not into her eyes. I had to maintain control, had to stick it out while the minute and a half of incinerate ticked down on my deep-dish pizza. I would not let her pull this again, not while I stood there. Maybe I couldn't meet her gaze directly, and maybe the words lodged like gravel in my throat, but at least I could stick my generous butt between her and my lunch. She was *not* going to get her claws on it this time, dammit.

"You know, Ellen, you don't have to be so difficult all the time." She let out an annoyed huff. "You should realize that I'm just trying to help."

I made a noncommittal noise, something too high to be a grunt, but too low for a squeak. My breathing was not deep, and I could already feel the tightness in my bladder. But I was not going to leave until that meal was cooked.

Her eye roll was audible, though I didn't actually see it. "Whatever." She turned to leave. "At least wash your dishes this time."

Excuse me? I looked up, but she'd already flounced off before I could ask what she meant.

The microwave beeped. I looked down.

The green stuff was there again.

My hunger vanished. Dread crawled through me.

I hadn't left the room this time. No one had touched the microwave.

Hard as it was to believe, for once, Tiffany wasn't to blame.

I pulled out the mystery meal, pushed back the wave of nausea that threatened just from smelling the awful thing. Studied it.

Little green, ovoid berries linked by stringy, fungal growths that wrapped around everything with a pale green fuzz. All globbed together like the meatloaf from hell—and reeking like a swamp where creatures went to die.

Who in their right minds could find this edible? This wasn't even worthy of sticking in the compost bucket. For all I knew, it would eat the worms, not the other way around.

This wasn't just my overcooked pizza, deformed by Incinerate mode. What if—

Tiffany's comment came back to me.

I tilted the crapulence into the trash. Ran the glass plate under the kitchen tap. The flow of water sent another painful reminder to my bladder—but I had to know.

When the plate was dry, I held it to the light.

Just as it had the day before, etchings flashed across the surface.

Grak, Bil, are you trying to get me arrested? You know I can't be caught with this stuff.

Ears roaring, I set the plate beside the sink. Uhh.

Had my food literally gone somewhere else?

I looked at the drying rack beside the sink. Both plates from the last two days still sat there, where doubtless Tiffany had left them as a passive-aggressive reminder of the problem she thought was mine. Heart racing, I grabbed the first plate. Held it to the light.

Nothing.

As for the second—

Very funny, Bil, it read. *Send the rookie banned substances. Don't do it again, okay?*

My poor bladder. I just barely made it to the toilet.

"Wow, that's like the third Dot burger you've had this week."

"Eh, I'm hormonal. I need the iron."

Nora chuckled. "Cow take your lunch again?"

"Much as I'd love to blame the office bovine, no," I lied. "This time I just really wanted a burger."

And much as I considered Nora my friend, someone who helped keep me sane even when things were at their worst, this was way too out there to be sharing with anyone.

Somehow, the microwave was switching my food with someone else's. But where was it going?

I didn't even want to think of the "how."

What really got me were the plates. Who would waste perfectly good dinnerware by scratching messages on it? And that "food"—if you could call it that—

"Earth to Ellen."

"Hmm?"

"Are you going to eat that fry, or keep staring at it like it's a carrot stick?"

I blinked and popped the cold wedge of grease into my mouth. "Hey, I like carrots, I'll have you know."

"Well, you should have seen the look on your face. Are you sure the T Bag isn't giving you trouble?"

I forced a grin. "I wish."

And though I never thought I'd say so, I think I meant it.

Day 4. Friday payday, and Tiffany's day off. And for me, experiment time. I went cheap: bean and cheese burrito, three for five bucks at Save-Mart. Two for home. One for my food-stealing friend. And since I clearly couldn't trust the machine, a hefty meal replacement bar for myself.

I kept my note simple. Direct. *Why don't you like my lunches? And why do you keep taking them?*

With no looming threat from my darling coworker, I was finally able to watch the microwave in action. Everything seemed fine as the Incinerate setting ticked down the seconds. But at the :45, a haze formed around the burrito. The haze became a smoky cloud. By the :30, I couldn't see through the pane that was normally clear. And then, with fifteen seconds left, the cloud had vanished, and the Soylent Something had taken over.

No surprise there. But the note that came back with it?

Oh, I knew my penpal's response would be to yesterday's threat, not the question I'd just asked. Our exchange was weird no matter how you looked at it, and I was the one asking the questions, which would lead to the one-day delay. But this—

Impossible. Unions ceased to exist following the Hydro Wars of 2089.

Lovely, I thought. *And here all my union reps have been worrying about is how much is covered for chiropractic.* I made to stow the plate on the rack—

Waitaminute.

A chill sliced through me as I realized what I'd just read.

2089? And said with such irate certainty, referenced like a historical fact.

I couldn't call this a prank. Couldn't blame it on anyone in the office, or even at the school. Phokas College was hardly a research institution. And as of today, I'd seen the food switch places with my own eyes.

There was no denying what was happening. My lunch was going to the future.

N ever had I looked more forward to a Monday.

I'd burned the weekend rabbit-hole jumping, stationed in front of my laptop with a bowl of Cheez Poppers, clicking on every time-travel link I could find, only to resurface more confused than ever.

All I could tell was that it was an icky-sticky hot mess that, depending on one's opinion, was either a splintered mass of possibility or an interconnected loop. But I worked in instructors' services and basic tech support, not the physics department. Every concept hurt my brain.

Sunday night I met Nora at Fishy Rice for sushi. I over-ordered on purpose and planned the leftovers for dinner the following evening— except for a small portion of the chicken teriyaki. That bit, I saved for my futuristic friend.

By Monday lunchtime, I'd decided to be honest. *I don't know why this is happening,* I wrote. *I just want to reheat my lunch in peace.*

I signed the note with my full name and the year.

I closed my eyes before Adventure Number 5. Took a deep breath. Calmly opened the microwave door—

"Why don't you like yourself, Ellen?"

Ignoring the woman, I went through the usual steps. When the clock started ticking down, I lifted my gaze. "Excuse me?"

"Everyone is concerned about you," she went on, her brows lifted in apparent sympathy. "You continue to eat all this unhealthy food, like you don't care."

Oh, give me a break. We both know the only "concerned" one is you. "Uh-huh," I managed. It was all I could do to focus on my breath.

Tiffany locked stares with me, but when I didn't say anything more, she threw up one hand. "Just tell me when you're done," she said, holding up a carton. "You're not the only one who uses the microwave, you know."

I recognized the box of LeanGreen Ez-Cook. The one the commercials called *The super healthy meal that's ready in a flash!* I wanted to make my own comment about double standards, since even that "nutritious" option was loaded with chemicals to keep it fresh, but she was gone before I could muster the courage.

My silent conjugation of insults halted with the microwave's beep.

I retrieved the plate, disposed of its nasty contents, rinsed it off, and checked the message.

And forgot to breathe.

Every Terran schoolchild knows that additives, preservatives, and artificial flavor enhancers have been banned from our food supply for decades. Dealing in illegal toxins is a crime subject to punishment without mercy.

We have identified your frequency. Whoever this is, cease your activities at once. If not, your next "lunch" will be a bomb.

I put the plate on the dish rack, next to the drying cutlery. Crap, crap, crap. What could I do this time? Tiffany would be back any moment, demanding to use the machine, and there was nothing I could do to stop her.

And in the rush to make my food, I'd forgotten my usual bathroom detour.

Dammit. I was going to hold it this time. For all I knew, the teriyaki would be enough to provoke the other side, and Tiffany's own "health" food would make it worse. *Focus on your breathing, Ellen,* I told myself, over and over. *And think.*

What would stop a microwave? It ran on electricity. I yanked its long black three-prong from the wall. That was a start—

"What are you doing?" Like bloodthirsty mosquito, Tiffany was at my side.

I had to think fast. "Uhm. The microwave's been acting funny. I was just—"

She took the plug from me and stuck it back in place. "Probably allergic to the trash you call food."

Something like that. But she had no idea.

I stood there as she put her carton in the Cook-Box of Doom, dread pooling in the place I'd normally put food. She punched in the time; the near-hysterical part of me almost giggled that she chose ninety seconds, too. Her fingers hesitated over the panel—

"Don't!"

I started forward too late. She'd already pressed Incinerate.

"Jeez, Ellen, what's your problem?"

I raised a finger, trying to interject. "I don't think—"

"No, you never think, do you?" she sneered, hands on her hips like an overbearing mother. "You're just a lazy slob, taking advantage of the union—are you even listening to me?"

I ignored her, my eyes on the clock.

Fifty-seven seconds. Then we were doomed.

I swallowed. "Wh—where did you get the microwave?"

"A Gregslist ad," she said, clearly confused. "Someone was giving it away, practically brand new! What does it matter?"

Forty-nine. The pain down there was a throbbing ache. I clenched tighter. "And you didn't keep it for yourself?"

"Well, it was acting up. But you seem to have got it working—"

"Really?" Glowering, I threw out a hand at the machine that had just hit forty-five seconds to go. "Does that *look* like it's working right?"

Tiffany's eyes widened at the shimmering box.

Thirty-eight. Smoke was already fogging the glass. The microwave rumbled. Started to thrash. Thirty-four. Watching in horror, I tried to think of what to do. Tiffany edged away.

"If you knew it was broken, then why did you keep using it? This is your fault, Ellen. You should really—"

My eyes had settled on the drying forks.

"Out of my way!" I lunged for a handful of cutlery. Pushed her aside. Jabbed the release button.

The microwave stopped at twenty-six.

Smoke poured out. Maybe that would have been enough. But this couldn't continue—it had to be stopped for good.

Jamming the forks inside, I closed the door and hit "resume."

A web of blue lightning enveloped the awful machine, pulsing like a beating heart. The microwave screamed. It gave one final thrash, hurling itself straight off the side of the kitchen counter and onto the linoleum, where it crashed into a smoking heap.

Which was just enough to activate the sprinkler system.

Dammit. I clenched tighter. I wouldn't run away this time.

"Omigod!" As the fire alarm sounded, Tiffany's face contorted with rage. Her mascara was running, and her white blouse looked like a prime candidate for a wet t-shirt contest. "For the love of—augh, Ellen, you should be reported for this reckless behavior!"

"*My* behavior," I repeated. Already we were no longer alone; the other five employees in our department had appeared, all watching the scene. Even Milo. "No, Tiffany, *you* should back off. You keep trying to change us all, and for what? Just to feel better about yourself?" I laughed, short and harsh. "No. This ends now. What I eat—what all of us eat—is none of your damn business. Stop acting like it is."

Tiffany looked around. Maybe she was trying to find support. Around us, the others were nodding. A few murmurs of "yeah" followed, too.

"But—you all don't *get* it! You all deserve to be healthier! Right, Milo?"

Milo shifted like he didn't want to speak, but then his jaw set. "For the sake of departmental harmony, Ellen's suggestion is probably best."

With a curse, Tiffany threw up her hands. "Fine," she spat. "See if I ever do anything nice for the department again." She stomped out of the kitchen, tracking a wet trail down the hall.

I bit my lip. "Better watch what you say," I called after her. "You don't want anyone to file a grievance."

———

"So I hear you took Miss McPissy down a peg."

Nora and I were eating outside again, enjoying the June sunshine. The day was warm and bright, and for once, I had nothing to bitch about. I shrugged. "You know, I'm sure she meant well. Road to hell, good intentions, and all that."

Not like any of the future freakiness had been her fault. Just the part where she'd made a savory battleground of my eating habits.

Nora raised both eyebrows. "You're not going to report her, after all that?"

I chuckled and waved it off. "Nah. Something tells me she won't be a problem anymore."

Nora nodded, and from her expression, she seemed to get that the subject was closed, so she moved to the next bit of gossip. "Hey, did you hear? The union's looking at pushing for nutritionist coverage in our next contract."

I rolled my eyes. *Of course they are.* "I'm just grateful we have a union," I said, with a grin. And I took a big bite of my new favorite lunchtime meal.

A sandwich.

NULL AND VOID

ALEX GIDEON

Null's blade slid between the guard's fifth and sixth vertebrae. Her blade struck at the correct angle giving her a clean slice. The man's head separated from his shoulders with such ease, the rest of his body remained standing. Blood spurted from the stump of his neck. She stepped back, and the blood splashed across the lobby floor.

She heard the click of a safety, and she spun toward the second guard hidden behind the reception desk. The man leveled his gun at her head and squeezed the trigger. The power of the gun's leystone sizzled across her skin as the tiny magick missile rocketed toward her face. She stood straight, meeting the man's gaze.

The magick missile hit her between the eyes. The spell fizzled at the moment of impact, leaving her skin numb but otherwise unharmed. Behind her the first man's corpse finally fell with a thump to the floor. She took a step toward the guard behind the desk, drawing her second blade from its place at the small of her back. The second man's eyes flew wide, and he squeezed the trigger again, firing missile after missile at her.

Nearly every shot hit its intended target. Anyone else would have been long dead. Instead, Null picked up speed with each shot. She vaulted over the counter and landed behind the man. She brought her blades together in a scissor motion, and the man's head went flying out into the lobby.

She did not have time to dodge the gout of blood, and it drenched her face. She wiped at her face and stared at the blood on her glove. The second guard's body was slumped over the reception desk, and she wiped her glove clean on it. The radio in her ear crackled.

"All units in position. Have the security personnel been dealt with?" a gruff voice barked at her. She reached up and pressed the com button on her earpiece.

"Dead," she said. The word came as barely more than a whisper, but it was hard as stone.

"Good. Lock down the main entrance, get to the third floor, and secure the mainframe before someone pulls the alarm." Her radio went silent.

"Yes, Father," she said, though she didn't bother to press the com button again. She vaulted over the security desk, careful to avoid the rapidly pooling blood. The front entrance of the Kiseki Magickal Research Facility was solid glass. It stretched up almost thirty feet above her, giving one full view of the surrounding mountains of Hokkaido.

The complex was hidden away in the forests of Shiretoko. Tucked away under wards and magicks that would have made even Tesla proud. That the Takeda Group sullied Japan's last pristine wilderness with their secrets came as no surprise. No more than a whispered rumor, the Kiseki Magickal Research Facility was the most infamous in the world. The atrocities committed within its labs grew more horrendous with each telling. Those stories were not far off the mark.

The Takeda Group denied all rumors, but their continued standing as Japan's most successful Medical Corporation failed to quiet them. The Guild took interest years ago and followed their progress closely. But not even *they* could confirm its existence. Then, the Daito Group approached the Guild claiming they found it nestled among the mountains of Hokkaido. They jumped on the request.

The Guild bought the information for a small nation's treasury.

They made it clear that should the intelligence prove false, the entire board of the Daito Group would die. It was no idle threat. Luckily, they indeed found Kiseki. Unluckily, Null still killed them all. With the research and data they would secure from Kiseki, the Guild stood poised to become the most powerful force on the planet. The Daito Group's existence was now too volatile.

Null pulled a black box from a pouch on her thigh. It was small enough to sit neatly in the center of her palm. A magickal seal, etched in silver, marked each side. On the top was a gleaming purple stone. A leystone, and a powerful one at that. Its energy made Null's skin crawl. She set the box in front of the double doors and pressed the leystone down into the box. The seals on the box began to glow one by one. Then the box began to expand. Unfolding again, and again. It sprawled across the glass like a veil until the windows were solid black.

Null reached up and pressed the com button. "Barrier kindled. Front entrance secured," she said, calmly.

"Good," her father crooned back. "Now scour the Shire."

"Understood." She slid her blade back into its sheath. She turned and made her way to the emergency stairs. The elevators were quicker, but they wouldn't operate with her inside. No magick did in her presence. Since the world was powered by it, it was a useful trait at times, and an inconvenience at others.

The emergency stair was simple poured concrete with a steel railing. She took the stairs two at a time, her feet silent even in haste. The door to the third floor was solid steel and could only be opened by a charged ley card. Null placed her hand on the card slide, and the little red light on it blinked out. She heard the snick of the lock disengaging and opened the door.

She stepped through the doorway and was met with a long floor. The walls and doors around the edge were solid glass, and she could see offices through them. Personnel sat behind desks and conspired together in meeting rooms. Executives in their suits and researchers in their white coats. None noticed her enter. If their magickal ability was high enough, they most likely couldn't even see her.

The tile was gray here, and it stretched across the hall to the switchback stairs that led up to the upper floors. She walked to the center of the hall and looked up. She could see the high ceiling, eight floors above her. Each floor was lined with a balustrade, and glass walkways spanned the gaps at each, making the open center look like a spider's web. The main control room was located on the top floor. The mainframe for the complex was there, so she could secure the research data, as well as disable Kiseki's wards.

"Who are you?" A woman in a white coat stalked across the floor toward her. Her heels click-clacked against the tile, and her long, sleek black hair fanned out behind her. A sneer marred her face, and the lines it made spoke volumes about how often the woman wore it. Null remained silent, though her hands strayed to the hilts of her blades. The white-coated woman stopped in front of Null and planted her hands on her hips.

"Show me your credentials, or I'm calling security." The woman huffed. Null said nothing. Instead, she studied the personnel who stopped to watch. Too many. Father would not be happy.

"Come with me." The woman reached out to take hold of Null's arm. Lightning fast, Null pulled her blade and brought it up and through the woman's wrist. She staggered back with a scream, cradling the stump of her arm to her chest, drenching her coat red.

"Don't touch me," Null said, calmly. Then she put the point of her Wakizashi through the woman's throat. Wide eyed, the woman scrabbled at her neck. Null planted a foot on the woman's chest and pushed. The blade slid from her throat, and the woman collapsed onto the floor. She sputtered for a moment, then fell silent.

No one moved, all too shocked to do more than just stare in horror. Null stood straight, and ever so slowly slid her second Wakizashi from its sheath. The sound of the metal echoed through the complex. They moved then, and almost as one, they began to scream. Null watched them flee, knowing it was pointless. Every exit was sealed.

They were all going to die.

Yuki was a connoisseur of screams. All the test subjects of Kiseki were. After years of tortuous research, they were far too familiar. She wailed through those tests so many times herself that she could tell the experiment simply from their subject's cries. Magickal Energy Level checks brought short, breathless barks. Spell Endurance tests brought ululating wails. Magickal Energy Amplification was the worst. Desperate shrieks, like a thousand demons howling in the deepest, blackest pits of Hell. She hated the eerie silence that followed more than anything. Because Yuki was the only one who's ever survived the Amplification process.

The screams that echoed through the ventilation were new to her. There was pain and terror in them, but those they came from unused to it. These didn't come from test subjects. The woman holding her food tray stared up at the vent in the top of her room, face frozen in horror.

"What is that?" Yuki said, as quietly as she could. The woman with the tray jumped at her voice regardless. Yuki's heart sank when her food smeared across the white tile. Meal times were the only thing she looked forward to during the day. The woman dropped to her knees, hastily scooping the noodles and rice back onto the tray. Yuki slipped off her bed and joined her. She gathered a handful of rice and dumped it on the tray, her hand brushing against the woman's. The woman recoiled as if she'd been struck by lightning. She scrambled away, her brown eyes wide and dark hair flying.

"I'm just trying to help," Yuki said, hurt. More screams filtered down, and the woman's eyes snapped up. She looked back at Yuki and ran. She fumbled with her key card to get through the door and bolted through it. The door slammed shut again, and Yuki heard the magickal locks engage. She sat for a moment, hoping the woman would come back. She didn't, of course. They never did.

Yuki survived the Magickal Amplification process, but that didn't make it a success. Her power tripled, but she couldn't control it. Worse yet, her magick spiked spontaneously and unpredictably. The first time it happened, she burned six researchers alive. The second time, her power sliced her caretaker in half. Yoko-san was the closest thing to a mother Yuki had. Yuki still had nightmares of that night. She could still feel the blood on her face.

Now, no one dared to be around for more than a few moments. The nurses dashed in to leave food the way the woman before had. If it weren't for the screams, she never would have stopped. The researchers perform their experiments from afar, using machinery and robots to torture her. Yuki was sure they still hated her for the deaths of their colleagues. Only the other subjects treated her kindly, but they were just hoping to die.

Hot tears streamed down Yuki's face. She hated this place. She hated the men in their lab coats. She hated the nurses and their cowardice. She wished the Amplification killed her like the rest. A high-pitched wail speared through the vent. She knew the sound of a death rattle all too well. She didn't know what was going on, but the thought of the facility personnel meeting their end brought a smile.

She could only hope.

With a cry, a man came charging from one of the offices, a lamp held aloft in his hands. Null backed toward the balustrade as he came, white coat and blond hair flying. He swung, and she ducked under the blow. Her blade bit into his leg, severing it just below the knee. He pitched forward and struck the railing. Moment carried him up and over, and he toppled into empty space. For a moment he screamed; then with a thump of impact, he fell silent. Null peered over the balustrade down four stories to where the man lay on the tile. His neck was bent at an unnatural angle, broken. Blood seeped from stump of his leg, surrounding him in a field of crimson.

Nearly two dozen other dead laid around him, most missing limbs as well. When she first started her assault, many tried to stop her. She cut each and every one of them down. As she made her ascent to the top floor, she had not gone out of her way to kill, though. She didn't need to. The extermination units would handle that when she disabled the facility's security measures and the scouring began in earnest. Still, she showed no mercy to those who attacked her.

There was a surprising lack of security personnel. It seemed the Takeda group lent little thought to protecting Kiseki. Most likely they expected the wards would be sufficient, as indeed they had until today.

She rounded the switchback stair that led up to the fifth floor. Here the offices gave way to research labs, though they retained the glass facades. The gray tile also became white again here, and the floor had a decidedly sterile, medical feel to it. The air changed, and there was a chemical tang to the air. She saw the researchers cowering in their labs, but she paid them no mind. When she had passed, and they thought they were safe, they fled their hiding places and bolted for the doors. They would find them barred against them, and all hope dead.

She gained the top floor without spilling any more blood. The control room was on the other side of the floor, and here Null found the reason for the lack of security. They guessed her destination and marshaled here. Two dozen of them stood between her and the mainframe. Each held a strange black handle, and blocks of energy protruded from them. Ward shields, more effective than steel. They formed a phalanx from glass to glass, an impregnable rainbow wall.

"Stop where you are," one of the guards yelled to her in the tongue of Japan. A woman, which came as a surprise. They were armored head to toe in black leather, and Null had assumed they were all men.

"You cannot stop me," Null replied in the same tongue. "If you wish to live, remove yourselves from my path."

"Drop your blades and we won't kill you. The higher ups want you alive for study. You can't get through our shields, and you can't fight us all," the woman said, and the others laughed in agreement.

"I can, and I will," Null said, and she launched toward the phalanx. They squared their shoulders and prepared for her to break upon their wards like water on rock, confident they could hold her at bay. They were wrong.

Like a spirit, she passed through the energy of their shields unscathed.

She fell on them with a frenzy. Their leather armor, enchanted against hostile spells, was no protection from her blades. She took two heads from their owners' shoulders with her first pass, drenching the rest in gore. She let her momentum carry her through the rest, sending them sprawling. She rolled, gaining her feet again and launching back into the fray.

Those who she crashed against still fought to right themselves. Those on the edges tossed their useless shields aside and began their assault in earnest. These men and women carried rifles instead of the handguns the lobby guards had. They fired on her, confident again that their weapons would shred her before she could attack again. Once more, they were wrong.

Their missiles could not harm her, but they fired much faster than the hand guns. The air they displaced buffeted her, and she staggered slightly. Her blade, aimed for a guard's neck, hit his chest instead. It bit deep, flaying both his armor and skin. He cried out in pain and fell back, clutching at his chest. She followed him down and drove the point of her blade through the bottom of his jaw and into his brain.

Booted feet stomped across the tile behind her. Null wrenched the blade from the man and pitched forward. Placing all the weight on her hands, she raised her legs into the air and wrapped them around the guard's head. With a twist and a crack, she broke the man's neck.

Many of the others continued to fire on her to no avail. These she cut down with ease. Others threw their rifles aside and tried to bring her down by hand. They were untrained in hand-to-hand combat, and these, too, she made short work of.

One woman managed to get Null in her grip, her hands around Null's throat. Null took those hands from the woman before putting a blade through her heart.

One by one, the guards fell until only one was left standing. The woman who commanded Null to lay down arms. She still held the handle of her ward shield in her hand. At some point, the woman had removed her helmet, and her sleek black hair played about shoulders and down her back.

From a pouch at her side, she pulled out a baton. With a flick of her wrist, the baton extended out and she took her stance. Null faced her, dropping into her own stance. Unlike the others, this woman had some training. Null could not afford to underestimate this one.

"You have killed my men. Now I will enjoy killing you," the woman said calmly. Almost formal.

"You will try," Null said, both her expression and her words blank. The woman let out a cry and pounded across the floor toward Null. The woman's hand spoke of a strike to Null's head, but her feet said differently. The blow came, but it was changed at the last moment, going low toward the abdomen. Null stepped around her, batting aside her baton with one blade, the other coming like a scorpion's tail at the woman's temple.

The woman threw up her arm, blocking Null's blade with the handle of her ward shield. While its energy was of no use, the handle formed a shallow metal dome over the back of her arm, and this she used like a buckler.

The woman's second strike came, swift as lighting. Null parried, attacking again, only to be thwarted by the woman's buckler. For several long moments they struggled, and it seemed that they were evenly matched. It was rare for Null to meet one who could match her skill.

But the woman left Null an opening. The woman spun around Null, hair flying. Null dropped her blade and reached up. She grabbed the woman's hair in her fist and jerked her backward. She gasped at the sudden motion, and Null drove her blade into the woman's kidney.

The woman's eyes widened at the pain, and her mouth opened, but no sound came. Null stepped up against the woman and brought her lips to the woman's ear.

"You were a worthy foe," Null said in the woman's tongue. The woman's lips moved, though Null did not know what words she tried to speak. Then the light fled her eyes, and the woman died. Null pulled her blade from her corpse and let her fall.

She turned and made her way toward the control room, carefully stepping over the bodies that littered the floor. The control room's door was made of solid steel, a far cry from the glass fortress the rest of the complex seemed. Heavy wards and sealing spells were laid upon the door. The unnatural feel of the magick had a sharp crack to it, which told Null that the spell work was recent. Most likely placed when she began her assault.

Null placed a hand on the door, and in the moment before the magick died, she felt that the spells had been cast from the other side. Someone sealed the door from the inside. No longer powered, the spelled lock clicked open. Null turned the handle, pushed the door open, and stepped back.

A chair came down in the space just inside, swung by unseen arms. The assailant stumbled when their weapon met only air, and they fell. It was a girl, a rather odd one. She was dressed in a t-shirt and jeans, which was much more casual than the other personnel Null had seen thus far. Her black hair was styled in a short bob cut and shot through with streaks of acid green.

Null strode into the room, and the girl looked up. Null lashed out with a kick, catching the girl full in the face. Her head snapped back, her horn-rimmed glasses snapping in half, and she collapsed back onto the floor. Null stalked after her, sheathing one of her blades as she went. She bent over the girl and wrapped her fingers into her multicolored hair. The girl screamed when Null jerked her up. Blood streamed down her face from a broken nose, and she scrabbled at Null's hand in her hair.

Black mainframes lined the walls, with small interfaces set sporadically throughout. The room was dark, lit only by the bluish screens on the computers around them. In the center of one wall was a bank of screens, and beneath it was the main interface board. Null dragged the girl over to the chair in front of the screens and forced her into it.

"You are going to do exactly as I say." Null said, not loosening her grip on the girl's hair. She brought her face close and noticed a name tag pinned to the girl's chest. "Do you understand, Miseki?"

"Screw you," the girl said, voice cracking. "Why should I?"

Null drove her blade deep into the meat of the Miseki's thigh. She screamed, the sound echoing harshly off the metal of the mainframes. Wanting to be sure the girl didn't bleed out before she could be of use, Null left the blade in her. "I will continue to cause you pain as such until you cooperate," Null said, her tone flat. "Will you do so?"

"Yes. Yes," Miseki said, breathless.

"Good." Null let go of the girl's hair and turned her toward the board. She reached into one of the pouches strapped to her thigh and pulled out another black cube, which she handed to the girl. "You will transfer all data to this hard drive."

Miseki nodded and took the hard drive. She popped open a panel on the box and pulled a cord from within. She attached this cord to a slot on the board, and the screens kicked on. For several minutes, Miseki clacked away at the keyboard, her shoulders shaking as she sobbed. Null kept a close eye on the screens to be sure the girl did not attempt to sabotage the data. At last, a file transfer progress window popped up on one of the screens.

"The data is transferring, but it's going to take a while," Miseki said. Her voice was shallow, and her skin was pale from loss of blood and shock.

"That is no matter. While the program runs, you are to disable all security systems in the complex," Null said.

"I've only got access to a couple of the systems. I'd need the rest of the codes to do that," Miseki said. Null threw a folded piece of paper onto the desk in front of the girl.

"That should be all the codes that you need. Now disable them." Miseki unfolded the paper and got to work. Null watched her log in to each system directly. Cameras, locks, wards—she shut them all down. The process took the better part of a half hour, and by the time she was shutting down the last of the systems, almost all the data had transferred.

"That's everything," the girl said at last. She had lost quite a lot of blood by now, even with Null's blade still in the wound. Her skin was starting to go blue, and her eyes were beginning to glaze. The radio in Null's ear crackled.

"Good job, Null. The systems are all down and the Extermination Units are moving in to scour the facility," her father's voice crooned into her ear. "I have a new task for you. I've been tracking the data as it comes through. It seems there are sub-levels that we were unaware of. The lowest level is comprised of holding cells of some sort. You are to get down there and kill anyone and everything you find."

"Yes, Father," Null said, pressing the com button on her earpiece. Miseki had collapsed onto the interface board, and Null wrapped her fingers into the girl's hair once more. She dragged the girl upright and reached down to pull the wakizashi from her leg. Blood burbled from the wound without the blade to stop it, and Miseki whimpered. Null brought her lips close to the girl's ear and whispered, "Thank you for your assistance."

Then she drove her blade through the spot just beneath the base of the girl's skull. A quick death. If they did not force her hand, she would give all her victims the same. But it didn't matter. She sheathed her blade and left the girl and the control room behind.

She had orders to fulfill.

Yuki paced the walls of her cell like a tiger seeking escape. More and more screams filtered down to her through the vents, and she had her hands clamped over her ears to try and keep them out. It didn't help. Everyone who worked in Kiseki had exceptional magickal capabilities, and their power leaked out with their deaths. All the fear, pain, and anguish were magickally saturated into their cries and pierced Yuki's being like spear.

She had been trying to ward herself against the magicks, but her own power was unreliable. She tried once again, making the signs and whispering the words, digging deep to make the power come. This time it did, and the ward that settled over her was nothing short of salvation. She still heard them, but the magick twined about them no longer affected her.

She breathed a sigh of relief and collapsed onto the bed. What in the world was going on above to cause such desperation? She shivered in her white slip, her arms wrapped around herself for both warmth and protection. She rocked slightly, wracking her brain for what she should do. An hour had passed since she first heard the screams above and her nurse had bolted. The tray of food sat on the little table next to her bed. She had scraped everything that was spilled back onto the tray. Food was too precious to waste, especially now that she had no idea when another meal may be coming.

Her captors were dead and dying. That she was sure of. But why? How? Was another organization responsible? Or maybe another experiment? Perhaps the Amplification Process worked on another and they were now wreaking havoc on the researchers. It was a pleasant, hopeful thought, but she doubted it. If another like her was responsible for what was happening, Yuki was certain that she would be able to feel their magicks. Maybe there was something else the scientists created that was responsible? Some monster sprung to life from their depravity.

Whatever the cause, Yuki couldn't be certain that anyone would come for her again. If they didn't, then she would starve to death in this bright white hell. She glanced at the door. Solid steel and so heavily spelled and warded that she had no hope of breaking through. Not when she barely had any control over her power. And even if who or whatever were responsible for the carnage above did come for her, they may just kill her and be done with it.

She shook her head. She could sit and speculate until she was dead, and it wouldn't make any difference. She needed to know what was going on above. But how? She couldn't get out of her cell.

Or could she?

She went still at the thought of the possibility. She couldn't physically leave her cell, but perhaps she could project her consciousness out. She had never attempted it before, but then she had never been able to try. The researchers punished her harshly for any unauthorized usage of magick. But there had been no response to the ward she cast moments ago. Why not try?

She slipped from her bed and settled herself in the middle of the floor. She crossed her legs in the position the scientists taught her. Her hands rested in her lap, clasped together except for her little fingers, which jutted outward together in the hand sign for the Gate of the Crown, the portal for the spirit. Her heart was beating quickly, and she took a deep breath to calm herself. While she knew the theories behind this particular brand of magick, she had never attempted it before. And her failings were much more explosive than the regular person's. But she needed to know, so she had to try.

She closed her eyes, listening to her heart pounding in her ears. She breathed, in through her nose then out through her mouth. She kept the rhythm. In. Out. In. Out. Her muscles relaxed, her heart slowed, and she began to slip. Down. Down. Down into herself. She reached for the energy she knew to be there, searching for the Gate of the Crown. She found it, a great swirling mass of magick. She touched the gate, and the energy surged at her touch, desperate to be released. So she let it free.

The energy erupted from the gate like a bolt of lightning. It swept her along with it, and suddenly she found herself standing in her cell once more. For a second, she thought it hadn't worked. She turned and stopped with a jump. She was sitting on the floor still, hands clasped, eyes closed. She took a step closer and reached out toward the vision of herself on the floor. Her hand passed through the other her with no resistance. She held her hand in front of her, turning it this way and that. She seemed so solid.

She lifted her eyes to the dark ceiling above her, and her breath caught. She could see. Everything was laid bare to her. The physicality of the painted concrete was stripped away. She saw the energy that made it whole. The push and pull of the atoms upon each other. She could see the circuitry that powered the building, and she followed it to its source in the leyline that ran beneath the complex. She felt tears threatening at her eyes as she perceived the leyline in all its glory. A great vein of the world that pulsed and flowed with creation. The Earth was a living, breathing thing, and it was absolutely enthralling.

With a great effort, she wrenched her attention away from the beauty of existence. She had a reason for this ritual, and it would do her no good if she was discovered and killed while she marveled at the world. She focused on closing her sight, and the room solidified around her once more. She wondered a moment how she was going to get out of the room in this form, and the answer twinkled in her mind as if she had always known. With a thought, she lifted from the floor toward the ceiling. Then she was through and lost in darkness. She was in solid stone. She kicked herself for not noting the layout of the complex while she looked at creation. She could open her sight again, but she wasn't sure she wouldn't lose herself completely if she did.

She closed her eyes. A long time ago, before they performed the Magickal Amplification on her, her handlers would take her on walks through Kiseki. There was a particular spot she was fond of during those excursions. On the top floor of the main building, there was a place where she could stand at the railing and look straight down on every floor. She would stand there as long as they would allow and watch the people scurry about on the levels and walkways below. A giant ant hill with a task for every worker. In that moment, she was their queen. It was the closest thing to happiness that she could remember.

She opened her eyes, and memory became reality. The railing she remembered was in front of her. The bronze still held the blemishes from where her tiny hands gripped it hard in excitement. She strode forward, placing her hands in the exact same spots. Her hands engulfed the railing, which was so much smaller than she remembered. For a moment it felt like all those years since the last time she stood here fell away. With a smile, she leaned over the rail to peer at the floors below, expecting the busy ant hill.

What she got was horror.

The walkways and levels were stained so red, it was as if Kiseki itself were bleeding. There were corpses as far as she could see.

Broken, smashed, severed, and defiled. Hundreds of unseeing eyes stared up at her from every floor and walkway. At the very bottom, the bodies were piled so high that she had no way to count them.

A sob rattled out of her throat, and she felt a tear trickle down her cheek. A hundred million times she had dreamed of this very scene. Imagined them all dead, and her free. She realized now that dream was, in fact, a nightmare. The dead below were, by no means, innocents. Each and every one of them had caused more than their fair share of pain and death. But even they didn't deserve this.

There was a ring of people surrounding the pile of bodies. Each was dressed head to toe in black. Most carried rifles or handguns, though a few held blades. As she watched, another of the black-clad men dragged a body over to the pile. It was the woman who had brought Yuki her food not even an hour before. The man drug her by the hair because she had no limbs. He tossed her onto the pile, and those standing around the circle laughed.

Shaking now, she backed away from the railing. Those were no saviors. It was murderers who had seized Kiseki. If they found her physical body below, they would kill her. She knew that with a grim certainty. She was going to die. Whether she starved to death, or was put on the pile with the rest, she was going to die.

Magick, sudden and sharp, rippled across creation. Her sight blasted open when it did, showing her once more the threads of the world. This burst was coming from the same sub-level that her body was on. She recognized this power. It belonged to one of the other research subjects. The energy rasped across Yuki's being. Pain, fear, dread. This was a death rattle. Someone was on the bottom sub-level. And that same someone was killing the other subjects.

Panic struck Yuki like lightning, and she threw her will back down to Kiseki's sub-levels. In the blink of an eye, she stood in the long corridor that ended at her own cell. Another death rattle shook the world, and she raced along the hall toward it.

She came around a bend and stopped dead. In front of her, it was as if existence ended. The energies that crossed and colored the world suddenly died. A black void yawned across the corridor, devouring all energy that it came in contact with. Before she knew it, she felt herself being drawn toward the void. It was as if it were a black hole, and her own energy was being caught in the event horizon.

Suddenly she was afraid in a way she had never been before. With a scream, she ran from the void, fighting its pull for dear life. At last she broke away and sped back toward her cell. The steel door of her cage raced up to meet her. For a split second, metal filled the entirety of her vision. Then she was through the door as if it had never been there. Her body still sat in the center of the stark white, and she raced toward it.

Yuki's consciousness slammed back into her body with all the force of a battering ram. The reconnection drove her backward where she sprawled on the floor. Her breath came in short shallow gasps. With effort, she rolled over and got her feet under her. Supporting herself on the table, she stood and turned toward her cell door. Something was coming for her. Something black and cold.

The lock clicked, and slowly the door swung open.

The boy gasped when Null slid her blade into his heart. He did not fight, and beyond his first exclamation, he remained surprisingly silent. This was one who knew pain much greater than this. He held her eyes with his own until Null saw the life flee. She settled him onto the little bed and drew her blade from his body. He seemed peaceful, and for just a moment, Null wondered what had caused the boy to greet death as a friend at such a young age. He could not have seen nine years after all.

She left the boy's concrete and iron cell and made her way to the next cell. The first few sub-levels she encountered had been more labs, these more grandiose than those she saw in Kiseki's main building. This level seemed to be nothing more than a cell block. Most stood empty, yet she had already taken close to two dozen lives, and there were still more to end.

She continued on, offering each cell's occupants their choice of death. Each of them had the same haunted look about them. They were thin, skeletal. More wisp than human. Once she had seen photos of the victims of the Holocaust. The prisoners of Kiseki reminded her strongly of those photos. Not one of them fought her. Each accepted their death in the same way the boy had.

One by one, she made her way through the sub-level until she came to a turn in the corridor. She rounded the corner, and magick, sudden and powerful, welled up to meet her. The power stretched across the hall before her, and she came to a stop. For several long moments, she stood there, and she had the distinct feeling that this new power was studying her.

Then it was gone. Or rather, it fled from her. Rushing back down the corridor. She stole into motion, following it back to its source. Eventually she ran out of hall and ended up at the largest cell door she had seen yet.

It was far too ostentatious for what it was. Where the other doors were of black iron, this one was all gleaming silver and bronze. Runes and magickal symbols crawled across it, forming seals and spells. It oozed magick like a miasma, and Null knew that if all of the greatest spellcasters that her father employed at The Guild worked together to counter the door's power, they would fail.

Null placed her hand on the metal, feeling the raised bronze runes under her palm. The power surged and broke against her like the sea upon a cliff, leaving her undamaged. One by one the spells snapped, until none remained. She turned the handle and pushed the door open.

There was none of the gray stone and cold iron bedding in this cell. Instead it was a pure, medical white. All the white blended in such a way that it was hard to see the transition from floor to wall. Null took a step inside, and it felt to her as if she had stepped into a vast, snow-covered landscape.

In the center of the snow stood a girl. Tall and slender, with skin so pale that she seemed more like a porcelain doll. Her feet were bare, and she clenched her thin white slip in her hands. It was her hair that kept her divorced from the rest of the room, though. It fell to her waist, and was a bright, soft pink. Her eyes were the same shade, and while it would be most unnatural for a normal person, it was somehow right on this girl. She seemed to Null like one of the Sakura trees of Japan, bloomed in spring while winter was all about her.

Null halted just inside the door, and their eyes met. The girl was shaking, and her fingers worked her slip in obvious fear. Several times the girl opened her mouth as if to speak, yet no words came out.

"Are you going to kill me?" the girl said at last, her voice soft as spring wind. Slowly, Null nodded.

"I am."

Yuki couldn't stop shaking. There was no emotion in the girl's voice when she sentenced Yuki to death. Yuki stared into the girl's eyes, and she saw nothing. No feelings of any kind. This girl was the void that her soul encountered in the corridor. She could still feel it. The vast emptiness was inside of the girl, and Yuki was afraid.

Her executioner stood stock still, her head tilted to the side as she examined her target. It seemed to Yuki that this girl was her polar opposite. Her skin was dark, and her shoulder length hair was black and curly. She was dressed head to toe in black, armored, blood-stained leather. Fresh blood dripped from the blades she held in each hand, and when she walked, her heavy boots left crimson footprints behind.

"You may choose how you die," the girl said, her voice as hollow and dead as her eyes. Yuki looked down at her hands and realized just how badly she was shaking. She let go of her slip and rubbed her hands together.

She didn't want to die.

So many times when the scientists were poking and prodding, she had. But faced with it now, she realized just how much she wished to live. The fact that only she survived the Amplification showed just how strong that wish was. She took a breath, relaxing her muscles, and her shaking stopped. She wanted to live.

She looked up at the dark girl, still waiting for a reply, and she felt something tighten inside her. She raised a hand in front of her, concentrating hard, and a swirling ball of flame appeared in her palm.

"I'm not going to let you kill me," she said, aiming the fireball at the girl. Her eyes flicked to Yuki's palm then back.

"You cannot harm me." She said it the same way a person says the moon comes out at night, and Yuki laughed.

"Watch me," she said, pouring her magick into the fireball. There was enough power in it now to consume a whale. This girl had no hope of surviving the attack.

Then, just before Yuki released the spell, a vision of her nurse mother swam in front of her eyes. She saw her face twisted in pain when her power ripped through her. She saw the scientists she killed with a fireball just like this one, writhing in agony as her flames ate them alive. She saw the face of the woman who brought her food only a little while before, and she saw the fear that covered her face like a mask.

"I don't want to kill you," Yuki said, a tear running down her cheek. "I can't kill you. So just get it over with."

She focused on the spell in her palm, and she reached out to take the power from it. She couldn't do it. She blinked, reaching out again. And still the power wouldn't drain. It was as if there were a ward around the spell she had made. It continued to draw from her, and the flames crept out of her palm to cover her hand.

It didn't burn her. It was her spell after all. But it was getting stronger. She stepped back, still trying to draw back the magick. She tried a counter spell, but it was drawing from her too fast for her to catch any power for anything else. She had lost control. Just like all the other times.

"No. I don't want this. No!" She yelled at the flames. They didn't listen. The spell covered her arm now and was moving across her shoulders. Yuki looked up at the dark girl. She stood in the same place, watching. She was going to die if she stayed.

"Run!" Yuki shouted at her. She didn't move. The spell covered both of her arms now, and she could feel it kindling. The spell was about to be cast whether Yuki wanted it or not. Once more she shouted at the girl, "Run!"

Then the spell exploded.

F lames exploded out of the pale girl, engulfing Null in an instant. The white room was gone, and everything was painted in reds and yellows. But there was no heat. These flames were magickal, and they could not touch her. She could hear them, though. The fire roared around her in a deafening hurricane of flame. Null reached up and plugged her ears with her fingers, careful to keep from cutting herself.

Finally the spell ran out of power, and the firestorm died. The room was visible again, though no longer white. Everything was charred, and the bed and little table were gone, the mattress burned, and the metal melted into a pool on the floor. The pale girl was on her knees in the middle of the room, head in her hands, her pink hair flared out around her. With the roar of the flames gone, the sound of the girl's sobs filled the room.

"I told you that you could not harm me," Null said as she stalked toward the girl. She looked up, and her watery pink eyes widened.

"You can't be alive," she whispered in disbelief. "No one can survive my magick when it's out of control."

"There is no magick that can affect me because I have none of my own," Null said. She stood over the girl now.

"That's impossible. Everyone has magick, even if it's just a tiny trace."

"Everyone except for me," Null said. She pulled her arm back, the tip of her blade aimed for the girl's throat.

S he should be dead, Yuki thought. *There's no way she could have survived.* And yet, here she was. Completely untouched by her flames. She claimed that she had no magick of her own. Maybe she didn't, that would explain how she survived, as well as the void she had seemed in spiritual form. Maybe having no magick meant that she couldn't be touched by it.

Which meant that Yuki couldn't hurt her.

Yuki went still. She couldn't hurt her. Not matter how powerful her spell, or how badly out of control her power. She couldn't hurt her. She wouldn't be afraid of her. She wouldn't run at the sight of her.

She watched the woman draw her arm back, and she knew she was going to be killed. But she didn't care. Before she realized what she was doing, Yuki launched herself at the woman. She wrapped her arms around her and hugged her for dear life. The woman was a murderer, but it didn't matter. Because she was the only person in the entire world that Yuki couldn't hurt.

Tears streamed down Yuki's face to run red across the woman's armor. The last person she hugged was her nurse mother. It was the night her powers went out of control and killed her. No one had touched her since, and to be able to hug someone, even the woman sent to kill her, was a blessing.

She expected to feel the bite of the woman's blade at any moment, but it never came. At last her tears were spent, and she stepped back. Yuki smiled, and an odd look crossed the woman's face. The first emotion out of her that Yuki had seen.

"Thank you for letting me do that. You don't know how much it meant," Yuki said with a little bow. She spread her arms wide and closed her eyes. "I know I can't stop you. But it's okay. I'm ready."

N ull raised her blade again and stopped. Something was different. She didn't know what. It had started when the girl embraced her. It felt as if something inside her woke. Something she had never known was there.

It was warm. Warmer than anything she had ever experienced. It started in her stomach and spread until it touched every limb. For a moment, she was contented. She couldn't bring herself to let her blade fall upon the girl while she was in her arms. And she couldn't bring herself to do it now, not after the memory of the...the...

Feeling.

That's what it was. A feeling. The first she ever had in waking memory. Slowly, she lowered her arm. It had been fleeting, but she knew it was real. This girl made her feel...something. She didn't know what. She didn't have enough experience with the sensation.

She gazed at the girl in her charred slip, standing ready for death. While she had never desired to take a life, she had also never cared to spare one either. She did not want to kill this girl. Another first. What else could this girl show her?

"What is your name?" Null asked. The girl opened her eyes, and they flicked down to Null's blades, now resting at her sides.

"Are you not going to kill me?" the girl asked, confused.

"I asked you for your name," Null said, brushing the question aside.

"Yuki," the girl said, her voice suddenly very small. "My name is Yuki."

She was named after snow? It seemed fitting to Null. Somehow. Null slid her blades into their sheaths at the small of her back. "My name is Null, and I am not going to kill you. I am going to take you with me."

Yuki's eyes narrowed, and there was fear in her voice when she spoke. "Where are you taking me?"

"I do not know yet. I shall decide that once we are out of Kiseki." Null turned and gestured for Yuki to follow her. "Come with me."

Null stepped through the door and walked a few steps down the corridor. She did not hear Yuki's feet following her, and she stopped. When she looked over her shoulder, Yuki hadn't moved. She stood, wringing her slip with her hands again, indecision etched into her face.

"If you do not come with me, the extermination units *will* find you here," Null called back to her. "They will not spare you as I have."

Yuki bit her lip and glanced around at her burned-out cell. She took a shuddering breath, and Null saw resolve settle about her shoulders like a mantle. Yuki nodded to herself and stepped forward.

Null didn't move until the girl stood next to her. Yuki looked up at her, worry and hope both etched into her eyes. Null nodded to the girl, then turned and struck out down the hall.

"Stay with me, and do as I say. If you do, I will get you out of here," Null said, her eyes scanning the every shadow of the hall ahead. It had been some time since the extermination units penetrated the complex. Her father very well could have sent them down to check on her.

"Thank you. For rescuing me," Yuki said. She was almost running to keep up with Null, her bare feel slapping against the concrete.

"Do not thank me yet. I have not decided what I am going to do with you," Null replied. Yuki fell silent after that, sticking close to Null as the weaved up and out of the sub-levels. Null kept a close eye on the girl as they went.

Truthfully, she did not fully understand why she wanted to rescue the girl. She made her feel things. Things that normal people should feel. Feelings that she long ago accepted that she would never experience. The girl was full of firsts for Null, and she was not sure whether or not she wanted to experience these emotions. But she knew that Yuki was her only chance to find out. In the end, she may decide she did not want to feel these things. She would kill the girl, if that came to be.

But until she could come to a decision, she was going to protect this girl. Even if it meant she had to slaughter the world.

GOLD MOUNTAIN

AMY BAUER

The lightning bolt struck with no warning, blinding me in a sea of foggy white. Thunder cracked, sharp and immediate, and a tangy odor filled my nose. Crying out, I threw my arms over my face.

My horse stopped, shifting weight to her hindquarters. Before Diaochan could rear, I lunged at her head. Her muscles shuddered under my body, and I hugged her, singing a lullaby from home as much to calm myself as to ease the mare. She, at least, loved to hear the old language.

Gradually her tremors eased, and I dismounted. On my right, the North Fork American River cut through Green Valley's canyon with a soft gurgle of whitewater. Towering cliffs loomed over a wilderness of trees. It was lovely I suppose, but I still preferred the bustle of Guangzhou's crowded streets to the wild beauty of California.

I walked slowly, leading Diaochan, trying to calm myself. The cloudless sky was bright and sunny, with no hint of storm clouds. I'd never get used to this rough country. Maybe if I'd been allowed to pan gold and stay in a mining camp, I'd feel more settled.

Diaochan whinnied, shying sideways. I didn't have to look far to see what had spooked her.

A tall, broad-shouldered man lay face up on the riverbank. Unblinking, wide, ice-blue eyes stared at the sky, his spirit vanished. He was pale-skinned, with hair the color of strong tea, shot through with iron-gray. The lightning bolt must have struck him as his shirt had shredded into blackened char.

I stroked Diaochan's neck as I drew her away from the body and tied her loosely to a pine tree in the woods. A small cabin nestled in the trees. Walking back to the river, I chewed my lip.

At home, I would have owed this elder my prayers. I would have fought to find his family, lit incense for his spirit, but I was no longer in Guangzhou. Did the spirits of my ancestors follow me this far away from the Flowery Kingdom? Did I owe anyone anything in this land of everyone for himself?

A shovel and rocker, gravel spilling from it, lay abandoned in the river. Last time I was in Green Valley, Cheng Fan had been beaten for working a white man's abandoned claim too well. Would they think I'd stolen gold from the rocker? Should I pretend I hadn't seen the dead man? Just move on?

I rubbed my face. I had letters to distribute and money to gather so I could return to Dai Fow.

Dai Fow. Big City. San Francisco. City of hills and fog with a harbor full of ships abandoned by the forty-niners.

I'd never make enough money to return home or fetch my family to Dai Fow if I angered the bosses who lived there. Actually, money would be the least of my problems. Straightening my shoulders, I started toward Diaochan, but a nagging, soft *bzzz* like an angry bee drew me back to the body.

I peeled away the blackened shirt. The lightning must have fused shirt and skin together as large chunks of skin ripped off in my hands revealing glittering insides. *Glittering?* I'd once seen a man, chest ripped open by a sword, his insides open to the weather in a bloody mess, smelling like rotting fish in the summer sun. This man's insides gleamed with only a tinge of oily smell. Long skinny lines, maybe made of metal, shone and glistened. Small sparks arced light like tiny lightning flashes, making the *bzzing* sound I'd heard.

I froze for a moment, and then shook myself, wiping my hands on my trousers. I wasn't far enough removed from Guangzhou to abandon a dead man to the river, no matter what his insides looked like. I'd leave his mining equipment scattered in the river. With luck, I wouldn't be accused of stealing his gold.

I pulled the body to a sitting position. With several grunts, I heaved him over my shoulders, carrying him the short distance into the cabin before depositing him on the rope bed set against the wall.

Sweat poured down my face, and my breath came in harsh pants. Muttering a curse I'd learned in Dai Fow, I collapsed on a roughly carved wooden chair by a small table. I closed my eyes, losing myself in a daydream of my wife's lively face with her shining dark eyes and soft, black hair. Then I thought of my two-year-old son, born after I left the Flowery Kingdom, and remembered the miserable poverty towering over us all like White Cloud Mountain over Guangzhou.

Opening my eyes, I search for a distraction. Maybe there was something in the cabin I could use to identify the dead miner. I stood up and wandered the room.

Near the bed was a small dresser, empty except for a change of clothes. Besides the chair I sat on and the table, the only other item in the room was a huge floor-length mirror made of a beautiful dark wood with the finest quality glass I'd ever seen, completely out of place in the plain cabin.

My reflection looked back at me, crisp, not wavy like most glass. A series of knobs ran down the right side of the wood frame. I pushed the top one, and my face and body faded away, replaced by the image of a stall, similar to a horse's in a barn, with stone-like walls.

I extended a shaking finger and brushed the glass. Instead of bending when it pushed against the surface, my finger moved through the mirror like a dolphin gliding through water, disappearing from sight. I stared at the spot where my finger had vanished for a heartbeat before I pulled it back. I let the mirror swallow my entire hand. Ignoring the thought of my disapproving mother, I stuck my head through the glass.

The cabin disappeared. The stall I'd seen previously appeared in front of me, well lit and empty. Through the opening ahead, I heard noises that could have been people talking, and whirrs and grinding I couldn't identify. I pulled my head back, and the cabin with its reassuring dullness embraced me.

Muted shouting wafted in through the open door. I tore myself away from the mirror and went outside. A man stood by the river, cursing with an impressive vocabulary, including some strange expressions unknown to me.

The swearing stopped abruptly.

"Who are you?" he said, his words terse.

"Lau Zing," I replied, nodding my head. "May I have the honor of your acquaintance?"

"Reykirk." He turned from me, circling the ground like a sheep dog.

Before I could decide if Reykirk was his first or family name, he asked, "Did you see a body lying here?"

"Yes. How did you...?"

"Where is it?" He ran his hands through shoulder-length blond hair. Brown eyes bored holes through me.

"In the cabin. I took..."

Brushing past me, he ran toward the cabin. I followed and found him staring at the dead man. Unsure what to do, I sat at the table.

Reykirk was repeating in a low voice, "I can't lose this job." He looked at me, eyes narrowed.

"Were you the one who removed his shirt?"

"I needed to see if I could help him."

"You saw the open wound?"

"Strange, yes?"

He didn't answer, and the silence hung thick, like Guangzhou summer air.

"I can't let you tell anyone. I'm sorry," he said, his low voice chilly. He withdrew something the size of his palm from his pocket, pointing it toward me.

I didn't know what it was, and I didn't want to find out. I threw myself from the chair, falling to the floor. A beam of light streaked over my head, sizzling against the cabin wall. I froze, my heart pounding like waves during a storm, staring at the blackened spot, before I backpedaled, scurrying like a sand crab and kicking the table toward Reykirk.

He tripped, falling across the doorway. As he fell, he shot off another beam of light. The strike caught my arm, and I sucked in my breath. My head spun, the cabin walls shrinking in on me. Gasping for breath, I searched for an escape.

Nowhere to hide, and I couldn't outrun light. Reykirk was climbing to his feet. My eyes locked on the mirror. Desperate, I threw myself toward it. Another shaft of light flew past. I fell through that strange glass, landing on a hard floor with a grunt. My arm throbbed, and my body ached. I struggled to my feet.

A small room with three smooth walls the color of spring leaves surrounded me. Murmurs of conversation and strange mechanical sounds drifted in from the area outside the stall. Where the fourth wall should have been was an opening onto a large smooth, stone-like floor.

Turning back from the opening, I was nose to nose with the man trying to kill me. His brows furled, he glared at me from the other side of the mirror I'd just fallen through. He pounded at me with his fists. Shaking, I moved to one side of the mirror so Reykirk couldn't see me.

My arm throbbed. The sleeve of my burnt shirt hung in shreds, revealing a blistered, angry red spot the size of a silver dollar. It hurt, but I didn't know what I could do about the pain.

Needing to get away, I stepped outside the stall but stopped, unsure what to do. A huge room stretched before me, mostly open space with nowhere to hide. The walls stretched at least two stories tall with windows set near the roof. A large window the size of a wagon near the floor on one end let in sunlight. I glanced back. A small label on the outside of the stall read 1852.

The whirr of machinery turned me back to the room's center. A moving belt traveled the length of the room. A number of oddly dressed people, mostly men, stood near the belt, shoveling and pouring rocks and liquid into containers that passed. They ignored me. Fascinated, I forgot my fear and shuffled forward.

One man in a short tunic shoveled white-gray rocks onto the belt while another dumped reddish-orange stones from rough pottery. A woman in bright orange and a strange hat poured out black liquid.

Looking across the activity in the room's center, I saw a number of openings similar to my stall. The entire room was ringed with them, identical except for different numbers on the wall.

Something touched my arm, and I jumped. A dark-haired man stood beside me, in a silver shirt and black pants. Something about his face reminded me of the man who'd been struck by lightning.

"Why did you not check in, 1852?" he said in a low, choppy voice.

"My name is not 1852. I am Lau Zing," I protested.

"You arrived through one of the 1852 gates. You are 1852. Where is your gold? You have not met your quota. We need your gold. Report."

His nonsense words washed over me like a cold rainstorm. Frustrated by everything I didn't understand, two years of repressed anger exploded like gunpowder. "My name is Lau Zing. Someone named Reykirk is trying to kill me, and I don't know why he didn't follow me here. I have no gold. I traveled to Gold Mountain to mine gold and get rich, but my huigan boss didn't care. As soon as he discovered I came from a family of scholars and could speak English, he insisted I become a courier. You don't say no to the Dai Fow bosses unless you want to die far away from the Flowery Kingdom. Now I ride back and forth through the California wilderness like a witless ant. I'll never get rich enough to send for my mother and Mei and my son."

"The gate closes for fifteen minutes after each use so the natives can't follow. You know that, 1852. Where is your gold, 1852?"

I threw up my hands. The huge window over his shoulder beckoned with a taste of the outside. I needed to see outdoors and left the man sputtering to himself.

"1852, report!"

I looked out the window and breathing became difficult. Shiny structures, maybe buildings, rose through the sky. Sunlight glinted off them forcing me to squint. I thought I was on the ground, but if my eyes could be trusted, I was hundreds, maybe thousands, of feet high. Clouds drifted below. An oval shape the size of a small boat flew past. By all my ancestors, I saw people in it.

My head swam. I clutched at the window frame. I must be mad. Madness would make sense of everything. I grasped for an explanation like a child grabs at sweets.

I'll never know how long I stared at the strange view before my head began to clear, my mind to work again. I remembered I'd left Diaochan. Maybe I could return to the mining camp through the mirror? Maybe I just imagined Reykirk? Maybe if I returned to work, this madness would pass like a flock of herons in spring?

I turned from the window and almost ran into a woman in a bright yellow shirt and slim black and white trousers. She was striking with black, curly hair hanging loose and dark brown eyes.

She frowned. "Why did you ignore the check in? What is your employee number?"

I stared, not knowing what to say.

She repeated the question, the words sharp.

Deciding on truth, I answered, "I have no idea what you are talking about."

The woman really looked at me for the first time. She glanced from my dirty brown trousers to my dark blue shirt, finally to my face and straw hat, eyes lingering on my queue. "My name is Shariandra," she said. "Are you human?"

What sort of question was that?

"What else would I be?"

"A bot. A machine that looks like a person."

"I'm not a machine. I'm just a courier trying to support my family from half a world away, and I think I've gone mad."

She held out a hand toward the red burn on my arm and, in a much gentler voice, asked, "How did you get here?"

Her kindness drained my anger. "Through the mirror. This man fired something at me that burned my arm. I'm so frightened. I just want to go home."

Right as I said it, I realized I didn't know which home I meant.

Someone shouted. Swiveling my head, I locked eyes with Reykirk, who stood on the opposite side of the moving belt. Forgetting the woman, I ran for the mirror, only pausing long enough to ensure I had the correct stall. I needed to be free of the noise, crowds, and things I didn't understand. Praying to my ancestors with all my might that the trip would work in reverse, I launched myself at the glass.

Stumbling into the cabin, I nearly fell, somehow staying upright. The dead miner was gone from the bed. I didn't stop to wonder and ran for Diaochan.

She stood where I left her, whuffing happily when she saw me. Quickly I untied my horse and climbed on. Turning toward the mining camp, I urged her to a canter, hurrying away from the cabin.

I rode in a fever. I needed to reach my friend, Wong Hing, and ask for help. We had traveled about a mile when I abruptly reined Diaochan to a stop. Unused to such a fast pace, she took deep, shuddering breaths.

A man was trying to kill me. If I went to Hing's, I would lead Reykirk to one of my few friends. Last time I was in camp, Hing told me the Carter brothers had abandoned their claim. Their cabin was away from the Chinese section. I'd hide there.

I led my horse to the river, and she drank deeply. When she was ready, I remounted and turned her toward the Carters' claim.

A half hour later, I sprawled inside the shabby cabin eating dried fish. Diaochan sheltered in the tiny shanty the Carters had used for their mules. If only I could get Mei to California. The natives might be hostile, but at least only one person was trying to kill me here. Back in the Flowery Kingdom, the warring armies killed any who got in their way. Maybe we could open a restaurant in Dai Fow. I hear people are making fortunes serving food.

I'd left my sleeping roll in the shanty, and I stalked through the twilight to retrieve it. Diaochan whinnied. I froze, listening. Beneath the soft wind and rustling leaves, I heard the sound I'd been dreading. Light footsteps approached. Steeling myself, I left the shanty.

Pain blossomed in my leg. I staggered, falling to my knees. A few feet away, Reykirk pointed his tiny weapon at me.

"At least tell me why you are trying to kill me before you do," I said, surprised by how calm I felt. Only half of me believed I was going to die. The other part still thought I was mad.

"I need this job," he said.

"You keep saying that, but California has lots of work. Miners, sailors, launderers, grocers."

"I fell asleep." His voice and body trembled. "You found the bot before I woke and could send the retrieval team. I'm going to be fired." He stared past me at the river.

A stick cracking was the only warning. Glowing light surrounded the man. He arched his back, dropping his weapon. His mouth opened in a soundless scream. The light vanished, and he crumpled, moaning in pain. I stared at the body on the ground so close to mine and began to pray, waiting to join my ancestors.

Two people appeared from the trees. Close-fitting clothing covered their entire bodies, including their hair, only their faces revealed. Somehow, I couldn't focus on them; my eyes kept sliding over them. Ignoring me, they walked to the other man, securing his arms, before they searched him.

"Reykirk Lorenzo. You are under arrest for multiple violations of the Time Travel Security Act. You are charged with the attempted murder of Lau Zing and causing bodily harm and emotional distress."

One of them tossed Reykirk over his shoulder before walking off into the trees. The other yelled, "Clear!" and also disappeared into the tree line.

A woman wearing a long silky dress emerged from the shadows, and for a moment, I imagined I saw Mei. As she drew nearer, I recognized Shariandra. I tried to pull myself to my feet, but my throbbing arm ached, and my wounded leg would not support my weight. I remained sitting.

"Close your eyes and relax, Zing. I'm here to help you."

A small sting punctured my shoulder. Within minutes, my head and arm stopped throbbing. The agony in my leg receded, and I breathed easy again.

Shariandra sat down beside me, her arms stretched behind her while she stared at the darkening sky. The sweet vanilla scent of the pines drifted on the night breeze.

"So beautiful," she murmured. "We don't have any more wilderness back home."

"Where is home?"

"Same as you. California." She looked me in the eyes. "You're not mad. I promise."

I wanted to believe her. "How'd you know my name?"

"The factory bot recorded what you said. You were right when you said 1852 wasn't your name. It was your year. The factory you found will be built five hundred years from now."

"Maybe you're mad, too." I hugged my knees to my chest, the lack of pain like spring following winter.

She pulled a book from her bag. A solemn couple splendid in ceremonial clothing from The Flowery Kingdom gazed from the cover.

"That looks like Mei and myself, but so much older than we are now." My voice shook.

"Some years from now, after finding a stash of old letters, your great-great-grandson will decide he wants to write a book about the history of his immigrant family." She opened the book. "The Americans are so different from us, so raw and fresh, often uncivilized, but determined. A fresh wind blows through this land."

The same words I had written to Mei last month in a letter now traveling to Guangzhou.

"It's all true," I whispered.

"Some of my people wanted to relocate you or silence you. However, we couldn't do that without changing our timeline. You have too many descendants."

"I have a large family?" The ice that had chilled my spirit since I sailed into Dai Fow began to melt. My eyes watered. I blinked a few times before I spoke again.

"What was that place I went to?"

She watched a cloud float across the moon and sighed.

"Over the centuries, we've stripped our world nearly bare of ores, gems, and other resources. We discovered time travel and started sending bots into the past to blend in with the locals and gather resources we no longer have."

With the wilderness all around us, I couldn't imagine a barren world.

"Was Reykirk sent by the ones who wanted me dead?"

Her face hardened. "No. We assign humans to monitor the bots and remove any that malfunction. Reykirk shouldn't have let you find the bot in the river. He thought he could kill you and hide his mistake."

"Now what to do with you? You need to keep silent about all you've seen."

"Who would believe me?" I said, knowing it to be true. "I don't believe me."

Shariandra smiled. "We do rely on that."

I thought I could feel Mei's patient dark eyes on me.

"Could you help me get my family to Big City, I mean San Francisco? I thought I wanted to return to Guangzhou, but I realized today all I want is to be with my family and keep them safe. That will be easier here than in the middle of the Rebellion back home. The bosses will let me settle down if Mei is with me. Maybe we could stay in San Francisco and open a restaurant.

"That's a lovely idea. We'll find a way for you to afford their passage that no one will question. We owe you."

A weight lifted from my shoulders, but I had to ask, "How did you and Reykirk know where to find me, and more importantly, why are you helping me? It would have been much easier not to interfere, safer too."

The silence lingered so long I thought she was not going to answer. When she finally did, I had to strain to hear her over the night sounds of the forest and the river's whitewater.

"When I return in seven months to wait with my many-times removed grandfather while my many-times removed grandmother

190

sails into San Francisco Harbor, you'll tell me how to find where you were hiding, and I'll write it down where Reykirk and my future self will be sure to find it."

She leaned close and kissed my cheek.

My fingers touched my skin where she had kissed me as if holding a fragile orchid. I would see my mother and son soon, and Mei, my beautiful Mei. Our family tree would descend for at least five hundred years. Tears flowed down my cheeks, but my heart was as light and free as a sky lantern drifting over San Francisco Bay.

ALONE

FAITH HUNTER

From the world of the Rogue Mage, a story of Young Thorn

I had been in Enclave. Sitting at a sidewalk café on the corner outside of the priestess's home with my twin sister, Rose, reading aloud a poem written by a Pre-Ap poet named Henry David Thoreau. The language was formal and wandering, with images so intense it seemed to uplift me to some higher plane. I was reading a line about the full moon when my gift fell.

Hammered me.

All the mages and all the *voices*.

All of them.

In my mind.

The cacophony, the wild blast of need and outrage and want and love and lust and *power*. The voices in my head. The voices of every mage in Enclave. Desires, hatreds, petty angers. So little kindness. So little love.

Puberty and my gift descended like a seraph in battle armor, brutalizing me, sending me screaming, falling to the street. Moaning. Gasping. My mind invaded by voices shouting, demanding.

And then Lolo's voice, soothing, a bitter tea at my lips. And then nothing.

When I woke, it was in an odd little bed that was rocking beneath me. The wool sheets were rough compared to the mage-touched sheets I slept under in the priestess's house. The clothes I was wearing were cotton, my socks knitted wool. Human-made clothes. Around my neck was a leather thong, the opal disc pendant lying on my chest. My mage attributes didn't glow, and I intuited a connection to the opal: I assumed it blanked my skin, making me look human, dull and ugly, keeping my secret from the human world.

There were hand rails on the side of the bed. I levered myself over them and down to the floor to find myself in a private cabin of a sleeper car on a train moving out of Enclave. Alone.

Six hours after waking, I was still here. *Alone.* I hated that word: *Alone.* And bored, with nothing to do but stare out at the world beyond the frosted glass as it rocketed by. For *days* more according to the porter, a tall, broad man with one blue eye and one brown eye. He also had the scar of a kirk brand on his face, but from the way the light diffused slightly around his cheek, I could tell he wore some sort of glamour. The branding was probably a response to the odd quirk of genetics that had given him mismatched eyes. Humans were afraid of anything different. Brandings were designed to be visible, as lessons to those who saw them. Facial scars could be horrible, and if the porter's was still partially visible through the glamour, it must be worse underneath. The glamour could have been worked to completely hide it, but the humans probably would have considered that a sin worthy of more punishment.

I was curious, but I didn't ask. That would have been rude. And foolish. So I just tipped him well when he brought me meals and answered my few questions about our destination and the length of the trip and when and where on the train I could eat.

His name was Taft. And he didn't ask questions, which I appreciated.

He withdrew as I stared out the window into the falling night, eating the excellent grilled cheese, spinach, mushroom, and tomato sandwich and drinking the tea—black tea with real cream. Not thinking. Not feeling. Just staring out at my new, frozen world, so different from the New Orleans Enclave, with its damp heat and the smell of coffee and gumbo and beignets on the air. And the feel of creation energy dancing along my skin.

Beyond the ice-rimmed windows of the train were mountains and evergreens and the stark branches of leafless trees. Snow and ice covered everything. Everywhere. Except the vertical walls of rock the train passed between. The stone was cracked, split, splintered, and coated with an ice glaze, but so full of power that it called to me, called to my mage gift, the ability to work the energy stored in the stone heart of the world.

Beyond the windows of the train car was this unfamiliar place, this impossible scenery. The scent of ice on the ground, snow in the air, the stink of the steel rails and wheels, steel-against-steel, all assaulted my Stone mage nostrils with each breath. Yet even here, so far from Enclave, the distance growing with each moment, there was the presence of mage magics. The engine was powered by mage might, bartered and paid for. The rails kept free of ice, also by mage power. Despite the cold outside, the window didn't have ice covering it, except for a little frost in one corner. I touched the glass and felt the tingle of magic there too. The glass had been treated with a warming spell; the magics in the corner had begun to wear thin and would have to be recharged.

Mages were everywhere. We were nowhere. Humans used our magic but hated us for making it, for having access to it when they didn't. Humans were vile. And if I slipped up, they'd kill me.

The stories we'd been told in Enclave of what humans did to unlicensed witchy women had been vivid and intense. Remembering them now left my mouth dry, my heart pounding, my breath coming too fast. My reflection in the window changed as my skin began to glimmer, to glow, shining through the working of the amulet. In my panic, I'd released my neomage attributes, my eyes mirrored in the glass with the gray-blue of labradorite, my flesh like pearls. Even my red hair glowed scarlet. And my scars were pure white, evidence of my damaged body and a childhood lived in danger.

I stared at myself, terrified. If the wrong person saw me like this...

But I had been trained since the crèche to control my powers and myself. The simple mantra taught to every neomage child forced its way up through my panic. "Stone and fire, water and air, blood and kin prevail," I whispered. "Wings and shield, dagger and sword, blood and kin prevail."

I said the phrases over and over, breathing deeply with each repetition, each breath fogging a round spot on the window only to have the conjure evaporate it away. I kept it up until I was calm, until my fears weren't somehow overriding the opal *Glamour* amulet's preprogrammed conjure.

The mage glow faded to human-ugly. Tears blurred my reflection, making it waver. My *Glamour* amulet was a comforting warmth in my fist, my true nature protected once again.

And my body calmed, my hunger returned. I finished my sandwich and the tea and then drank several bottles of Mason's Pure Godly Deep Well Water. Most local streams, lakes and wells were perfectly safe to drink from now, since the Apocalypse had eliminated diseases, overpopulation, and industrial pollution. But well-to-do humans still preferred expensive brand-name water imported from trusted purified sources. A neomage in hiding could piggyback on that affectation. We needed to know where our water came from, since some waters interfered with our elements. Well water was safest for me, and Lolo had probably ensured that the train was well stocked with Mason's.

Once again the window drew me. I turned off the light, crawled close on the small couch, and studied the new world beyond. And for the very first time, in the dark, I began to experiment with my Stone-gift. All by myself. Because I was *alone*. I would have no teachers. Never would, ever again. I knew that—despite Lolo's promise that she'd find a way for me to return.

But I still had the lessons I'd been taught in school. They would help. They could steer me.

Remembering the lesson of *sight*, I let my eyes fall out of focus. Within minutes, I figured out how to use mage sight. It wasn't nearly as hard to achieve as I'd feared, but it was a lot harder to hold onto. Mage sight was disorienting, made worse by a vague motion sickness from the movement of the train car. But when I could hold onto it, I was able to see the foulness of allergens, of ice and metal and trees and even air currents, bright but sickly.

Beneath my clothes, my prime amulet was glowing softly, automatically protecting me from the effect of the allergens, the elements that I couldn't use. But when we passed rock, I could see the might of stone, the granite glowing a warm and perfect blue/pink/lavender of might. The rock called to me. I hoped that wherever I was going I'd have access to stone. To the heart of the world.

A handful of pre-conjured amulets were in my pockets. I wasn't sure what they did, but I had days to figure them out. They would need to be charged when I got...wherever I was going. To the mountain "city" where Lolo had decided to send me. *Alone.*

Alone with my worthless, dangerous, extra gift. A gift that allowed me to read the minds of mages. Any mage, all mages I was close to. *Forced* me to read their minds. Though the train car was warm, I shivered remembering the horrible things mages thought.

Tired, I turned on the lamp and slid into the bed that Taft had made for me when he brought my dinner. The sheets were cold, and I pulled the heavy coverlet up. I withdrew the letter I'd tucked into my shirt, unfolded the single sheet. The note was dangerous to have, and I'd read and reread it so many times already that I almost had it memorized anyway, but I hadn't been able to destroy it. Not yet. It was written in Lolo's crabbed penmanship and with her Cajun phrasings.

T*horn.*

When you wake, you be far from other mages, as safe as I might manage. You should still have you memory, but if not, know this. When you gift descend, you develop a condition I am calling mind-openness, allowing you entrée *to all other mages' mind. It was more clamor than anyone could handle, especially a mage so young and inexperience. Thus, I have you on a train, sending you away to safety, for now.*

I sending you to a human man named Lem in Mineral City. No one there has ever seen a mage. They won't know what to look for. They won't expect one to arrive via train. You weapons case is in luggage with you chest. It will arrive with you, never fear, along with other necessities. In the sleeper compartment is enough to get you to Mineral City, including amulets and a Book of Workings. *You recharge the stone and keep you mage attributes muted. The simple spells you need to survive be easy to follow in* Book of Workings. *If you have question, answer in the* Book.

Tell no one what you are. Not even Lem.

Know that I begin search for a cure for you mind-openness. Practice you savage chi and savage blade. You and Rose will *be battle mages, together, a weapon against Darkness.*

Learn how to use and control you Stone-gift.

I send supplies.

Lolo

PS – destroy this note

W hat Lolo hadn't said was that I was now *rogue*. From the bitter taste in my mouth and the carpet fibers on my clothes when I woke up, I figured out that I had been drugged, smuggled out, and sent away. A mage away from Enclave, without a visa, without ID. Without protection. If discovered, humans would have the right to rape me, torture me, and kill me.

If there was a sin in being out of Enclave, it wasn't mine, as all children are innocent, but that wouldn't stop humans if they learned what I was. Humans were inherently bitter and violent. Everyone knew that.

Yet Lolo was sending me to a human. What kind of man was Lem?

Was a better human than others of his kind? How did Lolo know him? Or of him? Not that it mattered.

I was in so much danger that I should have been immobilized by fear. But I had survived being trapped in a nest of devil-spawn. I had the scars to prove it. I could survive this too. If I was careful.

I refolded the letter and hid it away again. Tears threatened, tickling beneath my lids. Missing Lolo. Missing Rose. *Alone.*

"Stone and fire, water and air, blood and kin prevail," I whispered again. "Wings and shield, dagger and sword, blood and kin prevail."

The train rocked me, soothing in its own way. I slept at long last, clutching the opal amulet.

Morning broke and Taft woke me with a three-tap knock. I pulled the coverlet over me against the cold and for the modesty that the human would expect me to feel. He took my breakfast order and fired up the water heater in my shower alcove. I had no idea if I would be able to use the shower. If the water the train had taken on at the last stop was collected rain water or river water, water that had been in recent contact with air, I might be in trouble. Everything about living with humans was going to be difficult.

I was in luck. When I tested the water with a fingertip, the shower water didn't drain all my energy on contact.

Refreshed, I put my red hair—human drab—up in a big messy bun and dressed in clean human clothes in somber greens and blues instead of the vibrant shades I was used to. It was no secret to the world that mages had flamboyant style, whereas humans were chaste and dull and unimaginative. I made my own bed. I knew it was Taft's job, but I figured he would be busy with all the old humans who had boarded at the dawn stop in Opelika, Alabama, a day outside of Atlanta. There must have been twenty, all self-important humans, all traveling in the sleeper cars.

I could tell Taft was harried when breakfast was late. As he opened the door, I could hear a human woman demanding, "More towels, more wash clothes, and hot tea. And hurry up about it, you genetic abnormality."

Her words made me angry. She was insulting the man who was waiting on her, which seemed foolish, cruel, and unnecessary. If it had been me, I'd have cooked something slimy into her eggs and given her salt instead of sugar for her tea. But then, I'd been called impulsive all my life.

I leaned until I could see out the door, beyond Taft's bulk as he maneuvered my food tray inside the small space, and took in the blonde, blue-eyed woman. She had diamonds on her fingers and wrists and around her neck, and she was tall and lean, with perfect skin and that look that only money can buy—"money" meaning expensive amulets full of glamour that hid the imperfections. In her case, she was glamoured all over, from her hair, eyes, skin, and waist, to her elegant ankles. In reality, the woman likely looked totally different.

I wondered who she was faking for, but then the middle-aged man behind her said, "It's all right, dear. He'll get to us."

"He'll get to us *now*," she snapped, "or I'll see his other cheek branded too."

Taft paled.

"It's okay," I said to Taft, my voice soft. "Go help her. I'm fine."

"Thank you, Miss," he said, and he was gone.

The moment I was alone, I sat down on the couch so I wouldn't make the motion sickness worse, and calmed myself down. It took a while. By the time I turned to the food, it was stone cold. So was the tea. And with the glamoured woman giving Taft so much trouble, I'd never call for fresh.

Instead, I pulled out my amulets, looking for one that might contain a pre-programmed conjure to reheat the food, the sort of convenience that would be commonplace in Enclave. The stones were brilliant in mage sight, glowing red, blue, emerald, and purple-black. They were mesmerizing. I could stare at them all day. But they were obviously more than pretty. The crystalline microstructure of the stones contained power. Each amulet's structure was different and told an experienced mage what the amulet did. To me they weren't as obvious.

One of the simplest, a small carved soapstone cat-paw, looked like it should store and release heat. Most amulets require a spoken word or a physical gesture to activate, and I had no idea what sign or word would work. After several attempts, I placed the cat-paw on a small bit of egg and said the word, "Warm."

The soapstone glowed red and then orange...and burned the egg to a crisp. "I need to learn control first," I informed the scorched egg as I waved away charred-egg smoke. "Then I need to learn how to recharge you pretty little amulets. You'll make my life much easier in Mineral City. And yes, Lolo, I am talking to the stones you sent me."

More carefully, I heated the rest of breakfast and the cup of tea, and enjoyed the meal immensely.

I traveled alone in my private cabin all day, curled up on the couch with blankets, reading the *Book of Workings*, and trying different conjures with the amulets—simple ones that didn't require a mage circle. The *Book* itself didn't really contain detailed, spelled-out, step-by-step conjures so much as discussions of them, descriptions or what happened when the magic went wrong (things went boom), hints, and other writerly examples of non-helpfulness.

Through trial and error, I learned how to spark a flame with the handy-dandy cooking amulet, and how to use the black and clear agate healing stone. It looked roughly like a frog and, if I was still in Enclave, I'd take the agate to the stone-working class and get them to show me how to carve and polish it to enhance the froggy shape. Still, it was cute.

The white onyx fish likely held a sphere of protection or battle shield.

The clear quartz was used for illumination in the dark, like a flash-light or torch.

There was a pink quartz rose I had shaped and polished myself in class. Now just holding it filled me with a sense of calm and peace. I tucked it into my chest pocket.

I'd need a necklace for them all, like other Stone mages wore. But that would be foolish because then humans might discover what I was. I'd have to hide it beneath my clothes somehow.

I fingered a large cabochon of picture jasper, the lines of minerals looking like a scene as viewed from a Pre-Ap airplane—roads across a hilly desert landscape. In one corner was a greenish diffusion that looked like a desert oasis. It was beautiful and felt warm in my hand. I wasn't very good at it yet, but I focused my mage sight on it. It lit up as if I'd pointed a lantern at it, the light fracturing through the green minerals. It was a disruptor charm, but I had no idea what it was intended to disrupt, which would make it dangerous to test. What if it disrupted the train and the cars flew off the tracks? But Lolo had given it to me, so I assumed it would reveal itself to me eventually.

Then there were two amulets I couldn't figure out at all.

One, an onyx Arctic seal, seemed to be empty of energy, but it had a pathway to...somewhere inside of it.

And the last amulet was carved out of wood, which meant it had most likely come from Lolo herself. The microstructures of the wood were alien to me; I couldn't read them to tell me what the amulet did. But it had to be something special.

After lunch, I went through the carry-on luggage Lolo had packed for me. Her gifts didn't include salt mined from below ground, the only salt a Stone mage could use in workings. And the wood floor of the train car would have made a working circle impossible anyway. She didn't provide any personal items from my past except my comb, brush, toothbrush, and a silk-stitched needlepoint in shades of beige and brown framed in painted wood. The needlepoint had hung above my bed for all fourteen years of my life, stitched with the prophecy given by Lolo when my twin and I were born: *A Rose by any Other Name will still draw Blood.* Birth prophecies were usually obscure. Mine had been interpreted to say that the rose and the thorn worked together to draw blood—that Rose and I, together, would be warriors unlike any other. Meaningless now that Rose and I were separated.

The only other thing of real interest was a small jewelry box, black velvet with a hinged lid. I opened it to find a tiny chip of teal and aqua stone, zoisite. Crammed inside the lid was a folded scrap of paper—a note in Lolo's crabbed hand: *"This here a one-time charm. Use once, then it nothing but a rock. You in danger with a conjure, you drop stone in water —any kind—and it activate. It stop all conjures except them in contact with you body. Use with care."* Lolo was canny. Some said she had second sight. More than useful, this charm was important.

She'd also packed three books for me, though I wasn't particularly interested in reading. Two were Pre-Ap fantasy novels, and one was a mystery set in the Last War. By mid-afternoon I was bored beyond belief—almost bored enough to try to read a book—and wandered down the train to the dining car for tea. The car was only sparsely occupied, so I had my own table. Taft, moving quickly and economically despite his large frame, took my order and left me to the book I'd carried in, one of the novels. But I left the covers closed, sipping tea and staring out the window, surreptitiously watching the half-dozen humans in the car. I saw how much the well-dressed, upper-class humans used magic. They wore it as cosmetics, as charisma enhancers, as luck inducers. Some of them fairly glowed with applied creation energy.

When the dining car emptied, I left too and returned to my cabin.

After dinner, late on that full first day of consciousness, the opal *Glamour* amulet that hid my mage attributes stopped working. It was sudden and shocking, and I instantly began to glow. At first I tried what had worked before, reciting the "Stone and fire, water and air" mantra over and over again, but it had no effect.

When I finally gave up on that, I turned mage sight onto the opal disc. The *Glamour* amulet had run out of power.

For a continuous conjure, my prime amulet should have picked up the duties of the working, automatically recharging the *Glamour* amulet. That's how things worked for other neomages. But it hadn't.

I pulled out the *Book of Workings* again. Things in the *Book* weren't arranged in any obvious way, but after some false starts and cross-referencing I found my problem in a section on puberty. Since my gift had opened, my prime was no longer fully attuned to me. All I needed to do was to reset my prime to adult specifications through the Ceremony of Attainment, the ceremony all mages went through when their gift fell upon them.

That brought me down hard. That clearly would not be happening while on the train. I'd need blood and massive amounts of stone. Stone like the huge, broken cliffs and mountains we passed. I'd need to get off the train for that. "Seraph bones," I muttered, cursing. I wondered when that would occur to Lolo and what she would do about it.

I went through the book again and found that there was no Ceremony of Attainment in the *Book of Workings.* "Of course there isn't. The one thing I need most I don't have access to."

Desperate, I paged back and forth through the *Book of Workings* and found an entry that taught me how to recharge my amulet stones from an elemental source when they ran out of power. In an addendum, someone had written how pre-conjured amulets could be recharged from primes in an emergency. Which this was.

I had no idea if the method would work with my poorly attuned prime, but the recharge conjure seemed simple enough: Just press the empty stone against my prime and place both in contact with my body, then push power into the empty, assuming I could figure out how to do that. I didn't even need a circle to contain the energies, as they would be in constant contact with my body. It sounded easy.

But it didn't feel easy to me. It felt terrifying. What if the poorly attuned prime ruined the amulet? And itself? I'd heard of such things happening and the mage having to be given a brand new prime amulet. "Yeah, that door's shut too now."

I pulled the blanket up higher, reheated my tea, and tried to figure out what to do. Back before Enclaves had been created as safe havens in which to test our gifts, before the *Book Of Workings* had been compiled through decades of trial and error, neomages developing new conjures had been known to disintegrate, to burn to death, to explode. And that was before mages had prime amulets. Maybe the primes helped to prevent that. Maybe not having a fully functional prime would leave me open to all that danger.

Mages were supposed to have help in their first, most important year of settling into their gifts, of finding a niche in Enclave. I would be going it alone. I didn't know what I'd do if my prime ran out of power before I got to my destination, but for now, I could try to transfer some creation energy from my not-quite-perfect-prime to the pre-conjured disguise amulet.

I double-checked the lock on the outer door, opened the small door to the minuscule bathroom so I could see myself in the mirror, and pulled my tunic top up, exposing my belly. I pressed the stones together above my navel, on bare skin. Not because there was anything in the entry in the *Book* that specified contact with bare skin or the navel, but I knew that some older mages wore their primes inside their clothes on long chains, so it seemed to make sense.

Moments later my mage attributes flickered off, then on, and then off again. And they stayed that way. Mage sight showed the prime holding steady and the opal fully charged. It was a beautiful stone, but not so valuable that it would look out of place adorning a teenaged girl.

Relieved, I washed my face and was about to change into my night clothes when I heard voices in the hallway, a woman's shrill voice shouting, "You stupid defect! Look what you did!"

I cracked open the door. The blond woman was standing in the corridor in her night-robe, a luxury that mage sight confirmed was mage-touched, the velvet catching the lights, glowing as it flowed across her body, emphasizing breasts and hips, hiding belly and soft underarms. She was rich, like Midas rich. None of the other humans on board wore so much magery. Most wore none. Mage magics were expensive.

On the floor near the woman were trays with empty wine bottles, lipstick-smeared glasses, china plates and bowls, and silver utensils. Somebody had been having a party.

"You stained my dress!" the woman screeched, lifting a royal blue formal gown to the lights. Her voice climbed higher, "It's *ruined*."

"No, ma'am," Taft said, quietly, deferentially.

The woman stepped forward, her face inches from Taft. "What did you say?"

He hunched as if afraid, but his right foot slid backwards, stabilizing his center of gravity; his right hand fisted behind his back, invisible to the blonde—all one motion. The reflexes of a man with plenty of martial arts training.

Then his fist opened, his muscles relaxed, and I wasn't sure what I had seen.

"I didn't stain your dress, ma'am. I was just taking it to be cleaned."

Her eyes went wide, and she shook the dress at Taft. "I'll have your job and you branded again. I'll have you stripped naked and flogged in the streets."

"Please, ma'am. I didn't stain your dress. It was—"

"Are you calling me a liar?" Her voice dropped into a hiss that would have done a water moccasin proud. "You despicable, flawed, aberration. You *dare* to call *me* a liar, you malformed...*deviant.*"

I pushed my door fully open and said, loudly, "Taft, thank you so much for the excellent dinner tonight! I appreciate..." I let my words fade away, paused, looked around wide-eyed, then asked, even more loudly, "Is this woman hitting you?" I stepped fully into the hallway. "Help! Help! There's a woman hitting the porter! Help!"

Doors opened all along the corridor.

I continued shouting. "She's drunk, and I think she's beating Taft!"

"I am not drunk, you—"

The door behind her opened and her tirade abruptly cut off. The middle-aged man traveling with her said, "Koren, it's all right. Come back inside."

"It's not all right. Look what he did! You always say it fine, that it's all right when it isn't. That porter ruined my dress!"

"No, Koren," the man said. "You dropped whiskey sauce on it at dinner. I asked Taft if he'd try to get the stain out. He was taking it away to work on it."

Koren's face shifted from fury to embarrassment to calculation and back to fury. She glared at me, and I dropped my shoulders to make my already small frame look smaller and opened my eyes really wide to look younger.

Koren turned to Taft and whispered, "You fix this dress or I'll see you lose your job."

"Yes, ma'am. I'm sorry, ma'am. Thank you, sir. I'll try to get the sauce out of the dress." Taft skittered down the hall, the dress in his hands.

I gave Koren my meanest look. "You're nasty. And spiteful. And cruel. And selfish. And now your boyfriend knows how mean your personality is."

Koren turned and looked at her man friend. His eyes were downcast, embarrassed and humiliated for Koren's behavior. "Hope your beauty glamours don't fail. Then he'll know how you really look physically. He'll have the full picture of what you actually are." The man looked up quickly, taking in his mean-spirited girlfriend, his eyes narrowing. Maybe he'd finally figured out he'd been bamboozled. I shut the door.

I slept deeply, with a sense of malicious satisfaction. But in some of the stories I'd been taught as a child in Enclave, doing good and doing evil could both result in something the Pre-Ap humans called karmic payback. So evening up the score for Taft by standing up for him and pointing out the glamoured woman's flaws, might result in a case of seraphic punishment, if it was discovered that I had taken pleasure in my acts.

I woke up just after dawn as the train braked and rapidly slowed. I gripped the hand rails on the bed. Steel screeched on steel. The car shuddered, making my jaws clack together.

The jarring, quaking, deep vibration faded as the train came to a stop.

Nearby, I heard a loud crack. I leaped from the bed, threw on yesterday's human-ugly clothing, with the amulets still in the pockets. Barefooted, I rushed into the corridor along with most of the other occupants of the sleeper car. The woman, Koren, was standing there, dressed, her blond hair up in a twist. Behind her the door stood open, her compartment revealed. Her traveling companion lay on the floor, head turned to the side, in a pool of blood. His chest was unmoving, his eyes open.

I heard voices shouting, "Get down! Get down on the floor!"

In an eye blink, I realized several things.

The man was dead.

Koren held a pistol. Pointed at Taft. Who was on one knee on the floor. Hands raised.

Koren was surrounded by masked men. All dressed in black. All with guns. Pointing at the people in the hallway and away from Koren. And they were the ones shouting.

Also, Taft was armed. The outline of his gun was visible beneath his clothes, at his back. Taft was far more than he seemed.

Last, I realized that the train was being robbed.

My fingers twitched for the sword I had been learning to use. But it was safely stowed in the baggage car. I had no weapon but my wits. I figured that meant I'd be dead in seconds.

My amulets warmed up. My prime and one in my pants pocket. The disruptor jasper. Was it for guns? Oh. *Wrath of angels.* Lolo and her second sight.

"You've been nothing but trouble, you twerp." Koren shifted her aim, pointing the gun at me.

I gripped the jasper, whispered, "Guns."

Koren pulled the trigger. Nothing happened. Not a thing. "*Yes*," I muttered.

From the floor, Taft struck in a long, loose, easy, and deceptively powerful kick. His foot hit Koren's arm. The gun flew. Bone broke with sharp *crack.* Taft rose from the floor, fast, in the lion stance. He spun in a complicated set of moves that incorporated parts of several advanced techniques. Hands and feet snapping out. In less than two heartbeats, the men wearing black were down, disabled, incapacitated, dead, or unconscious.

My mouth fell open. Taft knew savage chi. He was a half-breed. Half-human, half mage.

Taft stood and adjusted his white jacket. "You folks go on back in your cabins. Everything is under control here."

A man down the corridor gasped, "You're a...*mule*." The last word was filled with distaste, his face pulled down into harsh lines, as if he was disgusted to have been rescued by a half-breed.

Taft's disfigured face twisted, but before he could speak, I said, in my best little-girl voice, "And he saved our lives. Taft is a *hero*." I clasped my hands in front of my chest and stared at Taft with what I hoped looked like adoring eyes. I wasn't much of an actor, but the man who clearly hated half breeds went silent. "*Our* hero!" I added just in case the humans were stupid too.

Taft chuckled and raised an eyebrow at me in a look that the others couldn't see. He turned his attention to them. "Not a hero. Just a train marshal, a Hand of the Law doing his job, and unspeakably grateful to the Most High for a misfire." He shook his head in wonderment, completely missing my horrified expression. "Seraphic intervention. Surely an instance of seraphic intervention."

Taft was *police*. Taft was undercover. Sweet seraph. I was in trouble.

I swept the horror off my face and tried to restore the adoring expression I'd been wearing only moments before.

Koren was on the floor of the cabin amidst the bodies of the men in black, holding her arm, making a piteous mewling sound.

"Koren Steinwald," Taft said, his voice officious, "I hereby place you under arrest for the murder of Harold Meechum, and for attempted train robbery. You and your men will be kept in the mail car under the watchful eye of my partner and remanded over to the proper authorities at our next stop. May the High Host have mercy on your soul, for the court system will not."

Turning back to me, he continued in his normal voice, "I've got it all under control. You're safe now. Go back into your room, little miss. I'll bring you breakfast soon."

I backed away and closed the door. Leaned against it. Tried to remember how to breathe.

Behind me, I could hear Koren curse as Taft handcuffed the prisoners, and then dragged them down the corridor to the next train car. The doors closed.

A Hand of the Law would arrest me. Torture me. Turn me over to the kirk. I was an unlicensed neomage who had just released a conjure in his presence. But maybe he hadn't noticed. "Misfire," he'd said. Was I safe? I must be safe. He hadn't arrested me and dragged me away with Koren.

I fell on the bed and pulled the covers over me, shaking with cold and shock.

It took quite a while to get the train back up and running. And then more time at the next stop. It would put us a day late getting to Mineral City, but I didn't care how long the trip was. I would be spending the rest of the trip locked safe in my room, having my meals left on the other side of the door.

T he days dragged on. I practiced with my amulets. Studied the *Book of Workings*. Got bored again quickly and read one of the Pre-Ap books. It was about a place where dragons and humans were friends and worked together to try to save their world. A world where people could *ride* dragons to fight a menace in the sky. It sounded so exciting and made me want to soar on a dragon. But no way were dragons in my world going to work with anyone. No way were they going to allow a human to ride them. Humans—or at least their souls —were tasty treats to dragons in my world.

F our days passed. We were a little over thirty-six hours late so far, making the trip far longer than Lolo had expected. Four days as my opal *Glamour* amulet faded and died several times and had to be recharged from my prime. And then my prime began to fade. It needed to be attuned to my energies. It needed to be recharged. And for that all I needed was a long train stop at a depot near rock. Lots of rock.

We had been climbing into the Appalachians for days now, our forward progress hampered by the meandering route necessary for a train to rise in altitude. And the Appalachians were stone.

Most of our stops to take on water and supplies were near towns, and towns were usually built on at least marginally farmable land, the soil of centuries overlaid on the bedrock. The train sometimes stood still for an hour or more, and passengers would leave to shop in the stores near the depot. But even with the town built on soil, there would have to be exposed rock somewhere—the dirt could be thin in the mountains.

Given time and rock, I'd be fine. I just needed to know when the next stop would be.

Summoning my courage, I dressed in long sleeves and thin gloves to cover my softly glimmering limbs, a kerchief over my hair. Lolo had packed human makeup, and I used some of that, inexpertly, on my face. I was surprised that Lolo even thought of makeup.

When Taft knocked on my door to deliver breakfast, I opened it wide and backed away.

"Are you okay, little miss?" he asked. "I know the robbery attempt was a terrifying thing for you. I promise you're safe now."

"Thank you. I do feel better. But I need to get out a bit. I want to buy a present for my adoptive father. Do we have a long stop soon?"

"We'll be pulling through Hendersonville at 10 a.m. and our layover there is close to four hours. We'll be shuffling the deck." At my blank look he said, "The cars have to be uncoupled and recoupled to a different kind of engine, one that's equipped with the proper devices

210

to melt snow and ice as we climb the last leg. You can shop, eat a meal, even take a tour of the old ruins, if you want."

Hendersonville had been badly damaged in the Last War, and a tour might give me a chance to get close to stone. "I'd like that," I said. "Thank you."

"Any time, little miss." He backed away and closed my door. I had to wonder why Taft was still on the train; he had foiled the robbery. But maybe train marshals stayed on the trains all the time.

<hr />

P romptly at ten, I was standing at the vestibule at the end of the car, holding a large bag and dressed in heavy layers, a knitted hat, and thick gloves for the weather, which had gone from cold to glacial with the elevation change. My makeup-covered face was the only skin showing.

The moment the train stopped, I scrambled down onto the platform. Rushing into town, I found a shop, where I bought a candle, a pair of knife-pointed hair-cutting scissors, and a box of salt that had a healthy mine-salt glow. Then I found a rickshaw with a runner who was willing to take me to the ruins. He was a strange little creature, not much taller than I and stick-thin, with an accent I couldn't place.

As he trotted away from the town, I lied, "My great-great-grandparents' home is supposed to be over that way." I pointed in a random direction. "It's a brick house that was destroyed by a stone spear in a battle with Darkness. According to my grandmother, it's a little off the beaten path. Do you know any houses with stone like that?"

"Aralbet knows everything about these ruins, missy ma'am. Everything. I know of five such destroyed houses, but only one with a spear of stone through its heart. I can take you to it, lady."

We passed numerous boulders and rocky outcrops, but they'd all lain exposed to the elemental damage of ice, snow, and air—useless to me. But in less than an hour Aralbet had delivered me to what I wanted. The remains of a brick house were scattered around a single shaft of mountain heart stone. Luckily, the stone didn't glow with the remembered taint of Darkness and it had been partially protected from rain by the metal roof that was still partly in place. "This is it."

Aralbet stopped the rickshaw and I slid to the ground. "I'm going to walk around it, okay? And stop to pray. My grandmother lost her entire family here, and I promised I'd light a candle and pray for them."

"Not until Aralbet sees if it's safe, missy ma'am." He pulled a short spike from the floor of the rickshaw beneath my feet. It was a flame-blackened and hardened stick with a makeshift iron point affixed to one end. He jogged around the house, stopping every now and then to poke the spike into holes. He wasn't very bright, but he had been working for tips for a long time, and he knew how to look important. He was also awfully sweet. Missy ma'am? Odd. "Okay, missy ma'am. You're safe to say your prayers. I'll stand here and guard you and wait."

"Thank you, Aralbet," I said, gravely. Satisfied that I might get away with my less-than-half-baked-plan, I walked around the house and chose a spot where brick and stone met and Aralbet wouldn't be able to see me. I'd forgotten to bring a blanket, so I emptied my bag and sat on it. With the last sparks of the handy-dandy cooking charm, I lit the candle and set it as close to the north as I could figure. Then I poured a narrow salt ring around me. And then I stabbed my left thumb with the scissors.

"Fire and feathers," I cursed, then quickly hushed myself, "that hurt!" I smeared the welling blood on my nearly dead prime amulet, and then on the roof-shielded side of the upthrust stone. I leaned into the rock, head bowed as if I was praying. "Stone and fire, water and air, blood and kin prevail," I whispered. "Wings and shield, dagger and sword, blood and kin prevail."

Beneath my fingers the prime hummed, the vibration high-pitched and fast. And it...sucked up my blood, pulling it into itself. Even the blood still dripping from my wound hovered in midair and then slapped wetly onto the amulet.

Light glowed. Energy, raw and intense, flooded from the stone spear into my prime amulet. Energy flowed from my prime to me, and back to the prime. The microstructures in the amulet shifted, realigned, reformed themselves. All of a sudden I felt...whole.

And the white onyx Arctic seal amulet that has been sitting dormant in my shirt pocket for the entire trip began to glow through the cloth. With mage sight I could see energy flowing into the seal from somewhere else, much more energy than even the stone spear had given me, energy waiting for me to tap it. Lolo had given me a lifeline: a preprogrammed link to an alternate CE source!

I wasn't sure exactly what I was doing, but with my prime amulet properly attuned I didn't have to know. I could just let creation energy flow from the *Link* amulet to my prime, and then into each of the pre-conjured charms. Relief left me breathless. My skin stopped glowing. My throat, which had been sore because my prime wasn't protecting me from elemental allergens, stopped hurting.

I sat back. I wasn't tired anymore, but I was hungry. Starving. I wanted peanut butter and jelly sandwiches. Muffins. Even tofu would be good about now.

I stood and scuffed the salt into the grass, knowing this much salt would kill even weeds, and feeling sorry for that. My Earth mage twin would have been furious. *Rose. Gone. Alone.* I forced tears away, snuffed the candle, and repacked the bag. I was alone. But I was surviving. That's what mattered.

Feeling better than I had since I left Enclave, I climbed back into the rickshaw and asked Aralbet to return me to the train depot.

I went to bed that night and slept well, knowing I could keep my secrets as long as I wasn't searched.

O n the next day I sat in the dining car with the other passengers. I read the dragon book again and enjoyed it just as much the second time. And I went to sleep knowing that it would be my last night on the train.

As my thoughts drifted toward slumber, I felt warmth against my skin coming from the amulets I'd placed under my pillow in the bed with me. The wooden charm that I hadn't been able to identify was hot. It was activated now, and I could feel a spell of forgetting. Lolo. What had Lolo wanted me to forget? *Seraph bones!*

Sleep took me.

When I woke, it was in an odd little bed that was rocking beneath me. The wool sheets were rough compared to the mage-touched sheets I slept under in the priestess's house. The clothes I was wearing were cotton, my socks knitted wool. Human-made clothes.

Memory returned, of my gift descending. Of the bitter tea Lolo had forced down my throat. I had been smuggled out of Enclave and put on a train. And—where was I?

Around my neck was a leather thong, the opal disc pendant lying on my chest. My mage attributes didn't glow, and I intuited a connection to the opal: I assumed it blanked them, making me look human, dull and ugly, keeping my secret from the human world.

There were hand rails on the side of the bed. I levered myself over them and down to the floor to find myself in a private cabin of a sleeper car on a train moving out of Enclave. Alone.

But, oddly, it didn't seem as terrifying as I'd expected it to be.

I dressed in the unfamiliar clothing and then looked to see what Lolo had sent along with me. Not much.

There was a knock at the cabin door and a branded man with mismatched eyes asked what I wanted for breakfast. When he returned with my meal, he told me to pack and be ready to leave. "We'll be at Mineral City at the 3 p.m. stop. I'll be bringing the rest of your luggage here shortly."

"Thank you," I said. "I'll be ready." And I tipped him well. He looked as if life might be hard for him.

At 3:10 the train stopped, though I could still feel it moving in my muscles and nerves. I was sitting on my luggage. The porter knocked on my door, and when I opened it, he said, "Little Miss, this is your stop."

"Little Miss" because I was only four feet tall and skinny. The porter thought I was a pre-teen human traveling to family. Rich family, hence the private compartment in the sleeper car.

He stacked my stuff on a cart, and I followed him down the narrow corridor, through the crush of people, my eyes on his mop of hair high above everyone else. The porter was tall, which was handy.

Outside, the smells hit me: ice and water and snow and the smoke of wood fires. The scent of stone, which was amazing. There was no natural stone in Enclave—New Orleans was built on centuries of accumulated river silt. The only rock was carried in by traders for use by Stone mages like me. But here, the very ground oozed Stone power!

"This way, Little Miss. Your grandmother said the man meeting you would be in the station and that I was to see you personally into his hands." I followed, feeling a hint of excitement. "Lemuel Hastings," the porter called out, his voice nearly as penetrating as a conductor's. "Lemuel Hastings! Got a passenger for you!"

"Thorn St. Croix?" a gravelly voice demanded. I turned, the anticipation quivering in my chest. He was a grizzled old human, maybe forty-five or even fifty years old, though I had little familiarity with old humans. The humans in Enclave all looked young, healthy, strong. This one was red-faced, his skin lined and browned, his head covered by a hat, his lanky body mostly hidden by layers. His eyes, brown as swamp water, landed on me. "A *girl*? What in saints' balls good is a girl?"

I felt as if I'd been hit with a mallet. All the air left my lungs. My excitement evaporated.

Hastings turned to the porter. "It was supposed to be a boy! Someone I could train up for my business, who'd get strong when I got old. Someone to take care of me." He leaned in, examining me, and the scent of the old man hit me. Pipe smoke and aftershave—something Lolo might mix, with sandalwood and sweet orange. And the scent of stone dust. I surprised myself by picking out the smell of raw hematite. There was reddish dust ground into his clothes.

The porter said, "Sir, I—"

I interrupted. "You've been working old bloodstone. You mine it yourself?"

Hastings spun back to me. "What do you know about *old* bloodstone?"

"Not heliotrope. Reddish bloodstone. Hematite. Full of iron. It can be used in cosmetics and industry and traded to mages in the Enclaves."

"How would I mine it?" he barked.

"Very carefully," I said, smirking.

"How old are you?"

"Fourteen," I said.

The porter's mismatched eyes widened as he took in my small size.

"I haven't hit my growth spurt yet," I lied. I'd hit one. There might be another. Or not. Neomages are much smaller in stature than humans.

Hastings grunted, and dug in his pocket, pulling out a stone. "What's this?"

"Heliotrope," I said instantly. "What a rock-hound would call bloodstone in these days."

"And this?" He handed me another rock, coarse to the touch, vaguely pyramidal in shape. There was a crystal buried in the rough, but not enough of it exposed to tell for certain by color alone. The rough was grayish, with maybe a hint of faintest lavender.

I rubbed my thumb over the sliver of exposed crystal. The gem hummed at me, rich and nigh unto perfect. I squinted up at him. "You sure you want me to say this out loud? In public?" I left the last of the phrase silent. *Where someone might steal your find and jump your claim.*

The man snatched the rock from my hand and the cart handle from the porter's. He glared at the porter. "I'll take her. You tell the old witch we're even now."

I didn't know what that meant, but when Hastings whirled and left the station, I followed, until the porter put a restraining hand on my shoulder. "I'm through here every month. He mistreats you or..." He stopped and rubbed his chin. "He mistreats you *in any way*, you meet me here next month, same date, same time. I'll take you back to New Orleans."

That was odd, for a human to feel such interest in—maybe compassion for—a person just met. "Thank you." I took his hand and shook it. "You're a good hu—person."

Before he could figure out that I'd nearly called him a human, I spun and followed Lemuel Hastings out the door and into the frigid air of Mineral City.

ROAD TRIP

JANET WALDEN-WEST

One

I kicked the bejesus out of my tire, wishing the rubber was something more flesh and blood to vent my irritability on. I had missing campers, a possible will'o'wisp to blame, and no backup.

And my last temporary-partner possibility had just called from the hospital, beat to hell by a poltergeist, with a "Sorry, Samantha, I'm out." Although she'd taken the initiative, sending me a replacement.

Hard to say which pissed me off more—not having help or getting set up like that one friend who can never find a date on her own.

I paced around the truck, swatting gnats and no-see-ums. The tail end of September, and Tennessee hadn't gotten the memo it was pumpkin spice and cozy sweater time.

The minutes ticked by, dread climbing up my spine and raising the hairs on my neck, like a late-season tick crawling up my leg. Two separate, experienced hikers had disappeared in southeast Georgia over the last week. The only survivor of the latest disappearance swore his missing friend babbled about lights in the forest before they bedded down for the night. The next morning—no friend.

A sweep with Search and Rescue dogs, and the forest service hadn't turned up a trace or a body, same as the first disappearance. With Fall Break approaching and leaves coloring up, people would turn out for day hikes on those trails, or weekend camping trips.

Boozy, happy, oblivious prey.

And I was standing around useless, waiting on some asshole hunter with time management issues.

I whirled for another go at my innocent tire. A gleaming gold and white SUV wheeled in, gravel spitting, taking the turn to the deer camp too fast.

The Escalade settled in a cloud of gray dust and pinging rock.

My irritation turned darker. I shook my arms out, shaking away tension and loosening muscles. Popping the knives from each forearm sheath, the hilts hitting my palms but hidden under my sleeves.

My supposed backup took her time, flipping the visor to check her lip-gloss. She finally popped out and surveyed me, a critical sweep from head to toe.

We'd never met, but I knew all about her. Hard not to. Not many creatures dared hobnob with human hunters.

Like she read my mind, this one smiled, showing unusually square, perfectly white teeth. "Well, as I live and breathe. It is the infamous Sam Vasquez. I thought Andi was pulling one of my legs."

The Kelpie might not be living and breathing long.

"And what are you going by these days?" Not that I expected her true name.

"Rachel Alexandra."

If you were going to use the moniker of famous female racehorses as your alias, why not go with the best?

"Go away, Rachel Alexandra."

"Fact—you needed a second. Fact—I owed Andi a favor. Fact—here I am." She checked the cuff of her suede blazer, tugging it straighter.

"Fact—I don't know you, I don't want to know you, I don't trust you. Bye."

Big liquid-brown eyes narrowed. "Fact—monsters never put their killing sprees on hold until your preferred backup gets her casts off. This creature isn't going to hold off snatching tourists because you're a snippy bigot."

True, but I wasn't hunting one supernatural with another breathing down my neck. Especially this one. "There are no swim-up bars or suites at the Bellagio for you to crash in where I'm going. You aren't qualified to help."

She smiled, slow and ugly. "I was a predator before your grandparents were born. I'm also difficult to kill. Say what you mean—you won't deign to hunt with me because I'm not human." She crossed her arms and stared me down. "And you'll sacrifice innocent lives for your bigotry."

I swore, fingers closing over the knife hilts until my knuckles creaked. I doubted her generosity came from giving a damn about human lives as much as it did the burning need to discharge whatever obligation she'd bound herself to.

My obligation was to oblivious people out for a weekend of fun and fresh air.

But she wasn't wrong. I chewed on the inside of my cheek and rolled the idea around, poking for weak spots. Andi had been my last resort, and Kelpies probably had little to fear from wisps. The incorporeal elementals used compulsion to mesmerize the unwary and lead them away. Kelpies shared a similar form of psychic suggestion. Maybe they were immune.

"I hope you've got something you can actually hike in." I eyed her Prada flats.

The Kelpie would make an acceptable stalking horse for this job. I just had to survive working with a creature who won human trust, then carried them to a watery death.

R achel's version of suitable outdoor wear consisted of old jeans —i.e. a pair worn twice—polished riding boots, and a luxurious, long-sleeved tee. An eye honed from side-gigs guarding the red carpet estimated her ensemble cost as more than peoples' mortgages. Maybe the wisp would be so taken with her fashion élan, I could kill it before it noticed me.

Her lip curled in a similar opinion of my wardrobe. I finished lacing my beat-up hiking boots and rose, tying a flannel shirt around my waist. It was warm enough to get away with a short-sleeved tee during the day. Plain cotton, three to a pack, thank you very much.

I tucked the two wrist knives in a duffel, since Tennessee Highway Patrol were not understanding souls. I kept the smaller blade though, tucked out of sight in my boot. Fallback in case of unreliable partners. "Truck's loaded. Thanks for the help, by the way."

"I'm the talent, not the roadie." She flicked a careless hand at me as I pushed past.

"Hope the talent packed or she's going hungry and naked."

Rachel waved a bag—one of mine, not that she'd asked to borrow it—and sashayed to the truck. She waited at the back bumper, dangling the pack from a fingertip.

She spent the first part of the drive fiddling incessantly with every button and gadget, lowering and raising the seat, messing with the air, and adjusting mirrors. The final straw came when she screwed up the radio presets. I slapped on the satellite station, queued a playlist, and cranked the volume past conversation-appropriate levels.

I watched Rachel out of the corner of my eye as music cycled from Daddy Yankee to Rob Zombie to scratchy Delta blues. I had no idea if Kelpies liked anything other than the song they sang as they dove underwater with their prey.

"I met him once." By some Kelpie trick, her statement rose over the song, without raising her voice.

I lowered the music and took my eyes off the road as a lonesome opening twang filled the truck. "Robert Johnson?"

She shrugged. "Joint below Memphis. Some cash and a little sweet talking got the white girl in."

Somehow, I imagined more than sweet talk was involved. "Were you the devil at the crossroads?"

She purred out a laugh made for rumpled sheets and luring men into damning deeds.

She switched her attention to me, and my skin crawled at the intensity. "Tell me, why all alone? All you hardcore live-by-the-gun-die-by-the-gun types seem driven to form adorable paramilitary thingies, or at least partner up with another camo-clad bestie."

I clenched the wheel, grief and stale coffee burning up my throat. The rumble strip under the tires whined a sharp warning. I relaxed my grip, edged back into a lane, and turned the question on her. "Why don't you have a partner?"

"There are few enough of my kind, and I don't care for other Kelpies even if we were more numerous."

"Human, then. Lots of people make poor life choices. You know, like those wealthy yet short-lived CEOs you enjoy marrying."

"Your sort don't seem to trust me. Besides, we know how human-supernatural partnerships end."

Maybe she was simply talking about humans aging faster.

Maybe not.

Not that human-human partnerships lasted, either.

Time for a new topic. "How about we discuss business?"

She yawned and tilted the seat, slouching lower, digging her shoulder blades into the seat and stretching. The rubber soles of her boots squeaked against the dash.

"Feet off my dash. Seriously, were you raised in a barn? Is that how it works?"

"FYI, I was raised in one of the first townhouses erected in Glasgow. As for plans, that's your area. You plan and find, I'll dispatch." Her boots tapped to the beat of Beyoncé's "Formation."

"*We* have to destroy its link to the world, or if it's too large, foul and desecrate the link beyond use."

She pushed her shades down her nose, glaring at me over the linked double-C emblem. "I was promised action and adventure, not a day of manual labor and polluting the Little Pigeon River."

"I didn't promise you jack. Besides, you'll probably get your chance. One of us has to distract it while the other handles the landscaping. Most wisps have unaddressed anger management issues."

That mollified her. Right up until we pulled into the state park.

"Day trip or will you be camping?" the park officer asked.

"Camping."

He handed over the form, but frowned at my ID, taking extra care to copy the information down.

I kept a smile plastered on and handed him back the form and extra fee. I was a brown girl, but at least my last name was Vasquez. He might not like it, but he wouldn't send in an anonymous tip to Homeland about supposed terrorist activity in the park. ICE might get a call though. Seemed to be happening a lot lately.

The auburn haired, porcelain skinned non-human beside me got a dopey smile and nod.

He handed me back a sticker and trail map, pointing to the sign displaying park rules.

"Camping?" Rachel's voice was ominous, some of the creepy Kelpie voice magic filtering in and visibly darkening the atmosphere in the car.

"We have to find the wisp first. The hikers all disappeared from the same general site, but that's still a crap load of acreage to cover."

I pulled into the farthest parking slot and hopped out, stretching for the sky and loosening stiff muscles.

The pissed Kelpie mouthed something that involved my ancestry and farm animals, glowering through the closed window and not moving from the comfort of the truck.

"You say the nicest things." I opened the hatch, transferring items into backpacks, and dropped her pack to the dirt outside her door. "Saddle up or go hitch a ride out."

Her fair skin colored, eyes going swamp-gas green around the edges.

"You can sit your ass in the truck for three days, 'cause I've got the keys and newer trucks are almost impossible to hot wire. But you still won't have fulfilled your oath to Andi. Alternately, you can risk getting Georgia clay on your lovely shirt, discharge your obligation, and get to kill something in a thoroughly gruesome and satisfyingly horrific manner." I buckled my pack, pulled out the map and compass, and ducked into the soft shade of the trail.

A metal door thumped forcefully, accompanied by swearing in Scottish Gaelic. Rachel appeared beside me, heavy pack dangling from one shoulder.

She hitched the pack higher, only to have it slip down again.

Without thinking, I reached around and pulled the other loop over her shoulder, shaking the pack to settle it, same way I'd done hundreds of times with my partner.

Rachel growled, the vibration accidentally helping center the pack.

I froze, the sound thrumming against my bones, a visceral warning.

This wasn't my partner. I was too close and personal with a creature I didn't trust. I stepped off and forced my voice to come out bored, despite my tripping pulse. "Hush and try to fit in, please. Act normal."

"Normal is another word for boring."

"Then you're golden." Shoving the compass at her, I folded open my map, tapping the rough circle I'd sketched in earlier. "These are the known vics. There are two backcountry official campsites in the area and who knows how many unofficial. One vic came from an official; one picked their own."

"So we wander all day. Glad insects don't care for Others." She lifted a perfectly filled-in brow at me.

The no-see-ems had already coalesced around my eyes and nose in a transparent cloud. The coating of bug spray on my face seemed to be more of a condiment.

I thought about zapping Rachel with the bug spray. "*Anyway.* We quarter the designated search area. Wisps can manifest during the day, but only if it's extremely overcast. We'll have to wait until dark to know for sure if I guessed right." That's when they lured victims. "For right now, we search for magic weirdness or bodies."

Once she gave up sulking, the Kelpie moved like she belonged in the forest. After leaving the marked trail, something in her seemed to shift. No twigs crunched under her feet, and she avoided briars and berry thickets. Or they bent away from her. I'd heard the old tales.

I followed Rachel's sure-footed progress and studied her. To her credit, she stayed focused. Her intense gaze swept the dark forest in slow arcs, nostrils flaring in and out, searching for changes. All she got for her effort was the constant trilling of crickets and the occasional deep thump of a bullfrog. Warm-blooded critters large enough to serve as prey kept a safe distance from the Kelpie.

Except me. So basically, I wasn't as smart as the average 'possum or trash-panda.

She also froze and tilted her head whenever the breeze shifted, searching for magical traces and decaying flesh.

I shivered in the sticky heat. No one knew if Kelpies were also scavengers or only ate fresh.

My fingers crept to my neck, and I played with the aged metal disk threaded on a thong. The charm helped against things messing with my head, but the ancient metal pendant was originally created to cut through artifice. It let me see Rachel as she really was. It was both disturbing and reassuring that my vision matched reality—tall, all lean muscle, and a few lines garnered from real-life tribulations etching dark-rimmed brown eyes, auburn hair in a modern cut. Her image moved through a faint watery haze, like seeing her through heat rising off scorching asphalt in summer.

A woman content enough in life.

That was more alien than the magical haze. I let thoughts of a lonely future I couldn't imagine go. "Break time."

I kicked at a log, waiting for any legless inhabitants to slither away before dropping down on the mossy bark and shrugging out of my pack, wiping sweat. A swig of cool water helped re-center me. The protein bar I dug out would help even more.

Her nose wrinkled. "How can you stomach those? They smell like plastic."

"They're cheap fuel. I'm assuming you don't always get the food source you prefer." My hand dropped to the knife in my boot.

"True. I haven't found a decent deli below the Mason-Dixon line, and it's impossible to find a fish taco here that isn't fried catfish." She pulled an honest to God cold pack and container of some sort of soup out, and I caught hints of curry and coconut, my stomach growling.

Her other brow lifted in challenge.

Check and mate.

She drank soup and lolled back on the pack, one leg bent, watching me over the top of it. "Talk to me about hunting wisps."

"Since you haven't picked up any traces, we quarter until dark, and see if anything comes after us."

"If it does?"

I tugged the neckline of my shirt lower with one finger, displaying the disk with its stylized Norse eye. It popped a faint, angry spark against the hollow of my throat. It didn't approve of Kelpies. "This'll keep me from naughty-wisp influences."

"I suppose you have one for me?"

"Nope."

"Ahh. I'm the bait."

"You probably have a natural immunity, but if not, hey, you won't have to pretend to be ensnared. We still need to find the thing's locus, which is where it kills the victims, so win-win."

Her eyes hazed to a watercolor effect, delicate aqua tinting the sclera. "Smart girl. Now, unlike you, I tend to avoid incorporeal annoyances, so tell me—what do we do with this locus thingy?"

"Depends. Smash or burn it if it's a small enough site. Magically deface it if it's too big."

"How...vague."

"Why do you think the packs are heavy, princess?"

The green changed back to soft brown. Maybe she thought I complimented her.

I buttoned up the flannel and slumped farther down, pillowing my head on the lumpy dual-purpose pack for a quick nap, and closed my eyes. Knife loose under my fingertips, in case soup wasn't the only thing on the menu.

Two

I glared up at the sudden influx of giant, filthy dust-bunny clouds, just in time to catch a fat raindrop in the eye.

"I don't do rain." Rachel was completely serious, voice reverberating with the same deep boom rolling in from the far-off coast. "Fix it."

'Cause, yeah. I could totally alter the weather. Although I wasn't crazy about seeing first-hand what rain did to water-based supernatural's self-control.

This far into the edges of the Okeefeenokee, we'd left caves and mountain behind. All we had were trees, too much obscuring underbrush, and hundreds of tiny springs, creeks, and rivulets.

Not that I was any fonder of autumn downpours than Runway Kelpie. Unlike summer's short, cheerful bursts, these tended to grab on and dig in with strong bear claws, here to stay. Even under a thick canopy, rain fell in a heavy sheet of water. The wind picked up, whipping my pony tail into my face and dropping the temperature a good twenty degrees in as many minutes. The flannel was soaked before I had time to dig out a thin rain poncho, and all the soft cotton did was wick up the chilly water and hold it close to my skin.

I consulted my coated map. As long as my map was accurate-ish and no one had seen fit to do a park clearance project since they map was updated, I had a possible solution.

An hour later, we didn't stumble onto our destination so much as I smacked nose to crumbling chimney with the old cabin. While Rachel jerked the tough fibers of kudzu and overgrown mulberry vines free in economical sweeps, I scrubbed at the stinging scratch on my nose.

I skirted the iffy remnants of decayed wooden steps in favor of the relatively solid narrow stone lip, more a projection of the rough foundation than a true porch. Since the shack was ninety-five percent stone, I gave it decent odds of not crashing down on us.

A thick layer of leaf mold and stuff better left to the imagination covered the floor and mounded three quarters of the way up the rear wall. Rachel deigned to step in once the floor held my weight.

Crawling on hands and knees like a human bulldozer, I shoved the debris to a corner, revealing moss and tannin-stained floor. The walls and chimney held out the rain, tiny stones between the tightly-stacked rocks acting as mortar. I raided Rachel's pack, rigging her sleeping bag over the narrow open door. The room warmed with that simple barrier between us and the storm.

I didn't notice her absence until a puff of damp blew in and Rachel materialized, dumping a clattering load of old, seasoned wood by the fireplace.

The liberal use of dry leaves from my cleaning spree finally generated a tidy blaze, the chimney either clean enough or full of enough cracks to draw without suffocating us.

The threat of possible pneumonia trumped modesty, and I fought the buttons on the flannel over-shirt that felt like it weighed ten pounds now.

Rachel pivoted to face the wall in an oiled move.

I stripped off jeans and socks, draping them in front of the fire, and pulled out dry replacements. "Your turn."

She turned back, swiping a graceful hand through her hair, the thorough soaking and humidity causing her careful blow-out to melt into loose curls. "There's little point." She stared at a particularly fascinating rock just over my head.

It took a minute for me to catch on. "Seriously? *You* under packed?" I hadn't inspected the small bag she'd *borrowed* from me for her use, simply stuffed hunting necessities in the outside pockets after she finished packing.

She looked down her nose at me. "I packed one civilized change of clothes; however, the weather forecast mentioned nothing about rain."

Meaning she'd merely tossed clothes in the fabric bag with no other protection. The packs were water *resistant*, not water *proof*.

I bent back to mine, unwrapped the plastic sheet from my sleeping bag and winged the bag at her.

"Pardon?"

"Stay wet, or use the bag. You won't fit in anything of mine."

She bristled, proving some hang-ups crossed species boundaries.

I smiled, sweet as fresh churros, and turned away. The squish of her wet shirt coming off and the longer, sucking-squelch as she peeled away reluctant jeans followed. Both landed by my toe, splattering me. I twitched her crap in front of mine to dry and hoped she never got the bitter stink of wood smoke out of the cashmere tee.

I brushed by her, not difficult in the one room building, evading a drip from the surprisingly intact metal roof and inched the makeshift door aside to peer out. No signs of it letting up and visibility sucked, rain and heavy tree cover creating a murky pre-twilight. Overcast. Dark. Something, some nagging fact, tried to come up for air in my waterlogged brain...

"How did you stumble on this hole?" Rachel's tone dripped disdain like the roof did water.

"Map."

"I saw the map the ranger supplied. There was nothing about tumbledown shacks."

Nosy Kelpies. "My own map." I tapped the laminated version, folded open on my pack.

"Which does not explain here." Her gesture took in the dilapidated refuge and sent the blanket off one arm.

"Real hunters make notes of important things and occasionally pass them on. Important things like abandoned homesteads."

The place might have been left during the removals of the 1800's. More likely though, it was a sad remnant of forced Relocations during the Depression, when FDR created jobs by way of his New Deal and Public Works, and expanded state and national parks.

"You need a map featuring better bolt-holes."

I dropped down in front of the hearth, hogging most of the heat, and pulled my hair out of the pony tail to help it dry, and shifted the focus, putting Rachel under the interrogation spotlight. "Why do you hate camping and the great outdoors? You're a Kelpie, a water horse. Last time I checked, lochs were outdoorsy."

Rachel draped over her pack the same graceful way she did everything. No wonder her résumé mostly included hunting the kinds of urban creatures that inhabited Tokyo, or pests that annoyed people vacationing in Cannes.

The sleeping bag slipped again to reveal hard, spare muscle. The kind produced by unyielding physical labor and sparse diet.

"I wasn't born to a loch, and I had my fill of wilderness after." For the first time, a hint of accent tempered her words. "Thirty or forty years of felling trees, moving stumps and boulders, and living in the weather cured me of any ridiculous concept of the desirability of getting back to nature. Nature doesn't like it when you try." She shifted, unconsciously leaning closer to the fire's comfort.

"When did you arrive here?" I made an expansive sweep with both arms to accommodate North America in general. "You have little to no accent."

"Just after the Revolution."

That'd be the American Revolution. I curled up facing her, intrigued.

"Escaping to nothing, carving trails, creating a home and a viable town—none of it was a thrilling experience. Don't believe all those documentaries that paint it as harsh but rewarding. Mostly, it was dirty and painful."

"Then why come?"

"We all have our reasons."

"Killed the wrong villager and stirred up a mob with torches, hmm?"

She flipped the sleeping bag so that fabric shielded her face. "There was a death, but it wasn't at my hands."

Something in her voice and the remote look haunting her face hinted it might be wise to stop with the reminiscences.

Unused to feeling pity for supernaturals or party princesses, I let it go. The fire danced and crackled, drawing me into its dance. The heat and low drum of the rain lulled me.

Fire. Light. Daylight...

"What are you thinking about?" Rachel's hypnotic voice snaked around the room, low and soft. Adding to my reverie, not pulling me out.

"It's darkish out."

"Umm-hmm," she replied in a lazy sigh.

Missing hikers and times and weather clicked, snapping me out of the almost-trance.

My pulse jumped, and I glared at the Kelpie. "Try to bespell me again and you'll never live to discharge that debt you're carrying. Wonder what happens to a 'supe's soul in cases like that?"

"I tried nothing. Although I'm not above using a lazy, distracted hunter's self-hypnosis for personal amusement."

Not lazy, but definitely distracted and careless. I wasn't used to protecting my back from my own partner. I stuffed that pain away, of having a missing piece in my soul, and shook my phone out of the case, gyrating and contorting like a Cirque de Soleil performer until it got one grudging bar. "Put your brain power to good use. You ever wonder why now? What roused this wisp? They're tied to objects, and not exactly Mensa material on top of that. The likelihood of one getting an itch to mix things up and move locations? Not instinctual."

The Kelpie made a noise under her breath, either agreement or amusement.

I wobbled in a one arm up-one out position, awkwardly typing and waiting while the line crept slowly, searching.

"Hah!" The website opened, confirming my guess, and I slapped the phone across my palm.

"Get the latest celebrity divorce gossip?"

"Did that before we hiked in yesterday. Those hikers? There was a storm the night before one disappearance, and the day of the other."

"Meaning what, in relation to my life and ending this adventure?"

Water sprites. It could be coincidence: rain, water levels peaking, the deaths. Except coincidence was just another word for clue. My heart plummeted from Everest heights to Grand Canyon depths.

Water. Which we were surrounded by in the form of creeks, stream heads, rivers, ponds, marshes and, eventually, the ocean. Tracking a sprite to its source here was worse than searching for a specific grain of sand on the beach.

Frustration rose, a headache tapping at my temples.

"—am. Samantha!"

Rachel's exasperated voice whipped at me like a cat'o'nine tails, causing me to wonder how long I'd been lost in my own head. "Jeez, what? And knock off the voice theatrics." I rubbed at non-existent lash marks along my bare arms.

Her teeth gleamed, larger in the firelight, a green-blue haze outlining her.

I dropped into a crouch, knife flashing between us. Her image wavered and reflected back from the silver like she was underwater.

She snorted and dropped to sit cross-legged, fingers tapping an annoyed rhythm on the warped floorboards. "Enough foreplay. What were you thinking about?"

I waited for her to spring, hazy after-images still flickering, screwing up my vision.

She stopped tapping, leaning to the firelight and holding her fingernail out for inspection, frowning at whatever chip or hangnail she discovered.

After a few seconds, I tucked the knife away and stood. Heart still pounding out of rhythm. "I was thinking. Clearly you aren't familiar enough with the action to recognize it."

She cocked her head, attention drilling into me. As if she was burrowing past the surface, looking for my lie.

"I'm ninety-nine percent sure we're not dealing with a wisp," I blurted, before she amped up the weirdness. "I think this is a water-based wraith."

Lean muscles corded, then relaxed. "Interesting."

Not the response one usually received when mentioning a power-ful, sentient monster that ran on hate and vengeance. I collapsed in front of the waning fire, crossing my legs and leaning elbows on my thighs.

The fire leapt as Rachel skillfully arranged more leaves and cracked up branches to feed the flames.

Wisps were elementals. They didn't think. Just flickered and led anything that followed them to its death in a swamp, a mindless one-trick pony. Wraiths had been human. Screwed over innocents. The worst and the most powerful creatures because they had some sort of legitimate grudge that lent them strength.

Murders. Suicides. Ungodly acts.

"Killing wraiths?" Rachel prodded. "The condensed version."

"Wraiths want revenge, justice, or closure. Depends on why they died. And the culture they came from, its rules, limits, and expectations at the time of their death. I doubt this one is a recent creation. It takes time to stockpile the power to manifest and kill." I turned to her. "You've been around longer than I have. What groups were most likely here, on this stretch of dirt?"

Rachel's coppery brows knit in concentration. "My territory and what passes for the northern part of Georgia now was primarily the English and my Scots. They left the Carolina colonies to find their own way. More Irish came after the potato famine." Her accent and speech pattern altered, becoming more clipped and formal as she relived those days.

In a whisper, I asked, "What about here? Did you hear tales or rumors? About the folk here before and after you arrived?"

"Aye. The Native Nations. Us. Others came to these shores much later. Wars create lasting aftershocks."

I cast through my eighteenth and early nineteenth century European history. Rampant expansion. Constant conflicts between monarchies. It involved...everyone, even into India and the Far East. Those wars nurtured the seeds leading to the first World War so much later, displaced Europeans from the continent venturing over, well after evicted Highlanders and starving Irish had. All of Europe eventually, west to east...

"Rusalka." I breathed it like an evil prayer, skin pebbling while a full-body shiver followed.

Out of nowhere, a sleeping bag fell around my shoulders, smelling faintly of peanut butter and banishing the chill.

Backlit by a flare of her power, Rachel's dark eyes seemed to float in front of me, framed by the two devilish red waves that had dried and fallen on either side of her face. "I taste your fear. What are these creatures?" she asked, soft as warm velvet brushing bare skin.

"Slavic," I whispered back. "Whatever name you want to give to the Eastern European countries now. Unwanted daughters. Virgins raped and murdered. Pregnant women drowned by lying, cheating lovers. Wives killed by suspicious or unfaithful husbands. Both our victims were male. Rusalkas are wronged women."

"What do they want?"

"Their honor back. Revenge. Neither of which they can usually ever achieve." Anger knifed through me.

I turned at the rasp of fabric and *hiss* of a zipper. Rachel was donning the driest pair of her jeans, shirt already on and face turned away.

I exhaled hard. "Doesn't matter, beyond knowing they are the strongest sprites out there. Their locus is where their bones came to rest, even if there's nothing much left. It has to be obliterated." Regret coursed through me over the sheer unfairness. There wouldn't be any justice in the afterlife, if one existed.

"Let's go."

"Charms or no, I can't see my hand in front of my face, much less I.D. a site, even though we are in the general area. It will be subtle. Right up until the owner pops up and tries to kill us. You?"

Reluctantly, she shook her head. "Fair point. My ability to sense the Other is intolerably heightened with the rain, and this land is steeped in magic. I'm drowning in it. I'd need someone with me to discern a ley-line from a wraith."

"Fine, then. We wait 'til it lets up and hope no one else is closer or more appealing than us." I upended both packs, re-sorting now that I knew exactly what I required.

Rachel had joked, but she was one thing I especially needed now—bait.

The rain mocked us all afternoon, spiced up with the occasional boom of thunder and lightning. A sharp snap followed by a long, shredding groan-thump announced the demise of branches and a smaller tree, adding to the fertile loam. Our tree-covered roof leaked faster, but held. Fall was still tornado weather in the South.

Rachel withdrew, lurking in a corner. Fairly pointless in a ten-by-ten space. She seemed downright flirty at the meet site. Now, she was standoffish.

I didn't know why being ignored bothered me.

I requisitioned our bags, since they were really my bags, pulled out my last apple and her last container of soup. I nestled the container by the fire and rotated the bowl every few minutes.

When the contents felt warmish from the outside, I swirled it temptingly in her direction. "You should tank up because I'm expecting a fight." The food and blackmail coaxed her out, and I scooted, opening a spot in the miniscule circle of hearth fire.

I drew my knees up to my chin, wrapping arms around them and exhaling. In the confined space, I bumped Rachel's shoulder, catching a fading hint of something green, almost clover-like, from her hair.

She twitched, then settled. "You have doubts about our success. Doubts that I'm capable of helping."

Startled, I rolled my chin so my cheek rested on the worn denim, facing her. She hadn't touched her liquid meal. "Where'd that come from?"

"You wish you had someone different in my place."

"Don't poke around in my head."

"No need. Let's say I understand loss. Yours sits fresh and heavy on you."

Bitch.

But I still had to work with her. I did my best to mimic diplomacy. "I wish we had more backup because Rusalkas are major league. This is more than Andi and I anticipated."

"What else is bothering you?"

At my sharp look, she shrugged. "Again, no magic involved. I've had generations to understand body language. It's far more reliable than spoken language."

"I don't like relying on a partner."

"Lie." Rachel cocked her head, hair falling around her white neck like sugar maple leaves on frost.

She looked completely relaxed, ready to keep up the lie-detector bit all day. "Fine. I don't like working with a partner I don't know. It's nothing personal."

"Mostly," she said, smiling. Less feral this time, more a soft curve of lips than bared teeth. "You don't care for this job, either. The endorphins you give off changed once you discovered it was a Rusalka."

I wanted to bitch at the minor invasion, except we were sitting shoulder to shoulder. Almost like friends. Almost like real partners.

I rolled my head, vertebra popping. "It's... I eliminate evil things. Black and white scenarios with a high level of personal job satisfaction. This Rusalka thing? It feels so unfair." There was that word again. It had been jackhammered home this world had nothing to do with fairness, and yet I couldn't shake the concept.

"These women died horribly." I played with a string hanging from the edge of my sleeping bag. "They were likely frightened and ridiculed right before they died. And now, I'm planning to do more bad things to them. Rusalkas are strong because an actual portion of that person remains. Don't get me wrong—they don't get a free pass, but this doesn't feel like justice. They suffered once, and now they'll suffer a final time." Sitting in a moldering, leaky shack with only a Kelpie for companionship, and a puny blaze—those were still comforts. Something lost forever to the dead women, basically thanks to trusting or being entrusted to the wrong person.

"You don't believe they go somewhere better after they're released? That human souls ascend at death?" Rachel asked, hunching almost imperceptibly.

"Let's say I've seen an enormous sampling of evil things, evil acts, and magic of every variety. I've never witnessed inexplicable miracles or any reprieve that wasn't the direct result of human actions. So no. No heavenly choirs, no open bars populated with honored warriors and big breasted women in chain mail, no fields of magic butterflies and roses." I faced the fire again. "You're into the rest of this humanity thing, so are you religious? A devout woman?"

She hesitated at that. "Believe what you will, but Selkies are human until…later in life. I was raised in a time where society's laws were God's laws. They were impossible to separate. I used to pray, once." She wrapped her arms around herself.

"Did you pray for yourself?"

"No. For…for others."

"What happened?"

"Nothing," she said, flat and hard.

"Exactly."

Three

R achel did her best to mesh with the stonework after our theological discussion, cold and silent.

I couldn't stay still, so I monitored the weather, ducking under the soaked door cover every few minutes.

Once I clearly made out a mimosa frond fifty feet past the house edge, I pronounced the storm done. Fifty-ish feet was shooting range. The fact there was no way to shoot a Rusalka was beside the point.

As soon as I tore the blanket free in a harsh rip of used duct tape, Rachel reanimated, balling the sleeping bag into a more or less circular mass. I rolled mine tightly, stomping to express rainwater. Both went on her pack, since it was the lightest, only holding clothes, odd bits, and the last of our food. Mine was heavier because it had the fun stuff.

I tightened the charm around my neck. Maybe the disc was strong enough to penetrate a Rusalka's illusion. Mostly, the beaten metal was simply one of my miserably small stash of keepsakes from someone no longer here.

Rachel's preparations consisted of Calvin Klein's version of autumn hiking gear, a green plaid button-up with French cuffs, and the riding boots. By most standards, she was gorgeous. The kind of true auburn hair that couldn't be replicated by dye and stylists, arched brows, good cheekbones, and mobile lips. She was sex appeal and arrogance in high-end denim.

I hoped it was enough. That just looking at Rachel and her glowing health and confidence, her obvious privilege, would piss off a creature that had been sacrificed because she wasn't a powerful enough woman.

"To be clear, once we find this thing, we work together. You do what you do best—entertain and flatter—while I do the heavy mystical lifting." I doused the last of our fire, telling myself the request had nothing to do with my guilt over using the Kelpie.

"Careful. You almost sound concerned."

"I don't want to listen to Andi bitch. She seems to consider you a friend, although why escapes me."

"She seems to hold you in the same esteem, for some equally unfathomable reason." Rachel tossed my pack at me in an unsettling display of strength.

I caught it and staggered, the wall saving me from ending up on my butt.

"You're still lying though. You have another reason to act like a concerned Girl Scout leader."

I whirled and plunged outside. Better a vengeful Rusalka than more psychoanalysis.

"This way." I ducked under a vine, a drop of water finding the opening in my collar and rolling down my spine to join the dozen others already soaking my waistband and the tied-up shirt. Storm done, the temperature had jacked back up, leaving a suffocating mist.

"Why?"

"We're close to the second vic's campsite."

"And?"

"Gut feeling, okay? This feels right." I leaned my rear against a coastal pine and rechecked the map. "Near the campsite" was still a hell of a lot of acreage. Nothing of note, other than a small stream that tapered off, going underground.

Rachel ghosted up beside me, cocking her head and watching me. Intense. Predatory.

I folded the map away, something about the stream nagging at me. The stream that just disappeared. Cut off before its time.

"Brag," I whispered.

"Pardon?"

"I think the Rusalka is close. Brag about your fantastic, glam life. About your endless conquests. Career. Travel. Talk about all the traveling you do."

I linked an arm through Rachel's.

She jumped and dragged us sideways a foot, like a horse shying, muscles turning too cold and too hard to be human.

I pinched the snot out of the inside of her elbow, a vicious twist guaranteed to leave a bruise on anything warm-blooded.

She gaped at me, jaw dropping. But she regained control.

I made *get with it* eyes, raised a brow at her and my voice to the forest. "So, how was your last date? Where was it? Paris?"

"Yeees," she finally answered.

"Is he still around?"

"No."

"You dumped him, huh. Sex no good?"

The corner of her lips twitched up. "You could say that. Not terribly adventuresome."

As we walked, Rachel got into character, recounting trips and lovers.

Girl was a player.

During a particularly vivid description involving a tryst in the Winter Palace and a stolen Faberge egg, the air seemed to quiver.

A *splash* sounded. Silence followed, spreading like ripples from a rock tossed in a pond. Large wildlife froze while smaller creatures hunkered down or went to ground. The stink of mold and things found rotting under dark, dank logs and better left that way replaced the normal wetland and clean ozone smell from the storm.

A glow twinkled to my left, like old-fashioned Christmas tree lights. If anyone chose bilious green as a festive color.

I squeezed Rachel's arm then dropped it, freeing us both, and patted the row of mesh pockets along the side of my pack, double-checking artillery. "Tell me more about what you did with that egg."

"In a moment. I need to catch my breath. *In silence.*" That was a warning, as the light vanished. The Kelpie tilted her head, attempting to pinpoint it again.

The lights reappeared, ran together as a ball, and flashed into brilliance, streaking at us like a meteor entering the atmosphere.

Then, the Rusalka was there.

Pretty, in that first flush of youth, her cheeks still faintly rounded with the last traces of baby fat. She had an apron over the sack dress, only a line of embroidery at the hem. Her hair was still in pig-tail braids, tied with bits of twine.

She focused on Rachel.

Since I wasn't her intended victim, I wasn't supposed to be able to see her. Playing along, I kept eyes on Rachel as the creature slipped behind me and nearer Rachel. I had to trust her to clue me in if things went bad behind my back.

She's not your real partner, and she's not human.

"God, you're bossy." I made a show of jerking several steps away, giving me room to fight.

Rachel's eyes shifted in the opposite direction. I backed farther so the Rusalka was in my peripheral vision. Not that I needed confirmation. The hairs on the back of my neck and arms were trying to hop off my body.

The iron disc circumvented glamours and showed truth. Audio? Not so much. The girl's lips moved, and I caught the occasional whisper of a word. "Lover. Lay...arms."

As the litany continued, I drifted farther away. The Rusalka inched closer. She fixated so tightly on Rachel, I wasn't sure the creature knew I existed. The stench of dead fish and disturbed mud intensified.

She cajoled, and Rachel answered in excited Russian.

I hoped the Kelpie was faking. My Kelpie compulsion-immunity theory wasn't exactly field-tested.

Rachel stepped closer to the girl, seemingly mesmerized, and my stomach bottomed out.

When the girl held out a hand, Rachel slowed, keeping just out of reach.

Okay, she wasn't spelled, and we weren't screwed.

I paced them, on the periphery of their intimate chat, and tried to blend with flora and fauna.

The Rusalka bent her round face, eyes to the ground, then peeked back up at Rachel, a sweet smile curving youthful lips. Rachel said something, and the girl clamped hands over her mouth to cover an unheard giggle.

Maybe *we* weren't screwed. Maybe *I* was.

Rachel wasn't *nice*. She didn't make girls giggle. She had a cultivated appearance and smooth charm to lure in prey. Expensive soup aside, generations' worth of men and women had undoubtedly fallen for her, and died.

The Rusalka was a water-wraith. Rachel was a Kelpie, a water demon.

Rachel gave that devilish, mega-watt smile. The Rusalka twirled, skirt lifting slightly and braids flying.

Rachel laughed and followed when the girl skipped away, looking back over her shoulder with a silent giggle.

Letting the Rusalka lure her, or the pair of them working together to lure me?

I slipped and regained my balance, adrenaline leaving a metallic taste on my tongue. Dampness wicked up my ankles. I glanced down to wet rocks and a newly swollen stream, water lapping around the tops of my boots.

The Rusalka whipped her head around, finally noticing me.

I pretended to frown at my soaking boots, looked up to the heavens as if asking for patience, and complained loudly while avoiding *seeing* the wraith. She paused, then went back to dimpling and beckoning at Rachel, while I bitched about wet socks and horrible camping trips.

This whole section of park was a giant mud puddle. The significance of the Rusalka's abrupt shift in attention when I touched this stream meant something.

I stepped clear of the stream, paralleling it on land.

The knives on my forearms were a comforting weight, and I squinted hard, keeping my maybe-friend, maybe-foe Rachel in focus. Whether they were double-crossing me or not, we all had the same destination, the Rusalka backing closer to where the stream vanished. To where I hoped its focus was.

I could dump a backstabbing Kelpie body in and destroy it with the Rusalka's link to this world, if need be.

Whatever tale Rachel spun, the girl enjoyed the attention.

The cozy courtship flew apart with the shock of a stealth-bomber attack.

The Rusalka skipped, grabbing for Rachel's arm. The Kelpie threw herself sideways in a haze of non-human speed, a wink ahead of the Rusalka's fingertip.

Rachel flashed out of sight for an instant.

I spun, searching for her, and tripped.

My hand slammed into rock. Knuckles split and my blood smeared over uneven stones. Worked stones, not much different from the base of the shack we'd hidden in. The remnants of a well.

The Rusalka whirled to me.

Bloated, fish-nibbled skin replaced the sweet baby face. The clothing turned to torn, rotted strips, allowing bone to show through. The braids vanished, leaving long, trailing patches of bleached hair between skull and shredded gray-blue flesh.

The lipless mouth opened, and keening tore the air, her voice audible now.

Her song hit me with physical force. I dug fingers into mud and leaf layers, but the sonic impact shoved me across the ground, belly scraping through dirt and over stone.

I clawed and scratched. Finally rammed fingers deep in muddy earth and stopped face down. My head hung over a dark hole.

The well had held together, with ground water so close. Narrow and plenty deep enough to drown and hide a body though, two hundred years ago or now.

Another subsonic shriek tore through the air. I jammed toes in and braced my knees hard against the rocks. My head banged ground, and un-mortared rocks tumbled, ending with a series of splashes.

Pushing me closer to drowning head first in a haunted well.

The Rusalka burst into view, hovering over me, her dress hem and bare feet replaced by a glow from her waist down. Fingers stripped of flesh and muscle, overly sharpened at the tips, flashed at my face.

I pitched left, losing another inch of safety. She missed me, nails sparking against the well.

I rolled hard. Hit a root and stopped belly up.

The Rusalka drove both hands down, aiming for my stomach. I twisted, shirt cuff hiking up and losing flannel and skin. The charmed silver knife strapped on my arm caught her sulfurous light, reflecting it back.

The wraith hesitated, twirling in place. I shook the hilt free, flipped the blade, and sliced outward.

The metal passed through her.

Her arm dissolved to vapor. Reappeared unharmed.

She grabbed my shirt, pulling me closer to the pit. Her hand melted fabric and brushed bare skin over my ribs. Fire shot through me, fritzing nerves along the way. Cloth sizzled, and the stink of burned cotton and charring flesh fought the smell of river muck and rot.

I added my scream to hers.

A deep, throaty roar joined ours. Arrogance and disdain coated me like mud, Rachel's Kelpie skills sending emotions at us like weapons. Her hatred didn't need words.

I was an annoyance.

Rachel was the chosen prey.

The Rusalka's keening took on a malevolent pitch. Warmth trickled down my jawbone. Blood from my ruptured eardrum, human ears not made to withstand the supernatural acoustic assault.

The creature launched at Rachel.

They whirled in a mad dance, the wraith's form flashing from the diseased, bruised ball of light to sharp bones. A neon green glow from

Rachel's eyes created a freakish counterpoint, her hands turned to claws.

Rachel lashed out, and the Rusalka faded to mist. A gobbet of mist flew away, leaving a trail like ichor until both winked out. The wraith shrieked in surprise.

I couldn't touch her, but Rachel could.

The Kelpie pressed her advantage, lunging again.

The Rusalka's arms lengthened, mist and bone twisting together. She reached inside Rachel's space and sank long, glowing fingers in the Kelpie's side.

Rachel spun in a furious arc with a neighing shriek. Wet tearing and a crunch reached me. Flesh, and at least one of her ribs, giving under the wraith's fury.

Instead of diving for the stream, increasing her power, Rachel spun farther. Leading the wraith away.

Away from me.

I scrunched into a precarious half-crouch. The pack hung, angled wrong, the waist strap burnt through. I grunted and wrestled it. The bottom pouch was empty, burned as well, its load lost while I rolled around. I patted higher. Found mesh and hard metal and plastic inside. I ripped at the drawstring, fingers closing on the last two explosive discs.

Something smashed into me like a pissed off linebacker.

I flew back, knocked off my heels. My spine bent over the rim of the well.

Rachel and the Rusalka twisted and slashed over me.

One clipped me, shooting me farther over the yawning hole, ass dropping into space.

The heavy, unbalanced pack twisted and plunged into the opening. Folding me in half and jerking me the rest of the way into the well with it.

I fell-slid several feet, before textured rubber boot soles and desperate fingers found purchase. My harsh breath filled the tunnel, pounding blood in my temple almost covering the snapping and crashing from the fight above. I arched, pressing the pack into the opposite side as a brace.

My arms shook, more adrenaline than fatigue—for now. Fingers cramped, wedged in slick notches, crap clogged under the fingernails not torn off. A hard edge pressed into my palm. The disc.

Only one, though, the other lost in the fall.

Another wail echoed. An answering roar sounded, the feel of pain in this one, even with the stones muting sound.

Willpower loosened one of my fingers, then the other four. Time was cold molasses as I inched my hand across my chest to the opposite arm. Blood and nastier crap slicked it, but the second knife was still there, and came free for me.

I angled the blade, sharp edge against fabric, and finished off the torn shoulder strap. Inched the knife farther, muscles in my forearm burning from the constricted motion. I misjudged, and the metal tip drew more blood before I got the edge under the wide chest strap.

This time, sawing the undamaged, sturdy nylon took forever. Fight crashing overhead, Rachel's screams coming faster together, the time rushed.

The last string parted. I shrugged and straightened my knees to keep wedged, shoulder blades aching, bending enough the shoulder strap slid, freeing the pack.

It landed, splashing hard enough that bottom muck flew up to hit me.

I cycled through options.

Weighed the influx of civilians in the next days and weeks and the awakened Rusalka, strong enough to shred a grown, powerful Kelpie.

Hunters all accepted that we had shelf lives with short expiration dates. Once I didn't show back up, Andi would know what happened.

There wasn't anyone else left to do more than raise a glass in passing.

My pack was filled with salt, holy water, and blessed charms, enough to purify my death. I wouldn't come back like the Rusalka, a monster for another hunter to put down.

I still closed my eyes, not able to watch. Head bowed against the disgusting, slick wall, I depressed the button on the charge, and opened my hand.

Claws wrapped around my wrist. Jerked up, toward the open air, my shoulder joint popping and pain lancing down my arm.

I fell face down in the sludge and twisted like I had no spine, rolling to get face up.

The Rusalka rushed me, lips stretched and hands bathed in dripping green flame.

Rachel reared between us, looking less human than the Rusalka. She towered over me, blocking out the sky, skin pulled tight and translucent, eyes glowing fresh, pure green. Fangs to put an ancient cave lion to shame framed her upper and lower jaws.

The explosive's booming quake hit.

First on the physical plane, knocking Rachel sprawling on top of me in a crushing heap.

The other charges, and the magic inside my pack, blew. A second wave rocked us.

This one hit the metaphysical plane.

The claws sinking through Rachel's wide back to reach me blew apart. Insane green fire drifted to mist and disappeared before it touched the churned-up ground.

My vision faded away with the mist.

Four

"Samantha?"

The Gaelic-accented whisper welcomed me back to consciousness.

I tried for Rachel's name, and wheezed instead. I coughed, feeling like something in my chest was coming loose, but finally made it from flat on my back up to one scraped, bloody elbow. "Yeah."

Rachel grunted something back, bent in half and breathing hard.

Wisps of disturbed dirt, mold, and tinted smoke trailed from a foot away.

No adorable, vengeful Rusalkas.

Just silent forest and us.

I flopped back, mud splattering. The cold coated my side, and I sighed in relief. Duty finally won out, and I levered up on both elbows.

The last of the cursed well made a sunken depression, no longer marring the landscape. Water bubbled up in gasps yards past, the streamlet re-emerging.

"That was a spectacularly stupid play," I confided to my sorta-partner.

The palm-sized scorch on my ribs contributed to my general crankiness. I found one clean-ish square on the inside of my shirt and scrubbed away the muck clogging my lashes. When I blinked hard, tears washed away the last irritants, and I could focus.

The sucking clay grudgingly gave up its hold, and I hauled up to my ass, then to my knees.

"Stupid, but it worked. Go, us," I said.

When Rachel didn't snark back, I crawled the few feet separating us, looking up since she was still bent over.

Oily sweat beaded her face. She breathed in wet pants, ribs heaving, like a spent horse.

"How bad?" I scooted closer.

Her eyes stayed closed, deep lines etched around them and her mouth, lips pressed into a tight line.

She grunted, hands on her knees as muscles quivered, bracing to stay upright. "Feels as though it's still clawing from the inside. Burns."

I touched the back of my hand against her forehead. Her skin was clammy-cold under mine, even with the exertion and humidity.

I scooped up her abandoned pack and double-checked for anything else we'd lost, finding one knife buried under mud. What-ever the Rusalka had done to Rachel, sitting around in a national park after we'd just blown a chunk of it to hell, a chunk that would reveal who knew how many human remains, wasn't an option.

"Ready?" We weren't partner-partners but seemed to have developed our own shorthand.

She gave a tiny nod.

I arranged the pack so it only occasionally thumped my raw side and got a shoulder under her armpit, painfully raising us both.

By the time we stumbled into the empty camp where the second victim disappeared, I was ready to throw up on her riding boots. Rachel grew heavier with every other step, the exact opposite of what should be happening with her supernatural healing ability. My burn was an angry throb, movement and sweat not helping.

Dropping the pack, I kicked it, blessing Rachel for her halfhearted packing. The sloppily rolled sleeping bag on top fell free and unfurled. Our descent was more a controlled fall.

"Hey, you still with me? I'm gonna be super pissed if I went through this trouble for a corpse," I said as I helped her flat on her stomach.

Her rough exhale wasn't all that reassuring. I wiped my reclaimed knife clean on my jeans and slit the remains of her shirt from collar to hem, rolling each half down an arm.

I almost made good on the throwing up, bile rising.

Burnt Kelpie flash smelled worse than seared human's. The gash started over a rib, the break clean. The snap I'd heard during the fight. Deeper gashes continued around her torso, one exposing an edge of lumbar vertebra. Another jagged tear showed deep red-brown liver. None of them were closing up, a slow trickle of rank, dark pus oozing out.

I dug around in the pack, finding my phone in the bottom. Even better, the screen woke when I pushed the side. Tilting it got me a bar and I hit speed dial, hoping for my version of a miracle.

A sleepy surfer-dude voice answered. "Man, do you know what time it is?"

"Yeah, Sylvester, I do. After lunch, even Pacific time. Get up and earn your retainer." At least he only sounded sleepy as opposed to baked. He was the only surfer-stoner witch I'd ever met. He also happened to be the most powerful one anybody had run across. The combination got him in a lot of trouble that I often ended up getting him out of.

"Hey, boss lady. How's it hanging?"

"By your dangly bits if you don't sober up and pay attention. I've got issues here."

"Sure, sure. What's the problemo?"

"Wraith attack. Real Old World type, a Rusalka. Got some wounds that aren't looking good. What gives?"

His voice cleared, scary talented brain taking over, curiosity piqued by the conundrum. "Since you're walking and talking, at worst it should be a bad second- or third-degree burn. Normal first aid. Oh, and scar powder. I'll mix you up a new batch and ship it out ASAP."

"I'm seeing some nasty black goo and the wounds are—I dunno—widening? Still burning, but in slow motion?"

"Not possible on a human. The only time they can work mojo outside luring and burning involves other supernaturals. Our best guess is a metaphysical poison," he said. "Since Rusalkas are wronged humans, they carried mortal hate and fear of the supernatural into their new existence. Even a scratch could poison a magical being."

"Bingo. So, how do I counter this poison?"

"Uhh, like fix it? You sure? If it hasn't been more than six or eight hours, you've still got time to interrogate your catch before the venom finishes it off," Sylvester added.

Given my job description, the assumption that I was torturing a supernatural for information before killing it was depressingly understandable.

"Sly, that is not what I asked. You want to keep yourself in reefer and Sex Wax on my dime, answer my question."

"Right, man, right. Gotcha." The shuffle of papers and odd clinks came through as he got to working. "What kind of creature we talking here?"

"Kelpie."

He whistled. "Must have been a solid hit. Okay. Antidote's not too difficult, even if you're in the field. None of the ingredients will do more damage to a mudhorse." He reeled off a short list of common herbs. I gave thanks again for my well-stocked ride. Reduced fuel mileage was worth it sometimes.

"Hope you left something though. You gotta mix these with a bit of the Rusalka essence. It serves as the potion's base." Sylvester burst my prematurely optimistic bubble.

"Let's suppose I left my Witch to English dictionary at home. Translate. What counts as *essence*? It went poof. No ectoplasm, no dust, nada."

"Essence is what tied it to this world. Usually, the remains and their resting place."

"Tell me that, say, water from its well counts?"

"Theoretically. But it's only theory."

Not his fault there weren't peer-reviewed articles on this stuff. "Thanks, and you're still my favorite, no matter what anybody tells you."

"You have the gnarliest problems, boss." He cut the call, cheerful now that he knew I wasn't on my way to swipe his complex basement lighting arrangement.

The truck was close, if I made my own path. Then onto the bomb site next. Sylvester's "six to eight hours" looped as background noise while I worked out logistics.

I dropped down on dirty knees in front of Rachel and pushed ropes of sweaty, matted hair out of her eyes. She looked worse than when we'd arrived.

I pitched my voice low. "I don't know how much of that you caught, but I need to leave for a while and scrounge up the supplies to undo the angry dead chick's handiwork. The weather's pretty much cleared the park out. You should be safe enough 'til I get back. Okay?"

She cracked a lid, blinking slowly. Her soft brown eyes were hazed with clotted green strands.

I hoped she understood. I pulled the rest of the bedroll up to cover her. At a glance, she'd pass for a sleeping camper.

I emptied a water bottle and headed for the truck.

This trip sucked as hard as the first.

No Kelpie to carry, but fatigue took her place. At least the truck was fine, and the lot empty of prying eyes as I peeled back carpet to reveal the concealed compartments and their contents.

Digging out a crap-ton of plastique-leveled landscape was not fine.

Too many hours later, I uncovered a trickle of water crossing over a bit of mossy, hand-cut stone, all that remained of the well. I angled the container to catch the moisture. The sky put on evening fireworks, even more spectacular refracted through the misty air, as the contaminated water inched to the fill line.

Rachel lay exactly as I left her, too still and small to be the opinionated, powerful woman I'd first met.

I dumped the pack on the edge of her blanket and sorted. Packets of herbs colored the water, changing hue with each addition. I winced as I shook in salt crystals, swirling the tie-dye mixture together until it all dissolved.

"Okay." I chewed the inside of my cheek. "If you're listening, I have to wash your wounds with this magic gunk in order to stop the Rusalka's poison. I'm gonna go out on a limb and say it'll hurt. Please don't go insane water horse and try to kill me." I gave the bottle a last swish and crept closer.

Spreading my knees for leverage, I draped a hand on the nape of her neck, reassurance and early warning both. Taking a deep breath of pus-scented air, I upended the contents, making sure it covered her side and back, dribbling down to her stomach.

The solution hissed and bubbled, and more of the black toxin poured from the wounds. Rachel quivered under my fingers as the potion did its job and boiled the venom away. Her hands turned to claws and dug knuckle deep into the Georgia clay.

I dropped the empty bottle and transferred my grip to the undamaged small of her back, steadying her. My insides twisted and roiled just watching, and the temperature felt like it jumped ten degrees, sweat beading along my upper lip.

The bubbling phase stopped. I waited another minute before swiping my face on my shoulder and ripping open a packet of gauze, wiping the opaque mess away. The gashes were still there and still deep, but nothing flowed out, and the edges held a healthy pink tint. I un-stoppered the glass vial by my elbow and tipped it onto a fresh square of gauze, stroking the saturated fabric down each gash, trying to be gentle.

Rachel's erratic breathing steadied, and she unclenched the claws. They turned back to elegant hands, and she got them folded under her head.

"Wh—" She cleared her throat, coughed, and finally found her voice, though it was too quiet. "What are you doing now?"

I passed the cotton over the vertebra and babbled. "Looks like my boy was right. Which means you owe witches a big thanks in general, and my witch in particular a generous bonus." Since witches and Kelpies had some sort of magical Hatfields and McCoys thing going, I hoped the teasing distracted from the fact I was poking at raw wounds.

"Why do you insist on lying to me? I heard enough to know the first bottle nullified the Rusalka toxin. What's in this bottle?"

I shifted the pad to coat another cut, and despite trying for a light hand, Rachel flinched.

"Big, tough Kelpie or not, this is going to take you longer to heal than normal. This will help deaden the nerves 'til it does."

Her brows dipped. "Big, tough Kelpie? You aren't a very accomplished flirt."

Heat tickled up my neck and face. I finished dressing the last slash, took in the miniscule amount of fluid left in the vial, and sighed, dumping it in the deep crevice that still showed an unnerving lobe of her liver.

I pushed up and chucked dryer kindling in the lined pit, coaxing a fire into being. Flames lit up the early dusk so I could see, instead of work by feel. I pulled off my ruined shirt and pitched it into the pile with Rachel's, both destined for the fire pit.

She rolled her head, cheek pillowed on her arms, watching. Her eyes held more brown than green now, but I had my doubts as to how present she really was.

I debated a whole second before shucking the bra and adding it to the heap. It was intact, but completely disgusting, slimy, sweaty, and reeking of fish and rot. I took my time washing the burn and my scraped-up hands, my back to Rachel, damning betadine antiseptic and Rusalkas. I slathered a thick layer of burn cream and Sylvester's black powder on my burn, then taped it with one of the non-stick bandages that never lived it up to their claim.

The duffel produced one last tee and another light flannel, identical to the trashed ones.

I squatted by Rachel again. In my non-professional medical opinion, she looked like the aftermath of a bad bout of flu, a vast improvement over her corpse-ish vibe earlier. Lifting the edge of the bedroll, I tented it to rest over her back. No bandages, on the off chance they healed into the wound.

"You are injured, too. Yet you used the last of the pain potion on me," Rachel said.

"You needed it more."

"I'm not human. I heal quickly. You don't."

"Pain is pain, all right?" I rose, trying to get away from the questions and the weird tightness in my chest.

I'd sworn I wasn't going to care about anyone again.

I hadn't thought I was able.

Rachel jumped at my sudden movement, eyes still drugged and only half focused. I dropped to my heels and laid a hand on the back of her head, reassuring her. "Easy. We're good. I'm just taking care of housecleaning." I waited until she subsided, eyes closing, before arranging the filthy remnants of our wardrobe in the fire.

I rummaged through the last of our supplies. Settling cross-legged beside Rachel's head, I dug out smushed crackers and sports drink.

Rachel frowned, lashes fluttering up and down instead of giving in to drugs and sleep, for God knew what reason. She lost the fight, lids finally dropping and staying down.

I followed suit, weirdly content despite my throbbing side.

Two days. It seemed a hell of a lot longer since we'd skipped off the civilized graveled lot and into the forest.

My passenger door slamming brought it all full circle. I squinted against the glare bouncing off the window. Leave it to Mother Nature to get cooperative now. The sun shone, highlighting the bright, festive leaves and emerald green grass.

I tossed the remaining crusted pack in my clean cargo area and slapped the hatch shut. I climbed in, careful of my side, and cranked the engine to a happy growl.

Rachel had her shades on, hiding dark under-eye circles. She'd made the trek to the car on her own, though I got left hauling the depleted pack. Her color wasn't quite normal yet, but her breathing was a careful, even, in and out rhythm.

She fiddled with the seatbelt, the seat still in the canted position she left it, probably trying for an angle that kept the seatbelt off her wounds.

"The rear seats all fold flat into the floor. It'll be more comfortable if you lie down back there," I offered.

Rachel abandoned the front, and the thump and whir of the seats folding filled the truck. "We're taking my car on the next hunt," she said on the end of a yawn. "Three words. Heated leather seats."

"Okay." I backed the truck out of the slot and waved cheerfully at a different park attendant on our way out.

ANTHOLOGY CONTRIBUTORS

Lillian Archer

My novel, *Prodigal Spell*, is available on Amazon. I am part of *TheMillionWords.net* blog, as well as my own writerly musings on my website, *www.lillianarcher.com*.

I first met Melanie over ten years ago, when we both attended the same writers' conference in South Carolina. Her wit, quick smile, and quirky sense of humor defined the way she navigated life. She thought nothing of jumping in the ocean at night with a New York editor (clearly, she had not seen *Jaws* as many times as I), nor of offering help to a crying stranger in the bathroom who'd just been rejected by her dream agent. Melanie had a *joie de vivre* that was infectious, and I am a better writer and person for knowing her.

Outside of writing, Melanie was a photographer of great talent, and she loved the steampunk genre. For my story, I blended a true historical occurrence with a talented photographer and a bit of steam-powered items as an homage to Melanie's interests.

Melanie, I hope this story brings you joy. We miss you greatly.

~Lillian

Natania Barron

Natania Barron is a word tinkerer with a lifelong love of the fantastic. She enjoys mixing horror and mythology, epic fantasy and the weird. Basically, she likes genre cocktails. Her first novel, a myth-punk space and travel adventure, *Pilgrim of the Sky*, debuted in late 2011. Her short stories have appeared in a wide variety of anthologies and publications, from *Weird Tales* to *The Mammoth Book of Kaiju*.

She lives in Durham, NC with her family. When she's not trying to figure out how to get to Narnia, she can be found cooking, playing guitar, painting, and plotting her next adventure (on a tabletop or otherwise).

Find more at *nataniabarron.com*.

Amy Bauer

One June day, I followed the Roaring Writers home, and to my surprise, they let me stay.

I currently write speculative fiction. Past travails in academia led to a few peer-reviewed papers and co-authorship of *An Introduction to Marine Mammal Biology and Conservation*.

When not writing, I enjoy historical reenactment, tea, travel, politics, and too many other things to name and remain under my word count. I live in Northern Virginia with one patient husband and five impatient cats. Six cats are required to be a crazy cat lady. That's my story and I'm sticking to it.

Melanie and I bonded over cat anecdotes. I remember standing in the kitchen at my first Roaring Writer's retreat talking with her. Her laugh was infectious and her eyes would light up as she held forth on various topics ranging from animals to writing to photography to anime. Her sunny personality and quick wit added zing to our group conversations. Melanie's death left a hole in our group, and I miss her.

For more information, visit my individual website (*www.storycurrents.net*) or the Roaring Writers at The Million Words (*www.themillionwords.net*). I'm on twitter @*AmaronB*.

Judy Bienvenu

I don't write. I have a lot of friends that do, which is how I found myself at ConCarolinas in 2013. The panels were interesting, the costumes were amazing, the craftwork was beautiful and the people attending were fun and engaging.

I found myself on the last day, at the last panel, talking with others who I had become friends with over the weekend. We ended up chatting about having a writer's retreat next year, right after ConCarolinas. I happened to mention that we had some time shares we might be able to use, and before I knew it, I was in charge of finding us a place to hold the retreat.

As fall rolled around, I started looking for someplace that would hold all of us. In the meantime, Melanie contacted Faith to tell her about our plans for the retreat. Not only did Faith agree to come as a guest writer, she also connected me with someone who had a beautiful mountain cabin we could rent. By Thanksgiving we had everything all lined up, now the waiting began. I hate waiting.

Since I don't write, but I do cook, the group invited me along as the "Chief Cook and Bottle Washer." Since there was no dishwasher, I really earned my title!

The mountain cabin turned out to be a beautiful log home at the top of a mountain in Roaring Gap, NC. It was as lovely a place as I've ever stayed. The weather was beautiful and the views of the night sky were amazing! With no light pollution, the stars filled every corner of the sky.

I spent my time shopping, cooking, washing dishes, and doing what I love: taking pictures. I am experimenting with infrared photography, and the mountains were perfect for my endeavors.

The evenings were fun, with plenty of giggles, cold beer, wine, Tiger Butter, good food, and great conversations.

I made new friends, reconnected with old friends, and watched the writers bloom with understanding when their work was being critiqued. I witnessed quite a few "AH HA" moments.

I am a camera repair technician (38 years) and a photo equipment reseller on eBay. I love photography, but am content doing it as a hobby. I travel where and when I can. I love the desert southwest, and the red rock canyons of the Four Corners area of the US. You can find my eBay store at *http://stores.ebay.com/The-Marmot-Burrow*.

Some of my earlier images can be seen at *https://haveacookie.smugmug.com*.

for Melanie

As dawn's first light warmed the horizon, Melanie left us. Always a photographer, she went to chase the light.

We had 20 amazing years together. We traveled, we laughed, we sang, we cried. We buried our parents, loved our families, built a home, adopted our fur babies. We made friends.

So many amazing wonderful friends.

Most of all we loved.

I will miss her beautiful smile and infectious laugh. I will miss her ability to see the good in everyone. I will miss her stories, both verbal and written. I will miss her ability to create the most amazing art.

I will miss her love. She made me a better person and made me believe I could do anything.

She was taken too soon. I will never again be able to tell her how much I love her.

So, go tell your loved ones how much they mean to you. Give them a hug. Call an old friend just to say hi. Hug a puppy. Pat a cat. Be kind.

Janet Buhlmann

I am an immunologist by training (piled higher and deeper) and currently work in the pharmaceutical industry doing drug discovery. I became a scientist because back in high school and college I hated to write. Little did I know how much writing was involved with a science career. In addition to writing at work, I've written our class notes column for Mount Holyoke's alumnae magazine for the last 19 years.

I met Melanie in college. We lived on the same floor freshman year, and second semester she became my roommate. We lived together again sophomore year. Things that I remember most about Melanie-her unique laugh, her black and white Sherlock Holmes hat, that she always had her camera at the ready, and of course that the collars on her shirt were always popped up.

I had another "purple planet" moment today. In February I went out to Minnesota to see my sister, and when I got home I was looking for some silver barrettes that I had brought with me. I couldn't find them anywhere, and I looked in every pocket of everything that I had taken with me on the trip. Today I took my luggage out because I needed to pack for an upcoming business trip, and I found both barrettes. When I first thought they were lost, I asked Melanie to tell the guy to give them back to me. When I found them today, I just laughed and thought of Melanie.

David B. Coe / D.B. Jackson

David B. Coe/D.B. Jackson, is the award-winning author of twenty novels and as many short stories. Under his own name (*http://www.-DavidBCoe.com*), he is the author of the Crawford Award winning LonTobyn Chronicle, the critically acclaimed Winds of the Forelands quintet and Blood of the Southlands trilogy, the novelization Ridley Scott's *Robin Hood*, and a contemporary urban fantasy series, the Case Files of Justis Fearsson (Baen Books). He is also the co-author of *How To Write Magical Words: A Writer's Companion.*

As D.B. Jackson (*http://www.DBJackson-Author.com*), he writes the Thieftaker Chronicles (Tor Books), a series set in pre-Revolutionary Boston that combines elements of urban fantasy, mystery, and historical fiction.

He is currently working on a new fantasy trilogy for Angry Robot and a tie-in project with the History Channel. David has a Ph.D. in U.S. history. His books have been translated into a dozen languages.

Remembering Melanie

I have so many memories of Melanie, most of them revolving around her wit and her mischievous smile, her kindness and generosity and compassion. I was fortunate enough to be able to count myself as not only her friend, but also one of her writing mentors, a role I cherished.

As it happens, though, Melanie was also a bit of a mentor to me. I am a dedicated amateur photographer, and Melanie was a talented professional. During the first Roaring Writers retreat that I attended as an instructor, I used a bit of free time one day to take some photos around the lake house at which we stayed. One photo in particular came out pretty well, and I, ever the eager student, showed it to Melanie. She looked at it, bestowed upon me one of her wonderful smiles, and told me she had taken nearly the exact same photo that very morning. I spent the rest of the day on cloud nine, basking in the approval of my teacher.

Alex Gideon

Born in Nashville, TN, Alex Gideon quickly decided he wasn't a fan of the N, and now lives in Asheville, NC. He enjoys writing fantasy of any kind as long as it's dark, and he dabbles in sci-horror. He enjoys exorcising, taking long walks on extraterrestrial beaches, relaxing demon hunting trips, and fishing for Old Ones. Find him on Facebook/A.G.R.Gideon, and follow him on Twitter *@AlexanderGideon*.

Melanie Griffin/Otto

Melanie was a storyteller. She was an incredibly gifted author who penned several novels, short stories and anime fan fiction and told stories through her gorgeous photography. Melanie also loved teaching and had a lifelong passion for helping others learn. In her lifetime, she taught thousands of students how to master their cameras and take beautiful pictures.

Melanie's warm smile, sense of humor, and her distinctive laugh are what we will all remember. She was a wise and kind soul, a gentle spirit with a wicked sense of humor and a love of bad puns.

Her motto was: It costs you nothing to be kind. So she was kind.

She went out of her way to compliment people, complete strangers, if something about them was nice--hair, jewelry, outfits. Everyone appreciated her compliments.

She loved vests, cowboy boots, and shirts with the collar turned up.

Melanie loved life with a passion. She gave her all into anything she was doing.

Her love of photography gave her the artistic outlet that she needed. And she shared her love by teaching photography. Her enthusiasm was contagious, and she had many repeat students--some went on to careers in photography.

When her health made it hard for her to really engage in the photography she loved, she turned inward and jumped feet first into writing, which was her first love. She wrote her first story in second grade, and the teacher told her mom that she was going to be a writer someday. She joined the Maryland WOW and the Roaring Writers groups, which helped her fine-tune her writing skills and taught her more about the commercial aspects of being an author.

She also felt the urge to create more visual art. Woodworking, leather craft, and jewelry making became a big part of her life. She loved steampunk and designed her work around that concept.

She often said that the best decision she ever made (other than falling in love with Judy) was her decision to attend Mount Holyoke College. As a legacy student—both her grandmother and her aunt attended—she had some pressure from her family to attend. She told them that she didn't want to hear *one word* about how great a school it was, that it was her decision to make. One trip to the campus was all it took, and she fell in love with the school. It was a pivotal decision that helped define the wonderful woman she became.

Melanie's photography is still available for purchase at *https://griff-ingraphx.smugmug.com.*

Faith Hunter

Faith Hunter is a *New York Times* and *USAToday* bestselling author. She writes dark urban fantasy and paranormal urban thrillers.

Her long-running, bestselling, Skinwalker series features Jane Yellowrock, a hunter of rogue-vampires. The Soulwood series features Nell Nicholson Ingram in paranormal crime solving novels. Her Rogue Mage novels, a dark, urban fantasy series, features Thorn St. Croix, a stone mage in a post-apocalyptic, alternate reality. Two of her fantasy series have been nominated for Audie Awards.

Under the pen name Gwen Hunter, she has written action adventure, mysteries, thrillers, women's fiction, a medical thriller series, and even historical religious fiction. As Gwen, she is a winner of the WH

Smith Literary Award for Fresh Talent in 1995 in the UK, and won a Romantic Times Reviewers Choice Award in 2008. Under all her pen names, she has over 40 books in print in 30 countries.

In real life, Faith once broke a stove by refusing to turn it on for so long that its parts froze, and the unused stove had to be replaced. Her recent hankering for homemade bread and soup resulted in fresh loaves each week, and she claims that the newish stove feels loved and well used—because Faith talks to her appliances as well as to her plants and dog. She collects orchids and animal skulls, loves to sit on the back porch in lightning storms, and is a workaholic with a passion for jewelry making, white-water kayaking, and RV travel. She likes the shooting range, prefers Class III whitewater rivers with no gorge to climb out of, edits the occasional anthology, and drinks a lot of tea. Some days she's a lady. Some days she ain't. Occasionally, she remembers to sleep. The jewelry she makes and wears is often given as promo items and is used as prizes in contests.

For more, including a list of her books, see *www.faithhunter.net* or *www.gwenhunter.com*. To keep up with her, like her fan page at Facebook: *https://www.facebook.com/official.faith.hunter*.

John G. Hartness

John G. Hartness is a teller of tales, a righter of wrongs, defender of ladies' virtues, and some people call him Maurice, for he speaks of the pompatus of love. He is also the award-winning author of the urban fantasy series *The Black Knight Chronicles,* the Bubba the Monster Hunter comedic horror series, the Quincy Harker, Demon Hunter dark fantasy series, and many other projects. He is also a cast member of the role-playing podcast *Authors & Dragons*, where a group of comedy, fantasy, and horror writers play *Pathfinder*. Very poorly.

In 2016, John teamed up with a pair of other publishing industry ne'er-do-wells and founded Falstaff Books, a small press dedicated to publishing the best of genre fiction's "misfit toys."

In his copious free time John enjoys long walks on the beach, rescuing kittens from trees and playing *Magic: the Gathering*.

Emily Lavin Leverett

Emily Lavin Leverett is a writer, editor, and English professor. She is the co-editor of *Lawless Lands: Tales from the Weird Frontier* and *The Weird Wild West* with Misty Massey and Margaret McGraw. Her first novel *Changeling's Fall*, co-written with Sarah Joy Adams will be followed in 2018 with *Winter's Heir*, the second novel in their contemporary fantasy faerie tale series *The Eisteddfod Chronicles*. She is currently working on another urban fantasy novel set in Raleigh, NC. Her scholarship focuses on the connection between Medieval English Romance and the *Discworld* novels of Terry Pratchett. She lives in North Carolina with her spouse and their three cats, where they remain stalwart Carolina Hurricanes fans.

Melissa McArthur

Melissa McArthur is the founder and president of Clicking Keys Writer Services, a full-service editing, cover design, and layout company based in the upstate of South Carolina. She also serves as an Acquiring Editor for Falstaff Books, and is an accomplished editor and proofreader.

Her urban fantasy series, *Guardians of Eternity*, will be published by Falstaff Books beginning in 2018.

A graduate of Winthrop University, Melissa has published short stories with Mocha Memoirs Press, Falstaff Books, and other quality small presses throughout the Southeast.

Melissa can be found hiding in the deep corners of the library or at home with her laptop and cat. For those of you out in cyberspace, she can also be found at *www.clickingkeys.com*.

Margaret S. McGraw

I don't write clever bios. I do make random comments like, "Wouldn't it be great if we could get together and write sometime" and end up in a remarkable writers group with annual retreats and amazing mentors like Faith Hunter, David Coe, and John Hartness.

I may have answered Misty Massey's "I wish there were an anthology of Weird Wild West stories" with "Why don't *we* produce one"... Together with Emily Leverett, we are co-editors of not one but two anthologies of short stories about the wildest West that never was: *Weird Wild West* (eSpec Books, 2015) and *Lawless Lands: Tales from the Weird Frontier* (Falstaff Books, 2017).

I write speculative fiction and blog on *WritersSpark.com* and *TheMillionWords.net*. I am a repeating guest at many regional conventions in Virginia, North Carolina, and Georgia, where I occasionally say something original and even entertaining. When I'm not at cons, I live in North Carolina with my daughter, an array of dogs, cats, Macs and PCs, and too many unfinished craft projects. Find me on Facebook or Goodreads at "Margaret S. McGraw", or on Twitter *@MargaretSMcGraw*.

Remembering Melanie

The first thing I remember about Melanie, always, is her beautiful smile. Her delighted laugh as we shared our love of stories, books, authors, movies, photography, nature, friends, and life. We met at ConCarolinas 2013 in Charlotte, NC. Afterward, she emailed this wonderful summation of the weekend: "Truly, a person never knows what fine folk or fortunate things one might discover coming one's way." Through email, phone calls, and our eagerly anticipated annual retreats, we shared stories, editing advice, writing goals, travel adventures and dreams, and so much more. I knew from the beginning that Melanie had some serious health issues, and to her chagrin, they often impeded her participation in our retreats and activities. Even so, I could never have been prepared for the shock of losing her so suddenly.

But Melanie hasn't left the Roaring Writers. If anything, she continues to bring us ever closer together. In honoring her, in sharing our grief together, in committing to this benefit anthology project, we continue to write and grow and learn and succeed together. And I still see Melanie's beautiful smile, just beyond the light.

Mindy Mymudes

Mindy Mymudes is a gardener based in Milwaukee Wi. She has a BS in horticulture and MS in biology, her thesis specializing in the population structure of an endangered plant species. While on a collecting trip for *Plantago cordata*, a Native American man led her to a location that contained the plant, which was well known to his tribe as a medicinal herb. His stories captivated Mindy and led to her strong interest in ethnobotany. She worked as a university greenhouse manager, cultivating medicinal, ornamental, edible, research, and unique plants. These days, she breeds and trains English springer spaniels, cultivates hundreds of plants, mainly in her basement. When her hands are not covered in mud, Mindy runs a small business called Let's Talk Promotions for writers, and she writes fantasy books written from the dog's point of view, for ages 8 to adult, with an environmental message.

For Melanie

Like most of us, I met Melanie through the internet long before we met in person. There was never a question we wouldn't hit it off, it was always easy between us. In the last e-mail she sent me, she called me her tribe. We shared a lot of things in common, and one was to make others laugh. I loved making her laugh, and so I contributed something I hope makes her laugh from wherever she is: comedic horror with a touch of the cartoon. *Love you, Melanie.*

Ken Schrader

I am a science fiction and fantasy writer, a shameless Geek, a fan of the Oxford comma, and I make housing decisions based upon the space available for bookshelves. I collect books, movies, and music.

I sing out loud when I think there's no one around, and I try to get a blog post up once a week – both with varying degrees of success.

I love music of all kinds, books, the big sky off my front porch, *Star Wars*, *Firefly*, Blind Guardian (to which, I write almost exclusively), rugby, stargazing, jasmine tea, and the smell of rain on the air.

My favorite flavor of ice cream is chocolate. My favorite food is a grilled steak, and I can suspend disbelief embarrassingly quickly.

I live in Michigan, am co-owned by several dogs (especially the Border Collie), and I am one of the rare breed of folk that enjoys mowing the lawn.

Laura S. Taylor

Laura S. Taylor lives in Vancouver, Canada, where she works as a library technician in post-secondary accessible textbook services. She likes to attend writing panels at science fiction and fantasy conventions, where she takes extensive notes and shares them at her blog, *lstaylor.blogspot.ca*. When not writing, she can be found swinging a sword or, in the summer, jumping off cliffs.

Remembering Melanie

It was our very first Roaring Writers retreat. Melanie and I hit it off right away. One afternoon, while the others were deep in chatter, we snuck off to another room to quietly write. That afternoon was as wonderfully productive as it was memorable, as we each worked on our own projects in pleasant, albeit silent, company.

Janet Walden-West

Janet Walden-West lives in the Southeast with a pack of show dogs, a couple of kids, and a husband who, sadly for him, didn't read the fine print. Among other vices, she's obsessed with dusty artifacts, great cars, bad coffee, and a never-ending supply of Mead notebooks. A member of the East Tennessee Creative Writers Alliance and Romance Writers of America, she writes urban fantasy that tends to escape the neat confines of the city limits in favor of map-dot hillbilly towns, and inclusive, feminist romantic suspense/contemporary romance.

The Spirit of What If

We all have our reasons for loving and writing speculative fiction, be it urban fantasy, science fiction, high fantasy, grimdark, steampunk, etc. However, a uniting thread for most is that magical, alluring sense of *"What if?"*

What if, when you kick over that mundane rock on your morning walk, instead of a familiar earthworm, you find a tiny basilisk underneath?

Melanie Otto, one of the founding members of The Roaring Writers, embraced that concept of "What if?" every single day.

After the last panel of a con one year, a group of stragglers, loathe for a great weekend to end, stood around chatting. High on lack of sleep and the energy that comes from being surrounded by like-minded artists, one blurted out, "What if we had a writer's retreat?"

Standing among eight people she'd only met days before, Melanie immediately chimed in with, "What if Judy and I used our timeshare rental to find a site for it?"

And The Roaring Writers, the greatest influence on my writing and writing career, was born.

Melanie was one of the first writers I met in real life, and from the time she jumped in to help me lug a monster of a cake halfway across the con's hotel complex, we clicked. Through epically long e-mail chats, rambling conversations at retreats, messaged song snippets, and spur-of-the-moment joke and anime recommendations, she shared her creative joy. Everything from *Rat Queens*, to accidentally writing romance, to the best version of *Walking in Memphis* for road trips was fair game. She truly led by example, reminding me to be kinder, more compassionate, and to approach life with enthusiasm.

That enthusiasm—that sense of adventure, optimism, and embracing possibilities—was all Melanie. She embodied creativity, building her own workshop when one room was too much to contain her artistic visions—photography, writing, leatherwork, metalwork, and Steampunk/cosplay fashion, to name only a few.

Although this collection is titled *Chasing the Light*, as a tribute to Melanie's photographer's eye, even when choosing her time to leave this world, in reality she was made of Light. I have no doubt wherever she is now, she's still asking "What if?" and, along with a beloved feline familiar, is jumping full-bore into new adventures.

Until we meet again—follow the light and safe journey, Melanie. I had Marc Cohn's version of *Walking in Memphis* on repeat when I wrote Sam and Rachel's road trip.

Made in the USA
Lexington, KY
28 May 2018